THE THRONE OF BROKEN BONES

A WEAPON OF FIRE AND ASH NOVEL

By Brittany Matsen

The Throne of Broken Bones
A Weapon of Fire and Ash Novel
© Copyright 2020 Brittany Matsen.

Editor - Mariz C
Cover by Dean Packwood

ISBN: 979-8-683-60096-9

For every person who lives in imaginary worlds
and falls in love

Author's Note

Welcome back, readers! Since it has been nearly a year since you may have last spent time with Emma, Blaze, Adrianna, Tlahaz, and Levaroth, I'm going to give a quick refresher. This will encompass both *The Mark of Fallen Flame* as well as *The Spellcaster's Weapon*.

In *The Mark of Fallen Flame* you meet Emma, a seventeen-year-old high school senior that just wants to graduate and figure out what she wants to do for the rest of her life. Her mother—Laura—who has moved them both around the country nearly two dozen times, is beginning to relax her hold on Emma, realizing she'll soon be eighteen and no longer under her roof. A few days before school begins, Emma and her best friend, Adrianna are heading to a concert when they're lured into a dark alley and attacked by creepy Shediem called Nybasses. That's when Emma discovers she has the power to kill them with her touch.

Fast forward to her first day of the new school year and we meet handsome, enigmatic Rowek who all the girls fawn over. He tries to get close to Emma and reveals that he is a Spellcaster and tells her she might be part Spellcaster also. They spend time trying to find information on her specific power set while Adrianna keeps going home with "headaches".

After school one day, Rowek skips class and Emma comes across two gorgeous men with English accents, one of whom is Blaze Thomas. A two-hundred-year-old Giborim who was hired to keep an eye on her.

At the homecoming dance that Rowek takes Emma to, Shediem attack, including the sexy, yet terrifying Levaroth who brands Emma. The next day, only a handful of people have any recollection of the events that took place, and Emma makes it her mission to figure out how to return everyone's memories.

Levaroth is becoming increasingly obsessed with Emma, showing up wherever she is now that she has his mark. Especially after Seattle is bombed and Blaze picks her up, taking her back to his fortress up on the mountain. The Giborim are hesitant to trust her and Emma learns that her mother is one of them.

Then Blaze leaves to deal with international Giborim affairs, and Emma's mum gets abducted. She calls the only other person she can think will help—Rowek—and tells him to meet her at the stated location. Once inside the creepy house, she goes into the basement where Rowek is. He morphs into Levaroth where he spills the beans on his deception, then takes her to Sheol.

Emma meets her father, Asmodeus, as well as Blaze's long-lost sister Haddie. She is paraded around for all the six princes to ogle. And ogle Amon, the Prince of Lust does, making her dance for him.

Her father forces Emma to join him in the coming war by using her mother against her. She, Haddie, and her mother all try to escape but Levaroth finds her. There's also that super creepy room where Asmodeus shows her his breeding program, resulting in a bunch of hybrids like her.

When Emma rejects Levaroth, he decides to punish her by forcing her to watch Geryon—her father's guard—murder her mother, Haddie and a bunch of other servants. Emma sacrifices herself in their place, and is whipped, nearly to death for the exchange.

At last she is given The Mark of Fallen Flame and sent back to Seattle to play spy.

Starting from the end of TMOFF, we meet Adrianna in The Spellcaster's Weapon in a new light. Magic is exploding out of her and the freshman girl from book one, Sara, offers to help her learn control.

After nearly killing Sean, and the entire school regaining their memory of the homecoming dance, Adrianna and Sara flee…to her coven leader's house. We meet a bunch of powerful Spellcaster's as well as their familiars.

When Adrianna's familiar is coaxed from her, a multi-colored wyvern emerges and thus leads to the prophecy which basically states that Adrianna is the most powerful Spellcaster to ever live. During the war, she and her wyvern will fight to bind the ultimate darkness back in Sheol for all eternity.

On the flip side is Tlahaz, King Nakosh's Shediem General, who needs a powerful Spellcaster to break into Levaroth's mind and erase his humanity. He finds Adrianna at the Seattle coven leader's house and breaks through the wards with an army of insects and carries her out before taking her to Sheol.

Apparently, all of the Shediem Generals have a thing for kidnapping women.

Adrianna is immediately thrown into training and despite her multiple escapes gone wrong, she develops feelings for the broody general, as he does for her.

At the end, Tlahaz sees a vision of the future which tells him she will be his forever. He takes her back to see her family one last time where she erases their memories of her and Tlahaz agrees to keep them protected during the war.

And now dear reader, go forth and experience the penultimate book in the Weapon of Fire and Ash series.

TABLE OF CONTENTS

LAURA

During the days, Asmodeus kept Laura chained at the foot of his throne, ensuring the corpses that comprised it brushed against her. Reached for her. A promise that she too would be used as little more than parts to lounge upon.

The nights were spent in his private chambers. He didn't try to touch her at first. Instead, he entertained disposable humans. Still, she remained shackled to the bedpost, forced to sleep on the cold stone floor, trying with all her might to shut out the giggles and moans of his bedmates. And when they inevitably screamed as he fed from them or inflicted pain that went beyond their thresholds, Laura kept her eyes wide open, waiting for the time when she was next.

He only beat her when she voiced her disgust and horror, or attempted to warn away the young, foolish human girls looking for wealth and other fickle promises that would go unfulfilled. Human women didn't bed dark princes and survive. They either spent their short, fragile lives forever seeking violent pleasure by any means possible, or the absence of a prince's touch drove them mad.

His punishments were not all so easy as a slap across the face or a cut to the flesh. The poisons he fed her were worse, forcing her to drown in the depths of her deepest, darkest memories. Days on end passed with Laura trapped in the horrors of her childhood.

When the despicable prince came near, she disappeared inside herself, refusing to let his silky, venomous voice poison her further. He was killing her and she knew it. She was too weak, her mind too detached from her body. When had she last eaten?

Time was no longer measurable, though it felt like months spent as his prisoner. His plaything. Even while her brain forced her to relive the very worst memories, Asmodeus's touch was inescapable. His sultry caresses were worse than the beatings and the memories. The feel of his mouth on her body was too much to bear. His eyes glowed in those moments, high on her fear. She wouldn't let him hear her scream, so she retreated into her head, letting it fracture into a million jagged pieces.

And there would be no repairing it this time.

His kisses and gentle words dripped with false adoration that seeped into the fissures of her soul and wove into her with its lies.

When the worst of the poison's effects would wear off, he was there, taking what was left of her sanity piece by piece. His deep voice rumbled through her, words that her splintered mind couldn't comprehend.

In the rare moments of clarity, Laura saw her daughter's face, bright and smiling, keeping alight the flame within her that told her to stay alive. She felt her love's—her true love, Sergei's—breath tickle her cheek, saw his eyes in the darkness of her torture. *Sergei!* Her heart ached for him.

A burning sensation danced on her icy skin, causing her eyes to fly open. The light was too bright, her eyes watering as they squeezed shut. But the glimpse she caught of a girl allowed her to relax slightly. The girl's eyes were sapphire blue, her hair a honey color. But it was her belly, swollen with child, that stopped Laura from fighting. The cloth she pressed to Laura's brow again and again felt too hot.

"Burning," she rasped. She really needed some water.

When a cup was held to her lips, Laura wondered if she had said that last part out loud. She sipped the liquid inside, but it felt hot too. So why was she shivering?

"Your fever is out of control. I had some medicines put into the water. You're going to be okay, Nadia, just hold on a little longer." The girl's voice was melodic, and Laura felt her limbs grow heavy.

"Emma's coming," the girl whispered. "Just hang on."

Laura smiled to the strange, beautiful girl.

Emma. Her daughter.

She's coming.

She's coming.

She's—

LEVAROTH

Ice invaded his every cell, freezing every molecule of his being. It coated his skin with a million tiny glittering crystals, giving it a bluish tint. The chill wracked his body in violent tremors. Ice picks drove under his brittle flesh, peeling it off over and over until his ears could no longer hear his screams. He was a master of torture; it was used to strengthen him and make him less susceptible to cracking should his enemies ever capture him. There was one who knew his weaknesses best, the one that trained him: his prince, Asmodeus. But without his healing abilities or raw power to fight back, his limits had never been pushed so far. This was his very own hell.

He was blinded and bound by magic—incredibly strong magic. How long had it been since he'd seen anyone's face? Days? Weeks? Months? Too long without light. He was a creature born of darkness, yet he heard himself beg for sunlight at one point. A rumbling chorus of booms that might have been a laugh was his only reply before the pain split him apart again. He'd lost appendages, had his skin ripped off, burned off. A boiling bitter liquid ate away at his vocal cords, cutting off his roars.

He hadn't made a sound at first. His fingers and toes had been sawed off but he'd remained silent, his jaw locked tight. The first grunt he'd made had been coaxed from him by a gravelly voice that said, "Once she has served her purpose, she'll be Amon's plaything." It was his reaction that had brought on the gruesome description of her defilement. He had fought against his chains then, tried to smash his head into Tlahaz's smug face. But his weakness had cost him.

Prince Amon had visited him next. Just the sound of his voice, his lust-thick accent raking talons down Levaroth's resolve, brought forth a harsh growl. He didn't remember Amon's words, just the snap of the magic's hold on him and his fists connecting with the prince.

Then came the pain. Pain beyond any he had ever known. Perhaps it was his broken focus. The place of dead, emotionless control was inaccessible—invisible bars forced him to feel every ounce of pain and hear every word of his torture. Because of *her*.

Emma Duvall.

The images of her that flashed in his mind made every strike, every drop of poison that flowed through his veins sear white-hot. He was living flame with a heart made of stone. But something about her had cracked the surface. Levaroth was not human, but emotions swirled through him like a maelstrom of toxins, each more lethal than the last.

Asmodeus was burning them out of him. His torture sessions all ended with the words, "You are not a man. You are a soldier. Forget Emma Duvall; Nakosh is your king. The darkness is your master. You serve corruption. *In darkness the king was made. So shall I serve the darkness and my king.*" Even when his ears roared with his frenzied blood, he knew the words. He repeated them to himself when Asmodeus was present, but in the privacy of his mind, he changed them: *Emma Duvall will be queen and I her king. Together we will build a new Sheol and all living things will bow to us.*

In the brief reprieve of his agony, exhaustion consumed him, and he sagged in his manacles. Unable to keep his eyelids open any longer, he let them flutter closed.

When Levaroth awoke yet again, his entire body ached but every wound was stitched back together. Not healed, no. Torture here was meant to last as long as it was willed. No, he was literally stitched together like Frankenstein's monster. He felt them, the stitches. Their itch, their tug when his muscles tightened. Not that he could have healed on his own regardless. He was drained, weak. He couldn't recall when he had last fed.

His head lolled to one side as he pried a single lid open, silently pleading for a glimpse of something, anything. His heart dropped at the blackness, then raced at the sight of the glowing red figure leaning in the corner. He wasn't sure he wanted to see anymore, knowing who stood in front of him. His stomach clenched in anticipation.

"Ah, you're awake. Good," Asmodeus said. His thunderous voice echoed through the chamber, rattling his chains. The prince stood to his full height, his skin emanating a soothing heat as he stalked toward Levaroth.

"Please, Master." Levaroth's throat was raw, his voice the grinding of screws in a blender.

"Your loyalty is not the problem, General." A pickaxe made entirely of shatter-proof ice materialized in the prince's hands. He stepped closer and a choked noise ripped itself from Levaroth's throat. "You are my own creation. I made you to serve Sheol without emotion. Yet somehow, you fancy yourself obsessed with my daughter."

Without warning the prince raised the axe above his head and swung it across Levaroth's abdomen, severing muscle and skin. He roared in pain as the magically preserved weapon penetrated his veins once again. His body shook. His flame did not warm him, his rage buried beneath a cloak just out of reach to save himself. If he wanted out of there, he would have only his wits.

Asmodeus leaned close, smoke drifting from his beastly nostrils. "I will do this to you, over and over, until you no longer feel the pain. Do not forget the creed you swore fealty to. *In darkness the king was made. So shall I serve the darkness and my king.* You are a warrior. A soldier. You exist only for me."

Suddenly an urgent rapping came from the door. It swung open, sending a blinding beam of light directly into Levaroth's eyes. He squeezed them shut, focusing on driving the cold out and coaxing his fire nearer.

"Sir!" Geryon said.

Levaroth didn't open his eyes beyond a sliver, taking in his master's personal servant. The creature huffed, distress plainly written on its face. Asmodeus stared at it, reading its mind. Levaroth cursed his inability to listen in on their shared telepathic connection.

"When?" the prince thundered.

"Just now, my prince," Geryon answered.

The weapon of ice disappeared from the prince's hands in a hiss of steam. Whatever had happened was enough to postpone Levaroth's torment. Silently, he was grateful, but he wanted to know what it was.

"How many?"

"At least twenty."

Asmodeus's roar shook the chamber, rattling Levaroth's ribs, the threads that held his body together vibrating uncomfortably. Then the prince and his servant left him, the cell door slamming shut. He exhaled a rattling breath.

Whatever had produced such a rage in Asmodeus, he hoped it didn't have to do with Emma. He imagined her safe, smiling. Her emerald eyes shining with rare laughter. Deep within his chest he felt the cord that led him to her. It was stretched, the same as it had been every time he felt for it since his imprisonment. A flutter of satisfaction filled him, knowing the Mark of Fallen Flame had not erased his own brand on her skin. It wouldn't protect her the same in his weakened state, but he could sense her, which meant she was alive, and that thought was enough to ignite a spark in his blood.

He pulled on the cord, this time feeling himself lift from his tortured body in the cell. When his eyes opened anew, he stood on a sandy beach. Waves roared and crashed onto the shore, the breeze carrying the scent of sweetness and sunshine.

Emma.

He found her instantly, less than twenty feet away, staring out at the vast blue. The salty mist clung to her hair, making it frizz and curl. The sun highlighted the red strands dancing over her shoulders like a living flame.

The two of us could set the world ablaze. She could be who she really was with him. No hiding how the darkness suited her. No pretending that she wasn't capable of destruction and chaos. No denying that she didn't crave it. He could handle her fire, and she could take his.

Her eyes lacked their usual brightness today, and her luscious lips were pursed together as she allowed herself to get lost in her thoughts.

He started toward her, feeling his muscles ache. But looking down at himself, he knew he was in his preferred human form. Not as the boy she'd come to know and trust as Rowek, but as man.

She sensed him then, glancing his way, but not in surprise. They often met in her dreams and he liked that she expected him. He couldn't help the way his lips curved. It wasn't as if he thought she'd be happy to see him, but the lack of instant hatred she normally flung his way had filled him with pleasure.

"What are you doing here?" she asked, breathy.

He turned his attention to the ocean, unable to sense the creatures that hunted within its depths. "Came to enjoy a swim. Want to join me?"

She narrowed her eyes at him as she shoved her hands into the pockets of her tight-fitting skinny jeans. "The water would be freezing here, no matter what time of year it is." Her words felt more like a stated fact than a rebuttal to wade into the water with him.

He wanted to reach for her, to pull her along with him. If he was in her dreams, then the temperature of the water was entirely up to the imaginings of her subconscious.

"It's only cold if you want it to be. If you tell the sun to shine, then it will." He grinned at her. "You hold all the power in your hands."

Her lips parted as she looked at him again. "Because I'm dreaming?"

He leaned closer to her, the thrill of her breath mingling with his, shooting through him. "Only if you want to be."

She studied him for a moment, not pulling away, but not leaning into him either. "You're hurt."

Startled, he stepped back.

"Your face is gaunt, and your eyes look as though you're in pain."

As if giving her words life, his entire body throbbed with so much pain, he doubled over. He didn't let a single sound escape his lips, crushing them together to hold it in. She crouched down in front of him, eyebrows knitting together. She reached for him then stopped herself, pulling her hands back and fisting the sand instead.

"Adrianna is in Sheol," he grunted, forcing out the words. "I don't know why, but they want me to forget you. Your father wants to *cleanse* me of my *emotions*." He spat out the words like they tasted of rot on his tongue.

Emma sucked in a sharp breath. "She's there?" Her eyes closed and she shook her head, the despair plain on her face.

"Don't shake your head and look as if the entire world has fallen on your shoulders," Levaroth scolded. He met her tortured gaze, holding it for several beats. "You aren't beaten. If you want to make the world bow at your feet, you can. I meant what I said: the world is what you imagine it to be."

Her expression turned cold. "The entire reason I'm a slave to my father's will—a turned spy to my people—is because of you. My mother is in literal hell, because of you, and now, so is my best friend."

She stood and let the sand fall from her hands, and as each grain fell, the shared dream dissolved.

When Levaroth felt the full gravity of his injuries, he shuddered. Sensing he was not alone, he cracked open the one eye that wasn't completely swollen shut.

Dull, flickering candlelight illuminated his prison, though neither he nor Tlahaz, who stood behind Adrianna, needed the light to see. It was her mortal eyes that adjusted, taking in Levaroth's shredded and bruised skin. Her jaw went slack and she retreated a step, only to meet the unyielding body behind her. He was physically less lethal in the smooth, human skin he chose, but still his body was decorated with sheathed blades. Enough for an armory.

Tlahaz gripped her biceps, steadying her, and Levaroth noted the way he held her to him. It was a light yet firm touch. Not meant to hurt, or even to warn her from fleeing. It was to anchor her.

If Levaroth could snort a laugh in his state, he might have. "You seem rather taken with that witch, Tlahaz." The congealed blood in his throat made his words sound gurgled. Adrianna winced at the sound. "And you think she can erase my mind of Emma?"

Tlahaz's nostrils flared as he released a lengthy breath. "I know she can."

Adrianna glanced behind her at Tlahaz. From the way that she no longer looked afraid, he guessed she was a willing party in all of this. She nodded, as if agreeing to some unspoken demand, then stepped closer.

Levaroth's chest rattled as he breathed in deep. The girl walked closer, and he lowered his head to whisper, "If I forget her, then she'll be in even more danger than she's already in."

When Adrianna leveled her gaze with his, a resignation was etched into her features that made his breaths come faster. Harder.

"Adrianna." His voice was a plea as her hands raised. Her palms glowed with brilliant purple light.

"This may hurt a little."

10

His eyes squeezed shut and he withdrew inside himself. He sought his tether to Emma and clamped every ounce of his determination into holding it tight. He would not forget her.

He couldn't, or she'd die.

The pain exploded behind his eyelids, as if his skull was being melted from the inside.

His lips parted and he wasn't sure if he screamed, but when the searing, blinding pain began to recede, his throat was raw. His face was damp. With tears or blood, he wasn't sure. Perhaps a mix.

Adrianna stood hunched over, breathing just as heavy as he did. And Tlahaz was standing just above her, brows drawn together in a look that Levaroth might have almost confused with concern.

"Did it work?" Tlahaz asked.

Levaroth already knew it hadn't. He was clinging to every image of Emma: her wild waves brushing her delicate shoulders. Her shining emerald eyes filled with goodness and determination. Her curves and the feel of her skin beneath his fingertips, his lips.

"No," Adrianna rasped. "I couldn't even get inside his mind. I had no idea it was going to be so much more protected than humans.'"

Levaroth barked a laugh, then wheezed from the pain that jolted his ribcage. The flesh on the tips of his wings seared from pulling against the nails that held them pinned to the wall.

His body was utterly ruined.

But his mind was, so far, impenetrable.

For Emma's sake, he hoped it remained that way.

EMMA

E mma awoke with a start. The room was still dark, and the constant warmth and comfort that Blaze's proximity brought her told her it was the middle of the night. It wasn't the first time Levaroth had invaded her dreams, but his usual swagger and domineering obsession with her had been absent this time.

Always, when he arrived in her dreams, they were somewhere new. The first time, she'd been back in Sheol, searching for her mom, and Levaroth had appeared behind her and told her to give up looking for her mother. When she had refused, he demanded that she be "a good little soldier" and do what her father told her. All the while, his eyes focused on her lips, until he'd pushed her against the unforgiving stone wall and tried to kiss her. She'd slapped him, and then she'd woken up.

But each time she saw him, he was less like an abrasive scouring pad on her person, and more…defeated. Tired. He hadn't tried to kiss her this time. There was something about the way he spoke to her that was almost final. But she wasn't sure why.

You aren't beaten. If you want to make the world bow at your feet, you can.

Empowering words from a powerful being. The only thing she truly wanted right now was to save her mother and Hadessah and get her father's mark removed. It was completely invisible,

12

even to her own eyes, but she could feel it like a leech buried beneath her skin.

Every time she tried to communicate something about the curse she was forced to bear, her lips would mash shut as if glued that way. And pain would light up the mark in her shoulder blade, shooting down her spine.

There were no loopholes. No way of betraying her forced servitude to her father. For now, at least, she allowed herself to be the pawn. She had agreed to it after all. In order to ensure her mother's safety, Emma had traded her freedom to become her father's slave. Whatever he willed, she was forced to do. Any information she heard at the compound spilled from her lips without her consent whenever her father commanded it. Fortunately, he'd called on her only once in the two weeks she'd been back.

Her chest tightened as it always did when she felt the full weight of her entrapment. But she forced her morose thoughts away and after another hour of staring into the darkness, she let sleep take hold again.

Instead of blissful, dreamless slumber, the fiery depths of Sheol rose to encircle her. But this time, Levaroth was not there to pull her from her nightmares.

4

BLAZE

Her screams tore through him, jarring him awake. His heart jackhammered in his chest as he leapt from his bed and threw open the two doors separating them. He'd convinced Emma to keep them unlocked at night after he ripped them both off their hinges the first night she'd awoken him with her terrified screaming.

Twisted in the duvet, her limbs flailed wildly, fighting off an invisible attacker. His heart clawed up his throat at the sight, and he rushed to her, pinning her arms and crushing her to his chest.

"Shhh," he soothed as she still fought. "Shhhh."

Her efforts turned limp as a broken sob wrenched from her throat. Blaze swallowed hard, smoothing the hair away from her face. It was knotted and wild from the significant fight she had been putting up. The same every night.

He let her cry, hoping she'd be able to fall back asleep in his arms as she sometimes did, but when her tears stopped she pushed away from his chest.

"I'm okay," she said, her voice scratchy.

Blaze didn't feel like arguing with her. It never did him any good. She always refused to tell him anything. About her dreams, or her time in Sheol.

"Let's go get some training in before everyone else wakes." She slid from the bed, still not meeting his gaze.

14

He grabbed her gently by the forearm, stopping her from escaping him. "You need to talk about it, Emma," he said. "Every night you wake up screaming but you won't tell me anything. If you can't tell me, find someone you *can* tell." He'd meant Gertie or perhaps one of the forty-eight Giborim females housed within the protection of the magical wards after abductions of Giborim females began several months ago, but Emma just shook her head.

"I'm fine. Really. Let's go get some work in, please."

He sighed, running a hand through his hair. "I'll meet you downstairs."

She nodded, standing perfectly still as he headed back to his room, adjoined with hers.

From outside the training room he heard her grunts and punches thudding against the punching bags. He waltzed into the room, watching her as she huffed. Punched. Kicked. She didn't look up, though he knew she could sense him from the rigid set of her spine.

Over and over her hits echoed in the large space.

Jab.

Kick.

Spin.

Kick.

Jab, jab, jab.

Duck, jab.

Kick.

Spin.

Her entire body looked more toned. Every subtle curve and divet of hard-earned muscle moved and tightened with her repetitive actions. They trained together every morning, sometimes for hours, or at least until he was called away by the elders and region leaders for meetings on strategy and news of the world outside the compound. He was glad to spend time with her—at least with him, she was safe—but she may as well have been miles away. She was distracted. Stuck in her own head. He allowed her silence because he had plenty on his mind too.

Every nation had fallen into discord with more political leaders being murdered daily. Each time someone new tried to take charge, they too were thrown out of the mix. Riots and looting were how the humans fought for their survival, instead ensuring their deaths.

Wordlessly, Blaze slipped on boxing gear and made his way toward Emma. Knowing from experience never to let an opponent sneak up on her, he cleared his throat.

She whirled and lunged for him. He dodged; she rolled gracefully back to her feet, fists protecting her face. Her entire body was coiled, ready to defend or attack—an angry wolf staring down the larger alpha pack leader. Though she watched him, she didn't really *see* him. He wondered how much longer her disconnect would last. What would he do if she never recovered? The thought made him swallow hard, his chest aching.

They were both broken in different ways. Surely, they'd anchor each other.

He faked a left hook, then swung his right leg out to knock her off her feet, but she jumped over it. The ease in which they fought—like an elegant, yet brutal dance—made him complacent. It lowered his guard enough for her to spin away from his assault and land a kick—too fast to anticipate—to his chest, sending him sprawling back.

Sweat dripped from her brow, her eyes aglow with eerie green light. He stared up at her, forcing a smile. "Good one."

"Again," she heaved.

"How about we use strike pads instead? Then you can just go rapid-fire? Help you work through whatever the hell it is you can't tell me."

She glowered. "I will. Eventually. I just need time."

Blaze huffed as he got to his feet. "Time is not on our side right now, Emma. It's something we have very little of." The moment he'd spoken the words, he realized they were too harsh.

Her brows slammed down, anger coursing over her features. "Again!"

He shook his head, but obliged her, taking the offensive to throw three quick jabs toward her chest and face which she dodged and blocked. Not wasting any time, she threw two punches of her own that he easily leapt away from, giving him enough room to throw a kick to her abdomen, his foot stopping an inch from her heaving chest. She knocked his foot away and they reset.

He grinned at the flustered way she rushed him again, taking the opportunity to pull her to him, lock her arms to her sides, and force her to look at him at last.

"Not fair," she panted.

His lips brushed against hers, the spark of their touch rushing through him. He didn't have to fake any sort of attraction to her. Their touch was electric. And her body responded in kind, the steely way she held herself melting against him, fitting her every contour to his like two pieces of a puzzle clicking into place.

He made quick work of his gloves, freeing his hands. Her heart thumped hard against his bare chest as he snaked a hand up the curve of her hip and around her back, climbing until he grasped the nape of her neck and pulled her lips hard against his, swallowing her gasp.

Every ounce of his desperation to be near her, to feel her—to be sure she was really here, and he wasn't still living the nightmare her two-week absence had been—was channeled into the way his tongue delved between her lips, tasting her.

His loosened grip allowed her to free her arms. After getting her own gloves off—the soft thump of them hitting the mat lost to his ears—she wound her fingers in the back of his hair and tugged him even closer.

17

Then she broke away, grinning slyly, though her eyes looked a little dazed. She raised her hands, gesturing him to continue their sparring.

A rumble sounded in his chest as he launched himself at her, his blood thundering in his ears. "Picture whoever it is that attacks you in your dreams, Emma. Conquer them."

She faltered, and he barely had enough time to draw back the force of his blow so it didn't knock her unconscious. At the last second, she leapt right, and his fist hit her shoulder. She didn't even seem to notice.

"What? No, I can't."

He shook out his arms, expelling the excess force he'd fought to contain. "Just try it, it might help."

"I could hurt you," she protested, standing frozen and unprotected. But the vulnerability in her eyes kept him from taking that advantage.

"You won't hurt me."

She bit her bottom lip, seeming to consider it. Then she nodded.

He smiled, as though this were a small victory toward her being able to confide in him.

She backed up, rolling her shoulders then her neck. He tried to avoid staring at her impressive form. In every way, she was a formidable opponent and—he had no doubt—his equal. A woman more than worthy to fight by his side in this war, and if they survived, any wars that threatened humankind thereafter.

When she looked at him again, her expression hardened, and her eyes pulsed with emerald light. She stepped into a ready stance.

Then she lunged.

Faster than he had ever seen her move before, she blurred, and then in a burst of blue, yellow, orange, and red—

She ignited.

Dancing, curling flames covered her body. He shot back in surprise, but the sight of her distracted him enough that the first hit came to his jaw. Cold, then searing hot, exploded in his face as she landed blow after blow. Then his chest and anywhere else she could reach was filled with pain. Everywhere she touched, she burned.

He roared as agony pierced him, dropping him to his knees.

The smell of charred flesh and burnt hair was everywhere, and his vision blurred. But mercifully, she no longer touched him.

"Ohmygod! Blaze!" Her voice was choked and distant. She fell to her knees in front of him, her ivory skin unblemished by the fire that had covered her. Though his attention stuttered on the fact that he could see her knees when she had been wearing full-length workout pants.

He held up a hand, feeling himself sway. His body fell forward, onto his other fist, and he gritted his teeth against the jarring pain.

"Did you know you could do that?"

He heard her sob. "Yes."

"Why didn't you tell me?" His words were slow. Pained.

She didn't answer.

As his body worked to heal his wounds, he dragged his eyes up her crouched form. Which held a few burned scraps of clothing that did little to cover her. His gaze made her look down, and her face turned red instantly.

She jumped to her feet with a squeaked "I'm so sorry," then turned and ran from the room.

If his entire body hadn't been engulfed in enough pain to make his vision swim, he'd have chased after her. Instead, all he could do was wait until his accelerated healing eased the burning from his wounds.

He hung his head, his breathing shallow. It was clear that whatever Emma was dealing with in her dreams haunted her during the day too. He had no doubt she had faced many horrors in Sheol. But without her willingness to share, he wasn't sure how to help her get over it.

A low whistle sounded from the doorway. "Playing with

matches again, brother?" Axel called, amusement thick in his tone.

Blaze wanted to pummel his brother for cracking a joke when he no doubt looked like he'd run through a house fire.

"Ah, no, I get it!" His brother snapped his fingers. "You wanted to *look* like a Blaze, so you set yourself ablaze." Axel cackled with laughter.

"Dear god, why do you act like you're still sixteen?" Blaze muttered.

"It's quite common to go through another adolescent-type phase every few centuries. Without the puberty, thankfully."

Blaze groaned. "Your presence is more painful than these burns." But he could feel the sting receding enough that he sat back onto his heels, ignoring the way his head throbbed.

Axel smirked. "I could give you some more to even it out."

"I'll pass."

Axel strode toward him, stopping to stare at the smoking crater of blackened training mat where Emma had attacked him.

"Lover's quarrel?" Axel asked wryly, though his brows knitted together in a small show of concern. When Blaze didn't answer, he continued. "I'm actually here to tell you the happy news first." He paused, meeting Blaze's gaze. His sky-blue eyes seemed duller somehow, though Blaze was sure it was just the light. "Emerelda and I are engaged. We'll be wed in two weeks' time."

Blaze gave a humorless laugh. "And if we're at war in two weeks?"

Axel shrugged. "She's planning the engagement party for Friday. No doubt her whole family will try to find some way to make it over for the wedding."

Blaze shook his head and sighed. This certainly wasn't the time to be thinking about weddings. They were about to go to war with the Shediem, on top of the fact that they still needed to secure as many numbers for their side as possible. There was no doubt that the Shediem were taking Spellcasters and any other supernatural beings by force.

"Now just isn't a good time to—"

"When *is* a good time?" Axel snapped. He sighed, the brimming anger in his eyes fading. "Look, you know Emerelda and I have always had wrong timing and whatnot. I betrayed her once, brother. I won't do it again. I love her."

With the deep, oozing wounds on his body mostly healed, Blaze stood, keeping eye contact with his brother. He deserved happiness after being forced to break courtship of Emerelda fifty or so years ago, because their father didn't approve.

Blaze nodded. He clasped his brother's hand, shaking it with a smile. "I wish you both all the best."

"Thank you, brother," Axel said. With a dip of his head he turned. Stalking from the room with a jaunt in his step, he called back over his shoulder, "I'd hide that mat *and* that particularly unfortunate side effect of your girl's anger from Uncle if I were you."

Looking back to the blackened spot on the mat and then down at his obliterated shirt, Blaze sighed.

5

ADRIANNA

A message materialized on the mattress directly in front of her at noon. It was coal black with words inlaid with gold script, requesting her presence for dinner. Pushing aside the letter she had been writing to her siblings— letters she wrote but never sent, considering her family no longer remembered who she was—she picked up the thick card. She imagined the invite was extended to Tlahaz too, though it was addressed only to her.

The king had perfect, elegant penmanship. She stared down at the note for several minutes, her heart beating wildly. Athena—who had been snoring a low, rumbly sound, curled up beside her—lifted her violet, scaly head, no doubt sensing Adrianna's rising panic. Adrianna patted her wyvern's head just above the small, studded spikes dotting the crown of her skull. Her fearsome familiar snorted in contentment before continuing her snooze.

Adrianna had met the king already, but he'd never insisted on her presence at all since being brought to Sheol. She knew why she was here, and so did the king. Perhaps he wanted to discuss the little progress she'd made so far. Every morning she was marched down to Levaroth's cell, and every morning she tried accessing his memories. Levaroth kept a solid wall in place attempting to thwart her attempts, but today, she'd had a small success.

She'd gotten inside his mind. Seen his intimate memories of Emma, both as Rowek and as a suave businessman. She'd seen other things too, horrible things. Like murder. So much murder. He enjoyed killing. It sustained him; he needed it like humans needed food and water.

Tlahaz fed off emotions, not just fear, but it was blood that he preferred. He said the emotions were more potent in the bloodstream. It was why he'd fed from her.

A shiver coursed through her at the memory of how it had caused both pain and pleasure. Unwilling to stop, it had nearly driven him mad. Now, even when he looked worn down or just plain hungry, she offered him a little bit of her blood, and always he refused.

She couldn't decide if the twisting in her gut when he refused was due to relief or disappointment. They had a mutual attraction that was undeniable, but it ran a little deeper. He didn't want to hurt her, and despite the constant tricks and pranks she pulled on him, she had to admit she liked having him around.

As if her thoughts had summoned him, Tlahaz opened the door and stormed inside, looking agitated.

"Bad day at the office, dear?" she asked, smiling sweetly.

Tlahaz grunted, shucking off his armor with a clang. Black liquid was splashed across his ruggedly handsome face and arms. Training, he always said. She pursed her lips as her gaze slid from his face to his wings.

With a gasp, she leapt off the bed, ignoring Athena's rumble of disapproval. "Your wing!" Adrianna rushed toward Tlahaz, magic rising to her palms, filling them with gentle light. One of his wings was bent at an odd angle, dragging on the floor, many of the lustrous feathers ripped off and exposing the same leathery grey flesh as the rest of his lethal, muscular body.

With a low growl he held up a hand, and she stopped with a huff. His golden eyes flashed dangerously.

Folding her arms over her chest, she cocked a hip to the side. "I know you can heal it on your own, but it looks damn painful."

"I don't care," he said, his words muffled around his full, distended canines.

So that was why he didn't want her getting close.

"What happened?" Adrianna asked.

"Training," he answered.

She rolled her eyes. "Who could have possibly broken your wing like that? Is anyone that stupid?"

His answering grunt almost sounded like a laugh. "Apparently."

He started to move past her and toward the bathroom, but she stepped in front of him, blocking him.

"Move, Witch."

She smirked. "Please tell me your next words are 'Get out the way.'"

He lifted a single brow. "You say the oddest things sometimes. But yes, get out of my way, or I'll move you myself."

She didn't budge. "You need blood. When was the last time you fed?"

"I don't *need* blood, Witch. Your damn scent makes me hungry."

His words sent a little thrill through her—part fear, and part excitement. She loved that she had an effect on him, but she tried not to push him. She'd seen enough teenage vampire flicks to know that when a hot guy craved your blood, it was best not to tempt him.

"You say the sweetest things, darling. Now about your wing." Her tone was flat. "Who broke it?"

Tlahaz grumbled something too low for her to hear before scrubbing a hand down his face and huffing a breath. "I've been training the young hybrids—the half-Giborim, half-Shediem children that Prince Asmodeus sends to the king for testing. They have powers much like your *friend*, Emma."

She tried not to bristle at the way he said *friend* but stayed silent for him to continue. She'd heard about the newest little army the king was concocting. It was vile and sadistic, and most

Spellcasters were used to speed their growth. The resulting child had powers beyond the average Shediem, making them valuable weapons.

"One of the little hell-spawns can move things with its mind, and thought it'd be a good idea to try to remove my wing."

Her eyes widened as she clapped a hand to her mouth, stifling her gasp. "Holy crap. But at least the child was unsuccessful."

Tlahaz glowered. "No, it broke in four different places before it was ripped off. I had to hold it in place until it could reattach before the breaks healed. It looked much worse than this." Already, it was straightening.

She marveled at his accelerated healing. It would be a nice thing to have in the coming war, but she'd just have to settle for her magic.

Tlahaz, no longer wanting to chat, picked up Adrianna under her arms and lifted her like a bag of feathers. She sighed as he set her beside the doorway and stalked into the bathroom.

"Oh by the way, your king sent an invite for dinner tonight," she called in after him, peeking to catch a glimpse of him stripping out of the tight-fitting pants he wore, to no avail.

"You've got to be…" The last of his sentence was drowned out by the water turning on. Part of her wanted to invade his privacy, just to annoy him. Instead, she turned, a sinking sensation in her gut causing her to climb back to bed and burrow under the covers.

The heat of her familiar along with her soft, vibrating breaths gave her comfort and strength to face the evening ahead.

Tlahaz walked beside her in the echoing halls with only the sound of their steps for her to focus on. That, and imagining a million ways the night could end in her death, or worse.

The gauzy pink chiffon dress that had been delivered to their door an hour before they were meant to leave swayed about her ankles. Delicate layers fluttered behind her, giving the illusion of a princess trapped in the castle with a fire-breathing dragon preventing her escape. Except it was an all-powerful king of darkness as well as a surly Shediem general that prevented her from leaving her elaborate dungeon of sorts. And in her case, it wasn't a dragon at all, but a wyvern who guarded her. The fire-breathing thing was still not present, but as she and Athena strengthened their bond, Adrianna could feel the beast's strength growing.

Perhaps soon she'd be breathing flames.

When they reached the golden double doors with thick black vines creeping over them, Tlahaz straightened, his cool, detached demeanor slipping into place like a mask. Adrianna's stomach clenched, feeling like the doors would open and reveal a lion's den.

Inside these doors, Tlahaz would not protect her, if he even acknowledged her.

Without warning, the doors creaked and opened seemingly of their own accord. They stepped into what Adrianna thought was a room, though she couldn't say for sure. Vines and trees grew wildly. Underfoot were roots and soft, spongy earth that her heels sank into. Sounds of birds tweeting and a stream gurgling filled the space.

Above, a warm buttery sunlight streamed in through the canopy of trees. In the center of it all was a long wooden table. Nakosh sat at its head, a small smile playing on his full, sensual lips.

It had to be an illusion of some kind. She'd been outside the walls of the castle, where nothing grew and there was certainly no sunlight.

The coiling black shadows that danced and played over the king's body moved away from his hands when he stood, gesturing to the two empty seats on either side of him.

"Come, my children. Sit."

Adrianna didn't argue, instead heading for her seat as carefully as she could without screaming. At one point she was certain that something resembling a root had slithered away. There weren't live snakes in here, were there?

Tlahaz took his seat, back ramrod straight, his expression vacant. Adrianna sat in her own, her gaze on the setting before her: glimmering, meticulously placed forks in various sizes to her right, knives to her left, and two odd-looking spoons above where a plate should be. A silly, sparkling cage.

"Welcome, welcome," Nakosh greeted in his soft, velvety voice. "Do you like what I've done with the place?"

Adrianna nodded, glancing up to offer a small smile. His stunning silver eyes held her gaze for several moments.

Around them, people she hadn't noticed before—probably because they were dressed like trees—stepped forward to fill their crystal goblets with wine the color of blood. It smelled sweet, yet earthy. The one pouring hers truly looked as though their skin was made of bark. She tried not to gawk at the realistic foliage. Or at the caterpillar slinking up the server's trunk-like torso.

Her nose wrinkled involuntarily at the sight, drawing a soft, melodic laugh from the king, and she promptly schooled her expression.

Across the table, the tree-person looked like they might tip over at any moment from the tall, sprawling branches and vines hanging from them that swayed when they moved.

When the servers finished filling the glasses, they stepped back, materializing into the shadows again, their steps eerily soundless.

"The most powerful Spellcaster to ever live sits at my table," the king mused softly. "I just wonder…"

Adrianna felt a lump rising in her throat, but she fought the urge to swallow it down, knowing he'd hear it.

Tlahaz shifted in his seat, forcing both their gazes to him. "Master, we appreciate your hospitality, but may I enquire as to the—"

"You want to know why I've brought you here," Nakosh finished briskly, bringing his goblet to his lips and swallowing a healthy mouthful of the wine.

Tlahaz inclined his head respectfully. He avoided her gaze, just like she thought he would.

Swirling his cup, the king stared down into the funneled wine as though it held the answers he longed for. His host of writhing, dancing shadows picked up their pace, reflecting the unsettling feeling in the room. Setting his goblet onto the table at last, he pinned Adrianna yet again with his chilling gaze.

"How goes the memory work with our friend Levaroth? Asmodeus is most anxious to have his best soldier back in fighting shape."

Her heart sank as her mouth opened to respond, but it was Tlahaz that answered for her. "She was having difficulty breaching his mind until today. Now that she is past the first obstacle, I suspect his memories will be sufficiently twisted in no time."

"Hmm." The king's eyes never left Adrianna's, though he didn't seem upset by the news at all. In fact, no emotion crossed his features at all, though it was difficult to see with the inky blackness passing over his face.

Finally, he leaned back, crossed a lean leg over the other, and looked from her to Tlahaz. "Good work, my dear. And are the two of you enjoying your time together?"

If Adrianna had sipped from the wine—which she had decided not to partake of—it would have been the perfect moment to choke on it in a display of shock at his line of questioning.

Tlahaz shifted again, looking the slightest bit uncomfortable. Adrianna smiled to herself, enjoying the way he suddenly looked like he might flee the room.

"Fine, my king. The witch enjoys her practical jokes, but I have come to tolerate her."

Her "practical jokes" ranged anywhere from enchanting his cutlery to dance right out of his grasp to making his weapons and armor invisible. None of which he ever found as amusing as she did.

Before Adrianna could snort a laugh, the king burst out with shrill laughter, making him look even more unhinged than he usually did.

The room fell deadly silent. Even the creatures occupying the strange forest stilled. If the king noticed the veil of fear that covered everyone, he didn't let on. He smiled wide, flashing a glint of sharp canines.

"My dear, you are even more fascinating than I could have known." Nakosh studied her appreciatively.

Adrianna forced a smile, but Tlahaz scoffed. "More like a severe pain in the arse," he grumbled.

Her smile turned genuine. Looking toward him, she said with false sweetness, "It's only fair to play a prank or two on the demon that kidnaps you."

A softer laugh came from the king, but Adrianna was too busy staring down the general, who glared right back.

Their stare-off was interrupted only when plates of food appeared on the table, startling her back into remembering where she was and who had invited her there tonight.

She noted long trays of what looked like assorted sushi, steaming crab legs drenched with butter, and sizzling steaks with mushrooms. But other dishes made her skin crawl. A stuffed serpent, coiled on the plate with unblinking eyes. A plucked bird that was too big to be common bird yet too small to be a chicken, its neck far longer than that of a duck.

Further down she spied a mountain of something breaded and deep fried. But as she continued to stare at the wide bodies and eight long legs, she realized with a barely contained shriek that they were very large spiders.

"See anything you like?" Nakosh asked, his voice dripping with dark amusement.

Any appetite she'd previously had, vanished. And that was saying something for her. With a snap of his fingers, one of the cooked spiders disappeared from the pile. Nervously she checked her plate, releasing a sigh of relief to see it was still empty.

The crunch from beside her told her the king was now eating one of the vile creatures.

"Having flashbacks, Witch?" Tlahaz asked with a smug smirk.

Adrianna wanted to slap it off his face a few hundred times over. "Whatever breed of spiders those are, they don't exist in Washington. The ones you had carry me were far smaller."

"These are camel spiders, I believe," Nakosh interjected smoothly.

Adrianna's stomach turned, but Tlahaz selected several pieces of the sushi, looking unaffected. After a few minutes of both Shediem eating in relative silence, Adrianna plucked a half-dozen crab legs with lemon juice and butter from the serving dish.

She'd just cracked the first leg when the king wiped his mouth on a cloth he'd placed on his lap.

"The real reason I asked you here, Miss Adrianna, was to ask for your assistance in growing the Anakeem Asmodeus has been creating. When you're not working with Levaroth, of course."

"Anakeem?" she asked, feigning ignorance.

He smiled, already comprehending her knowledge on the matter. "The half-Giborim, half-Shediem children. They have shown a great many powers that would be valuable to us in the coming war. We are in need of a powerful Spellcaster to aid in speeding their growth."

Adrianna felt her stomach churn violently. She pushed her plate away with a sigh. Apparently the king was determined to ruin her dinner at every turn.

She chose her words with care, ignoring the look of warning Tlahaz shot her from across the table.

"If I were to help in this matter, I'd need something in return."

Nakosh smiled. "I thought you might say that."

"Thought, or knew?" she asked without any malice.

He paused, pretending to think. "I'll save you time by saying I know what you're going to ask for. I know whom you wish to protect. Did Tlahaz not already guarantee their safety?"

She inclined her head. "To the best of his abilities, but his true loyalties lie with you. Should you be displeased with my progress, I want your assurance that my family will not be used as bargaining chips. No matter what, they need to survive."

Tlahaz grunted his disapproval at her boldness, but she didn't care. There was no one but Emma who would miss her if she died. If the king got offended over her attempting to bargain, then there was nothing she could do about it.

But Nakosh merely smiled. The swirling darkness caressed the sharp angle of his jaw and the corner of his full lips that looked too sensual. Her cheeks heated and his smile grew.

"Very well, Spellcaster, I accept. You start in the morning."

EMMA

H is wounds were so bad, his skin bubbled and oozed when she fled. She blinked away the tears that burned her eyes—she wouldn't let them fall.

She'd only just entered the hall when a thought occurred to her. In an instant, the burnt scraps that dangled from her body shifted and spread across her body until she wore full workout gear again.

After two and a half weeks, the perk of Prince Belphegor's powers remained: the ability to transform an object into another. She practiced changing one object she owned into something else entirely for several days after. When her laptop had decided to stop turning on last week, she held it and focused on a newer, sleeker model. And it had changed into it, functioning as a brand-new device.

At first, the power had felt a little like theft, and she had wondered if somewhere in a shop nearby, a MacBook Pro had gone missing. But when she had tried to find out from Blaze, he'd asked too many questions that she couldn't answer, and so she'd left it alone. She didn't have a car—not that she could leave anyway—but she'd been told many times that the state of Seattle these days was bad.

No, *worse*. It was chaos.

A missing MacBook Pro wouldn't be a big deal in the grand scheme of things, she'd assured herself. And the more she used her new ability, the more she found herself looking around her room for things to upgrade. Until it occurred to her that there was nothing beyond her reach. She could exchange rocks for gold. Anything she wanted could be hers. It was a dangerous power. She couldn't will anything out of thin air—it was an exchange of sorts—but as long as she could envision what she wanted, it became so.

On the walk of shame back to her room, she'd spied Axel standing in the shadowed alcove, watching her with cool blue eyes. With a small, forced flash of a smile, she hurried past him, eager not to make any conversation with anyone.

She did that a lot lately. It was easier to avoid people than to make excuses for things her father's power forced her to conceal.

In her room, with the doors locked, Emma flung herself onto her mattress with a heavy sigh. Rolling onto her back, she stared up at the high beige ceiling. She felt beside her until her hand hit the wooden side table, and on it, her phone. It was a new phone that Blaze acquired for her after she broke the one from her mom. Emma held it up in front of her face, selecting Adrianna's number, then paused. Of course she wouldn't answer, but Emma wanted to hear her friend's voice. When she returned from Sheol she'd tried to call Adrianna, but every time, there had been no answer—now she knew why.

She hit the call button, and Adrianna's voice immediately filled the speaker. "Hey, losers, it's Adrianna. Sorry I can't answer the phone right now, so leave a message!"

Emma sighed, then dropped the phone onto the mattress. The ache in her chest every time she thought about her friend only got worse, especially now that she knew Adrianna was in Sheol.

She was rubbing the spot above her heart, as if she could soothe it from the outside, when a knock sounded.

Her stomach tightened, but the warm, soothing presence of Blaze wasn't on the other side of the door. She'd requested all of her meals to be sent to her room so she had one less reason to leave it, but the knock didn't sound like Gertie's either.

"Come in," Emma said, sitting up.

The tall man with tidy blond hair and goatee she'd come to know as Sergei stepped inside, carrying a breakfast tray with two steaming plates on top.

"Morning," he said in his heavily accented voice.

When Emma had returned to the compound, Sergei was there, red-eyed and worn. He'd already known her mother was in Sheol and unlike most of the Giborim, he hadn't asked many questions.

"Morning," Emma said wearily.

"Do you mind?" He gestured to her small table with two chairs. She shook her head and got to her feet to join him as he set the tray down. "We haven't really gotten a chance to talk much. I think you have questions, perhaps?"

Emma didn't reply as she sat across the Russian Spellcaster who was in love with her mother. Who had been helping them from a distance her entire life. His eyes were dazzling blue, his smile warm and inviting.

And if she was being honest with herself, he was a good-looking guy. Even though his suit trousers were wrinkled and his white button-up shirt was rolled up his toned forearms, Emma guessed his unkempt appearance had more to do with her mother's absence than an inability to properly dress himself.

She lifted a steaming mug of strong coffee and let the aroma wash over her, eyes closed. Her throat burned as tears prickled behind her eyelids. When she opened them, Sergei gave her a sad smile.

"I miss her too, *Lastachka.*"

She didn't know what that meant but she nodded, swallowing back the wave of grief.

"I'm working on a spell that would allow me to travel to Sheol without an invitation. I could get her and bring her back." He spoke the words casually while cracking open his soft-boiled egg.

Emma choked into her coffee.

34

His gaze flicked to her with concern as she pounded her fist against her chest.

When she was finally able to breathe again—her nasal passage burning—she said, "You can't do that."

"Why not?" His voice was stern.

Emma felt her lips press together tightly, and she rooted around in her brain for an explanation that wouldn't include any mention of Sheol or the Shediem.

"Besides the fact that it's not safe," she said, folding her arms across her chest, "who knows if you'd be able to locate her."

Her spine tingled in warning and her tongue felt heavy, but she'd managed to get the words out.

Sergei shrugged as he dipped his toast into the soft, gooey yolk and took a bite. He chewed, looking thoughtful, but Emma didn't attempt to eat a bite of her breakfast. Her stomach had begun to knot itself, and nausea replaced her appetite.

"With Gertie's help, the task should not be a problem."

She admired his confidence, but from the exhaustion that creased his face *and* his clothes she didn't think that it would be nearly as easy as he suggested.

A bulge appeared on his shoulder under his shirt and it… moved! Emma gasped when it moved again. Before she could shout, Sergei glanced down at it, frowning.

"Come on then, Ugo."

Her brows creased as a small, furry white face peered from under his collar.

"What is that?" she exclaimed.

Little by little the creature climbed out of Sergei's shirt, pausing to sniff the air, its beady red eyes locking onto Emma.

"This is my familiar, Ugo. He's actually a wolf but I changed him to a ferret so as not to alarm people."

Ugo the ferret scurried down Sergei's arm, darting for a slice of toast. It snatched the bread from the plate, carrying it between its sharp, tiny teeth to sit on the table. The sound of it crunching was all that filled the silence while Emma continued to gape.

"Familiar?" she asked.

"Uh, magical creature," he offered before dunking his own slice of toast in runny yolk and taking a bite. "It bonds to a Spellcaster in spirit and becomes physical to help protect us."

She blinked, a maelstrom of questions swirling in her mind. Did Adrianna have a familiar? Emma had never heard about them or seen an animal around Gertie.

"Do all Spellcasters have familiars?"

He shrugged. "Some Spellcasters lose theirs—they die protecting their bonded. In extremely rare cases, a Spellcaster has no bonded familiar. It occurs at birth, though a Spellcaster doesn't know what their familiar will be until their magic reaches its maturity."

Emma blew out a breath, feeling woefully uninformed. After a beat she asked, "Did my mom know about Ugo?"

Sergei nodded, sadness clouding his crystalline blue eyes.

She bit her lip, not wanting to upset him but also wanting to know more about him. About his relationship with her mother.

"How did you and my mom meet?" Emma asked, picking up her mug of black coffee again. She sipped as his lips stretched wide in a smile.

"Your mother told you that she is from Russia, like me, yes?"

She nodded as Sergei washed down another bite of yolk-covered toast with a large gulp of orange juice. Then he continued. "Our families lived next to each other, though not as close as houses in the cities. At night when her father was out conning the townspeople or drinking himself into a rage in a pub, she would sneak over to my mother's house." He paused to take a deep breath, his eyes misty. "My mother always made sure to send her back with enough food for her mother and her sister, Sasha."

Emma's heart leapt into her throat at the mention of her aunt. Her mother's sister. "Why did my mother lie and say she was an only child?"

Sergei forked a bite of eggs into his mouth and chewed in silence for a long moment. "She was ashamed to leave her sister behind. I think it was easier for her to believe Sasha had died than to deal with the shame of leaving her with the monster her father was."

"But he's dead now?" It seemed harsh to speak about her only grandparents that way, but from what her mother had told her of her grandfather, it was better she'd never known him.

Sergei nodded, his eyes icing over with clear disdain. "Terrible man. Good riddance. I'm not sorry he's dead. Only that his wife had tagged along that morning."

Emma blinked. "What do you mean?"

The blond man looked her over, deciding whatever he wanted to say was best left unsaid.

But Emma persisted. "No, it's okay. Tell me."

Sergei shook his head again and rose from his seat. "I should probably get back to work. I'll leave you to your day." He walked around the table and gently grasped her face in his large, calloused hands. Then he pressed a kiss to one cheek, then the next. His lips were warm, and when he stepped back, he pressed a final kiss to her forehead and whispered several words she didn't recognize.

"Thank you for having breakfast with this old man," he said with a smile, then headed for the door.

"Bye, Sergei," Emma said quietly. She stared after the man who had begun humming to himself as he shut the door, leaving her in perfect isolation once again.

Emma sighed warily as she grabbed her laptop and sat down on the bed, pushing the top open to boot it up.

School was out, probably forever with everything going on, but it brought her a small sense of normalcy to do something so mundane—even if she had to create her own school work.

She worked for an hour, researching the Second World War, though her concentration was sporadic. Her reading material slowly changed to weapons used in wars up through the latest one, before morphing into odd articles and journals by fanatics claiming to know parts of the supernatural races. It yielded little results, and she nearly gave up, until her gaze snagged on the words *demonic marking that possessed humans, making them mindless slaves.*

Heart racing, she read further, trying to find out if what the conspiracy theory blog was describing was what was done to her.

In ancient times, when demons commonly roamed, preying on humans at will, they each possessed a stone which when forced down a human's throat, placed them under the mind control of said demon.

The human possessed was capable of physical violence beyond the scope of the strongest human ever recorded, also granting untold speed and a thirst for other humans' blood. This pandemic of demonic control is what is thought to be the origins of vampires in human lore.

The only way to end the demon's control was to slay the human, carving open their gut and plucking the stone out before their powerful bodies could heal.

Emma's stomach churned at the thought. Was the mark that her father had bestowed upon her a common stone that all Shediem once had, or something more powerful?

The image underneath the paragraph depicted a human man with his mouth opened grotesquely wide and a long, rail-thin creature with fangs and red eyes shoving its lengthy arm down the human's throat. Emma cringed.

Her phone buzzed and she picked it up, still trying to piece together how much of what she was reading was fact, and how much was speculation. The text was from Blaze, saying that Axel had announced his engagement to Emerelda. A party was to be held at the end of the week.

Tossing the phone back onto the mattress, Emma heaved a sigh. She closed her laptop, admitting defeat for the day, when she felt the dreaded sensation in her chest that made her squeeze her eyes shut. Like hooks inside her ribcage, she felt her body ripped from the comfort of the compound.

Emma didn't scream this time. She hated that it made her father smile. The only sound that escaped her was the wince when she landed hard on her hands and knees, the cold stone biting her palms.

When she opened her eyes, the cruel smile of her father greeted her.

7

EMMA

Emma climbed to her feet, swallowing down the terror that clogged her senses. "I haven't found out anything new," she said. Her eyes searched for any sign of her mother, but only she and two other...*beings* were in the great echoing hall.

Asmodeus, prince of Sheol, looked like a man with a mess of dark curls. His lean body was adorned in an elegant black coat embellished with gold and red threads. He sat up tall, still managing to look intimidating as a man. Especially with eyes the color of blood. Beside him, cloaked in the shadows, was his personal guard, Geryon. The minotaur-like creature had the snout of a boar, beady black eyes, legs covered in tough blue alligator skin, and clawed feet like a dragon's. As far as Emma knew, he didn't speak. But his cold, empty stare never failed to send chills up her spine.

Her father leaned forward on his massive throne constructed entirely of human bones, his long fingers digging into the grooves between smooth, ivory pieces. "And what have you been doing this past week, daughter mine?" His voice was the thundering booms of boulders crashing together during a landslide.

Her lips parted of their own volition, spilling her secrets. "I've hid in my room during meetings and I avoid everyone in the compound." As soon as the words were out, she squeezed her eyes shut, waiting for her father's punishment.

In answer, pain flooded her head, trying to split it in two.

Her eyes felt as if they were being carved from her skull. She screamed, eyes flying open in silent pleading. Her knees knocked together as she gripped her head, vision blackening.

Then the pain fled, leaving only a dull ache.

Asmodeus smirked with chilling satisfaction. Rage burned in his bloodred eyes: a promise that her failings would not bring pain only to herself, but her mother would feel his wrath too.

"From this point forward, any meetings the Giborim hold, you must find a way to become a part of. Find out what their next moves will be. I want to know where and who they are recruiting."

Her skin prickled as she nodded. He didn't have to force her compliance in this—his glare was threat enough.

When she'd first arrived back from Sheol, she'd stuck to Blaze's side constantly. But then her father had forced her to tell him how many female Giborim were being protected at Blaze's manor and the name of the Spellcaster that provided the wards. To buy her out from under Blaze, Emma imagined. Thankfully Gertie was unfailingly loyal.

After that, Emma had purposefully feigned a headache every time Blaze suggested she sit in on a meeting with the Giborim leaders. Little by little, she withdrew, especially when more Giborim leaders and elders from all over the world began to arrive. And each of them demanded answers about her time in Sheol. About the ranks of Shediem, their numbers, any weaknesses they possessed. Unable to provide any answers, Emma had simply burst into tears and fled the room.

No one demanded anything of her anymore. Well, Blaze didn't, but she could tell he was just as desperate for any information she could provide. And she wanted to give it to them, anything that could be of use. But the Mark of Fallen Flame seared through her body and molded her lips shut to prevent it.

"I'll do as you've commanded. Now can I see my mother? I want to be sure she's still alive, and not impregnated with one of your creepy demon babies." She knew her words were risky, but she desperately wanted to see her mother.

Asmodeus tilted his sharp face in mock consideration as her heart fluttered in dread of his answer. "Get me what I've asked," he answered, stroking the top of a skull beneath his palm, "then you can see her."

An angry sound between a cry and a scream broke from deep in Emma's chest—a wretched, broken noise that made her seem like a wounded animal. She allowed his rejection to stoke the fires of her anger. One way or another, she'd break his control on her, then she'd rescue her mother. And Haddie. She just hoped she wouldn't be too late for either of them.

"Fine. Send me back—they're probably still holding a meeting."

"Actually, I have a problem that I want you to fix."

A shiver of trepidation ran down Emma's spine as Geryon disappeared from his spot. Without a word, a flurry of steps sounded in the corridor behind her, along with the rattling of chains. Her breath stalled in her lungs when a woman with matted, light brown hair was prodded ahead of Geryon by the tip of his double-edged axe. Her arms were secured behind her back with manacles, her face bruised and coated with dried, cracking blood. But Emma gasped at what she saw trailing behind the woman and Geryon.

Tear-stained and trembling, at least ten children no older than seven or eight filed into the hall.

Emma whipped around to face her father. "What is this?"

She could hear stifled sobs and sniffles from the children shuffling closer. The woman Geryon was watching as if she were dangerous appeared to be in her late thirties, and her tears fell, yet her expression was one of defiance. A thick, dirty scrap of cloth had been tied around her mouth, but she didn't try to speak. Didn't try to fight.

Emma's heart raced. Each face, even the children's, had dirt and bruises mottling their skin. They were all prisoners. But why? And why were they brought here? Her stomach twisted as she slowly turned to Asmodeus again.

"This is Elizabet," her father said like he was telling her a story. Emma listened, trying to ignore the way her heart pounded, sensing danger. "Formerly one of my Spellcasters in charge of accelerating the growth of the Anakeem—the hybrid children. She was caught hiding these pathetic creatures." Asmodeus gestured to the children, who trembled and wept silently. "Instead of disposing of the faulty ones with no powers, she hid them, lying and saying she *had* disposed of them."

Emma's fists clenched. She recalled the pregnant women her father had shown her. He'd explained how he wanted to use the children born of Giborim females, using Shediem DNA, to create powerful supernatural beings. And how they'd all be trained soldiers programmed for war and death.

She glanced back at the frightened children again. A jolt of pain ricocheted through her chest, sharp and cold, as the realization of what he wanted her to do sank in. She shook her head. They were supposed to be murdered because they were not the perfect, mindless assassins her father desired.

The woman, Elizabet, seemed to figure it out too because her sobs grew louder, muffled by the fabric stuffed into her mouth.

"No." The word barely made it past Emma's frozen lips. Her entire body was paralyzed with horror.

Asmodeus rose from his throne and glided down the stairs of his dais, his arms tucked behind his back. Ever the prince of war. He didn't have to worry about getting close to Emma now. He held her leash. She had no chance of attacking him when he least expected it.

He stopped in front of the tear-streaked faces, clucking his tongue like a disappointed father. They didn't all look like Emma or even resemble each other, which made her think he was not the father of many—if any—of these hybrids. Then again, his true eye color was not green, so perhaps his offspring only looked like the human form he chose at the time.

"In the beginning, most of the Anakeem died before they could be tested for powers. After that, few of those that survived had powers. But now, we've perfected the method." He smiled cruelly. She wondered what the hidden meaning was. "They have unparalleled powers, even for you. They know only the ways of the Shediem. They're bred for brutality. Except for these ones— the runts of the litter."

He circled the group of children as they cowered together. Many of them sent pleading glances in the Spellcaster's direction. She cried harder, knees giving out, and Geryon caught her with one arm before she could hit the floor. He held up the woman, who had lost the strength to stand. And Emma knew why.

She wanted to move in front of the children—wanted to protect them from her father. But whatever silent command he had given would not allow her to move.

"What about them?" she asked. "Sure, the woman shouldn't have been hiding them, but they're not to blame."

Asmodeus chuckled. "You cannot undo what this witch nurtured in them. As I found out with you, once there is human weakness, it cannot be rooted out. These ones are simply humans with long lives. They're nothing."

He stopped in front of Emma, and she felt her stomach drop. He was going to kill them. And he was going to force her to watch.

He leaned forward, his young, eerily striking features too close. His awful bloodred eyes fixed on hers. She almost thought she could count the drops of blood that filled them, but that would be an ocean. The bodies left in his wake were innumerable.

"Kill them all. Starting with the witch."

Her body went cold. Her tongue was cemented in her mouth. The sound of her heart hammering in her ears momentarily cut out the cries. Cut out the pleas, begging for their brother or sister to be spared. Bile rose in her throat, the wave of nausea making the room spin. She shook her head fervently.

"No," she choked out, stumbling back, fighting the full force of her father's powers. "Please, not the children."

Asmodeus shook his head in disgust. "Begging is beneath

you, daughter." He leaned close again, his mouth brushing her ear. His breath was hot when he spoke, "There will be no one who will refuse my will when this is all over. Not even you."

Anger shot through Emma like an electric current, heating her blood. She fought to contain it, to control it. "I have done everything you have asked so far; I took your stupid mark willingly. Let these kids go."

The prince's smile twisted into something cruel and hideous despite his unnaturally attractive features. "You have done the bare minimum to keep your mother alive, daughter mine. It will not do. When war comes—and it will—your hands will be coated with more blood than you could even begin to fathom. Better get used to it."

"I will not do this. I will not kill innocent children." Emma folded her arms over her chest, praying that by some miracle he would let her walk away.

His twisted, wicked smile stretched as he said the words: "Kill them."

The power infused in her blood thrummed at his command. Every muscle, every tendon fought, shaking and burning as she forced her body to not move. "Please!" she screamed. The pain consumed her, flooding her veins and scorching her until white filled her vision. Her legs moved until she came to stand in front of the Spellcaster, and she met the defeated gaze of the woman who had fought to save the lives of the children.

"I'm sorry," Emma choked out.

Acceptance filled the woman's eyes as she gave a stiff nod.

Emma's hands lifted, and orange flames danced to life on her skin. For her it was heatless, but sweat soon beaded on the woman's forehead.

Emma's body shook, fighting the pull, until it grew too strong. Every muscle in her body was on fire. With a grunt, she threw a blast of her fire onto the floor at the woman's feet. A column of orange and yellow with tongues of blue encased the Spellcaster, ensuring the children would not see their caregiver's gruesome death. It would be quick.

When the hungry licks of fire were sated, they dwindled, leaving only a scant pile of ashes. The scent of scorched flesh still wafted through the air, making Emma's stomach turn. She forced herself to swallow, but it felt like swallowing a deflated rubber balloon.

Automatically, her feet spun her toward the gathered children. Most of them outright wailed, while others covered their eyes, trying to hide themselves from the monster she was forced to be.

This time she fought with all her strength, though not much remained after expending so much energy already.

"I can't. I can't. I can't," she gasped. Her words fell on deaf ears as her limbs moved of their own accord. When her palms erupted in flame once more, Emma tried to scream, but her lips had been sealed shut.

She tried to fight. Tried to stop herself. But she was simply a passenger in her own body, watching the scene play out, helpless.

A few of the braver ones tried to run but Geryon was there at every turn, throwing them to the stone floor at Emma's feet.

She wanted to look away as she reached the first child. Her eyes wouldn't close, forcing her to memorize the small girl's frizzy mess of blond curls. To remember her delicate blue eyes, red and puffy from crying. Fear shone in them, and Emma screamed inside herself in anguish.

The little girl spoke—a tiny, musical voice in a language Emma didn't recognize. Even if she had, Emma couldn't respond. All she could do was raise her hand, engulfed in flame, and grip the thin, fragile arm.

The fire exploded, shooting from her hands in a ring around the children. She pushed it all out, ignoring the stabs of pain behind her eyes or the stars that danced in her vision. If she could grant them one mercy in this hell, it would be a quick death.

Their screams were deafening, ringing in her ears long after they had ceased. When her father's control lifted from her, she fell to the ground, her body heaving and retching. Tears streamed down her face and her own tormented scream echoed through the hall. Her body shook, her energy spent.

The stone floor was warm beneath her cheek. But nothing could chase away the chills—from using too much power or from the acts of horror she'd just committed, she wasn't sure. She didn't care.

Emma gasped as an explosion of pain erupted in her ribs. Her head turned to see her father standing above her, rage palpable on his face.

"You're weak!" he shouted. His voice shook the hall like rolling thunder.

He kicked her again, and she felt as well as heard something crack. She bit down on her scream, letting the agony devour her. She deserved every ounce of pain for what she had done. With her eyes closed, her lungs seared as they tried to pull in air. Let him kill her in a fit of rage. She deserved no less.

But the next blow didn't come. She peered through her damp lashes to see her father spin on his heel and stalk back to his throne. Her head fell to the side as she struggled to breathe.

From around the corner of the great hall's entry, she spotted a pair of familiar striking blue eyes and silky, golden-blond hair.

Haddie.

Her vision swam as the girl fled from sight, clutching a bulging belly.

BLAZE

T he stuffy meeting room was loud, and a headache had begun to form between his eyes. He clutched the bridge of his nose, trying to rub away the ache. Arguments between the dozen or so influential Giborim were like white noise as Blaze's mind wandered yet again. Emma's outburst of flame was just the tip of the iceberg. Ever since she arrived at the gates several weeks ago looking worn down, her usually sparkling green eyes darkened from her time in Sheol, she had been different.

It was to be expected. One as pure and as good as Emma Duvall did not spend nearly a week in literal hell and come back unchanged. She had been gone only three days in earth time. But Sheol time was roughly twice as fast. Her scent, which smelled faintly of Shediem when he first met her, had become an unpleasant odor of smoke and blood and decay. Then again, he supposed that being in their realm would have that effect. But as the days turned to weeks since she'd returned, she still smelled like one of them, and it had set the house's fifty or so occupants on edge. Jake and his uncle, especially.

She had been back inside the compound for less than an hour when Jake had sought him out, fists clenched, eyes wild with the need to kill her. Blaze had sent him to London to help his father's house, which was also filled with families seeking protection. His uncle, however, had been a different matter.

"She's clearly been compromised," Silas had insisted. "You don't know she won't murder us all in our sleep. She's a danger. The exact thing we are trying to protect our females from."

Blaze had shut him down, refusing to act without first hearing from Emma what had happened. But she refused to part with even a single word regarding her time there. For a while, Blaze had thought that her mother—the whole reason Emma had willingly gone to Levaroth in the first place—had been killed. But the weariness and grief in her eyes were shadowed by the hope that still burned in them.

If only I could get her to talk to me...

Now things seemed to be going from bad to worse. After Axel had shared the news of his impending nuptials—which would be a financial drain, but he wouldn't think of that now—his uncle had found him. Blaze's burns had mostly healed, but his uncle missed nothing.

"Good god, boy. What in the bloody hell happened in here?" He'd gestured to the charred crater in the mat, then at the blistered skin adorning Blaze's arms, chest, and face.

"Training mishap," he said with a shrug, getting to his feet at last. "What do you need, Uncle?"

Silas had visibly bit back the urge to pry for further information, but his pressing news had outweighed that desire. "Well, as you know, the UN had been able to hole up somewhere safe. They were all found dead late last night, and there was another attack on the White House. That's the last anyone has heard. It's complete madness. Humans are prematurely thinking it's the end of the world. They're shooting each other and fighting over supplies. We have to intervene."

Injuries forgotten, Blaze had immediately called a meeting, and here they sat, arguing about their next move.

"We can't restore order, it's too late for that!"

"—stretched too thin as it is—"

"We need allies!"

Blaze observed the men, many of whom were standing,

fighting to be heard. It was true. With the last of the elected human leaders being murdered, the final thread of order and peace would snap. Militaries were without a commander and from their intelligence committees, it sounded as though the majority were possessed anyway, using their weapons to kill and scare civilians.

They didn't need just allies; they needed time. And some way to assure the humans that, for now, life should at least try to go on as usual.

And by way of allies, they needed hundreds of thousands of them if they were to win the war that was already cresting on the horizon.

Blaze sighed, racking his brain.

"Gentlemen," he called.

The leaders fell silent, their eyes fixed on him. For years, he'd served alongside them, defeating the Shediem that threatened the human race. They respected him. Most looked up to him. And now they all stared at him, hoping he had the answer to their problems. He didn't, but they didn't have to know that.

"I have sent messages to some old contacts. If you would all just bear with me until I hear back from them—"

"We're running out of time," his uncle barked. "The Shediem are concocting something while we all sit here doing nothing! The desert giants refused our attempted contact, which means they've sided with the Shediem—"

"The giants will side with whoever brings them the best gift," Artair snorted. The traditional Scot was even bigger than Blaze in muscular build and sported a kilt in nearly every circumstance. As an old friend of his father's, Artair was often useful in keeping Silas in check. But Blaze couldn't help but feel as though his father had sent Artair in his place.

Blaze's anger rose, his hands balling into fists on the hardwood tabletop, but he pushed it down and forced himself to remain calm. "We are not doing nothing, Uncle. Within these walls lies the future of our race. We must protect them. We have

a full armory that you are all welcome to utilize. Train. Prepare."
To the rest of them he said, "Hug your loved ones, because before
long there will be bloodshed and many of us may not survive it."

The room grew somber, accepting the words he spoke.

"But we *will* win. The Shediem have run rampant for far
too long."

Murmurs of agreement went around the table.

"As for the giants"—he met his brother's gaze and held
it—"send another chest of gold. And send one to the giants in
the mountains. With more and more Spellcasters who previously
offered us their allegiance going missing, I think we need to
double our efforts there as well. Get them here where we can
protect them. Gertie can expand the wards and if we need to
set up temporary shelters for them, we will. But for the rest of
today, let's take a team into town, pass out supplies, and try to
calm the riots. We'll visit the smaller towns too, those that might
not have enough food."

They all nodded. At least now, they had a clear plan.

Pacified, the leaders dispersed. Axel showed a group to the
armory, renewed vigor to train palpable in their faces. Blaze ran
a hand through his hair with a sigh.

After assembling a team and loading up a truck with spare
medical supplies, nonperishables, and water, they set out. Blaze
had wanted to go up to see Emma, to tell her he was okay.
He knew she would be undoubtedly embarrassed and possibly
ashamed. Heat filled him as he recalled her near-naked form.
He shook his head, clearing away that image as they entered
the city.

Axel's grip tightened on the steering wheel as he let loose a
long string of curses. The buildings they passed were graffitied,
their windows shattered. Even the little huts that sold something
as trivial as coffee had been raided. Widespread panic had broken
out only a week or so ago, and already people had taken what
they could find.

"They're just scared," Blaze said through the lump in his

throat. "They have no government. Banks are shut down. Their currency is meaningless, and food will become scarce. Not even their vehicles will be of much use without petrol. We'll do what we can."

As he spoke, a grocery store came into view. The doors had been chained shut, the windows boarded up. A group of fifteen or so people stood outside as one man attempted to sever the lock with rusted bolt cutters. One of the women among them clutched a crying baby to her chest, and the lump in Blaze's throat expanded.

"Stop here," he ordered, and Axel turned into the parking lot. Abandoned cars remained in the lot, and all of them had been broken into. Tires had been stolen off many of them.

The group spun toward their approaching vehicle, eyes wild. A different man, tall and gangly with a ratty rust-colored beard, pulled out a knife from his pocket and brandished it in warning. The woman, still holding her hungry child, began to cry.

"Wait here," Blaze said, jumping from the truck before it had fully come to a stop. He held up his hands in a show of peace. "Are you guys in need of food?" His eyes locked onto the woman and her babe.

"Yes," an elderly woman cried out, and several members of the group echoed her response.

But the man with the knife took several steps forward, wearing a wary expression. "And who in the hell are you?" he asked, spitting a foul wad of tobacco-soaked saliva onto the slushy ground.

"No one," Blaze answered. He gestured to the truck. "We have some extra supplies. You're welcome to take what you need. There's medical supplies too."

The woman whose baby cried in pain walked forward. "Yes, please. My baby refuses to nurse. I need to get him formula."

Blaze nodded, then glanced at Axel and gestured them to get out.

The sight of Blaze and his men made several people step

back. Though their weapons were concealed, they all wore their black, bulletproof jackets, and he was sure they all looked like some form of military, given the solid muscular build of them.

He gave the humans a reassuring smile as cases of water and canned goods were unloaded and set on the ground in front of them. When they all hesitantly started forward, Blaze went to search for formula to give to the woman.

Hopping up into the back of the truck, he spied the stack of canned formula and grabbed an entire case. He doubted she'd be able to carry it back to wherever she was staying, and decided to look for abandoned shopping carts. But before he could jump from the back, he heard gruff voices arguing, then the first crack of knuckles on flesh.

He leapt down and was around the vehicle in a flash. Axel and Dominic had already separated the two men, one of them the idiot with the now-bloodstained knife, and the other the older man Blaze had seen trying to cut the chains. His eyes were dazed and his breathing was heavy. Crimson flowed from his bicep where the redheaded man's knife had cut through his jacket and flesh. It wasn't the spray of an arterial wound. But if the location of the cut on his jacket was any indication, it was damn close.

"Get bandages and antiseptic," Blaze barked to one of his men before pinning his glare on the redhead.

"He were tryna take it all," the guy whined as Dominic deftly removed the knife from the man's bony grip. The calm expression on his friend's face was a mask of the true rage that Blaze could see in his eyes.

The man continued. "We all got families to feed, ain't we?"

"What's your name, greedy?" Dominic asked, gripping the man, possibly a little harder than he needed to.

"I ain't gotta tell you nothin."

The man spit again, this time aiming for Dominic's boot. In a blur of motion, Dominic spun him onto his front in the murky, melting snow.

"I wasn't," the other man panted, "wasn't trying to take it all, I swear. I have five sons and a sick wife—"

Blaze crouched in front of the wounded man and helped Axel get him out of his jacket. "Save your breath, it's fine. What's your name?"

"Richard."

Blaze nodded, taking the supplies Eric brought to clean and bandage the wound. When he was done, he taped the hole in the man's jacket and helped him put it back on.

Axel passed him a bottle of water and several pills. "For the pain," he explained.

Richard's face was pale and shiny with sweat. He took the proffered items and swallowed the pills before downing the water. "Thanks," he rasped.

A few of the assembled people had taken their supplies and departed in the chaos, but others remained, watching the exchange.

"Now, greedy," Dominic said, still leaning most of his body weight onto the thin man. "Carrying a knife is for self-defense, not stabbing other innocent people, *khorosho?*"

The man whimpered as he nodded fervently. Possibly because the Russian both looked and sounded like he could snap him in half.

"Glad we understand each other." Dominic lifted himself off the trembling man, hauling him up to his feet with him before letting go. "Now grab what you need and get back to that precious family of yours, yes?"

The man nodded, grabbing only as many cans as his arms could carry before sprinting away.

Dominic shook his head, and Blaze searched for the woman and child. She stood a ways off, trying to get the child to latch, with no success.

He grabbed two stacks of formula and loaded them into a shopping cart, along with a case of bottled water and mixed canned goods. When the woman began shushing her baby again, he pushed the cart over to her.

She looked up at him, tears streaking through the dirt on her face. He could tell she was young and pretty beneath the tattered clothes that were several sizes too big, the various stains no doubt from her new babe. From as best as he could tell, her hair was a light brown, though it was too matted and greasy to be sure. She looked as if she hadn't showered in at least a week. As far as he knew, the city hadn't cut off the water supply yet, but perhaps the girl simply didn't have access to one.

"Do you live far from here?"

The woman shook her head, then looked at the overflowing shopping cart. Her lip wobbled. "Thank you."

"I'll push this for you, you just lead the way. No one will give you any trouble."

She bit her lip. "I can manage myself."

Blaze understood her hesitation and tried to put her at ease. "I just want to make sure you make it home safely and that no one tries anything, knowing you've got your hands full." He nodded toward the infant, who had begun to doze. Likely from exhaustion more than anything.

Her throat bobbed. "Okay," she whispered.

"I know it's none of my business, but where is your family? Your child's father?"

The girl looked away, and he sensed from the silent shaking of her shoulders that she was crying again.

Blaze inhaled a long breath. "If you have no one, you're welcome to seek shelter in my manor. It's well protected and there are many women around your age there. And they have children too. I have a lovely caretaker, Gertie, who cooks the best meals. There's running water, and no one will bother you if you don't want to be."

The woman stopped crying to look at him again. Skepticism was heavy in her expression, along with dread, though her chin tilted up to show she wouldn't be pushed around. Blaze guessed she'd had enough of that.

"And…what do I have to give in return?"

Blaze couldn't help the disgust that bolted through every fiber of his being.

"Kindness is something I give freely and generously. If I could fit every last person within my walls, I would do so. Besides, I have a…friend that I'd like to introduce you to. She's had a rough go of things, but she has the most generous and beautiful soul you'll ever meet."

The woman smiled slightly. Then she nodded. "Do you swear no harm will come to me or my son?"

Blaze nodded. "I vow to get you both to safety. And don't worry about my guys." He hiked a thumb over his shoulder at his brother and the other Giborim. "They just look big and tough, but they're all big softies."

She gave a small laugh, eyes locked onto one in particular—Dominic.

"What's your name?"

Her lips parted as if to answer, then she closed them again. After a moment, Blaze thought she simply wouldn't tell him yet. Then she said, "Breanna."

He smiled. "It's very nice to meet you, Breanna. I'm Blaze. And that's my brother, Axel." He pointed out his fair-haired brother, then turned the cart, leading her back to the truck, careful not to touch her.

Before they loaded up to go to their next location, Blaze pulled aside his men one by one and told them to keep their distance from the girl. Dominic, who cast frequent glances in her direction, was the first to offer up his seat in the warm vehicle, while he sat in the back with the supplies.

Breanna's closed-off, timid manner began to relax when she saw how Blaze and his companions simply offered what they had to those in need. And none of them touched her, allowing her the space she clearly needed to heal from whatever horrors had occurred in her past.

When the sun sank below the snow-covered treetops, they

headed back to the compound. Both Breanna and her son, who had finally gotten the full belly he had desired, had succumbed to sleep. They had found a car seat in one of the only stores that hadn't been entirely emptied, and the baby—whose name Blaze discovered was Isaac—slept soundly beside his mother.

The back of their truck had been emptied of supplies, barring the formula he'd set aside for Breanna, with the assurance that they would not run out any time soon. There were still a few factories running in remote locations, which kept the compound fully stocked, and produce was grown year-round, thanks to Gertie.

Once they arrived, Blaze had Gertie help clear out the movie room for Breanna and Isaac. Unless people began room-sharing, they wouldn't have room for anyone else. But Blaze forced himself to think about that later. For now, he wanted to see Emma.

He stood outside her door and knocked. The familiar warmth of her presence filled him, and he smiled. Though he was certain he needed a shower, he needed to see Emma even more.

A muffled sound came from the room.

"Emma?" he called, his smile fading.

"Go away." The words were gritted. Terse. Almost…pained.

He blinked. "Emma, I just wanted to talk about his morning."

"Later," she called.

Blaze shook his head at her stubbornness, then tried the handle. She hadn't said she was indecent, but there was an edge to her voice that made him shake the locked door handle.

She groaned, and this time he heard it—laced beyond her frustration was pain.

Blaze backed away, then spun and rushed into his own bedroom. At the doors adjoining their rooms, he tried to open the first one, then the second.

Locked.

"Emma, open this door, or I'll break it down."

She made another muffled sound, then he heard her shuffling out of the bed and toward the door. But her steps were slow.

When she stopped on the other side of the door, his breath caught in his chest.

Her breathing was uneven. As if drawing breath was a great physical feat on its own.

Just as he poised to rip the door from its hinges, the lock clicked.

The door swung open to reveal Emma, clutching her ribs. Face mottled with purple, green, and yellow bruises. Her accelerated healing had already covered up the worst of her injuries, judging by the dried blood on her lip and eyebrow.

Anger heated his blood. "Who did this to you?" His words were low and gravelly.

Emma squeezed her eyes shut, then winced. "Please go," she whispered.

"Not until you tell me who did this."

"I said get out!"

Flames jumped from her palms, punctuating her words. They were smaller than this morning's and didn't cover her entire body. At the sight of them she staggered back with a guttural sob. The sound broke him.

But before Blaze could stop her, she shut the door in his face, clicking the lock back into place.

LEVAROTH

The Spellcaster, Adrianna, was proving to be incredibly powerful. His link to Emma felt different somehow, but he couldn't put his finger on what had changed. Panic sliced through him as Adrianna left the chamber.

He needed to see Emma. With his eyes shut, he pictured her. Then he pushed his consciousness into her mind.

She was awake this time, lying on her back with an arm over her eyes. Fading bruises marred her arms and jaw.

Anger surged white-hot through his body. His beast snarled within him. Whoever hurt her would pay. He couldn't see the rest of her face, but when a tear rolled down her cheek, he sucked in a sharp breath—alerting her to his presence.

Her body shot upright on the bed, making her wince and clutch her abdomen. Despite her apparent pain, her eyes searched him while his did the same of her.

"Who did this?" he growled.

She swallowed hard.

Ah, right. Her father. He nodded in understanding, but it only made his rage burn hotter. "Same." He gestured to his bedraggled form, not sure what she could see.

But the shock in her eyes told him she saw plenty. Her gaze lingered on his wings, which he was certain looked like shredded skin and bone.

"You won't be able to tell me why he did it, I suppose?"

Her lips parted slowly, as if it took great effort. "Killed. Kids. Weak." She seemed surprised she could muster any words at all.

Clearly her father's gag order wasn't as tight as he'd thought. Perhaps it hadn't included speaking to other Shediem. But being in the home of a Giborim filled with the nasty little faux-angelic soldiers likely made it so she couldn't say anything they might overhear either.

He puzzled over her words for several minutes. "Asmodeus killed children because you're weak?"

Her eyes sparkled with tears and she shook her head.

An odd sensation curled in his gut as he tried again. "Your father made *you* kill kids and thinks your weak?"

She nodded.

He mulled over her meaning. The only children he could think of were the Anakeem Asmodeus was training. *Without his general*, he thought bitterly. Though the prince had been sure to gloat about Tlahaz taking up the empty mantle.

"The Anakeem aren't behaving, I take it?"

She gave a noncommittal shrug. "You haven't forgotten me yet, I see."

He shot her a wry grin. "Oh, if only you were easy to forget, sunshine."

He missed her warm scent, and found himself wanting to touch her. He moved closer to the bed, ignoring the stabs of pain that assaulted his body. She fisted the rumpled floral duvet on the bed, and he noted with amusement how strange the giant flowers looked near her. Light and frilly things clashed with her personality. Her stubborn will. Her need to fight for what she believed in. She was a snake in a rose bed.

She didn't scoot away when his legs hit the mattress. That answered his question: if he could touch things within her room, then he could touch her.

He leaned down, inhaling deeply. The faintest whiff of her warm, sugary scent reached him. It mixed with her blood, making his stomach tighten painfully as ravenous hunger shot through

60

him. He stilled with one hand outstretched, curling them both into fists.

"Why are you here, outside of my dream?" she whispered.

His face was only a foot away. He watched her wet her lips and shift uncomfortably.

"Because I wanted to be." He glanced down at the swirling pink flowers, lip curling like they were a disease. "Did Muscles pick the gaudy décor?"

She blinked at his rapid change of subject. "I doubt it."

He chuckled, drawing himself back up to full height.

Emma craned her neck to look up at him.

"I don't," he retorted.

She bit her lip. "Have you seen my mom?"

Levaroth released a breath. "No. But I found out why Adrianna is in Sheol. She's a Spellcaster—I mean, I knew that, but I can't remember if I told you or no—" From the alarmed expression Emma wore, he guessed he hadn't. "She's meant to be the most powerful Spellcaster to ever live, apparently. There's a whole prophecy about her. She's supposed to change my memories of you."

Emma's eyes were wide, her lips parted in shock. "She's…a Spellcaster? How is that possible?"

Levaroth rolled his eyes. "I can show you the basics of how babies are made but—"

She held up a hand, her dainty nose wrinkling. "I just… that's a lot to take in." She sat silently for a moment, her hands twisting in her lap. "She's supposed to change your memories of me? Like what, make me evil or something? And what do you mean, a prophecy?"

Levaroth shrugged. "I've resisted her so far, although I can tell something's different. I just don't know what." Shifting through his memories of her, he searched for gaps or inconsistencies, but it felt as though a wall was in place to keep him from doing just that. Finally he said, "The prophecy just states she has to bind the ultimate darkness to save the world from mass destruction or something."

Emma let out a shuddering breath. "During the war, right?"
He nodded.

"But I don't understand why my father would try to turn you against me when we're on the same team."

"It's not about you. It's about the fact that my loyalty has been compromised."

"How so?"

Levaroth rubbed the back of his neck, ignoring the tiny bursts of pain all along his neck where Asmodeus had been stabbing him with his enchanted ice picks. "I didn't know your father was going to force you to take the Mark of Fallen Flame. After you left, I went a little crazy, trying to get him to undo it."

"I..." She paused. "Do you know of anyway to-to get rid of—" She gestured over her shoulder.

Levaroth's gaze darkened as he began to pace. Emma watched him. Her emerald eyes glistened. An idea formed, a way to free her from her father's control. But the cost was steep.

Then he stopped, a smile spreading across his lips slowly. "A kiss for information?"

Her jaw dropped, expression morphing to anger in an instant. "And if I agreed, then killed you?"

He laughed loudly, and her eyes darted to the door beside him.

"Hmmm, let me guess. Muscles is on the other side?" The spark of an ugly, human emotion flared to life in his chest. He fought it down, hoping she'd take his deal.

"No, he left. But he'll be back, so keep your voice down."

He leaned over her again, lips brushing the shell of her ear. She shivered. "It's good of him to protect what's mine. Until I get out of here."

Emma scoffed, leaning her head away. "And here I'd thought you had changed. Glad to see I wasn't wrong."

Levaroth stayed where he was, watching her. "I can't help you remove your father's mark. But I'm guessing your little

Spellcaster friend can." He paused, wondering if he could really say the words that had formulated in his mind. "One kiss. And I'll make sure you go free."

He could hear her heart race and her breathing quicken. The moment she decided, he knew. A delicate pink rose to her cheeks. The bruising on her face was nearly gone now.

When she scooted toward him again, he didn't bother fighting his smile.

"Just a kiss, and that's it," she warned.

"If you can manage to stop after just one kiss, I'll need to see a physician."

Before she could add any further quip, he cupped her face and brought his lips down on hers.

The bite of pain from the pressure was eased by her softness. Her body stiffened at first, and he thought her power would kick in and finish him off. But when he deepened the kiss—desperate to taste her—her shoulders eased, and she sighed into his mouth. His tongue swept over the seam of her lips, parting them. The taste of her was a heady rush of sweetness and sunshine and he couldn't get enough. Her hands shook as they rose up the plane of his chest.

He crawled further onto the bed, forcing her onto her back beneath him. A groan ripped itself from his chest. He wanted to touch her everywhere, to please her. To claim her. His teeth nipped at her swollen bottom lip, eliciting a tiny gasp that made his blood roar.

Mine.

Mine.

Mine.

Her hands continued their exploration of his body, drifting up over the bulge of his shoulders and down his back, stopping less than an inch from the slope of his wings.

"It's okay," he panted, not wanting her to stop.

Hesitantly, her fingertips brushed the joints and he trembled, kissing her with more fervor. She palmed the ridge of them, making them twitch.

"Does it feel nice?" she asked in between the kisses he scattered between her lips, her jawbone, and the curve of her delicate throat.

The rumble in his chest was his only response, and he felt her lips tilt up against his cheek.

Then another presence touched the edges of his senses and his growl turned menacing, just as she stilled. His canines lengthened as he skimmed them along the hollow of Emma's neck, a threat to keep her pinned beneath him. Her shiver of pleasure made the beast inside swell with primal satisfaction.

A knock sounded at the door. Emma clapped a hand over his mouth, silencing his sounds of disapproval.

"Emma?" Muscles called to her.

Shameful tears sparkled in her eyes as she tried to push Levaroth off her.

"Good," he whispered into her ear. "Open the door and let him see my kisses on your body."

Her look of horror made him frown. This wasn't how he wanted her to remember him.

"Emma, please let me in," Muscles said.

It took everything in Levaroth to restrain himself from shouting at him to go away.

"You got what you wanted, now go away," she hissed.

Levaroth pressed a final kiss to her forehead. His throat thickened. "Don't forget me, *Ash-nesikah*."

Then the room evaporated, and with it, Emma's warm, perfect body.

His chest was hollow. Everything ached. As he tilted his head back a trickle of warmth seeped from his eyes, and he roared, letting the pain consume him.

When a dark, hulking figure stepped through the barrier into his cell, Levaroth leveled Tlahaz with a dead stare.

"I want to make a deal," he rasped with the dregs of his remaining energy. "I will stop fighting. Give up my memories. If your Spellcaster can remove her father's mark."

"That's not possible," Tlahaz said as he folded his lethal arms over his chest. "That mark is the only thing ensuring the Shediem-Slayer doesn't murder us all."

Levaroth shook his head. "She's not strong enough to contain all of our powers. And besides, if it were Adrianna, would you allow it?"

Levaroth had witnessed in the past weeks the way Tlahaz protected the Spellcaster, always stopping her before she exerted too much power, and hovering beside her like some danger might just appear out of nowhere.

And from the way the Shediem general's body tensed and his teeth audibly ground together, Levaroth had his answer.

"It may not be possible for her to remove it. And once you give up your memories you won't care anymore anyway."

Levaroth tugged on his bonds, letting the fresh wave of searing pain slice through his bones. "The mark needs to be removed first. Then I'll give up my memories."

He jerked harder, hearing the bones in his wings snap. He clamped his jaw shut to keep his agony trapped inside, trying to cover the emotional ache in his chest with physical pain.

Tlahaz's lips pulled up in a twisted smile. "Such the fool. However, I will consider it…brother."

He spun, leaving Levaroth huffing as blood coursed down his arms.

EMMA

At least one rib had been broken. Her father had deposited her back to her room only a few minutes before Blaze knocked the first time. She was both thankful for her quick healing and irritated by it. Irritated, because at least that would have prevented her from completely losing herself the moment Levaroth pressed his lips to her.

Like with every time she had kissed Rowek, his kisses were hypnotizing and all-consuming. Even more so when she'd felt the full, incredible, beautiful edges of his true form. No matter how much she knew she should hate him, over the past few weeks, seeing him in her dreams every night had lowered her guard. And somehow made it even more impossible to resist his ethereal beauty.

When Blaze had knocked, it had jarred her from the shroud of dreamlike pleasure that was Levaroth's kisses. Shame had filled her so completely, she hadn't answered the door. Instead, she'd jumped into the shower, determined to rinse Levaroth's scent and the feel of his mouth from her body.

And still, she felt it like a banner of shame for all to see. Especially Blaze. She'd opened a window too, trying to chase the woodsmoke and spice from her bed linens, but even after she balled them up, threw them into the wash, and replaced them with new linens, it lingered.

He lingered.

She'd just settled back onto the bed, hugging her pillow to her chest, when a knock sounded from her external door. But she didn't need to open it to know it was Blaze.

"You need to eat, Emma." His voice sounded pained, and she released a breath of relief. He'd arrived, delaying yet again the images of the woman and children she'd slaughtered from filling her mind.

She rose from her bed and strode to the door, pulling it open.

Blaze's brows were raised in surprise that she'd finally opened the door for him. "Can I come in?" he asked.

She nodded, chewing on her lip. As he carried a dinner tray and set it on her table, she watched him, waiting for a reaction. For him to catch a whiff of Levaroth, or see the evidence on her skin, even though it had long since washed off thanks to her determined scrubbing. But he didn't seem to notice that anything was off.

He stood awkwardly by the table, examining her from head to toe, brows furrowing. Maybe he did see something of Levaroth on her. She forced herself not to squirm, and not to touch her lips.

"At least you've healed."

She nodded.

"And your ribs?"

"They're fine," she replied tightly. In part because he was so observant, but also because the warning jolt down her spine forced her to reveal the very minimum.

Blaze nodded, running a hand through his dark hair. "And do you mind telling me how the hell you ended up looking like you were put through a meat grinder?"

Emma's throat tightened. The next flare of pain down her spine was worse, making her wince. Though Blaze seemed to mistake her reaction for his sharp tone, and his expression gentled.

"Did you go somewhere?"

Desperation to veer away from the topic made Emma lunge for him, grabbing his hands in hers. Her eyes pleaded with him to drop it. "Blaze," she gasped. "Please, can we just eat? I'm tired."

His lips thinned, and wordlessly he dropped into the chair across from her. With his elbows on the table, his hands clasped together, Blaze pressed his lips into his hands, looking like he was praying. But he wasn't. He watched Emma with a look that bordered on anger.

"I'm really sorry about this morning," she said after taking her seat too, though she didn't move to touch any of the food in front of her.

"Don't worry about it," he said, reaching for a steamy plate of chicken korma, one of Emma's favorite dishes. He scooped the aromatic curry onto a heaped plate of rice and offered her a rolled-up naan bread that had a warm, buttery shine to it.

The scent of garlic made her mouth water, but her stomach knotted. She hated that he was angry. She hated that she couldn't tell him the truth. And most of all, she hated that she was her father's pawn.

"So, a group of us went into the city to offer supplies and whatnot," Blaze started after a long stretch of silence. He scooped up another bite of curry and rice with his naan bread before continuing. "There was a girl with a baby. Breanna. She has no family, no protection whatsoever. We brought her back to the compound. She's a human obviously, so she'll need to be kept out of the inner workings of things. I figured since you've expressed your wish to be kept out of strategy meetings, you could kind of keep an eye on her. Help her acclimate, but make it so she doesn't discover the truth of us."

"Actually," Emma said, setting down her fork. Bile rose in her throat, and she nearly choked on her next words. "I was thinking about it today, and I'd like to take a more active role. I think I'm ready."

Blaze searched her face for a moment before nodding. "Okay. Sure. I can have Gertie help with Breanna and Isaac."

"I'd still like to meet her," she offered.

Blaze nodded again. "I suppose she'll have to be invited to

Axel and Emerelda's engagement party. Speaking of which, do you need a dress for that?"

Emma tried not to let her distaste for dresses show. "How fancy is it? I have a few dresses but they're more summery-type things that my mother wouldn't stop buying me. Although, my prom dress is still at my house—"

Blaze interrupted her musings by saying, "I'll make sure you have something appropriate."

She forced a smile in thanks, and they ate the rest of their dinner in silence. She offered to take her tray down to the kitchen and pop in to meet Breanna, but Blaze told her to give Breanna the night to adjust before meeting too many people.

Emma agreed, but still took their plates downstairs. Gertie gave her a sad smile and wrapped her in a hug that stretched on long enough to make Emma's eyes prick with tears. She pulled away before the floodgate of her tears was unleashed, muttering something about a headache, then fled back to her room.

Emma stared up into the dark, too afraid to close her eyes for fear of bringing back each tiny, terrified face of the children she murdered. At some time in the early hours of morning, exhaustion finally claimed her, sending her directly into the writhing pit of her nightmares.

She stood in the grand hall again, her father's bloodred stare on her, and ropes clutched in his monstrous claws. When he tugged them, Emma's left arm and leg moved. She looked down, finding the ropes tied to her wrists and ankles and one around her throat.

Tears pooled in her eyes, and tiny whimpers sounded behind her. Emma turned, seeing a small girl of only seven or eight with blond curls and bright blue eyes pleading with Emma to spare her. She saw a dozen pairs of eyes wide with terror as her flames burst to life around her, and around their small bodies.

Emma screamed, but no sound came out. She screamed, and clawed at the ropes, and ran toward the children, but her feet weren't moving. She reached for them, trying to save them, but it was already too late. The undulating tongues of blue, orange, and yellow had already lapped up the last of them.

She screamed again, turning on her father. But he was no longer there. Up on the throne, casually lounging, was the Dark King. His billowing darkness tumbled and curled over the throne, hiding nearly all of him from view, though she could make out the rough outline of him. And his devastatingly beautiful face with sharp cheekbones and pointed chin focused on her. His shadows caressed his face and wrapped around the top of his head. His black hair was bone-straight, falling somewhere past his shoulders. He was mesmerizing. She wanted to look at him forever, but the sight of him hurt her eyes. Like a star had fallen from the sky and walked upright as a man. That was the King of Death.

Then, his dazzling silver eyes turned to the girl beside his throne who looked exactly like Emma. But her features were harder. Sharper. Eyes filled with cruelty, she wore a crown that matched the king's. His shadows stretched over her too and wrapped up her legs, though she didn't seem to notice, or care.

Emma couldn't speak; she could only stare at the chilling likeness that stared back at her. Nakosh trailed his long, slender fingers over the other Emma's arm, but she was the one that shivered.

The king smiled, wide and terrifying. Then his icy voice filled her mind. "Don't you look lovely in a crown?"

Emma awoke with a jolt. Her throat burned, and she was sure she had been screaming. But Blaze didn't rush into her room to comfort her. He never came at all, but she could feel his presence near. As if he stood on the other side of the door, debating whether to see if she was all right.

She was glad he didn't, though. Turning onto her stomach, she buried her face into her pillow and wept.

She didn't train with Blaze the next morning, but she did attend the meeting. The mark had forced her out of bed and down the stairs, but she'd wrestled against it outside the door until the pain had become so great, she gasped.

Entering the room several minutes late, she noticed everyone's eyes sweep over her in curiosity or confusion. Blaze was especially stunned, stopping midsentence.

"Sorry, please continue," she said, taking a seat between Gertie and Axel while flushing with embarrassment.

Blaze straightened, clearing his throat. Before he continued, she saw the faintest curve of his lips. He was pleased she'd made an effort to interact with people again.

It made her sick to her stomach to know that he thought this was her breaking out of her metaphorical shell. That this was her beating back the darkness that consumed her. What he didn't know is that she'd just brought the darkness into the room. It waited within her, cataloging any and every piece of information that could be used against the Giborim.

In her lap, her hands balled into fists. Listening to Blaze report on the suspected and confirmed Shediem activity around the globe was one thing. But when another man—Donovan, she thought his name was—began listing the locations of other communities of Giborim and covens of Spellcasters who had confirmed they were preparing to fight, she wished she could tune him out.

Blaze stood, taking back the attention of the room. His expression was hard and emotionless when he said, "It was confirmed this morning that the White House was breached and the president all the way down to attorney general were found dead. With the others in line dead as well, there is no known chain of command any longer."

Emma's stomach plummeted, her lips parting on a sharp inhale.

"The humans are calling for a vote while others are trying to elect a leader in their own states. Stores are closing down due to the violence, and many places have lost power. We have people to work on providing backup power as most everyone will freeze to death without it. Of course, we experienced that here much sooner due to King Nakosh's message." Blaze's eyes met Emma's.

"What message?" she asked the eerily silent room. Not even Silas, Blaze's tall, wiry uncle who looked to be in his late thirties, spoke.

"Can you play it?" Blaze asked Donovan, who nodded, tapping frantically on the iPad screen before him.

A crackling sound came from the device, then a familiar voice that clinked like ice—yet caressed the senses—said, "Humans." Another series of cracks and pops echoed through the room before Nakosh continued. "By now, you will have guessed that your world is under attack."

Emma's heart rate spiked, her breaths coming faster.

"It is true," the King of Darkness purred as seductively as a lover. "I am the king of a race of superior beings, called the Shediem. Soon there will be a war that will kill many of you. I give you now a choice. When your princes arrive, fall at their feet and pledge your loyalty to them...or you will die."

The crackling sounded again, ending with a high-pitched squeal that made everyone cover their ears. Then there was silence.

Emma swallowed hard, looking to Blaze. "This transmission went out globally?"

He nodded.

"When?"

"A little over two weeks ago," Donovan answered, checking his screen.

When she was still in Sheol.

Her gaze snapped back to Blaze and stayed there, searching his face. "Why are you only just now telling me this?"

He huffed a humorless laugh. "You know why."

Because she'd been a husk of her usual self since she'd returned. Because she'd remained hidden to avoid inadvertently spying for her father. Because deep down, there was an overwhelming sense of guilt that plagued her at every moment.

She'd gone to Sheol to save her mother.

Instead, she'd returned a puppet and her father held her strings.

He'd promised that she'd kill them all, and she couldn't allow that. If she had been stronger, maybe she'd have put as much distance as she possibly could between herself and the compound. When she'd appeared at the gates, she could have turned around and walked away. Perhaps it wouldn't have lasted long, but she could have at least tried.

Or maybe, running away from Blaze would have forced her father to command her to slit each of their throats in their sleep.

Either way, it was her fault. What was to come was her fault.

"I'm sorry," Emma whispered. Not just to Blaze, but to everyone in the room.

Silas leaned forward. "Well, you seem well recovered after many weeks back being fed and clothed by the kindness of my nephew here. Perhaps you'd now like to tell us what took place in Sheol?"

An invisible hand wrapped around her mouth, holding back every possible response. Wincing at the bite of pain that zipped down her spine, she shook her head. "I'm sorry," she said again.

Silas scoffed. "You say those words an awful lot and never seem to mean them," he sneered. "Perhaps you're really one of them now and won't tell us anything because you're protecting them. Is that it?"

"Uncle," Blaze warned.

Emma gaped at Silas's accusation. "I would never—"

The words vanished from her mouth and she snapped her jaw shut. Bolts of searing pain flared in her shoulder where her father had placed the mark. It radiated through every vertebra, and her back bowed.

"That's enough!" Sergei barked from the other side of the table, rushing to Emma's side.

She wheezed, steadying herself with her hands flat on the table. Blaze's eyes were wide—everyone's were.

Sergei rubbed her back in soothing circles while she steadied her breath. Was she not allowed to speak ill of the Shediem now? If that were the case, she'd be in agony multiple times a day.

"I'm sorry," she repeated. The next words came out without her permission, flat and robotic even to her own ears. "I had…I had a spasm."

"Demon," Silas breathed, the shock on his face morphing to hate. He pointed at her, spittle flying as he bellowed, "She shouldn't be here!"

"Uncle!" Blaze barked. He nodded to his brother, and both he and Dominic rose to haul Silas out.

She watched in horror, the room quieting once more.

To Emma, Blaze said, "Do you need to go lie down or are you okay to hear the last order of business?"

There was something in his expression that alarmed her. *He knows there's something wrong with me*, she thought. Her back still ached from the sudden burst of pain. What would happen if Blaze figured out she took a Shediem mark that controlled her words and her actions with a single thought? Would he die? Would her father know?

She wasn't terribly eager to find out.

Emma gave Sergei a weak smile over her shoulder. In his wise gaze, she saw something worse than understanding: sympathy.

With a nod, he returned to his seat, though she still felt his eyes on her. Under the table, Gertie patted her hand, but Emma ignored her, unable to face anyone else's pity.

"While we've sent communications to every Spellcaster coven we know of, many have moved underground. They're unreachable. I propose that several teams be sent to request an alliance in person. Gertie has contacts in New Orleans and Sergei has many throughout Europe and Asia.

"I'd like Gertie and Sergei to be accompanied by at least three people as they journey to their separate locations to recruit their contacts."

Axel and Dominic reentered the room, but Silas did not.

"I'll go of course," Axel said.

Sergei lifted his hand into the air, speaking before Blaze had time to acknowledge him. "May I recommend that Gertie and I travel together on our quests? There is a certain level of unity among Spellcasters. Waltzing in with one Spellcaster and a host of Giborim may appear like coercion."

Gertie nodded. "That is quite true. My contacts are not disloyal to the Giborim; however, they've had reason to mistrust you." She smiled sadly. "It would be beneficial to bring as few Giborim as possible. And Emma should go as well."

Her eyes flew wide. "Wait, what?"

Blaze narrowed his gaze on her. "Something wrong?" He sounded genuinely concerned, but Emma still heard the underlying bite of anger.

He was angry—and rightfully so—that she was keeping secrets, but she couldn't deny the sting of having his anger directed at her.

"I'm just not sure why it would make sense for me to go. My mom is a Giborim."

"But your father is not," Gertie replied, addressing the elephant in the room. Everyone knew it. In fact, she was almost certain that everyone knew her father was a Shediem, but that was something the mark would not allow her to confirm.

She swallowed hard with a small nod.

Blaze's steely blue eyes bored into her as though he could see inside her mind and lay bare all her hidden truths. She almost wished he could.

"It's decided then," he announced. "Myself, my brother, Emma, Sergei, and Gertie will depart for New Orleans the day after the engagement party. You're all dismissed."

Emma leapt to her feet, determined to make it out of the room before anyone could corner her, but she was not so lucky.

Blaze's hand gripped her arm and yanked her around to face

him. Sergei lingered in the doorway that Emma glanced at with longing. The Spellcaster clearly debated whether to intervene or not, but one cutting look from Blaze made him sigh before stalking from the room.

"What was that about?" Blaze growled.

"What?" Emma snapped with a surge of anger she didn't understand. Sucking in a breath, she calmed the rage, but Blaze clearly saw and felt it.

"What happened, Emma? You can't say nothing, 'cause there's something off. You're different. You hide away, you won't say anything about what happened other than the fact that you failed to save your mother but she's alive, and then..." He took a steadying breath, his body beginning to tremble. "It was like you physically couldn't say whatever you were going to say."

Emma didn't respond. Didn't react.

His eyes cut back and forth, searching her face for a hint or a sign that she was correct. She couldn't risk him finding out without knowing what would happen to him if he did. For all she knew, the mark would instantly kill anyone who figured out the truth.

"Am I right?" he demanded.

"Blaze," she whispered, reaching for him.

He jerked away, glaring down at her. "Why won't you tell me anything, Emma? Is what my uncle said true? Are you one of them?"

His words hit harder than a physical blow, and she stumbled back. Pain erupted in her shoulder, warning her away from trying to answer.

"Why would you say that?" she asked, her chest heaving while angry tears filled her eyes. She wanted to reassure him, to tell him everything.

Instead, she was forced to endure his anger. His accusations.

"I don't know, it's like you're a completely different person. But whatever is going on with you, I'll figure it out. Mark my words—I've spent my entire life hunting down the truth. You can't hide your secrets forever. And until I do, you better expect to have me at your side every waking moment. I'm not going to let you out of my sight. My people need my protection, even if it's from you."

Emma was almost too stunned to speak. She knew each word came from a place of desperation, a way to provoke her into opening up. But she couldn't.

"I'd never intentionally hurt them, or you," she said, and expected pain. But it didn't come. A breath of relief rushed out of her, and she couldn't help the smile that curved her lips.

Blaze's shoulders sagged. Wordlessly he pulled her into a crushing hug.

The pent-up anger and frustration drained from them both. She relaxed in his embrace, his fresh scent of pine and soap wrapping around her. For a moment she was able to let go of the weight of guilt and despair. For a moment their fragile trust felt strengthened by their strange bond. It was more than friendship, yet she wasn't quite sure what it was.

She yearned to define it. To finally put a label on whatever they were, but she knew that she couldn't now. Not until she found a way to be free of her father's hold.

If she ever did.

No, she silently reprimanded herself. *I will be free. I won't be his slave forever.*

Despite Blaze's earlier threat to remain by her side, it wasn't long until he was called away to the training room. Not wanting to return to her room, she stopped by to meet the new girl, Breanna.

She knocked gently, hoping not to disturb the baby if it was asleep. After a moment the door creaked open just wide enough for a young, pretty face to appear. She was likely only a year or two older than Emma. Her light brown eyes were guarded.

"Hi," Emma greeted her. "I just wanted to introduce myself. I'm Emma."

The girl eyed her for a moment before answering. "I'm Breanna."

A shrill cry rang out from inside the room and Breanna whipped around, panic creasing her face. She sighed. "That's Isaac. I'm sorry, I've got to go."

"Okay," Emma replied. "Well if you ever want any company, my room is upstairs to the right, the second-to-last door on the left."

The girl nodded distractedly as the baby continued to fuss. Without another word she closed the door in Emma's face.

The rest of the week, Emma continued to research the mark, or anything resembling it, and trained alone. Though Blaze observed from his perch against the wall, he didn't offer to train with her. The way he watched her intently had her temperature spiking.

She knew he was only making good on his promise, but they rarely spoke, and the bars on her cage tightened ever closer.

On Friday morning, after training, she arrived back in her room to a large box sitting on her bed. She ran a finger over the violet satin ribbon before untying the bow and pulling off the lid.

Inside was a silky, emerald-green dress that matched her eyes. It shimmered as the wintery sunlight that poured into her room kissed the fabric. Emma held it up, noting the sweetheart neckline and knee-high slit on one side with a frown.

The dress was beautiful and not inappropriate, but the heavy feeling in her chest reminded her of when she'd been dressed in Sheol for everyone's entertainment. The small, rational voice inside her head told her this was just Blaze being kind. The dress had to cost a small fortune, and she needed something nice to wear to the engagement party this evening. Pushing aside her irrational fears, she gently laid the dress aside and typed a quick thank you to Blaze on her phone.

It was nearly an hour later when she received his short reply: **You're welcome.**

To occupy her time before the party, Emma showered, then went downstairs to see Breanna. Blaze stood in the foyer, talking with a few soldiers as well as his brother, but his eyes locked on Emma. Even as she turned from him and crossed to Breanna's door she felt the heat of his gaze.

Emma knocked once and waited.

Pulling the door open a scant few inches and seeing it was her, Breanna opened it further, her eyes nervously flicking to the men standing in the foyer.

"I was wondering if you wanted any help getting ready for tonight," Emma offered.

"I'm not going," the girl firmly declared, a sleeping bundle cradled in her arms.

"Why not?" Emma asked.

Breanna turned and walked back into the room, leaving the door open for Emma to follow. Milk stains and empty bottles littered the small space. Breanna's hair was in desperate need of a wash and tiredness lined her eyes. The poor girl needed a hot shower and a long nap.

"Because I don't really know anyone, and besides, I can't bring him along." She nodded at the tiny babe fast asleep on her shoulder. His plump lips were parted in sleep.

From what Blaze told Emma of the boy, he'd been skin and bones. Already she noted his cheeks were beginning to round.

She spied the same long, white box on Breanna's bed, the bow untouched.

"You already have a dress," she pointed out. "And I don't know anyone either. We can go together. And at least when your little guy has had enough, you have a reason to bow out. He's a baby. Everyone loves babies. You'll be the life of the party."

Breanna laid Isaac down in his crib with practiced care, then smoothed the stray strands of chestnut-brown hair that had escaped from her messy bun.

"I'll sit here with him; you go have a nice hot shower," Emma offered. "I'm sure you'll feel differently once you've gotten cleaned up."

Breanna opened her mouth, as if to respond, then sighed heavily. Emma noticed the flicker of unease in the mother's eyes.

"I promise he'll be perfectly safe," she added gently.

"Okay, I'll just be a minute. Come get me if he starts to cry."

She shooed Breanna into the bathroom. "Take your time. You deserve this."

Once the door closed, Emma peered over the rail of the crib at the sleeping child. She distanced herself from Isaac while collecting the half-full bottles of milk and carried them across the now-empty foyer, around the corner, and down the hall, into the commercial-grade kitchen sink where they could be sanitized. Then she hurried back, knocking straight into Blaze's chest when she turned into the foyer.

"Ah! I'm sorry!" She quickly backed away.

Blaze's lips tilted up, hinting at a smile. No doubt recalling the other dozen or so times she'd run into him. "How's the girl?"

"I'm watching Isaac so Breanna can have a minute alone. I was just taking the bottles to the kitchen to be washed."

Blaze nodded. "Good. She needs friends."

Emma followed suit and nodded as well. "Well, I should get back in case Isaac wakes up. I'm supposed to be watching him."

"Okay," Blaze said. "I'll see you this evening."

He turned and strode away without waiting for Emma to reply, and she scurried back to the room before Breanna could think Emma had left for good.

Breanna came out of the steam-filled room twenty minutes later, looking refreshed and cheerful. "I think I will go to the party. But only if you walk in with me."

"Of course," Emma said, smiling.

When Breanna finally opened the box, she gasped. Emma rushed to her side, immediately taking in the stunning floor-length grey dress, covered entirely with glittering crystals.

80

Even Emma's heart stumbled in her chest, taking in the elegant, extravagant gown.

Beneath it was a tiny black suit fit for a baby. Emma smiled.

And at the very bottom was a notecard. Breanna picked it up and flipped it over.

"What does it say?" Emma asked, feeling an unexpected pang of jealousy. Her dress had been beautiful but there had been no note card on the glittery tissue paper at the bottom of the box.

Breanna flushed from her cheeks all the way to the tips of her ears. "It's from Dominic."

Emma blinked, taking the card that Breanna offered for her to inspect. She'd expected it to be from Blaze, and something like relief flowed through her at confirming the signature at the bottom. An elegant scrawling script covered the notecard that read,

Breanna,

Please accept these garments as a token of goodwill and best wishes. I hope both you and your son will attend tonight's festivities.

I look forward to seeing you there.

Dominic

Emma tried to stifle her giggle but was unsuccessful. The color drained from Breanna's face, and Emma fell into abrupt silence. When the girl began to tremble, Emma wrapped her arms around her. And softly, Breanna dissolved into tears in Emma's arms.

Whatever horrors she'd suffered at the hands of men, it was clear she wasn't ready to receive another's attentions.

Emma made a note to speak to Blaze about it while she rubbed the girl's back until her sobs ceased. "I don't really know Dominic, but I know his friend, Blaze. He trusts Dominic and I sincerely doubt he would if the guy was untrustworthy."

Breanna nodded, wiping away her tears. "It's fine, I just…I have a hard time trusting men." She gave Emma a forced smile.

Emma nodded. "I get it. You don't have to go if you don't want to."

Breanna shook her head, squaring her shoulders. "No, I want to go. I can't live my entire life afraid to go outside. If you say I'm safe here, then I believe you."

Her heart warmed at the small token of trust the girl bestowed to her. "I'm glad. And I'll stay with you the whole time. You'll have fun."

Breanna nodded, biting her bottom lip as she turned to face the dress, wearing an expression fit for battle. And for her, it likely was.

When both girls were dressed and ready—along with Isaac, whom Emma had to admit looked adorable in his little suit—they headed out together. A symphony guided them through the enormous house. People filtered in and out of the elegant ballroom awash in white. Smiling faces filled the room and couples danced.

Long tables were draped with crisp white tablecloths. Strings of crystals hung from the high ceiling, drenching the room with refracted light. Everywhere they looked, crystal vases held red-tipped white roses—an odd splash of color that reminded Emma of blood on snow and made her stomach flip. One glance at Breanna told Emma she was thinking something similar.

Many noticed their approach and stopped to look at them both. Emma felt naked in her formfitting green gown, its back sweeping along the marble tile.

"Very…extravagant," Breanna commented quietly, trying to ignore the onlookers as she gently bounced Isaac, who had begun to squirm.

Emma didn't respond. She scanned the crowd, and her eyes landed on the tall man with dark hair artfully swept back, dressed in a tux. His grey-blue eyes were already on her, though his face remained expressionless, making her heart throb painfully in her chest. He was exquisitely handsome. Too handsome for this world, she thought.

Beside him, equally well dressed and built just as impressively as Blaze, was his blond-haired, blue-eyed friend, Dominic. He, too, was strikingly handsome, in a mob-boss sort of way. Unlike Blaze, he smiled, his eyes fixed on Breanna in her stunning, sweeping dress. Emma felt the urge to step in front of her new friend, to defend her.

He made his way through the throng of Giborim, and when Breanna spotted him, she took a step back.

"Hey," Emma said, calling the girl's attention back to her. "No one in this room would dare try to hurt you. Least of all, him." She gestured to Dominic, who was closing the distance between them rapidly. As if he sensed that Breanna was about to bolt.

Breanna swallowed, taking deep, steadying breaths. Internally, Emma wanted to find whoever had hurt the girl so badly and tear them to pieces.

"Breanna." Dominic breathed her name like a prayer as he flourished into a deep bow that made her blink in stunned fascination. "You make that dress shine."

His head-to-toe assessment of her was not exaggerated or inappropriate, but still Breanna blushed fiercely.

"And what a handsome wee man." Dominic bent over and stroke Isaac's hand. Immediately the babe's face lit up with wide eyes, and an even wider smile.

Breanna let out a breathy laugh. "He smiled," she said, astonished.

"Children tend to like me for some reason," Dominic commented.

Emma snorted a laugh just as Blaze said from behind them,

"Because you're a big, soft teddy bear, Dom."

Dominic's supple lips quirked into a grin. "That's all true," he admitted, before leaning close to Breanna and whispering conspiratorially, "Except the soft part." He smacked his fist against his chest like a gorilla, and Emma rolled her eyes. "Rock. Solid."

Emma glared at both men after taking in Breanna's pale face. "We're going to go get drinks now," she said loudly.

Dominic looked ready to follow, but Blaze caught his arm and gave a sharp shake of his head. Emma offered a grateful smile to Blaze then led Breanna to a table tucked in the corner. Before one of the servers could come take their order, Emma swiped two flutes of water from a passing tray and offered one to Breanna. She mumbled a thank you before tipping the glass back and draining it.

"You don't have to, but one day, will you tell me what happened? I mean, I can guess…" Emma heaved a sigh. "I just mean, if you ever want to talk about it, I'm here."

Breanna nodded. "Thank you."

Emma gave her a small smile in return. She wouldn't push, but should she ever get a name, she'd make sure that the man who had hurt Breanna never took another breath without great pain and effort.

Breanna's complexion steadily improved, especially when no one else bothered them. Emma convinced her to dance a little at the edge of the group when the symphony played an upbeat tune; the others moved to it in some sort of organized choreography that reminded her of the times she and her mother had watched *Pride and Prejudice*. Breanna bobbed and swayed with Isaac, who had fallen asleep again, and the girls laughed at themselves for being so wildly out of step.

Dominic approached when the tempo switched to a slow, beautiful melody. "May I dance with you, *Krasivaya?*"

"Um—I—my—" Breanna stammered, looking down at the sleeping infant.

"I'll hold him if you want," Emma offered, holding out her

arms. To Dominic she snapped, "Do not touch her unless she gives you permission."

He smiled. "I promise." Turning back to Breanna, he said, "Just one dance?"

Breanna worried her bottom lip, then slid Isaac into Emma's awaiting arms. Dominic offered his hand to help her to her feet. She glanced from it to Emma with rapidly increasing breaths.

When Dominic's smile faltered, he offered his elbow instead. "Truly, I mean you no harm, *draga*."

Breanna's throat bobbed. She hesitated for only a moment longer before taking it.

His answering smile could have illuminated the entire room; he wore it all the way to the center of the dance floor.

When they turned to face each other, Emma watched as Dominic lifted his hand. There was no hesitation this time. Breanna slid her hand into his, placing her other on his shoulder. He wrapped an arm around the middle of her back, keeping nearly a foot of space between them, then whispered something to her when she visibly tensed. She relaxed slightly before he began sweeping her around the room in a graceful dance.

Emma smiled, taking Isaac back to the table where she sat, holding the peaceful bundle. But when she looked at the child, the face of a small girl with blond curls flashed in her mind, replaced with nearly a dozen other little faces contorted in pain. Her smile vanished and she swallowed down the bile burning her throat. Suddenly, she wasn't sure she could continue to hold the baby without passing out or throwing up.

But Breanna looked almost at ease. She didn't so much as glance in Emma's direction, staring into Dominic's eyes, enraptured by the man's ethereal beauty, just as Emma was with Blaze.

When the first song ended, they didn't let go of each other. The walls Breanna had erected ten stories high around her heart were coming down, brick by brick.

"I think your momma is going to be just fine," Emma

whispered to the slumbering babe. "And maybe I will be too."

Axel and Emerelda paraded around the room, the latter clutching his arm like a lovesick puppy while the former barely took his eyes off her. When they came to Emma's table, Emerelda smiled brightly, thanking her for coming to the party. Up close, Emma noticed Axel's eyes looked a little bloodshot. Dark smudges lined his eyes. He almost looked tired…or sick. Did Giborim get sick?

A commotion outside the doors drew Emma's attention, especially when she heard Blaze's voice.

"Uncle, for the last time, I will not discuss this with you. Not now, not ever. Now excuse me."

Emma rose from the chair, careful not to wake Isaac, and peered into the corridor.

Silas called after him, "The girl is only here because her powers are the edge we need in this war. But it's clear from that display at the meeting and how she refuses to tell us anything that she is not on our side. You were supposed to be charming her, but what have you been doing, eh?"

Emma's heart froze in her chest.

Blaze stood at least ten feet away from his uncle, looking furious. His fists were clenched at his sides and his bowtie was undone and loose around his neck. Silas's back was facing her, but his spine was rigid.

"I've done everything you've asked, Uncle. She does trust me."

"But do you trust her, nephew?" Silas asked.

The beat of silence was too much. Emma turned before either one of them spotted her just as Breanna, smiling wide, skipped back to the table, Dominic in tow. Wordlessly, Emma gave Isaac back to his mother, then fled the ballroom.

The hall was mercifully empty, Blaze and Silas nowhere in sight, and Emma didn't have to contain the tears that filled her eyes, blurring her vision.

The kisses, the smiles, everything. It was all a lie. A ruse to get her to fight in their stupid supernatural war.

Another betrayal. Another lie.

And she had fallen for it yet again. First with Rowek, who charmed her into trusting him before revealing that he was actually Levaroth, and now this. When she reached her door, she slammed it shut behind her, making sure both locks were secured. Her tears fell hot and fast down her face, nearly causing her to miss the item sitting on her bed.

A trickle of ice spread through her veins at the sight of the crown. It was very Christlike, an arrangement of thorny brambles and red roses. Beautiful and horrible all at once.

It pulled her closer. Her arms lifted, reaching for the crown, even though her mind was screaming at her to stop. But she couldn't.

Her fingers felt the sharp jabs of thorns piercing her skin when she lifted the crown. Her body shook, fighting the mark's power over her. With jerky movements, Emma pulled the crown onto her head. It bit at her scalp and tangled in her hair.

Tears flowed faster from the pain. Her feet moved again, carrying her across the room, and stopping in front of a mirror.

Hot trickles of blood ran from her fingertips and her head, one trailing between her brows. A sob broke from Emma's chest.

All at once the invisible force holding her in place vanished, causing her shoulders to sag in relief. Emma shakily pulled the crown from her head just as the solid object gave way in her grasp, crumbling through her fingers. It dissolved into ashes that rained down the rug and arranged itself into words by an invisible current of icy air that brushed along her ankles, sending goose bumps up her body.

Emma watched transfixed as the words took shape.

I told you you'd look good in a crown.

BLAZE

At just after midnight Blaze found himself standing outside Emma's door yet again. His night had not been a success in any respect.

Emerelda, in her usual high-maintenance fashion, had screeched about the decorations until everything was glittering and sterile white, save for the red-dipped roses. A gruesome choice, he thought, but his brother hadn't protested. Axel had followed his bride-to-be around, catering to her every whim and calming her when he could. Even after people began to arrive, Emerelda had still found things to complain about.

He'd been happy to see Breanna out of her room and seeming to enjoy herself. Even more surprisingly was that his friend, Dominic, had taken such an interest in her. For all her nervousness and hesitation around him, she'd let him lead her around the ballroom floor and Blaze had caught her smiling once or twice.

He'd wanted to ask Emma to dance, but between keeping things running smoothly and the unwelcome confrontation with his uncle over the usual topic, Emma had disappeared before he could ask her. It struck him as odd that she'd left without him noticing. She always seemed to be slipping out from under his radar these days.

Shortly after he'd rejoined the festivities, the "happy couple" were seen shouting at each other in the hall. Well, Emerelda had been doing the shouting. Axel had looked as if he wasn't hearing a single word, though he nodded and muttered apologies that were grossly out of character for him. The purple smudges of exhaustion under his eyes had deepened in the course of four days, making his eyes look sunken. His skin had a light sheen of sweat, making him appear ill, and his usual arrogant, joking disposition was absent.

Perhaps it was wedding nerves. Or maybe he'd changed his mind about marrying her. Blaze couldn't understand why his brother was desperate to marry Emerelda when he already looked so miserable. It was customary for a wedding to bring out the worst in people; add in an impending war, and both of their behaviors seem a little more excusable.

Axel loves her, he'd reminded himself. *And she loves him, even if she doesn't always show it.*

At least Blaze hoped she did.

Though he wanted to go find Emma, he had pulled his brother aside and into the brisk wintry night, away from listening ears.

"Are you certain this is what you want? Wouldn't you rather wait to marry after the war, when you can give her the big, perfect wedding she wants?" Blaze asked.

Axel frowned, swaying as though he'd had too much to drink.

"Are you unwell, brother?"

"Quit asking me that," he'd snapped, gripping Blaze's lapels without any real show of strength. "I need you to be supportive of me and my future wife," he hissed, breath smelling of mint and other herbs. "Yes, she is a perfectionist and wants everything handled a certain way, but once this is all over she'll be back to her cheery self. Okay?"

Nodding, he'd removed Axel's bony fingers, excusing himself. In the foyer, he caught sight of Breanna, cradling a sleeping Isaac, looking brighter than he'd seen her in her glittering gown that flowed down her supple curves and pooled onto the marble tile.

Her back was against the wall, but there was no sign of her

usual rigidity. Dominic stood just to the side of her, propping himself up against the wall with a hand by her head, their faces less than a foot apart.

He whispered something into her ear, and she smiled shyly, looking down at her infant with all the motherly affection Blaze had seen in his own mother's eyes. He moved past them with care, heading up the wide, winding staircase to the top floor, where he stopped outside Emma's door.

Listening for sounds within the room, he let the warmth of her presence and her sweet, smoky scent fill him and clear his mind.

When the sounds of shuffling came from within Emma's room, he knew she was awake. He raised his fist and knocked gently.

There was movement. He heard her breathe in shakily. Then her soft steps as she made her way to the door. Another pause, then the door opened.

Her hair was mussed; some strands looked as though they'd been tugged on. The scent of smoke and ashes intensified. Emma's lips were pursed, her eyes filled with a look of betrayal that made him frown.

"What's wrong?"

"Nothing."

Blaze snorted. "I've been around long enough to know that when a woman says 'nothing,' it's most certainly something." When her expression didn't lighten, his amusement faded. "Please tell me."

An array of emotions played on her face, too quickly for Blaze to read them all. Then her head tilted down, her shoulders rounded.

"It's nothing. I'm tired."

A stab of disappointment flared in his chest. Another lie. Another secret. The wall she was building around herself was getting higher and thicker—so much so he wondered if he'd ever be able to knock it down.

Blaze lifted a hand and cupped her cheek, lifting her face to meet his gaze. "Whatever it is that you're keeping to yourself is a burden that could be lifted from your shoulders if you'd confide in me. I told you before, that no matter who or what you are, I don't care. I know you miss your mother, and I can't imagine how hard that must be for you. If you're blaming yourself, don't. It's not your fault. We will find a way to save her. Sergei and Gertie have been consulting every written text regarding Sheol—"

She shook her head and huffed a sigh.

Blaze switched directions. "I just want you to know that I'm here to help you carry this weight. Don't let it crush you." His thumb stroked her cheek. "I can help you."

Anger and hurt crossed her beautiful face, but her lips remained tightly pressed together.

He pushed down another wave of disappointment, but he didn't let her go. He stepped closer, leaning in to kiss her lips, but her face turned away from his, forcing his lips to brush her jaw. A cord of rejection snapped taut in his chest, bringing with it a sharp stab of pain. He sighed, dropping his hand, and stepped away.

As he did, his gaze fell over her shoulder, to the dusting of ash on the carpet in front of her mirror.

"Did something catch fire?" he asked before she could shut the door.

She swallowed hard, then nodded. "A candle tipped over and caught some of my school papers."

Blaze flicked his attention to her clenched fists. And the stain of smeared ash that coated her fingers. Then, with more scrutiny, he noticed the smudge of ash above her brow. And caught in the fine hairs was a fleck of crimson. The damp roots of her hair looked as though she'd washed something from it.

Something like blood.

His teeth clenched and his nostrils flared, picking up a trace scent of blood. She was lying to him again.

Something far worse had taken place.

"We're leaving in the morning. Be downstairs with a packed bag at six."

She nodded weakly, her eyes looking as though they were trying to say the words she wouldn't speak.

"Goodnight," he said, this time gentler. He started toward his room, flinching when her door slammed shut.

He entered his chambers with a long exhalation. The party continued downstairs, though the noise was barely audible to his hypersensitive hearing.

Just after his shower, a knock sounded at his external door.

He couldn't help but pause, trying to feel for Emma's presence next door. She was there, a tiny beacon of warmth against his skin, like the direct rays of the summer sun but without the blinding light. It wasn't her that had knocked.

Blaze hurried to his door, a towel wrapped around his waist, droplets of cool water trailing down his back. He pulled the door open, finding Manny and Garrett standing outside, with grim expressions.

"What is it?" Blaze asked. Neither bothered commenting on his attire, not that either of them cared.

Manny spoke first. "The gate was attacked. Shediem."

The words were a punch to his chest. "How many?"

"Six," Garrett said, rubbing a spot on his chest with a grimace. "We managed to capture one. Destroyed the rest."

Blaze's brows lowered. "Six? They couldn't have hoped to get past the gate with just six," he said, mostly to himself. "Have you questioned the one you caught yet?"

Both shook their heads. "Not yet," Manny said. "But we thought it was odd. Six Nybbases. Their packs aren't the type to attack the compound."

Blaze nodded. "No injuries?"

Garrett exchanged an uncomfortable look with Manny before saying, "One."

Blaze's spine straightened. "Who?"

Manny rubbed a hand over the back of his neck. "Emerelda."

Blaze frowned. "What was she doing on the other side of the gate?"

"See, this is where things get a little awkward," Garrett explained. His freckled face had gone red and his eyes were fixed on a spot on the floor.

When he opened his mouth to say more, Manny cut him off with a glare. "She claimed that earlier, one of the vendor trucks had dropped a box of tablecloths and she wanted to search for it."

Blaze looked between the two men, tasting the lie on the air like battery acid. From the way Garrett's face had begun to resemble a beet, Blaze was fairly certain he could deduce the truth. She'd snuck out to meet with someone. But *with whom* was the question.

He leaned forward slowly, stopping a few inches from Garrett's face. His voice was soft and menacing when he spoke. "Who was she with?"

"We couldn't tell," Manny said with a sigh. "He took off when the Shediem attacked. We didn't see where he went. Anyway, she just got scraped. Nothing major."

Blaze drew out a long breath. "What was she doing with this guy, and how do you know for sure it was a man?"

Garrett seemed eager to jump in. "We heard a gruff voice. It looked like they were just talking, but she seemed a little more than friendly with this bloke, if you know what I mean."

Blaze rolled his neck, trying to loosen the growing tension. How would he tell his brother that his beloved was not being faithful? He didn't have any proof.

Manny started to speak, but Blaze held a hand up, silencing him. "We need to keep a closer eye on her. Report directly to me if she sneaks off again. I want to know who she's meeting, and I want him brought to justice. My brother deserves that much."

Manny swallowed audibly. "Will she...will she be punished according to our laws?"

Blaze sighed. Their laws were harsh toward women caught in infidelity. An engagement between Giborim was nearly unbreakable. The blood ritual which was done early that morning had bound his brother to Emerelda and her to him. If she was found to be unfaithful, their law dictated she be stripped bare and stoned to death. Which for a Giborim often took weeks.

"We would need proof first. Does my brother know?"

"I doubt it," Manny replied.

With a final nod, Blaze gestured them away. "Now that the party is over, make sure the gate is guarded by five, starting tonight. And add seven extra men around the perimeter. I'll be leaving in the morning, and so will Axel. We'll be gone for about a week."

The men nodded, turning to go.

"Don't let her out of your sight, and stay vigilant. We can't let another attack happen."

LEVAROTH

Pain exploded through him like bombs, tearing through flesh, muscle, and bone. His eyes wouldn't open, but he could see the pain behind his lids, even though he was alone. He'd soon be paid another visit from the Spellcaster and Tlahaz.

He just hoped Tlahaz had agreed to let her try to remove the mark from Emma. The silky cord that stretched from him to her had vibrated with pain and fear only hours ago, while Asmodeus rammed magicked tools into his broken body, making him unable to visit her. To protect her. But the surge of protective rage had helped stave off the worst of the pain.

Now, he was strong enough, and tugged on the link, launching himself into her consciousness.

Her nightmare had already begun, footfalls echoing through the labyrinth halls of Asmodeus's palace, trying door after door. He didn't have to ask who or what she was looking for. He'd found her in a similar dream before, and it took only a moment for her desperate cry to confirm it.

"Mom!"

"Emma," he said behind her, making her turn.

She looked him up and down with cold anger. "Is it actually you, or the you that betrays me and gets me thrown in the dungeon? Not that there's really a difference." Then her eyes dragged over the wings tucked in at his back and some of the

95

tension left her. "It's you."

Levaroth nodded. She seemed more agitated than usual, like a caged animal. He knew how she felt. The only moments he could step out of his prison were the moments he spent with her. But this was only a projection of the two of them. Neither of them was truly here. The constant throbs of pain reminded him of that.

"I can get us out like last time," he suggested. Even though this was her dream, where the halls turned and forked to different halls endlessly, when she would let him take the lead he found the exit. But never her mother.

Emma glanced at the corridor filled with locked doors, her anguish plainly written on her face. It tugged on a deeper thread in his chest that he tried to ignore. She shook her head, shifting her weight to her other side as if unable to stand still for long, arms crossing and uncrossing. The behavior reminded Levaroth of the sensation that sometimes raced through his veins and tingled up his wings when he needed to stretch them: to fly. The girl looked as though she wanted to sprout wings of her own and take flight. The image tugged his lips to the side.

"I have to find her," she said.

"Let me help," Levaroth offered.

She shook her head. "I don't want you here. Leave."

Levaroth ignored her and walked past her to one of the doors, and with as much strength as he could manage, he gripped the handle and yanked. The door groaned and the hinges cracked as it was ripped from its frame. He tossed it behind him, the resounding smash against the stone wall causing Emma to jump. She sucked in an alarmed breath, then rushed to his side. The flames that danced and undulated from the floor illuminated enough of the room to see inside.

It was dark and monochromatic, stacked with dust-covered furniture. Levaroth snorted. This was what her mind thought of the Prince of Wrath. She didn't acknowledge Levaroth's amusement, only started for the next door.

She pulled and pulled on it, even tried sending balls of fire at it. But only Levaroth could open it. She folded her arms over her chest, huffing with frustration.

"If I were to analyze why only I can open doors and find exits in your nightmares, would you try to kill me?" he asked with wry amusement.

She flashed him a sickly-sweet smile. "Oh, I wouldn't try. I'd succeed."

He gave a gruff laugh, trying to ignore the flood of desire her words unleashed within him. They sprinted down corridor after corridor as Levaroth tore each door from its frame. But each room was uneventfully empty.

At last they reached a dead end: a door with chains across it, decorated with hundreds of locks. A white light seeped around the edges, giving an eerie vibe that made Emma shiver next to him. They both stared at it for a moment. Then Levaroth started for it.

Emma wrapped both of her small hands around his comparatively large bicep and tugged on him. He stopped, instead of dragging her entire body along with him, though the idea amused him.

"What?" he asked.

"This is my *nightmare*." She stressed the last word as though this was new information to him. Her eyes were wide, but there was no fear in them. Only wariness.

"That's why I'll go in first."

She swallowed hard. "I can't see my mother dead or beaten. I just can't. I need to wake up."

Levaroth raised a brow. "It's just a dream. Besides, if you conquer this fear, you likely won't have any more nightmares about it."

Emma bit her plump bottom lip, and Levaroth watched, wanting to taste it again. "We could always occupy ourselves in another way," he suggested, grinning.

Her gaze snapped to him like a taut rubber band, her brows

drawn and lips pursed. "By the way, thanks for all your help getting this mark removed."

Levaroth's jaw tightened. "I made the offer, but Adrianna hasn't visited in over a week."

Emma looked back at the glowing door. "Is she okay?" she whispered.

Though his answer could not be entirely truthful—seeing as he hadn't seen her in so long—he still said, "Yes."

He wanted to reach out and touch her. To assure her that he'd find a way to remove the mark. But deep down he wasn't in any hurry to forget her. He wondered, even if Adrianna was successful in removing all those memories, if she'd truly be able to wipe away all traces of Emma Duvall. She was a drug laced through his blood. An addiction that only grew stronger. He didn't need to remember her to crave her, though it would be more painful—an addict looking for a high but unable to determine what would set him free.

Her throat bobbed, as if she could hear his musings. He watched the nervous ticking of her pulse and let the sound of it fill his ears. With a deep inhale he closed his eyes, and her intoxicating scent wound through him. He shuddered, wishing he could press his lips to the base of her slender throat. To feel her strong, feminine body beneath his again.

A squeak came from directly in front of him and his eyes flashed open. He'd backed her against a wall, arms on either side of her head, caging her in. The tip of his nose rested against the silky curve of her neck, just below her jaw. His canines had lengthened, and he bared them with a low growl. Her heartbeat thundered in his ears. And though he had never been able to taste her emotions, he could see the hint of fear in her eyes.

But her heart thundered for an entirely different reason: excitement. Despite not wanting to admit it, she wanted him too.

"I'm the only one that can withstand your fire," he whispered against her skin, which pebbled in response. His breath skated to her lips. "I know your inner darkness better than *he* ever could."

She was rigid in his grasp, unbreathing. "*He* can't handle your fiery passion like I can. I set you aflame, I can feel it." Her eyes fluttered closed and he considered sinking his teeth into her at last, letting her taste coat his tongue. "I can make you burn hotter than you've ever felt before." His tongue flicked out, running along the sensitive area that thumped wildly. She sucked in a sharp breath.

Actual fire leapt from her skin, burning neither of them.

He chuckled deeply. The irony of his statement had come to life.

Her eyes snapped open at the sound of his laugh, realizing what had happened. With a hit to his chest, she managed to knock him back a step. A mixture of hatred and disgust filled her every feature. His rage roared to the surface at the sight of it, his beast fighting to break free.

"Don't you dare touch me!" Her chest heaved as she tried to regain a sense of calm.

"Why?" he challenged. "Why do you fight it? I can hear your pulse. I can sense your desire. Stop fighting it. You know we'd be perfect together." *If just this once* were the words he didn't say. Because soon, he wouldn't remember what it felt like, this raging desire that only she incited. This fight to make her his. To make her bow at his feet.

"It's not me! It's the mark or something, this isn't me!" Emma glared up at him as if every touch and kiss didn't drive her wild, while Levaroth fought the urge to crush her body against his, to feel her every curve. His frame trembled with the effort.

"You've been drawn to me since the day you laid eyes on me, sunshine."

"Don't call me that!"

He smirked, forcing himself to take another step back. The heatless fire still lapped at Emma's flesh, like a pet seeking affection.

"I haven't fed in weeks," he said, his voice still gravelly. "And your unique scent is impossible to resist in every way."

"What, are you some kind of vampire or something? I thought you could feed on emotions."

Levaroth snorted. "I'm far scarier than any silly human imagining. I don't feed on blood." His smiled turned wicked. "Unless I want to."

Emma scoffed, though she seemed determined to keep a safe distance between them. "Do you need to touch someone to feed off their emotions?"

"No. I can feed off a room full of humans if their emotions are strong enough. But touching someone is more potent. It tastes better. Usually because it's fear."

"Have you ever fed off mine?"

Levaroth glanced back at the waiting door. The light behind it poured out brighter than before, pulsing with urgency. "I can't taste your emotions," he said. Then he looked back at Emma, who now watched the door too. "I can feed off you, but it would be muted. And you wouldn't die like humans do. It would weaken you, but you'd be fine. And even if I *could* taste your emotions, I don't need to. They're always written so plainly on your face."

Her cheeks grew pink, but she didn't look at him, only stepped toward the door.

The feeling of hands gripping his spine made him stiffen. Then he felt a tug.

Shit. He lunged for the door and ripped it from its hinges before he could be pulled from Emma's dream.

"I have to go," he said. "Remember, it's just a dream." He pressed a gentle kiss to her temple. Her screams pierced him just as the palace floor fell out from under his feet and he jolted back into his body.

His eyes flew open wide, meeting the dark stare of Adrianna. A feral snarl exploded from his chest at being forced from Emma's mind. Curls of colored magic sparked from her fingertips when she staggered back a step with a yell. She clapped a hand over her mouth and stared back at the inky black barrier. How she'd gotten in without Tlahaz was a mystery Levaroth didn't care to solve.

100

She dropped her hand then moved closer again. "I'm sorry, but I don't know how long I have. I wanted to let you know Tlahaz told me the deal you're offering."

"And?" he snapped, temper still burning hot.

"Tlahaz thinks it's too complex for me. I haven't had much training, but—"

"Skip to the yes or no part, Witch," he growled.

Adrianna pursed her lips, eyes filled with irritation. "I'll do it. But I need some way to access Emma. I can't physically touch her, which complicates things. I'll need to establish a link to her before I—"

"I'm linked to her. She bears my tracking mark. I share a link into her mind and can project myself to her location."

"That's where you were," Adrianna said with a smile. Her expression turned hopeful—excited, even. "That should work!"

"When can you do it?" Levaroth asked quickly, his chest battered with conflicting emotions.

Her smile evaporated. "I'll do it the next time Tlahaz brings me to you. But...Levaroth..."

His name was stilted on her tongue, making him snort.

"In theory, if I do this, the link you share with her will vanish too."

A pang of something cold ricocheted through him.

"Not that it matters, I guess," she mused quietly. "Since you're trading your memories for her freedom."

Levaroth met her eyes and saw her approval in them. She offered a tentative and kind smile. He didn't return it.

"It matters to me," he breathed. "But her freedom matters even more."

EMMA

The nightmare sent her shooting upright, gasping. Her body was slicked with an icy sweat and she shivered, trying to push the horrific sight from her mind. Emma pulled back the covers and started for her bathroom.

As she passed the door adjoining her room and Blaze's, she felt him just on the other side. Part of her ached to open the door and let Blaze comfort her as he'd done the past few weeks, but she couldn't. Not after what she'd overheard. Had it all been a lie? Every time he'd held her after a nightmare, had he been doing it just to make her care for him even more?

It had worked, that's what stung the most. Maybe it had been because she'd moved around so much and couldn't retain a lasting relationship that had her throwing herself into every set of willing arms. Every charming smile flashed in her direction had brought her nothing but heartache.

The conversation between Blaze and his uncle played on repeat in her mind as she turned on the shower and stripped off her damp clothes. *I knew it was odd. What did a man of two hundred years see in an eighteen-year-old girl?* Sure, she'd been forced to mature faster than most girls her age, but she was still just a child to a man that had lived several lifetimes and would likely live several more. *But I...*

Tears of humiliation burned her eyes as she stepped under

the spray of the hot water. It did little to chase away the chills of her nightmare—of what she'd seen inside the room. Not to mention the visit from Levaroth that had turned her into a mess of heat and confusion. Emma bent her head, letting the water pour over her skull and neck. It ran in rivulets down her face, her tears lost to the warm cascade.

They had an unlimited supply of hot water, and though it was the middle of the night, Emma turned it off when her eyes had dried up and the images from her nightmare were no longer etched into the underside of her eyelids. She stepped out, grabbing a plush white towel and wrapping it around her slim frame. Her eyes avoided her reflection. She knew she was losing weight, but she didn't want to see it.

In the doorway, she froze, sensing the warm, soothing presence of a Giborim—not in his room, where he'd been when she'd entered the shower—but on the other side of the door. Tentatively, she peered out around it. Blaze stared back at her, and he looked angry.

He shot to his feet, movements stiff as he rushed toward her. Emma tried to stumble back, but Blaze clasped her by the shoulders, holding her in place. His warm, earthy scent made it difficult to remember why she didn't want to see him right now, especially with only a towel covering her. But the strength of his hands and the heat pouring from his impressive body made her want to lean into him instead.

Emma managed to mentally shake herself, and she looked up at him, craning her neck. "This is highly inappropriate."

His eyes narrowed, accentuating his intimidating expression. "I'd ask what you dreamt of this time, but since you won't tell me, I won't ask. I just want to know why you're shutting me out now. You won't even let me comfort you anymore when you wake up screaming."

Emma pulled in a deep breath, then instantly regretted filling her senses with him. "I heard you and your uncle. About your little deception."

Blaze went perfectly still for several moments, his eyes dropping to the doorway where carpet ended and tile began. "My uncle has no idea that I knew of you months before he did. He has no idea that Sergei had hired me to look after you for him when he wasn't around. And he certainly doesn't have any understanding of what I feel for you. Because I didn't trick you, Emma, no matter what you may think."

Her heart raced as she blinked up at him. Did she believe him? She knew that Sergei had asked him to protect her. They were friends. But even if it wasn't duty that tied them together now, it had been before. She questioned everything: their almost kiss in his garden. The actual kiss on her front porch.

"Why?" she croaked.

"Why what?" he asked harshly.

She couldn't look away from his cool, penetrating grey eyes when she spoke again, feeling childish. "Why do you like me? I'm a child compared to you." Her face was hot as his features softened.

Then he chuckled.

"You are very young," he confirmed. "But in every sense of the word, you are a woman. You know your mind and your heart. You fight fiercely for what you believe in." His head bent lower to her, making her acutely aware of the proximity of their lips.

"For us, our bodies remain young even as we go on for hundreds, if not thousands of years. It's easier for me to overlook your age because of it. However"—he straightened to his full height, serious expression back in place—"if my age bothers you, I need to know."

Emma bit her lip and considered. Then she shook her head.

His relief was palpable when he smiled, a dazzling, heart-stopping smile, and she couldn't help but return the gesture.

"And just so you know," he whispered as if imparting a great secret, "you're ten times as mature as my brother's fiancée and she's over eighty years of age."

After seeing Emerelda scold several servers over a crease in the tablecloths, Emma felt inclined to agree.

Blaze's intense stare dipped to the soft, white terry cloth that Emma held in place around her body, and she felt as if it wasn't there at all. He stepped back, though she noticed the stiff movement for what it was: reluctance.

"Well, I'll leave you to get dressed. And if you need me at all tonight, I'll come."

He turned to go, but she grabbed his hand. Blaze looked at it, then at her, brows drawn.

She bit her bottom lip, hoping her request wouldn't sound childish. "Could you...I mean instead of having to come back, you could just stay?" Her face flamed and she glanced down at herself, half expecting her fire to burst to life to hide her from her embarrassment. "I'd put clothes on, obviously," she added quickly, before looking up again.

Amusement lit his features, then he nodded.

Emma returned the gesture before scooting around him, careful not to let any part of their bodies touch when she snatched up a pair of sweatpants and her favorite worn band T-shirt and hurried back into the bathroom to get dressed.

When she emerged, her footsteps faltered at the sight of a shirtless Blaze lying on top of the duvet, denim-clad legs crossed. His hands were tucked behind his head of dark hair. His eyes remained closed, but she could tell from the uneven breathing that he was not yet asleep.

Nervousness fluttered through her, making her fingers and toes tingle. Standing at the empty side of the bed, Emma tried to work up the courage to pull back the comforter, but she felt frozen. It wasn't as if it was the first time she'd shared a bed with him. For weeks, when her nightmares woke her, Blaze had stayed beside her the rest of the night or until she had admitted defeat and gone to train.

He cracked one eye open as his lips curved. "I'll stay above the duvet the whole time." He drew an *X* over his heart.

Emma sighed, flinging the covers back like ripping off a

band-aid, and before she could talk herself out of it, climbed onto the bed and curled the thick, soft material over her, leaving just enough of her face exposed for her to breathe.

"Relax. If I had any ill intentions, a bit of cotton and goose feathers wouldn't be able to stop me."

That statement did the exact opposite of relaxing her—she clutched the blanket tighter before his rumbling chuckle shook the bed.

Emma scowled at him and he smiled. The lines of tension on his face had almost completely vanished. Her chest suddenly felt lighter. Then with a peck of a kiss to her temple that reminded her all too much of Levaroth's departing kiss, he sighed and switched off the lamp, plunging the room into darkness.

The guilt returned, weighing on her shoulders.

Blaze turned onto his side, facing her. "You okay?" he asked.

She nodded. "Yeah." Her voice was small in the seemingly infinite darkness around them.

Blaze said nothing and Emma felt his warmth begin to wash over her. She didn't want to close her eyes and get trapped in the same nightmare, but with Blaze so near, she couldn't fight the exhaustion.

Sleep pulled her under, this time dreamless and peaceful.

When she awoke the next morning, Blaze was gone, the spot beside her cold. But a tray of steaming hot food sat on her table, and Blaze's scent lingered in the air. He hadn't been gone long.

She smiled as she crawled out of bed and walked over to her table. Between a plate of eggs with sautéed vegetables and a mug of black coffee sat a note. Emma read the elegant scrawl twice, her lips tugging even higher at Blaze's neat writing.

Emma,

Get packed and be ready to leave by eight.
Meet you downstairs.

P.S. Last night was a success.
Perhaps we could try again tonight?

Yours,

Blaze

Her cheeks were flushed at the idea of spending a full night with him tonight, but she was certainly willing to try anything to keep the nightmares away. Though what she saw beyond the door would likely haunt her for the rest of her days.

Placing the cream-colored note aside, Emma sat down to eat her breakfast while it was still hot. She'd need to get dressed and head downstairs to assert herself in whatever official Giborim matters she could. The reminder of the fact that she was obligated to spy at every opportunity turned the food in her stomach to lead.

She pushed the plate away after downing her coffee, despite the churning of her gut, and stood. She selected her usual jeans-and-shirt look, pairing it with a stylish black leather jacket, before grabbing her small suitcase from under her bed and tossing a week's worth of clothing into it.

When she was done packing, Emma headed downstairs, spying Breanna outside her room, leaning against the doorframe. Dominic pressed his lips gently to the back of her hand with a small bow, then spun on his heels and stalked away. Her cheeks were red, and her chest rose and fell rapidly, as though she'd run several miles.

Emma suppressed her smile at the two's budding relationship. She was happy for them, but she worried that her new friend would get too attached to Dominic, a Giborim who lived in Russia. Breanna was never to know what he was or why he couldn't be with her. Giborim were forbidden from marrying humans. If they did, they were disgraced and cast out from their ranks.

The cold reminder of that ridiculous law stood in a shadowy alcove of shelved books. Silas's dark hazel eyes were fixed on Breanna, burning with disdain. She hadn't noticed the onlooker of her exchange with Dominic. But Emma had.

When she got close enough to Breanna, Emma was still issuing her own glare at Silas. He noticed her only a second before Breanna did. Switching her attention to Breanna, Emma smiled before turning back to where Silas had been, the space empty. *Good*, she thought. *The vulture can go be creepy somewhere else.*

"Where's Isaac?" she asked.

"Sleeping," Breanna replied, her voice light and dreamy.

There was no denying that the girl was starstruck by the impressive male. Emma was part Giborim and even she was enraptured by the Giborim's ethereal beauty. By their unnerving grace and their all-around vibrance. As if their angel-descendance made their blood glow.

Shaking away her far-off thoughts, Breanna said, "So I heard you're leaving today."

"Yeah." Emma felt a pang of sadness, being away from Breanna. Little Isaac, too. It was a relief to no longer see the faces of the children she had killed when she looked into the babe's deep blue eyes.

Breanna threw her slender arms around Emma's neck, hugging her tight. Emma returned the embrace.

"I should be back in a week. Maybe less."

Breanna nodded, looking as sad as Emma felt. "I'll miss you. Isaac will definitely miss you."

Emma smiled. "I'll miss you both." She squeezed her new friend once more. Her chest ached even more when the faces of those she wished she could hug, but couldn't, swam through her mind—Adrianna especially.

Footsteps approached and Emma turned, finding Blaze and a very tired-looking Axel making their way toward them. Emma cast a glance at Breanna, who went rigid as she did in every man's presence. Every man except Dominic, that is. Emma wondered if she should warn her friend away from the Russian to save her from getting attached but thought better of it. It wasn't her place to meddle.

If by some crazy miracle they won this war, Emma hoped the Giborim would learn to accept that love was unstoppable. That everyone should be allowed the freedom to choose whom they wished to love.

After all this…they deserved it.

Blaze smiled at her as if he'd heard her thoughts. She forced herself to smile back. If she somehow survived—if they both did—then she hoped that *they* would be accepted too. That even though her father was a Shediem, she'd be allowed to love Blaze without him being cast out.

But there was far more at stake than her future.

For now, they'd have to find happiness in the brief moments they had left.

So when Emma caught the scent of Blaze's cologne mixed with his unique musk in the air, her smile became genuine.

Sergei and Gertie entered the foyer, duffel bags and suitcases in hand. They stopped, Sergei nodding in greeting, which Emma returned.

Breanna muttered her goodbyes then scurried into her room, closing the door softly behind her.

"All right," Blaze said, inhaling a deep breath and running a hand through the stray ebony curls that had fallen against his forehead.

Raking them back gave him a deliciously tousled look that made Emma want to touch the silky strands too. An errant curl slipped forward again, brushing his dark eyebrow.

"Are we all ready to go?" he asked, glancing at each person.

Axel nodded with a wide yawn.

"You can get some beauty sleep on the way," Blaze quipped to his brother, who scoffed in mock offense.

Emma couldn't help but notice how loose Axel's clothes suddenly seemed to be. While he was nowhere near as packed with muscle as his brother, he was still well built. But today, his muscle density seemed to be diminishing. It brought to mind a type of parasite her mother had told her about. It starved the host, feasting on muscle, then fat, before boring into the bones to carve out the marrow. Emma's stomach turned even at the memory of her mother showing her pictures of those that had been infected with the parasite.

But Giborim didn't get parasites, at least not that she knew of. It made sense that diseases and illnesses didn't affect them. In Emma's short life, she'd never truly gotten ill, though she'd feigned sickness on more than one occasion to get out of school during a test or when there was a particularly nasty bully she wanted to avoid.

Somewhere, deep down, her mother had known Emma wouldn't get sick like other children, but she'd played along until Emma's own guilt would eat away at her. She'd burst into tears and confess her reasons for trying to get out of school. Her mother never got mad, and though she would use the same lecture about the importance of education, she would allow Emma her rare skip day. They'd eat soup and watch cartoons. A few of her supposed sick days were the happiest childhood memories she possessed.

They filed out of the mansion, and though Emma knew Gertie used her magic to keep the temperature inside the wards warmer, it was still cold enough for their breaths to puff in little white tendrils in the air.

A black SUV idled on the gravel road. After depositing her luggage into the trunk, Emma hopped up into the back and climbed over into the farthest row, allowing Gertie and Sergei to have the middle row to themselves.

No one really spoke beyond Blaze questioning both Spellcasters about their contacts in the south. Emma tuned it out, instead watching the world outside as they drove down the snowy mountain. The splashes of green from pine trees on a canvas of glittering white and the smooth, crystalline surface of frozen waterfalls were calming.

The route they took did not lead them into the city, but Emma saw plenty of what had descended upon mankind.

"Besides world leaders being murdered and the Shediem King's creepy message, what caused humans to descend into chaos so quickly? I mean, why did stores shut down and whatnot?"

Blaze cleared his throat before speaking. "Do you remember the Shediem attack at your school dance?"

She nodded, knowing he couldn't directly see her. "Yes."

"Everyone's memories came back the same day you returned. Not only that, the Shediem made themselves known. Instead of hunting in the shadows at night they began hunting in plain sight. It sparked terror that turned to chaos in less than forty-eight hours. People were too scared to leave their houses. They still are. It slowly began to happen around the world."

"The military was deployed but most of them were possessed. It was a bloodbath for a while," Axel added.

Her heart leapt in her throat. As far as she knew, only Levaroth could restore the memories of everyone involved, and he did so only once she'd left Sheol. Perhaps that move had been purposeful, but she suspected that if he'd been imprisoned from that moment on, it was more likely he'd done it to do the right thing, or he'd been forced to do so.

It didn't matter now. At least humans had the ability to figure out how they would defend themselves. Once the Giborim and Shediem were done with their slow game of chess and all-out war began, there would be nowhere to hide.

When Blaze's meaningful look met her eyes in the rearview mirror, she guessed he also had a theory as to who had returned the humans' memories and why. She looked away, just as another gate rose in front of them. Men in the same black canvas jackets and trousers as Blaze and Axel, holding massive guns, halted their pacing as the vehicle approached.

When the SUV came to a stop, more men with raised rifles crept toward them. Blaze rolled all four windows down, but didn't speak. Everyone inside sat still. Tense.

The guy leading the armed men walked around, peering inside each window, but Emma couldn't see any part of him through his helmet and tinted visor. They certainly looked ready for the coming war, though if they were worried Shediem would just drive up to the gates, then perhaps not. Searching the vehicle with guns wouldn't stop creatures that could make you see whatever they wanted you to see or enthrall you with their voice.

Then when the guy nodded and Blaze rolled up the windows, shutting off the frigid air that had drifted through the car, a thought occurred to her: perhaps it wasn't Shediem they were defending against.

"Are they Giborim? Is this another compound?" she asked.

The SUV rolled forward when the gates swung open and still the ten or so soldiers followed, looking ready to blow it away at a moment's notice.

"Some of them are. It's an ex-military stronghold and airfield, but it belongs to a friend of the family," Blaze answered as he drove through what looked like the back lot of an abandoned airstrip.

"Some friend," Emma muttered.

Blaze smiled, but it didn't quite reach his eyes. "They can't be too careful right now." It was clear he was familiar with where he was going, because Blaze never once seemed unsure. He sped across the lit painted lot to a hangar with a small jet sitting just outside. He parked the SUV inside the covered space and got out.

Heart still pounding, Emma felt that her backside and the seat had melded together permanently.

Once on the plane—and away from all of the guns that had been pointed in their direction—the excitement about flying in an airplane for the first time began to return.

Blaze helped her stow her small carryon bag into the overhead bin before she took a seat in a large beige armchair that didn't look anything like the seats she'd seen in movies. Sergei followed behind her, looking green and visibly shaking.

"Who is going to fly the plane?" Emma asked Blaze, who took the seat across from her.

He cast a sidelong glance at Axel, who had already fallen asleep in the chair opposite the side of the aircraft that now hummed and vibrated. "Usually Axel or I would fly it, but I know a great pilot that will take over for our trip."

Emma bit the inside of her cheek, unsure of why she felt nervous. "Why?"

Blaze offered her a small smile. "To be able to sit with you." Then his eyes drifted to the seat diagonal from her, out of her line of view. She turned, spying Sergei clutching the armrests of his lavish seat as if the entire plane would explode at any moment. "And to make sure Sergei doesn't try to fight takeoff," he whispered. With a wink, he rose from his seat and stalked over to Sergei.

"Can I get you a drink?" Blaze offered him.

A spark of relief flared in Sergei's eyes. "Anything with vodka."

Blaze chuckled, clapping him on the shoulder before striding to the back of the plane. Emma leapt to her feet and followed curiously.

The back of the plane was fixed with cabinets and a sink. A small metal fridge was wedged in the middle, containing a vast assortment of beverages, as did the cabinet in front of Blaze. He was pouring a great deal of clear liquid into a short, crystal glass. The smell was alarmingly strong, but Emma didn't comment.

Without looking up at her, Blaze spoke. "Coffee? Soda?"

She smiled. "I'll never say no to coffee."

He smiled too as he grabbed a mug and placed it under a black nozzle. A sweet yet bitter aroma wafted over to Emma before Blaze handed her the cup, and she breathed in the comforting scent deeply with a satisfied groan.

"You can have as many cups as you like if you do that every time."

Her smile grew as she sipped the scalding liquid.

Blaze stepped into the aisle and Emma put a hand on his arm, stopping him. She kept her voice low so as not to be overheard by the plane full of supernatural beings. "Is it just me or does Axel look…"

"Sickly?" Blaze suggested.

She nodded.

He glanced at the seat that held his sleeping brother. "Yeah, I'm not sure what's going on. I know he's under a lot of stress with the upcoming wedding and all."

She hummed noncommittally before following Blaze into the aisle. He held out the glass filled with what Emma assumed was straight vodka to Sergei.

His lips twitched in an attempted smile. "Thanks," he mumbled before taking a sip.

Emma stretched her thawing fingers around the cup and leaned back, staring out the small window.

"I'll be right back." Blaze turned then strode away.

She nodded, glancing out the window at the men wandering below, their guns relaxed in their hands. With a sigh she focused back inside the aircraft. Dull chatter from Blaze and another male voice she assumed was from the pilot accompanied the humming engine. Gertie met her gaze from the seat in front and sent her a reassuring smile.

She'd never been to New Orleans. It was one of the few places she and her mother hadn't lived in, but she was excited to see it.

Just as she allowed herself to feel excitement, the emotion fell flat at the realization that New Orleans would be just another husk of a city filled with terrified people. She wouldn't get the gumbo-and-beignets experience.

A voice came on over the speaker, interrupting her morose thoughts to announce that everyone needed to be seated with their seatbelts fastened for takeoff.

Emma set her cup on the little round table across from her and buckled her seatbelt. Blaze walked down the aisle a moment later and dropped into his seat.

With a jolt, the plane was moving. Emma couldn't help but glance over at Sergei, who was audibly panting.

"There's a sick bag in the seat pocket," Blaze said over the increasing rumble of the aircraft.

Sergei ignored him as the plane shot forward. It sucked Emma into her seat, a sensation that made her giggle. She felt Blaze's eyes on her while she watched the ground zoom past. The aircraft nosed up, and the wheels left the ground. Being airborne made her blood feel electric and she grinned wide, while Sergei sounded like he was having a panic attack.

The plane's intense shaking soon lessened, and it began to level out. When she glanced at the Spellcaster, his knuckles were white on the armrests.

"Have you not flown before?" Emma asked.

Sergei slowly looked toward her, clearly fearful that the plane would fall out of the sky if he made any sudden movements. He nodded stiffly. "I've hated it every time."

She frowned. "I'm sorry." She paused for a moment. "Surely you could just use your magic to stop the plane if it started to crash."

Her attempt at reassurance did not have the desired effect: Sergei gave a harsh bark that was somewhere between a wheeze and a laugh. "No, I'm definitely not powerful enough to do that," he said through gritted teeth.

The plane jerked slightly. Emma frowned and Sergei took a large gulp of his vodka, draining the last of it though he looked as if his body might reject the alcohol. Blaze sat forward in his seat, forearms resting on his knees.

When Emma glanced at him, he gave her a smile. To Sergei he said, "Just try to relax. We'll be there soon."

Even as Blaze spoke, Sergei's eyelids drooped and his death grip on the seat loosened.

"What did you do?" Emma whispered incredulously when Sergei's head slumped to the side.

"I may have given him a light sedative," he admitted, though his smile never faded.

Emma shook her head with a playful smack to his shoulder.

Blaze shrugged. "Didn't want the upholstery to be soiled. It's a relatively new plane."

She bit down on her lip to keep from laughing, then went back to looking out the window. Gauzy white clouds passed beneath them.

Through the rest of the flight, Blaze typed furiously on a laptop and Emma simply took everything in over several more cups of coffee.

When the pilot announced they were beginning their descent, she marveled at how they'd crossed the country in such a small amount of time.

The plane had just touched down when Emma began to feel her nervousness return. The clouds had obstructed most of her view of the city coming in, but from the small glimpses she caught, she knew this was not meant to be a vacation. What was she even doing thinking of vacations anyway, when her mother, Adrianna, Haddie, and countless other people suffered in Sheol?

Blaze roused Axel, who had slept through the entire flight and still looked like he was in need of several more days of sleep. Emma tried to wake Sergei, but Gertie laid a hand on her arm and offered a smile.

"Let me, dearie."

Emma nodded, then grabbed her bag and strode up the aisle before descending the steps onto the tarmac. Blaze had grabbed their bags from the cargo hold and loaded them into another black SUV that was nearly identical to the one they'd taken back in Washington, if a tad bit dustier.

A sleepy Sergei, followed by Gertie clutching his arm to keep him from falling, disembarked and climbed into the new vehicle. Blaze climbed into the driver's seat.

Emma followed, taking the seat directly behind him. "Where are we staying? Surely there aren't any hotels we can go to?"

"We're staying with some...friends of mine," Gertie replied from the back.

"Oh." *So, Spellcasters,* she thought. If they were staying with them, then had they already agreed to join their fight?

The drive to their destination was roughly thirty minutes long, though it felt longer, listening to Sergei ask Gertie questions about how old she was when her magic manifested and if she had ever lost control of it. Emma was surprised to learn that Spellcasters usually came into their magic around ten years of age. Yet according to Levaroth, Adrianna was somehow a Spellcaster, and Emma was certain her friend hadn't been hiding such a monumental secret. Adrianna had seen her power in all its morbid glory. If anything, she would have confided in Emma with something so important.

Her eyes pricked with tears. She wished she could talk to her friend. She wished she could properly talk to anyone, really. The loneliness she'd felt in keeping her powers a secret was nothing compared to the forced silence.

They didn't drive through New Orleans, and Emma wondered if Blaze thought it unsafe. The vehicle wound down a dirt road that quickly turned to mud. It splashed up the sides of the SUV, which rocked and bounced. More than once, the seatbelt dug into Emma's torso as the terrain attempted to send her crashing into the ceiling of the car. The vegetation grew thicker, and the path less clear, but Blaze drove without hesitation.

An invisible force hit her, knocking the air from her lungs, and the mark beneath her skin came to life. It pulled and flexed as though trying to rip out of her body. Emma swallowed down a shout, but just as everyone in the car began to notice her reaction to the wards, it stopped. Blaze's gaze remained fixed on hers in the rearview mirror while the vehicle slowed. She gave a small, reassuring smile that he didn't return.

When the car stopped, Emma turned to the beautiful house they'd arrive at. It was two stories tall, with a creamy-blue steepled roof and an ornate white wraparound porch. It didn't look dark or uninviting despite the thick canopy that shadowed the structure. The trim around the circular windows, as well as the railing that wrapped around the house, was covered with a thin layer of moss.

Gertie sucked in a sharp breath as the metal screen door— that was fashioned to resemble a drawbridge—flew open, and two women who bore shocking resemblance to the Spellcaster rushed out, their eyes flaring with violet light.

EMMA

Where Gertie was plump, with a frizzy mane of grey curls, the other two women were reedier. The woman who looked older, wearing a long, maroon cardigan and a scowl, stepped forward on the porch until the wooden railing prevented her from going any further. Although, from her expression, Emma supposed that not even a wild, thrashing alligator would prevent the woman from coming closer.

"Gertrude," the woman drawled in a thick Southern accent.

"Constance," Gertie said from behind Emma.

The strength in Gertie's voice surprised her, considering she wanted to recoil from the woman's hard stare. Behind Constance, the other woman—who looked like an identical but slightly thinner version of Gertie—rushed forward, looking on the verge of tears.

"Gwyndoline." Gertie's voice was a whisper.

Gwyndoline dipped her head in acknowledgement. "Sister."

Emma's lips parted in surprise, though she quickly snapped them closed again when a large mosquito flew too near her face. She'd already assumed Gertie and the woman called Gwyndoline were related, but were both women her sisters? Emma had never heard Gertie mention siblings.

Blaze stood perfectly still, save for the twitch of his fingers. Like he wanted to reach for a blade, if only to hold it in his palm.

"They knew we were coming, right?" Emma asked out of the corner of her mouth.

"Yes, we knew," Constance snapped.

Emma's eyes widened. From the twenty or so feet that separated them, it didn't seem likely they would be able to hear her. Yet they had.

"Constance, be nice to our guests," Gwyndoline scolded in an accent nearly as thick as the older woman's.

Constance nodded once toward Sergei. "Who's the other Spellcaster? What coven does he belong to?"

Sergei stepped forward and raised his palm. A silvery light emanated from it, and a small, white wolf appeared in the air in front of him. Emma watched in awe as the majestic animal loped through the air—as though it was walking on the ground—and stood taller than twelve inches. The last time she'd seen Ugo, he'd been disguised as a ferret.

The two women raised their palms unflinchingly. A rust-colored fox emerged from the orange glow of Gwyndoline's palm while only pale yellow light spiraled from Constance. Sergei's wolf trotted faster to the fox and briefly, Emma thought the two creatures would fight.

She didn't realize she'd grasped Blaze's arm until he leaned down and whispered, "Spellcasters have familiars. When they meet new Spellcasters, it's customary for their familiars, which are their protectors, to assess their master's magic. If there is a threat, it is eliminated."

Without stopping, the two small familiars leapt into the air. They spun around each other, the light flaring when Constance's magic joined the tangle. Emma waited for either creature to lash out, but slowly their twirling dance ended.

When the fox sat back, seemingly satisfied, it cocked its head curiously before leaning forward and rubbing its head against Ugo's side. The wolf dipped its head, resting it on the fox. Constance's yellow light simply vanished, and Emma felt her heart squeeze painfully.

Where was her familiar?

The wolf turned and padded back to Sergei's open hand, vanishing without warning. Emma's eyes were still wide and her hand still gripped Blaze's forearm.

Not for the first time, she wondered if Adrianna had a familiar, and if so, what it was. Emma desperately wanted to speak to her friend, and the worry for her safety crept back in like a heavy weight in her chest.

"Well you best come in," Constance said, though her features suggested she'd rather let an entire zoo traipse through her house than allow them in. Her hawklike stare remained fixed on Blaze as they approached, and all the way up the porch steps. Then she spun and stormed into the house, letting the screen door slam behind her.

Gwyndoline glanced around apologetically as she pulled the door open. Gertie went in first, then Sergei and Blaze.

Axel stood behind Emma silently. He clearly knew all about the exchange between Spellcasters. She flashed him a small smile, but his gaze was over her shoulder, already assessing the inside of the house.

In the first room, Emma's stomach dropped as a sharp reality hit her. From the dark storm cloud that hovered over Constance, Emma had expected the house to look dark and brooding too. Instead, everything was bright and cheerful—decorated for Christmas.

A tall, full evergreen tree reached up to the high ceiling, its coniferous foliage brushing the top. From top to bottom classic warm white lights shone, highlighting the multicolored ornaments.

In the chaos of everything going on around her she'd forgotten about Christmas. It felt like an odd display of normalcy to decorate for any holiday when the world could be destroyed by the Shediem in a matter of weeks, or possibly months. Christmas was just another reminder that her mother was still a captive in Sheol, and that her best friend as well as Blaze's sister, whom he still believed to be dead, were there too.

Yet the warmth that seeped into her heart chased back the horror of her circumstance, at least for a moment. It was always a happy time for her. No matter where she and her mother lived, a tree, lights, and Christmas music and movies were a comfort. On the weekends, the house would be filled with the sweet, sugary scent of cookies.

And this strange house smelled of cinnamon and peppermint. A crackling fire danced in the hearth, though the mild sixty degrees it currently was outside made Emma think the fire was magical. Her entire chest ached.

"What day is it?" she asked. She knew it was December, but she'd lost track of the days.

Blaze put a hand on her shoulder as Gwyndoline cheerfully replied, "December 19th."

The ache grew, squeezing her lungs tight. Christmas was in just six days. *I'll get you home, soon, Mom. I promise. And we'll have Christmas together, even if it's the middle of summer.*

"If you guys are still here, we'll celebrate Christmas altogether." Gwyndoline looked to Gertie while she spoke, and Constance scoffed from the doorway across the room.

Emma pushed away her sadness, focusing instead on the task at hand. Blaze straightened, giving Constance a loaded look. Words seemed to pass between them, unspoken.

"Why don't you show them to their rooms, Gwyn?" Constance said at last, looking even more sour than she did when she first spotted them.

Gwyndoline nodded, smiling, before heading into the hall. The bare wood-paneled walls were made more festive by the multicolored lights strung up at the top, and it seemed to occur to Emma that Gwyndoline was likely the one who had decorated the house. Candy canes hung from doorknobs of each door they passed. On the right was a large kitchen with mouthwatering aromas wafting out.

"Once you guys are settled, we can fix you up a late lunch,"

Gwyndoline said, likely hearing the grumble of complaint Emma's stomach gave.

At the end of one hall, Gwyndoline produced an iron skeleton key and handed it to Blaze. She refused to meet his eyes, even when he thanked her, only giving a stiff nod. To Sergei she gave instructions on the shower—how the nozzle didn't register hot water quite right and that he'd have to fiddle with it—and where to find fresh towels. She ignored Axel altogether, though he didn't seem the least bit bothered. Then she turned and began leading Emma and Gertie away.

Emma watched Blaze pause at the door, casting a small smile toward her. Axel looked at her too, cocking his head to the side. His expression was curious but she couldn't fight the shiver his gaze had caused. Even when she turned to hurry after the two older women, Emma felt eyes on her back.

Down another hall Gwyndoline paused outside a door to the left. She extended the key to Gertie, though Emma hadn't seen it in her hand a moment ago.

Gertie's eyes were sad as she took the key. "Thank you, Gwyn."

Gwyndoline threw her arms around Gertie's neck. "I'm so happy to see you," she whispered.

Emma suddenly wished the wall would swallow her up so she didn't have to stand awkwardly in the hall while the two women shared a much-needed moment.

She turned away, looking for some way to busy herself so they could talk. Instead, she caught a glimpse of blond hair and blue eyes lurking around the corner. Emma stalked toward him.

"Axel?" she called.

She rounded the bend and halted—the hall was empty. She stood, rooted to the floor by an unfurling sense of unease.

The room was elegant, yet small and simply decorated. A fake, half-sized Christmas tree lit up the back corner nearest the bed Gertie had claimed. A large window was opposite the beds, giving a view of thick shrubbery and very little light. With a sigh Emma tossed her bag onto one of the two single beds covered with thick, floral quilted comforters.

Gertie paused her bustling around the room. "You all right, darling? You look spooked."

Emma nodded, trying to muster a smile, though she imagined it looked as fake as it felt. "I'm just worried about Axel." Gertie nodded in agreement, and Emma happily changed the subject. "So, tell me about your sisters. Constance doesn't seem happy that we're here."

Gertie didn't respond for several moments, rifling through her bag until she pulled out a toothbrush and tube of toothpaste. She sighed.

"Constance is our older sister. Gwyn and I are twins. And Constance acts the way she does because Spellcasters are really only loyal to each other. We're meant to stay together, within our covens. But well…I didn't. I chose to serve a family of Giborim who took me in."

Emma couldn't help her curiosity. "Why? Why go work for Blaze and leave your sisters?" Perhaps it was the fact that she didn't have any siblings that she wanted to know. Not that working for Blaze was a bad thing, but she couldn't imagine it was very exciting.

"I wanted to be a cook, not a magician selling spells and potions to whoever offered the most. With Blaze I still get to practice my magic and be a cook."

Emma nodded. "Did you grow up here?"

"Yes." A small smile curved the older woman's lips. "And before you ask, no, I don't miss it."

Emma glanced down. "Can I ask…I noticed Constance didn't have a…a familiar. Do you have one? I've never seen you with an animal."

A flash of pain crossed Gertie's features, causing extra creases to appear. She sat on the edge of the bed and Emma followed suit, guessing this would be a long conversation.

"Constance is one of the only Spellcasters to be born without a familiar. She was often very jealous of Gwyn and me."

Emma frowned, but before she could ask the question loaded on her tongue, Gertie said, "My familiar died when I was just a girl." She paused and swallowed hard, her eyes shining.

"I'm sorry. I shouldn't have asked," Emma said.

Gertie shook her head. "It's all right. It's not a secret." She took a shaky breath. "One time when we were kids, it snowed. A pond that used to exist not far from here froze over. Gwyn tried to walk out to the middle of it and fell through."

Emma gasped, clapping a hand to her mouth.

"Naturally I jumped in to save her. The water was so cold it forced Tobias to try to come to my aid." A tear slid down her cheek. "He was just a kit. Just a wee thing. I pulled Gwyn out first but I was trapped under the ice. Constance came to save me at some point. By then my Toby had already drowned trying to pull me out." Her voice broke toward the end, but she pushed on. "He was scratching at the ice. He was so desperate to get me free that he didn't try to find a way out."

Emma's eyes burned with threatening tears. "I'm so sorry."

Gertie gave her a wobbly smile. "The pain of losing a familiar never goes away. Not ever. It's like losing a piece of your soul."

She didn't know what to say. An apology seemed painfully inadequate.

With a huff, Gertie brushed away her tears. "Now." Her tone became serious.

The pause while she seemed to grasp for the right words made Emma's heart thud against her ribcage painfully.

"I know you didn't have no silly spasm in that meeting."

Emma opened her mouth to argue but Gertie held up a hand to silence her. "Girl, everyone can sense the Shediem in you. Ever since you got back, it's undeniable. You don't leave with a faint trace of it and come back feeling like a general or greater unless something happened. There's a piece of one inside you."

Her eyes widened. A Shediem inside her? She was possessed?

In anticipation of offering any response, her lips sealed shut. A flash of panic ruptured through her. If Gertie knew she was under the Shediem's thrall, what would happen to Gertie?

The Spellcaster's lips twitched. Emma's silence had confirmed something, though she didn't know what.

She sat forward, placing her hands on her thighs, and she suddenly felt like Gertie was trying to see in her eyes what was affecting her.

"Are you currently in pain? That shouldn't trigger anything."

Emma breathed deeply, waiting for the strike of pain in her shoulder, but it didn't come. Slowly she shook her head.

Gertie nodded as though she had expected that answer. "All right, let's try... Do you know who your father is?"

The bite was instant, and Emma winced.

Gertie smiled. "Gotcha."

Emma's eyes widened. Had her admission of pain told Gertie that not only was her father a Shediem, but also that he was the Shediem responsible for giving her the Mark of Fallen Flame?

"Honestly, I don't understand how that boy hasn't figured it out already." Gertie shook her head, getting to her feet. "Matters of the heart are never straightforward though, are they?"

The hold on Emma's lips released instantly, and she sucked in a long breath.

Gertie smiled sympathetically. "Honestly, I expected something like this." The Spellcaster strode toward her, laying a hand on the shoulder that throbbed with phantom pain. "Don't worry, baby girl, Sergei and I will figure it out. Now do you want to shower first, or shall I?"

"Uh..." Emma stammered, "I'll shower quick." She started toward the bathroom with her things, happy to have a moment to herself.

Once she was dressed and Gertie had disappeared into the bathroom, a rapping sounded at the door. The soothing warmth she'd felt approaching helped loosen the knots in her stomach, and she threw open the door, smiling.

Blaze stood on the other side, looking like a modern Adonis with jeans and a T-shirt. His black hair was still damp from his own shower. But his stormy grey eyes and the slight crease between his brows made her smile disappear.

"What's wrong?" she asked.

His eyes took in every inch of her, assessing her for injury. Emma puzzled silently, noting the rigid set of his shoulders and the way his fists clenched and unclenched. His expression cleared suddenly, and he shook his head.

"Nothing. I wanted to see if you wanted anything to eat." His smile was stiff. "Gwyndoline was kind enough to set out a tray for us."

Emma nodded. Looking one direction, then the other, she whispered, "I'd be careful, though. They might be poisoned."

Blaze laughed softly, the last of his strange behavior fading. He took her hand in his, leading her down the hall. The physical contact sent a thrill through her. It seemed far too intimate to hold hands so publicly, but Blaze didn't seem to pay the gesture any mind.

He stopped, spinning her to face him. "Are you going to be all right tonight?" When her brows furrowed, he added, "The nightmares. It's a strange place; it's likely to trigger something."

She shrugged. "I'm sure it'll be okay."

His steel gaze searched her face. "I can talk to Gertie. It's probably best that she's warned so when you wake up screaming, she doesn't think you're dying or anything."

She bit her bottom lip. If Gertie spoke to Blaze—which

Emma knew she would—Blaze would be able to guess at Emma's strange behavior, which would only bring up more questions she couldn't answer yet. "I'll tell her." She secretly wished Blaze could stay with her, but she knew it wasn't appropriate, especially when they were guests.

Blaze's fingers wound tighter around hers, giving her a light squeeze. Emma tried to smile, but the closer they got to the kitchen where voices emanated, the more her heart stumbled over a beat. Most everyone knew there was something going on between them, but any displays of affection were forbidden by his kind. Axel had seen them kiss, but it was different now. The way he'd watched her made Emma think he'd changed his mind about being okay with the two of them.

In the back of her mind, she wondered if Blaze would still hold her hand when they got back to Seattle. It was foolish to hope for it, she knew. The consequences for their relationship, especially at a time like this, could be detrimental. She let the hope that had blossomed and warmed her chest chill. Nothing had truly changed. She couldn't let his people reject him—not when they needed him most.

Constance was absent from the gathering inside the dining area. Gwyndoline laughed cheerfully at something Sergei said when they entered. Gazes followed them and their clasped hands, but no one remarked on it. Sergei smiled down at his plate that still had a few crackers and slices of salami, making Emma's cheeks heat. Axel was seated in the corner, leaning against the wall. Emma avoided looking in his direction, hating how uncomfortable she felt every time she was in a room with him.

Blaze released her hand so they could sit at the table, both of them reaching for the trays of food. Beside her, she felt his warm gaze on her face, and she smiled.

"What time are we heading out tomorrow?" Axel asked, interrupting the lull of silence.

Emma looked up, stopping midchew. His gaze was fixed on her. Focused, yet relaxed.

It was as if he wanted to rattle her. To make her feel like she was going crazy. Maybe she was. Perhaps she was paranoid.

What if he simply sensed "the Shediem in her"—as Gertie had said—and was reacting like a hunter did when it smelled prey? Axel knew Emma was involved with his brother. It seemed only right for him to want to protect Blaze.

She tried to ignore any further looks from Axel the rest of the meal. Sergei shared stories of Russia at Christmas time and the traditions he'd been raised with, distracting them all with their own sense of nostalgia. Emma ate way too many gingerbread cookies, feeling the dull ache that her mother's absence brought. The traditions Sergei was used to were likely the ones her mother had also been accustomed to.

It was fascinating to think that her mother had grown up in a completely different country. She spoke a different language and understood the history of Russia better than Emma ever would. It made sense when her mother would make borscht every so often, though Emma had been convinced that it was just a way for her mother to get her to eat more vegetables when she was small.

Then it was Gertie's turn, sharing how Gwyndoline's magic showed up six months before her own. Gwyndoline smiled fondly at Gertie as they went back and forth with pranks they played on each other, on their parents, and on Constance. Their grandmother had been coven leader, and Constance had taken over less than a decade ago, Gwyndoline revealed.

Gertie's smile vanished then.

Constance stalked into the room a moment later. As if she'd stood right outside, listening. "I know why you're here, and if you think I'm going to fight in your little supernatural war, you're wrong. My coven will sit back and watch you lot tear yourself apart, but we won't choose sides."

Gwyndoline's face flushed at her older sister's harsh words. The room was deadly quiet.

Blaze rose to his feet slowly, staring Constance down. "When the Shediem try to claim the Earth as their new home, you'll just let them enslave or slaughter your coven? Your sister?" His voice was like rolling thunder through the heavy silence.

The woman's bony chin lifted in defiance. "Of course I'll protect them. But this fight is not ours. The Shediem may look like monsters, but you Giborim put yourselves on pedestals while you take whatever you want and seek to control the lives of everyone around you, even your own kind. The Spellcasters are forbidden from marrying humans by your laws, not ours. Anyone that goes against your precious rules is either forced to obey or killed."

The rush of heated words was colored with emotion—emotion that Emma thought belonged to experience. Had Constance loved someone and been forced to stay away from them?

"You're not wrong," Blaze said. His eyes met Emma's and held it for a moment; her heart leapt in response. "But letting the Shediem win won't bring about change. The Giborim were always meant to protect the humans and keep the supernatural hidden. But if we win, we can stand to make some changes. None of us should have to live in fear of discovery or be forced to give up love when we find it."

Constance folded her slender arms across her chest and glared at Blaze a few moments longer. "I won't ask my people to die for you or for anyone else."

Gwyndoline turned in her chair to look up at her sister. "I call a vote." Threaded in her words was a hint of magic Emma could feel. "Tomorrow afternoon."

The older woman's jaw tightened, and her thin lips knotted in disapproval, but she didn't fight it. Perhaps she couldn't. She simply pivoted and strode out of the room with a huff.

Gertie loosed a breath from across the table and shot her twin a grateful smile.

EMMA

N ight fell while their group drank hot chocolate and spiced cider together in comfortable company. Or mostly comfortable company, anyway. Constance didn't return, and Emma could tell that Gertie and Gwyn were affected by it. Still they laughed and sipped their beverages. For a few moments, Emma smiled too. She felt whole.

After yawning for the third time in the space of ten minutes, Blaze stood and offered her his hand. She accepted it, letting him pull her to her feet. Everyone smiled and bid each other goodnight. Axel stirred from his seat, having fallen asleep, but he simply nodded to Blaze before they left.

At Emma's door, Blaze tugged her around to face him before sliding a hand around the nape of her neck, then pressed his lips to hers. The kiss lingered, warming her entire body.

"Goodnight," he said, their faces barely an inch apart.

She swallowed hard, not wanting him to go. "Goodnight."

He hesitated as she pushed the door open, but when he didn't rush inside and insist on staying, she closed the door.

Emma climbed into the bed and switched the light off. She settled down under the covers, her stomach knotting itself. Without Blaze, she wasn't eager to sleep. No matter what horror awaited her, Blaze would not be there to comfort her once she woke. And Levaroth would likely not be there to help face them.

She stared up at the ceiling for at least an hour before the door creaked open and Gertie crept inside.

"Oh, I thought you'd be asleep," Gertie said sympathetically.

Emma didn't respond as the Spellcaster went to her bag on the floor and pulled out a vial of silvery fluid. She blinked in surprise—she's seen it before in her mother's bedside table.

"Here," Gertie said, holding it out to her. "This should help with the nightmares."

Emma took it, staring at it for several moments with uncertainty.

"It won't hurt you, just drink it quickly. It tastes a bit like dirt."

Emma's nose wrinkled at the thought. With a steadying breath, she unstopped the vial and tilted it back. The contents were bitter, and earthy tasting, though it coated her tongue and her throat, warming her. She fought the urge to gag and Gertie laughed.

"It's not pleasant, but it'll do the trick."

When it hit Emma's belly, her eyelids become nearly impossible to keep open. Long, silky fingers of sleep coiled around her, wrapping her up in blissful darkness.

She awoke the next morning to Gertie lightly shaking her. After rubbing the sleep from her eyes, a thread of shock ran through her: she'd slept through the night without a single nightmare. Part of her wondered if the reason Levaroth hadn't appeared was due to whatever Gertie had given her—but then she recalled that Levaroth had met with her while she was awake. Regardless, she felt more rested than she had in weeks.

They left the house and piled into the SUV with only a basket of warm muffins from Gwyndoline and a thermos of coffee. Morning light had only begun to chase away the stars, offering a faint pink and orange glow at the very edge of the sky.

"My first contact is quite near," Gertie told them. "We'd walk, but the wildlife out here isn't the safest to be around."

Not to mention the Shediem likely crawling around, Emma thought.

They truly didn't drive far, though there was no road to follow for most of the way, and Gertie had to direct Blaze through the swampy terrain. They pulled up to what looked like an abandoned coffeehouse on a gravel road. Its windows were boarded up and the wood slats were colored with profane graffiti art. The roof drooped inward, looking like one good, heavy rain would finally cause it to collapse. Thick, thorny brambles grew over the porch and climbed up the columns and exterior walls. All around, the foliage had gone unchecked for possibly a decade.

"Does anyone actually live here?" Emma asked through a bite of warm blueberry muffin.

Gertie nodded. "What you're seeing is just an illusion meant to detract people from getting near it. You'll see once we get inside."

They opened their doors and began to pile out, Axel standing almost shoulder to shoulder with Emma. He examined the structure, and with the hint of a smirk peeking out, he looked more like himself than he had in the past week. "Even without the illusion, it's certainly ugly."

Blaze nodded his agreement while Sergei barked a laugh. Gertie made a sound of disapproval, though paired with a smile it didn't have the same effect.

Emma glanced sidelong at Axel, smiling too, and his grin faded. Her heart twinged with guilt—she missed his cocky and easy manner.

In the distance, a chorus of shrill, animalistic shrieks rang out. Everyone in the group went rigid. Blaze's hand wrapped around the hilt of the sword at his back.

Gertie looked around with lowered brows, then motioned for them to follow her inside the old building. As Emma's foot touched the first step, the thick growth of bushes curled away out of her path. She gasped.

Sergei grinned over his shoulder—her awe of blatant magic was clearly amusing to almost everyone in the group. Axel brought up the rear, following close behind her and forcing her to keep moving. The screen door hung at an angle by only one set of hinges, but Gertie knocked on it anyway.

After a moment, when nothing happened, Gertie murmured something under her breath, and the solid wood door gave an audible click. She reached for the handle and her hand sailed right through the screen door, which flickered like a poor projection. Emma's mouth hung open in shock.

Gertie pushed the door open and disappeared inside. Blaze went next, then Sergei. Emma hesitated for a moment, until another round of howls in the distance made her step through.

Inside, a cobweb-covered bulb glowed with just enough light to keep them from tripping. From what Emma could see, it truly had been a coffeehouse at one time. Chairs and tables were stacked in piles, pushed against the walls, allowing only enough room to shuffle through the narrow space. A thick layer of dust coated the entire room, muting colors and making Emma's nose itch.

"August?" Gertie called as she led them into the back.

Three doors loomed before them: one in front of them and one on either side. But they didn't bear the usual pictograms for restrooms—instead, they were marked with outlined shapes and symbols that Emma didn't recognize. Gertie didn't hesitate, pulling open the door on the right, which bore twisting lines that might have represented snakes from the way they coiled together, and on either side had two crescent moons facing away from each other. It was visible on the inside of the door as well, as if it had been burned all the way through.

Gertie marched through, unafraid of who or what could hear them. Behind Blaze, Emma saw a dark staircase that led down to a basement. The memory of another set of stairs flashed in her mind. The darkness that reached out for her. The smell of bleach. Her mother's fearful cry.

Emma's breathing turned ragged. She pasted herself against the wall, leaning into it for support. Blaze turned on the first step, noticing her reaction, and his expression softened.

"Hey." He strode toward her and cupped her cheek. "I'm right beside you, it's okay."

Emma squeezed her eyes shut for a moment, blocking out the memory until her breathing normalized. Her hands still shook, so she balled them into fists and leaned back on them. When she opened her eyes, everyone watched her, but Blaze leaned forward and blocked them from view.

His concerned gaze held the question asking if she was ready, and after another moment, she nodded. He went first, glancing back after a few steps to make sure she was okay. For that she was grateful. Her heart picked up speed again the darker it became and her hand skated across the handrail for support.

"Is there no light?" she asked as quietly as she could manage, having to guess where each step was, wondering how far down it went.

Blaze's warmth directly in front of her reassured her, his soft steps pulling her deeper.

Instead of answering Emma's question, Gertie called out, "August! It's me, Gertrude."

When no answer came, Emma released a shaky breath. Her lungs felt tight. When she was no longer able to bear the inky black, she fished her cellphone from her pocket, but behind her a hand gripped her shoulder and squeezed.

"Don't," Sergei whispered.

"Why?" Emma asked, louder than she meant to. She flinched from her voice echoing off the walls.

"Down!" Blaze bellowed.

Yellow sparks shot toward them. Sergei pulled her back with him. The side of her knee slammed against the wooden stair, and she bit down on her bottom lip to muffle her cry.

The stairway went dark again for another moment before

little blue lights, like glinting fireflies, tentatively rose in the air a few feet in front of Emma. She could barely make out Gertie's form at the bottom of the steps.

The floating bits of blue light drifted forward, taking the shape of an elk that grew in size until its antlers were as wide as the staircase and its hooves clacked on the stone floor. The light that pulsed from it illuminated rows of shelves. Colored light spilled from Gertie's palm, meeting the creature and flowing over it like a lazy fog.

Emma didn't dare breathe as their magic connected. The elk held perfectly still, blinking up at the rest of them. When its attention turned to Emma, its enormous rack tilted with curiosity.

Finally, the elk shrunk, then vanished in brilliant blue light. Gertie's magic disappeared too, throwing them back into stark darkness.

"*Nzortica*," a gruff male voice said.

Lights from the room below came to life. A man in a pair of torn, tan corduroy pants and a matted wool sweater surveyed them. Slowly they all got to their feet.

"My apologies, Gertrude," the man that Emma assumed was August said. "Whispers of our kind being possessed, or frauds altogether, have made me a little jumpy." His eyes flashed with violet light before a crooked smile overtook his wrinkled face.

Gertie bounced down the last step and rushed to him, throwing her arms around his middle. He was at least a foot taller than her and looked to be in his late sixties, possibly early seventies.

The rest of their group descended the last few stairs and entered the dusty storage room that smelled of mildew.

"Who's the girl?" August asked, eyeing Emma with equal parts interest and caution.

Her jaw snapped shut—the mark had flared to attention.

"Doesn't seem like the type of company you'd keep."

Emma tried to ignore the mixture of anger and shame that

emerged at his statement. He could sense her Shediem blood and likely the mark. *Great, everyone can tell that I'm a freak.*

She glanced over at Blaze. His shoulders tensed, and a muscle in his jaw twitched, but he didn't meet Emma's gaze. On her other side, Axel stared unabashedly at her, a small, cruel smirk tugging at the corners of his lips.

"August, this is Blaze, his brother Axel, Emma, and Sergei." Gertie pointed to each of them as she said their names, and his eyes tracked from person to person, lingering on Sergei for a moment before looking back to Emma.

"Hmph," he grunted, then he spun on his heel and walked back to the rows of shelves.

Gertie followed at a brisk pace, waving the rest of them forward.

Emma passed shelves filled with murky jars and damp, sagging boxes. Her eyes snagged on one large jar that contained a dark mass. Though the grime on the outside made it difficult to make it out, it was clear that whatever was inside moved. She shivered, clutching her jacket tighter.

August walked quickly for such a frail-looking man. He was several paces in front of Gertie, leading them out of the musty storage room and into what looked like a small apartment.

The armchairs and lounges looked like they were from the seventies, their horrid rusty orange-and-brown upholstery torn, with stuffing as well as the occasional spring poking through. August gestured for them to sit, and reluctantly, they all carefully dropped into the sagging cushions. Sergei sat beside Emma on the small sofa.

"Tea?" their host called to them, though his tone didn't suggest he required a response.

She would have been glad for a warm drink to rinse out the layer of dust that seemed to coat her throat, but she wasn't sure it would do any good. The tea would likely be as old as everything else around them, and likely just as dusty.

"We're fine, August," Gertie replied tightly. "We were hoping to offer you and the *Loradoches* a job."

The loud clattering of china made Emma jump. A rusted spring in the sofa ripped through the striped fabric by her thigh, and she scooted over a fraction to avoid being infected with tetanus. Her eyes flicked up to find Blaze watching her with mild amusement.

August set down a tray with a pot and six mismatched mugs all filled with a steaming dark brown liquid on the table in front of them. The scent wafted into the air, reminding Emma of gasoline with the consistency of mud. She wrinkled her nose, unable to stop herself. Blaze regarded the beverage with as much disdain as one would a banana slug.

August took a cup and settled himself in the worn chair beside Emma. A twig floated to the top of the steaming brew, bobbing on the surface, but the man sipped it without a moment's hesitation.

No one else reached for a cup, until August's dark eyes darted to each of them expectantly. Gertie moved first, then Sergei. Finally, Emma bent over to grab one at the same time as Blaze, their fingertips brushing, sending a current of heat up her arm. Beside Blaze, his brother raised an eyebrow, and Emma's cheeks heated. Axel made no move to grab the last cup and no one said anything, though she heard August grunt in disapproval.

Louisiana was already much warmer than Seattle, but the hot mug still delivered a sense of warmth and security that Emma craved. She had to remind herself several times—while Blaze and Gertie took turns explaining why they were there—that the liquid was not coffee. She stared into the opaque sludge as something that resembled a leaf broke the surface.

Forcing herself not to grimace, she listened to Blaze telling August of her mother's abduction. Sergei offered bits and pieces—but not even he knew everything. There were gaping holes that they glossed over, and Emma waited for the usual questions. Waited for the weighted pauses for her to inject bits of information into, but they never came.

"In the past few weeks there have been reports of entire covens being abducted. The Shediem aren't going to ask nicely. This is about amassing as many powerful beings in their army as they can before war begins," Blaze said with urgency.

August sank deeper into his chair, as if hoping to become a part of it. His eyes didn't lift from his cup, even after Blaze waited for him to speak.

"Gertie," he whispered at last, shaking his head. Then his eyes lifted to her. They flashed purple once more, but there was sadness in them. "You bring these people to my doorstep knowing I don't belong to the *Loradoches* anymore?"

Gertie's eyebrows lifted. "Since when?"

"Surely you knew?" August replied.

Gertie shook her head, and he sighed.

"They kicked me out ten years ago. I haven't practiced magic since...until you came."

Emma swallowed hard. That explained the dusty apartment he clearly hadn't left in ten years.

"By who? Tabby?" Gertie asked.

August looked down at his lap, shrugging. His shoulders drooped as a sob escaped him. Emma turned to Gertie, who rose and placed her still-full cup onto the coffee table before moving to stand in front of him.

"She married that Daryl. You remember him?" August wiped his nose on the sleeve of his sweater.

Gertie nodded.

"He convinced her to force me out. Convinced the elders that I had lost my mind."

Emma's heart squeezed tightly. The man before them might have once been a great Spellcaster, but he was an old hermit now. Gertie patted his shoulder as he sniffled again.

When he had composed himself, he looked around. "I'm sorry, but I can't help you." Then he stood, dismissing them.

"Well that was a bloody waste," Sergei grumbled as they left the old man in his rotting house.

"Where to next?" Blaze asked Gertie once they were all back inside the SUV.

Above the rumble of the engine, a long, high-pitched howl made them all go still. Axel's frame began to tremble in the seat next to Emma. His hands were clenched into fists on his thighs, his knuckles white.

Since when did Shediem frighten him?

"This place is infested with Shediem," Blaze said darkly.

How much longer would it be until they figured out she was in their midst? That she was more Shediem than Giborim or even human? Emma didn't want to think about how they'd react to her then. Axel seemed to know, and Gertie knew she was carrying something resembling a Shediem inside her, but that wasn't it. Her father was a prince of Sheol. A full-blooded monster. Her mother was only a quarter Giborim; mostly human. But Emma had absorbed the power of a prince. Even if she managed to remove the mark, there was still the fact that Belphegor's power was in her blood. Soon, she'd be a mix of all the princes—assuming they didn't kill her first.

With every depraved sound from the creatures growing closer, the truth of what she was becoming settled further into her chest, a weight dragging her into the bottomless depths of despair. Each second that ticked brought her closer to the next time her father would steal her back to Sheol. When she'd betray those she cared for yet again.

This time they drove back on paved roads, passing abandoned vehicles that had been broken into and stripped for parts. Whether to sell or use for other purposes, Emma didn't know.

The exquisite French architecture that New Orleans was known for surrounded them, though the city looked like a ghost town. The only humans that milled about looked like they were either strung out on drugs or looking for another fix. The vehicle slowed, quieting the treads, and Gertie cloaked the vehicle so as not to draw attention.

In the shadows, tall, lanky creatures stirred, waiting for their prey. Their yellow eyes tracked the car's movement despite the spell that hid them from view. Emma swallowed hard at the memory of the Nybbases she and Adrianna had fought four months ago.

"Here," Gertie instructed.

Blaze parked the SUV outside a tall apartment complex. The double doors that led inside were chained shut, and thick iron bars covered them. Many of the windows in the apartments were also boarded or barred. Not a single light shone in any window, but Emma knew the city was not empty. Its inhabitants simply knew what monsters prowled the streets—and it wasn't just Shediem.

One man sat on his balcony, strumming on what appeared to be a ukulele as though the city teemed with life and vibrancy.

Slowly, they got out of the car. The man, who looked to be in his forties, had a thick, dark beard and a forest-green beanie that capped a head of long, greasy blond hair. He never paused his playing, though his eyes watched them approach.

Emma silently mourned for the great city. There was so much talent in New Orleans alone, it was like its own beacon for anyone looking to escape the monotony of daily life—to just come and live. Her heart bled for those forced to hide in terror all over the world. Their lives were now sport to the creatures that openly hunted on the streets. Would the humans ever get to live again?

Would she ever get to see New Orleans as the musical, artistic hub that it was? To come and enjoy the simplicity that places like New Orleans had to offer? She wasn't musically inclined, but she had loved to sketch, particularly when she was younger. She wouldn't win any awards for it or be able to make a living off it, but once upon a time, she had imagined having her own little space in this city, enjoying its warmth, the spices, the upbeat music on every street. The diversity of its people, the unification of all.

If it ever returned to its former glory, maybe one day she could just be an ordinary girl with a sketch pad, drawing whatever caught her eye for no other reason than for the pleasure it would bring her.

Gertie stopped and looked up to a closed balcony door on the second floor. Outside, on the pale bricks, was a silver carving that matched the one in August's coffee shop. It was small, and Emma might not have noticed it if she hadn't already seen it elsewhere. Blaze and Sergei exchanged matching quizzical expressions.

"Who you lookin' for, doll?" the man asked from above them.

Gertie didn't look like she was going to answer him, but at last she said, "Maria Oltos. Does she still live here?" She pointed to the apartment with the symbol.

The man strummed the small instrument with his head cocked to the side thoughtfully. "I've never seen anyone living in that space...and I've lived here fifteen years."

Of course, Emma thought bitterly. *Another dead end.*

Gertie didn't seem convinced at first. Then she nodded. "Thank you for your help."

"Anything for a sweet broad like you," he answered.

Gertie spun around, leading them back down the stone steps, but Emma caught sight of her cheeks taking on a rosy flush that made her smile.

They tried two more buildings in the city, with no luck. Many had fled, or—as Sergei had voiced after the second empty house—the Shediem had abducted every coven in the area. It made sense since the Shediem were everywhere, unchecked. The Giborim who usually resided in the area had moved to other compounds in more remote locations, though they passed a few helping the homeless and one covered in a spray of familiar shiny black substance. Blaze had nodded in respect, earning one in return, but they didn't stay and chat.

After the third unsuccessful call, Blaze made them head back to the bayou. They'd polished off the overflowing basket of muffins, and the sun was beginning to set. Soon, the night predators would be out in full force, and none of them were willing to risk being caught in a city full of Shediem, no matter how powerful they were altogether.

When they passed through the invisible wards surrounding Constance and Gwyndoline's house, Emma's breath hitched. It wasn't as painful as the first time, but whatever power existed in her shoulder twitched and writhed for several moments before going still again.

They coasted to a stop outside, and everyone's eyes landed on a sleek, silver Honda that hadn't been there before.

"Who is that?" Axel asked gruffly.

No one responded; instead they climbed out of the SUV in silence and hurried for the door, ignoring the distant sounds of Shediem and the screams of terror that followed.

Gwyndoline met them at the door, pulling it open before Gertie reached for the handle. Her twin's eyes were wide, her hands visibly shaking.

"You have visitors," she said softly.

Blaze met Emma's questioning look with one of his own, but the tick in his jaw betrayed his worry. He rushed past Gwyndoline and Gertie and into the house with the determination of an alpha wolf defending its pack. Emma practically had to jog to keep up with him, and when he reached the entrance to the dining room, he jolted to a stop, putting out an arm made of steel. She collided with it, giving an audible "oof" before throwing a glare up at him, but he didn't seem to notice. His eyes were trained on the two strangers sitting at the dining room table.

Constance stood in front of the stove, though she glanced at where Blaze stood in the doorway, giving off heat and violent energy. Sweat beaded her brow, and her usual mask of disdain was replaced with anxiety.

Emma swallowed hard, drawing two sets of violet eyes to her. Blaze shifted, trying to push her behind him, but she dug her heels in, meeting their stares.

A girl only a few years older than her, with vibrant purple hair cropped into a pixie cut that highlighted her sharp chin, smiled a crooked, twisted smile from her seat. Her pale skin gave off a shimmering quality that was undoubtedly magic. The boy across from her, who had dark skin and looked to be a year or so older than Emma, raked his gaze up and down with apparent interest. His eyes flared brighter with heat, and Emma looked back to the girl.

"Who are you?" Blaze asked, his voice harsh with impending violence.

The girl rose from her chair still smiling at Blaze in a strange, predatory way. "Taryn. And this is my brother, Derrik."

Derrik offered Blaze a nod before his gaze shifted back to Emma. He was handsome, she supposed, but when his irises extinguished their purple glow, Emma noticed the telltale signs of an addict: yellowing, bloodshot eyes sunken, and gaunt features. His frame was toned, but there was a sickness that seeped from him that not even his smirk could hide.

"I heard you lot were recruiting covens to help fight the Shediem," Taryn drawled, peering around Blaze's bulky frame to direct her next words at Emma. "And we heard you brought the Shediem-Slayer with you."

Emma's heart rocketed up another notch, and she was sure the whole room could hear its thunderous pace like a stampede of wild horses. Behind her, Axel let out a hiss.

He hissed. Like a cat.

Even Blaze turned to him. His brother's eyes were narrowed on Derrik in challenge.

Derrik laughed a lazy, rich sound. "Down, kitty. We're not here to harm anyone."

Axel's growl was cut off when Blaze lifted his hand, his glare demanding silence. Finally, Constance slammed the wooden spoon she'd been so vigorously stirring with onto the counter.

"And why would you be interested in fighting the Shediem, pray tell? Your coven is widely known for its brutality and ardent refusal to ever aid any other covens. When New Orleans fell to the Shediem, you did nothing to try to prevent it."

Taryn gave her a cold smile that was all teeth. "That's not entirely true. You don't have to trust us to be our allies." She paused. "No one wants the Shediem gone more than us, however."

"I don't believe that," Emma snapped, folding her arms across her chest. "Otherwise you would have tried to protect your city." She'd seen firsthand that there were few willing to protect the humans that remained, and it disgusted her. The Giborim, yes. But still, there were tens of thousands of humans that had fled because they had no one fighting for them.

The Spellcaster laughed. "It's always best to know when to pick your battles. My coven has had to fight and claw their way into even being recognized by other covens because we're misfits in their eyes." Her eyes flashed violet once again and flicked to Constance, who had her hands on her hips, lips pursed.

"You took the Spellcasters you wanted for yourself and slaughtered anyone that stood in your way," Constance spat.

Taryn didn't acknowledge the accusation laid at her feet, instead turning back to Blaze. "We're willing to offer you our combined magic to help win this war. But, we'd like to return to Seattle with you. I know you need the protection, and my coven goes where I direct them."

"I'll bet it does," Blaze muttered.

"And how do we know you won't betray us or any of the other covens in the heat of battle, just to be on the winning team?"

Gertie asked with more derision than Emma had ever heard from the kind lady's lips.

"You don't," Derrik confirmed, still smirking like a prince from his throne. "But I suspect you haven't gotten much help today."

Emma looked at Blaze. His expression was blank, but she could sense the war taking place inside him. On the one hand, they had volunteers willing to fight back in Seattle. On the other hand, they weren't nearly enough.

After a long silence where no one dared blink, Blaze responded. "You may accompany us to Washington. All the covens in the area were taken or pledged their allegiance to the Shediem willingly, so yes, we need you. You'll be protected and fed; in exchange I demand you swear an oath that you will not betray us."

Taryn's smile turned brittle. "I cannot swear it for all of my coven, but I will swear an oath that I will not order my Spellcasters to betray you." She cocked her hip to the side with a sniff. "Besides, they all know that the penalty for their disobedience is death."

Blaze's jaw was so tight, Emma feared he'd break it. Then he held out a hand to the coven leader, palm up. Emma's brows furrowed.

A sparkle of triumph lit Taryn's eyes, and Derrik's smile widened, flashing his white teeth.

The Spellcaster placed her small hand in Blaze's, and a deep purple light spread from her palm into his. "I swear my loyalty to Blaze Thomas, northwest regional leader of the Giborim. In battle my magic shall harm none but his enemies, until they or myself are vanquished."

Silver cords of light wrapped both their arms and flashed so bright Emma had to shield her eyes. She wondered how Taryn knew his full name, but even with a magical oath that made the Spellcaster unable to betray them, Emma still didn't trust her.

And her brother, who looked nothing like her, Emma trusted

even less. His eyes had never looked away from her. Their dark depths seemed to know the secrets Emma couldn't reveal. And his unnerving smile said he'd happily spill them all if she wasn't careful.

BLAZE

The duo of Spellcasters invited themselves to stay for dinner. They made uncomfortable small talk with the other Spellcasters, the forced proximity making the urge to haul them out and tie them to trees for the Shediem to feast on nearly impossible to dismiss. Their prejudice against the siblings' kind was palpable. Especially at Derrik, who watched Emma like a hawk circling a cornered rabbit.

"We're meant to stay a few more days. Where will you stay until then?" Blaze asked when the meal was decidedly over by everyone at the table pushing their food around instead of eating it. Well, except Taryn and Derrik. They ate like they hadn't had a decent meal in weeks, and from the look of both of them, it was probable they hadn't. Yet Blaze felt nearly certain they just wanted to put Constance out.

The hatred in the room was thick enough to slice into.

Taryn gulped down the last of her spiced eggnog and wiped her face with the back of her dainty hand—the same hand that now bore the imprint of an oath like shimmering glitter a preteen would wear. It reeked of her magic, which was not as pleasant as the other Spellcasters', apart from Derrik. He hadn't even used his and Blaze could scent the decay that occupied his body. A drug-addicted Spellcaster often smelled that way.

His bloodshot eyes were all Blaze needed to know that Derrik was still high off whatever substance held him firmly in

148

its grip. His sister's frequent glances also told him that she kept him close simply to keep him from overdosing on the Shediem-infested streets.

Taryn's reputation had preceded her. There were rumors of a witch down in the south that assembled a ragtag band of Spellcasters and formed her own coven by tearing families apart and killing any coven leader who stood in her way. She ruled the streets with much more than an iron fist. It was intimidation and cruelty, plain and simple.

Why she had sought them out still remained a mystery, one that Blaze intended to reveal. Before it got Gertie, or anyone else he cared about, killed.

"Ah well, Constance certainly has the room to spare us—"

"No, I most certainly do not!" Constance's cheeks were red, and orange sparks flew from her fingertips but extinguished the moment they hit the floor.

Taryn tilted back in the creaky wooden chair, grinning in that unnerving way of hers. "I swore to protect Blaze here." She gestured with her glittering hand at Blaze, whose body was bunched with building aggression.

Perhaps he and Axel would venture beyond the wards to hunt later tonight...

Derrik nodded. "Six Spellcasters is better than four." He glanced at Sergei. "More like three and a half."

Blaze's fists and jaw clenched, a snarl escaping him. Emma laid a hand discreetly on his thigh beneath the table. Her touch soothed the jagged edges of his temper, but he wouldn't let his guard down around Taryn or any member of her coven. "If you disrespect my friends, you won't be around long enough to offer any help when the princes rise."

Emma sucked in a sharp, muted breath at his words. It was true that Blaze was usually controlled and metered in his anger, but with his brother's odd behavior and Emma's secrets, he was beginning to wear thin. Not to mention that time was nearly up. War was a reality they'd all be forced to face any minute.

In his experience with past wars, it was always the unknown that drove people to brutality against their fellow man. Blaze reminded himself of that fact to reign in his loathing for the intruders. They needed allies. They were here for allies. And they didn't need to be friends in order to fight for the same result.

He stood before Taryn or her brother could respond, offering Emma a hand to help her to her feet. Her throat bobbed once before she took it and let him pull her around the long table and against his chest.

His body relaxed marginally at her nearness. The steady rhythm of her heart and her sweet scent put him at ease when all else failed. But he would stay vigilant. He couldn't afford to blink. People died when he looked away for even a second—a consequence he'd faced every day for over a century. He lived by two rules: never let your guard down, and never let them see your weaknesses.

Blaze turned to Constance, who had set her magic to work, clearing plates and scrubbing dishes with the same fervor she did everything. Unspoken, he made his request. She huffed and stormed from the room.

A moment later she tossed a skeleton key onto the table in front of Taryn. "Down the hall to your right. Second door on your left."

Which put them across the hall from himself, Axel, and Sergei. Blaze resisted the urge to roll his eyes.

"Thank you, Constance." Taryn's words sounded sincere— almost.

She said nothing, but stalked out again, leaving her magic to clean up the feast she'd prepared for them all.

"Come." Blaze led Emma from the room without another word to anyone.

She waved goodnight to Gertie and Sergei, but Derrik's whispered words made Blaze's grip on her tighten.

"See you soon, Shediem-Slayer."

He ushered her down the hall at a brisk pace, and once

he stopped outside her door, he hastily pressed her against it, needing to feel her against him again. He lowered his mouth to hers. His kiss was harsh and bruising, but she responded in kind, wrapping her arms around his neck and standing on her tiptoes, pulling him closer.

Another presence stepped softly down the hall. The familiar sensation of his brother made him groan internally—Axel always seemed to interrupt at the worst times. Reluctantly, Blaze broke the passionate embrace to search for Axel.

His brother leaned against the opposite wall ten or so feet away, hands in his pockets, eyes cloudy but watchful. He looked more lucid than he had when they left Seattle. Perhaps the distance between him and his betrothed was doing him some good. Another few days, and he might make a snarky comment the way he usually did.

"Generally, brother, when one of us is engaged in such activities, it is polite to *stay away*." Blaze's voice dripped with an irritation that he felt incapable of hiding lately.

Axel shrugged, then pushed off from the wall and strode toward them. "Just making sure you don't break the covenant of your existence."

His words were a slap in the face—Axel didn't believe in the prejudice nonsense that said Giborim could only marry Giborim. Even Emma blinked in surprise. Then color bloomed on her pale cheeks, her eyes brimming with shame. When her shoulders rounded, Blaze wanted to put his fist through his brother's face for making her feel bad about being with him.

"Go babysit someone else!" His voice was louder and more cutting than he'd meant—making Emma flinch—but Axel just shook his head with a scoff and walked away.

"I should go," Emma murmured, spinning away from him to dig the room key from her pocket and unlock the door with shaking hands.

Blaze grabbed her shoulder, halting her. He wanted to turn her around and show her just how unashamed of her he was, but her warmth slid out of his grasp and the door clicked shut in his face.

He growled. For several moments, he stood outside her door, fists curled tight. He considered knocking, but before his knuckles could meet the cool wood, his satellite phone buzzed in his pocket. Only a handful of people could call him on it, and three of those people were here with him.

Which left his uncle and Dominic, both under orders not to contact him unless it was an emergency.

He pulled out the phone and a chunk of ice fell into his gut at the sight of his uncle's number on the screen.

His strides were quick and long down the hall when he barked, "Yes?"

"I just thought you should know the wards were breached. Small attack, six injured, no fatalities." His uncle spoke with the same easy manner as one did when discussing the weather.

Blaze threw open the door to his room. Sergei and Axel both looked up from their separate mattresses. Sergei seemed concerned, but Axel just looked annoyed.

Blaze ignored them. "What? How many attacked? How did they get through the damn wards? Where's Dominic? I need to speak to him."

"Your cousin is busy consoling that pitiful human you brought here," his uncle sneered. "As for the wards, I have no idea how the Shediem got through. They weren't broken, but still intact."

Sergei jumped to his feet, looking ready to burst into action. Axel's pallid face lost even more of its color.

"Get him on the phone, *now!*"

His uncle's muttered curses were lost to the roaring in Blaze's ears. His pulse was wild as he paced back and forth, running his hand through his hair. He tugged on it, no doubt making it stand straight on end.

The phone made several garbled noises before Dominic's thick, Russian accent filled the speaker. "*Da?*"

"How many were able to make it inside the wards?"

"Twenty-six by my estimation. Easily taken care of, but they were able to make it into the manor."

Blaze swore. "How? Who was on watch?"

Dominic paused. "They were invisible somehow, cousin. They were only made visible once slain. We were fighting blind."

His lungs squeezed.

But Sergei said what Blaze was thinking: "A Spellcaster helped them attack."

Dominic grunted his agreement. Their keen sense of hearing made speaking directly into the phone unnecessary.

"Have any other compounds been attacked?" Blaze asked.

"Not that we know of," Dominic replied.

The anxiety in his tone was something Blaze recognized. He lowered his voice and asked, "Breanna and Isaac?"

"Safe."

The word spoken by his cousin was said like a vow. Blaze knew that Dominic had grown to care for the girl and her son. While his family and all the Giborim would demand he keep his distance, Blaze didn't issue any such sentiments. It was too late for that. And when the time came that Dominic made his intentions toward her public, he would need an ally.

There was no one more understanding than Blaze. His eyes drifted in the direction of Emma's room as if he could see her through the dozen or so walls separating them.

"Keep her safe," he said, accent thick with emotion. "We'll be there first thing tomorrow."

"*Nyet*," Dominic said firmly. *No*. "Finish the mission. We won't let them get close again."

The line disconnected, cutting off Blaze's reply. He pocketed his phone slowly, still feeling every fiber of his being pulling him back toward Emma. To wrap his arms around her and simply make sure she was safe.

But he resisted, looking to Sergei and his brother. "We need more allies, and we need them now."

EMMA

Gertie snored peacefully in the bed next to Emma's while she stared at the ceiling replaying Axel's cold distaste for her over and over. It didn't make sense—Axel had been kind in his own way, up until she'd returned. She knew people would treat her differently, but she hadn't expected it from him. It had stung.

Whatever his reasons, Emma decided to pull him aside tomorrow and have it out with him one way or another.

Her eyelids had just begun to feel heavy when she felt hooks under her ribcage, and her back leaving the bed. In a flash, she was on her knees, breathing heavily as she always did when her body was whisked away so violently.

Above her, Asmodeus perched in his ivory throne as the beast he truly was: skin coal black, with veins of glowing reds and oranges like molten lava churned inside him, eyes as red as the blood he spilled just for sport. Smoke curled and puffed from his dragon-like nostrils, dissipating up in the high ceiling. His expression was murderous. Terrifying.

"Time is up," he rumbled.

The warm stone floor vibrated beneath her hands and knees. His wrath shook the room. Emma climbed to her feet, waiting for the moment she'd been dreading for over a week.

"Tell me what you've learned."

Her stomach sank, and before she could try to keep her lips

sealed, the words poured from between them, damning herself, humanity, and the man she'd started to fall for in one fell swoop.

"Their strategy is to wait for your first move and then to use me to kill every prince and general so the Shediem are without orders, then to wipe them out. They have over two hundred compounds harboring humans, Giborim, and Spellcasters, all training and ready to fight. Estimated numbers are thirty thousand globally, but we've been recruiting more Spellcasters. Warding off whole regions and evacuating humans is their next step, so that when war starts, there will be enough survivors to carry on the population. They're scared, but they believe I'll be able to defeat you all."

Her tone was monotonous and flat, but her father still snorted in amusement. "Excellent. I've needed some good news."

Emma's brows drew together. Geryon was standing beside his prince, Levaroth nowhere in sight.

"Trouble in paradise, *Dad*?" she mocked.

Asmodeus's long, glinting claws ground against the bones beneath his hands, the only sign that he was unnerved. "My hybrid army is smaller than I'd anticipated. We're killing more than we're creating."

A sickness churned in her gut even as a triumphant spark of hope flared to life in her chest. It was disgusting, what he was doing. And worse still that he was killing innocent children and babies. But if they weren't developing powers, then perhaps he'd give up on the endeavor altogether. "I've done as you asked, now let me see my mother."

The prince's head cocked to the side, eyes still burning with fury. "I suppose. Geryon, go and fetch Nadia for me."

His servant disappeared, and several moments passed while Emma and her father stared at each other. There were no words to offer to the silence stretching between them. Nothing that she wanted to say could be said.

A woman's mutterings began to drift down the hall and through the open doors. Emma straightened, recognizing her mother's voice. But it sounded different. Grating. Coarse.

Geryon's audible clacking nearly drowned out her mother's shuffling, but when he came into view, pushing a frail woman ahead of him, Emma cried out.

The bruised woman's hair was matted. Dried and fresh blood pasted the dirty strands against her scalp. Emma's mother mumbled incoherently, her hands twisting together over and over.

"What's wrong with her?" Emma exclaimed.

At the sound of her voice, her mother stilled. Her wide, wild eyes no longer searched the room, unseeing. They focused on her, but recognition didn't register immediately.

Emma's blood roared in her ears as she spun back toward the monster on his throne. "What did you do?" she screamed.

Asmodeus waved away her fury as if swatting away an insect. "She's fine. Daddy issues have her receding into the recesses of her mind every time she is confronted with pain. I medicate her to keep her from hurting herself, but it makes it difficult for her to focus."

Emma didn't know whether to throw up or set the room on fire. Her legs reacted before the rest of her could, sending her sprinting through the room toward her mother. "Mom!"

Her mother's eyes filled with fear as she dropped to the floor, hands covering her head. "No, stop! You're not real!" she wailed.

Emma's heart tripped in her chest and her breath left in a whoosh. But she faltered for only a moment. She dropped to her knees, skidding the remaining distance to her mother's shaking, weeping form. She placed her hands gently on her mother's arm and back. "Mom, it's me," she choked.

Her mother cried harder. "No, no, no."

Emma felt her chest crack open as she too began to cry. She buried her face into her mother's side, trying to keep the unwashed stench from making her stomach revolt. Her sobs grew, swelling with the sense of anguish at what her mother had become in such a short time. Though it was likely that months had passed in Sheol.

156

Through ragged breaths, Emma tried over and over to soothe her mother, until at last her bony frame no longer shook and her cries fell to sniffles.

"I miss you so much, Mom. Sergei misses you too," she whispered.

Her mother froze. Then, slowly, she turned over, looking up at Emma as if just noticing her. Lips cracked and bleeding, cheek bruised and swollen, she finally began to understand that this was real.

"Emma?"

She smiled so wide her cheeks hurt. "Yeah, Mom. It's me."

Laura Duvall searched Emma's face, then scanned her body as best she could from the floor. "Have you come back for me?"

Those six words broke her. Emma's head fell forward as sorrow crashed into her harder and faster than she could bear.

She couldn't answer. Her tears spilled over, and Laura's bottom lip quivered.

Then she placed a hand on Emma's cheek, forcing her daughter to meet her gaze. "It's okay, sweetie. It's okay."

It wasn't okay. Nothing was okay. But before Emma could voice that, Geryon jerked her mother to her feet and began carrying her away again.

"No!" Emma reached for her mother. She couldn't let them take her. She was being tortured. She was dying. "NO! Let me take her home! She's dying!" Her voice cracked on a wail.

She hadn't heard her father speak, but the mark that bound her to him pulled her away from her mother, who fought against Geryon to get to her.

A woman appeared around the corner, cheeks glistening with tears, and with a small round belly that made Emma stop dead.

"Haddie!"

Her sapphire blue eyes met Emma's, and she shook her head in warning as Geryon tossed Emma's now-unconscious mother into her friend's arms. She lifted her with ease, letting Laura's head slump against her shoulder.

"Haddie," Emma said again.

All the fight left her body—Haddie was pregnant. Emma had failed her. She'd failed her mother.

She'd failed.

The mark drew her back like she was a fish at the end of the line, reeling her to him. When Haddie disappeared with Emma's mother, she stopped fighting the pull and let it slam her back onto her knees.

Asmodeus rose from his throne and stepped toward her. Every step shook the castle floor. Every step sent fire licking through her veins, but she couldn't move. There was no one to save her. There had been no one to save her mother or Haddie.

I failed. The words in her mind drew another choked sob from her.

A black claw hooked beneath her chin and forced her eyes up to his.

"Do you see now, daughter? You may have *some* free will, but I own everyone you love. I can and will destroy everyone you care for. The Giborim is next."

A flash of silver directed her attention to his other hand, where a small blade sat. A dagger to her, but just a small toothpick in his massive palm.

He held it out to her. "Take the blade and plunge it into his heart."

ADRIANNA

Adrianna chewed her food slowly, not tasting any of it. Across the table, her handsome, broody captor took another long swallow from his goblet.

"You're quiet this eve," he remarked.

She shrugged, forcing her heart rate to remain even. "It was a tiring day. A sad day." After she'd watched the handful of Spellcasters she'd been working with kill a dozen or so small children when they failed the tests that were meant to show what their power was, it had been difficult to concentrate.

His goblet paused at his full, pink lips. "Sad?" He spoke the word without an ounce of comprehension.

"Yes, sad," she snapped. With a sigh, she forced her tone to remain even. "I'm sick of watching babies die. I'm sick of helping enslaved women give birth to their fifth or sixth child since they've been in captivity. I can't get the sound of all the crying out of my head!" Without meaning to, her voice had risen again, ending on a shout that made Tlahaz's dark brows rise.

He set his cup down with a barely audible clack, but it still sounded like thunder to her ears. "How did you imagine a supernatural war to look, Adrianna?" he asked calmly. "There will be far more death and tears before we've claimed the Earth."

Adrianna hung her head. He'd never see her side of things. Though he cared for her and she begrudgingly cared for him, he was still a Shediem who craved bloodshed. "It's wrong," she said softly.

Tlahaz's lips tilted to one side as he rested his chin on his clasped hands. His gaze was almost sympathetic, though Adrianna didn't fool herself into thinking he was capable of sympathy. "Perhaps take a day to rest. You've been working a lot and I know you're not accustomed to our way of life just yet."

Her ire flared. Standing up so fast that her chair fell back with a deafening crash, she said, "I will never be *used* to killing. I'm not like you."

He leapt for her.

Too slow. Her magic shot out from her, wrapping around her general, immobilizing him. She was stronger now. More powerful, she could feel it. Athena stirred in her chest, but Adrianna quickly quieted her familiar before marching out of the room. She didn't run; she knew her magic would hold Tlahaz for as long as she needed.

Taking the stairs two at a time, she raced toward the one who'd assigned her this miserable position.

Nakosh lounged in his throne, head hanging back as he stared up at the ceiling. His skin was paler—almost translucent. The host of shadows that splayed across his lean body rolled over him as though trying to consume him.

"I've been expecting you, Adrianna," he said to the ceiling. His tone was deadened.

"The prophecy says I have to bind the ultimate darkness. It didn't say when." She lifted her palms, throwing as much power as she could at the wicked king of darkness.

The room was filled with blinding light and her ears with the roaring rush of blood.

For a moment, she thought it was working. Then a blast of inky black shot out—a wall of impenetrable shadows.

Adrianna panted, lowering her hands. A laugh echoed through the room, from behind the barrier of darkness.

An even darker shadow appeared behind it before the king

strolled through like it hadn't just blocked her magic from even touching him.

Though darkness still crowded around his body, writhing and twisting anxiously, a striking smile split his beautiful face. He stopped just in front of her trembling body.

"You can't bind me here, I'm already bound," he explained, a hint of sadness tingeing his silky voice. "Besides"—his smile grew—"the prophecy says you need to bind the ultimate darkness. Should the Shediem-Slayer slay me and another rises in my place, they will become the ultimate darkness."

Adrianna's breathing slowed, but her heart continued to hammer away.

Leaning close like he was about to share a secret, he said, "Better pay our prisoner a visit while your lover is sitting still, eh?"

She gaped. Sputtering, she managed, "He's not my—we're not—"

Nakosh chuckled. "That was very convincing, well done. Now run along before it's too late."

Obeying, she started from the room.

He called after her, "And take a few days off. Wouldn't want you doing anything reckless."

She paused, turning. His gaze was glacial, a dark power radiating from him, and suddenly Adrianna fully understood why he was the king of Sheol.

"Make no mistake, my dear: here in my realm, I could easily steal your breath from your lungs and watch you flounder until your weak little heart gave out."

Unshed tears burned her eyes while her nails bit into her palms from clenching her fists so tightly.

"I understand," she answered.

"No keeper again? How do you keep getting out without him noticing?" Levaroth asked weakly. He tried to smile but every muscle in his body spasmed randomly, turning his expression to one of pain.

"Last time, I made sure he was going to be gone for a long time before I snuck out. The wards and locks that are meant to keep me in are actually quite pitiful. This time, I just bound him with my magic. It won't last much longer, actually, because I just tried it on your king too." She shrugged despite the choked laugh that came from Levaroth.

"Never trust a Spellcaster. I found that out the hard way."

She wanted to ask what he meant, but decided against it due to time constraints. "We made some progress last time, but I'll try to break the marks this time. You ready?"

"Yes," Levaroth answered roughly. "It already feels broken. I haven't been able to project myself to her in…I'm not sure how long it's been."

Adrianna nodded. She rubbed her palms together, and a pale pink light spread between them. She placed her hands on his chest where she thought his heart was. His skin was burning hot. Feverish. No doubt his body was riddled with infection. She shook away the urge to heal him, instead focusing her magic into him, hoping to cool the fever at least.

He jerked, and Adrianna felt the thread that was tied to him move along until she felt Emma's presence. She was in pain. So much pain.

Adrianna gasped. "She's hurt."

Levaroth nodded. "It's emotional pain. I can sense the difference."

She tried to push that tidbit from the forefront of her mind—her friend was in pain and there was no way she could help her. "I'm going to try to find her father's mark."

Levaroth didn't answer. She could feel his pain too, and it was nearly overwhelming. If she wasn't careful, she'd drown in their collective agony.

Adrianna spread her awareness into her friend, sensing the strong, foreign Shediem presence recoil from her magic.

"I found it!" she cried, her voice sounding strange and garbled in her ears.

Adrianna's body trembled violently. It cost her so much to be like this, sending her awareness into one person and then into another who was impossibly far away. The gaping hole between them felt infinite.

"What are you?" she whispered to Emma. "You're so far away."

Like a serpent she slithered toward the beast trapped inside Emma's body. It was ancient and powerful. Terrifying. Inhuman.

Adrianna shrieked, and warmth trickled from her nostril. She tasted the coppery tang of blood on her lips.

Shit.

"What's happening?" Levaroth growled, his words slurred.

"Oh, god, what is it?" she cried.

"Keep going!" he urged, the guttural sound of his pain making Adrianna want to break away.

But she couldn't. The creature lashed out at her and she coiled around it. Every bit of Shediem energy that didn't belong to her friend, she gathered to herself.

And pulled.

Levaroth's roar shook her. Shook the floor, the walls. Her eardrums felt like they'd burst.

The Shediem entity fought while she pulled. Emma's pain and his rushed together and filled Adrianna. Her lips parted and she thought she cried out, but she couldn't tell.

The pain flooded her every cell, and both of her nostrils spilled blood.

"Witch!" a voice bellowed.

She choked out a cry. *No! He shouldn't be here.* "I'm not done!" Light flared bright behind her eyelids.

"Don't stop," Levaroth ordered, but his voice was weak. Too weak.

A tall, hulking figure crashed through the barrier she'd

erected around them and barreled into Adrianna.

"No!" she and Levaroth screamed in unison as Tlahaz ripped her away from Levaroth, the connection severed.

EMMA

The throne room vanished, and Emma stood in a dark room not hers. The chorus of three breathing, softly snoring males just confirmed what she already knew. *No*, she pleaded silently.

Slowly her eyes adjusted to the darkness, and she began to make out the slumbering forms. One in each of the two beds, and one curled up in a blanket on the floor. She didn't need to see their faces to know which one was Blaze. Her feet carried her forward, her grip tight on the hilt of the black dagger in her hand. Every muscle in her body rebelled, protested each step. She hoped to shuffle her feet and wake him, but the magic forced her steps to remain silent. Not even her tears would fall.

Too soon, she stood above the beautiful man whose usually stern face was softened in sleep. He lay on his back, one hand behind his head, the other laid across his stomach. It was so relaxed, and he looked so heartbreakingly handsome that Emma wanted to cry.

She tried.

Her heart felt like a wild animal had burrowed inside it and was tearing it apart from the inside. Real, physical pain flared in the mark on her collarbone. Not her father's—Levaroth's mark. With her lips sealed and her voice gone, not even a grunt of pain escaped her. But internally, she screamed.

Emma knelt softly beside Blaze, gritting her teeth. His dark waves cascaded over his brow. It was such a stark contrast to see the fierce warrior at rest. He looked younger. Gorgeous and strong.

The mark seared beside her heart, and her legs trembled. Something was very, very wrong. Was Levaroth dying?

She barely registered her arm lift, and finally, the first tear fell.

NO, she roared, hoping her father could hear her. *I won't kill him for you!*

She tried to open her mouth, to scream the words out loud, but her lips were locked tighter than a safe. Her flesh smelled like it was burning. Fire shot down her spine, wrapping down her limbs, stabbing into her fingers and toes.

Too much pain.

Her vision blurred. Shaking, she fought for control. She managed to lower the blade by several inches, and she fought harder, squinting with effort.

Something snapped inside her. Like a cord that stretched on and on, tying her to something. To someone.

Levaroth.

A choked sob finally broke through.

It was gone. He was gone. She looked down, but she couldn't see beneath the collar of her sweater to check if the mark had disappeared.

The pain eased, and she wobbled.

Then the dagger rose higher, her strength nearly gone. It was poised above Blaze's chest.

She brought it down, hard.

Eyes like steel flashed open.

In a blur Blaze rolled to the side, but the blade still caught flesh. He didn't make a single sound when he shot to his feet. Crimson bloomed on his bicep where the dagger had sliced. Like a waterfall, the red flowed down the contours of his muscular arm.

They stared at each other, and she hoped that the anguish

shone in her eyes.

His were filled with betrayal. Twin blades she hadn't seen anywhere near his person glinted from his hands in the sliver of moonlight between the curtains. He watched her like the enemy she was, feet spread and body ready to spring.

"Emma, you don't want to do this."

I know! She hoped her eyes reflected the words she couldn't speak.

She lunged for him, their training sessions coming back to her. She slashed at Blaze's face while he dove to the right. An animalistic growl that wasn't hers tore from her throat. Shock jolted through her, but her body moved like a puppet dancing for her puppeteer.

She wanted to scream at him to run before she set fire to the house or was forced to slit everyone's throats—even Sergei's and Gertie's.

"How long have you been a spy?" Blaze snarled.

Both his words and his tone broke her anew. Pain flooded her again, and her feet stumbled. A whimper vibrated in her throat. Her hands and knees hit the floor.

Sergei shot upright in his bed, indigo sparks flying from his fingertips.

"Get Gertie!" Blaze shouted.

Sergei's eyes were wide, staring at Emma, unsure of what to do. Then he tore off his blanket and stood.

Emma got to her feet, not sparing him another glance before she charged. Blaze feigned left then shot his arm out, the tip of the blade grazing her cheek. She knew he'd pulled back on purpose. He couldn't kill her even though his uncle had demanded he do so if she ever betrayed them.

"Let me help you, child," Sergei said gently.

She made a low, menacing sound deep in her chest. Little by little she was becoming less and less like herself. Her actions and sounds were not her own; she was just a passenger in her own mind.

Emma lunged for the Spellcaster, ready to slice into whoever got in her way. Blaze's solid body knocked into her from the side, sending her to the floor hard before her blade could catch flesh.

"Stay back," Blaze ordered.

Even Axel was up now, though he made no move to interfere.

Blaze circled her as she spun like a caged animal, tracking his movements, preparing to strike, snarling like some deranged creature. "You don't want to hurt me, Emma," he said. Confident, yet cautious.

She sprang at him again, swiping for his abdomen, then his arm, then his face, moving faster than she could register. But he stepped and dodged her with ease.

Kill him.

Kill him.

Kill him!

LEVAROTH

"No, I almost had it!" Adrianna screamed, thrashing in Tlahaz's arms, but he held her fast. "Let me go!"

"You're killing yourself!" Tlahaz's eyes burned with rage that he leveled on Levaroth.

"Please, brother," Levaroth rasped.

They stared at each other for a long moment.

"I can do this. But you have to let me try before I lose the connection for good." Adrianna's voice was gentler. Pleading. Even her body went still in his arms.

Tlahaz growled a low, wretched sound. Then he released her.

She rushed to Levaroth and laid her glowing palms on him once more. His chest heaved with the pain still coursing through him. He clenched his jaw, preparing for more.

It hit him hard, rushed through him like lava melting his insides.

His vision flashed, and Emma's bright smile filled his mind. Her soft body caressed his rough palms. Her sweet, spicy scent filled his nostrils. Her wavy auburn hair flowed like silk over his fingertips when he ran his hand through it. He pulled her closer, and she came willingly, pliant in his firm grasp.

He lowered his mouth to hers, kissing her with needy desperation. To ease the pain. To kiss her one last time. To finally tell her what he felt for her was true.

But her body grew cold. His eyes flew open, searching her face as it contorted in horror. Then she crumbled to dust. He reached for her, screamed for her, until her face faded from his mind.

Her name dissolved on his tongue.

The chamber surrounded him once more.

Adrianna falling into Tlahaz's arms, spent and unconscious.

Then blackness devoured him whole—an old friend that wrapped him in its eternal embrace.

His eyes flew open. Everything ached.

Tlahaz stood before him, arms crossed, expression blank. "Well?" he barked.

"Well, what?" Levaroth asked.

"Why are you here?"

The question puzzled Levaroth until he took stock of his brutal injuries. His restraints, both magical and human.

"I don't know," he answered.

"Who is Emma Duvall?" Tlahaz asked. His eyes were two burning flames of hatred that Levaroth had never seen before.

But that name…

Emma Duvall…

He didn't know it. Human in origin, he guessed.

"How should I know?" he scoffed. "Now what the hell am I doing here?"

A cold smile spread across his comrade's face, but it didn't quite reach his rage-filled eyes. "Welcome back, brother."

EMMA

Pain sharp and blinding sent Emma to her knees, giving Sergei time to escape. Agony stretched through her and she retched, expelling the contents of her stomach onto the floor. Something warm fell from her nostrils and ears. When she wiped it away with the back of her hand, it was stained red.

Was she dying?

The door flew open and the light flicked on as Gertie marched forward, hands raised. Blue sparks flew from her palms, then transformed into what looked like arrows whizzing for her.

"Don't hurt her! Try to get it out of her!"

A gust of wind broke the arrows into a million particles that disappeared before they ever touched the floor.

"I'm not strong enough on my own," Gertie barked as Emma's eyes darted back and forth, considering whom she should attack.

Emma didn't wait for whatever hocus-pocus they were attempting before loosing a bellow of rage, then leaping through the air toward Blaze. He barely moved back in time.

The searing agony tore from her back, and she was sure her spine had been ripped out. She collapsed on the ground as another roar filled the room and shook the house, but this time it wasn't from Emma's mouth.

A tall, shadowy creature with long claws and glowing red eyes screeched before it lunged at Blaze. He tore his blades through it in rapid succession. It screamed so loud the windows rattled.

It dove for Emma, and she curled into a ball with the dregs of her remaining strength. A bright light flashed behind her eyelids and the creature screamed again.

Then the unmistakable voice of Prince Asmodeus boomed through the room. "You have betrayed me for the last time, daughter. None of you will make it out of this place alive."

Her eyes wouldn't open.

It doesn't matter, she said into her mind, not caring if her father heard. *I'm dying already. I just hope someone saves my mother.*

Her lungs were on fire. She tried to breathe, but it felt as if a car had landed on her chest. She felt herself slipping away.

This is it, she thought as another tear rolled down her cheek, fiery hot against her icy skin.

I'm sorry, she tried to say, but her lips wouldn't move.

Then the darkness swallowed her whole.

EMMA

Muffled voices floated through the fog. Her body felt heavy; especially her eyelids. Every inch of her ached. Like she'd just spent the past twenty-four hours working out.

"...explains so much..."

"...seen this before..."

"What was it?"

An older, female voice spoke the words Emma could not. "The Mark of Fallen Flame." *Gertie.*

A younger woman spoke next, and it took Emma longer to place the voice. "I didn't think those things existed anymore. Then again, it's not like princes just wander around on Earth." *Taryn.* Her indifferent tone made Emma want to fall back into the dense fog that clouded her mind, but little by little, her awareness was returning.

"Why isn't she waking up?" Blaze growled.

"Calm down, Hulk. She was possessed by a prince for who knows how long," Taryn said. Blaze must have given her his death glare because a moment later she muttered, "Hey, at least she's alive."

Emma almost snorted. Just because she was alive didn't mean this was over. Her father's promise replayed in her mind over and over. She needed to get to her mother. To Haddie. To Adrianna.

Adrianna! Had she been the one to remove her father's mark?

"Why was she in Sheol in the first place?" Darren asked.

The reply came from Sergei, accent thick and voice gruff. As if he'd been crying. "Her mother was abducted."

Emma swallowed hard, and the room fell silent.

"Emma?" Blaze stroked her cheek with warm fingers.

"Is it…is it gone?" Her lips felt glued together and the words were garbled. She tried to open her eyes, and her lids reluctantly parted for a blink. The bright light made her squeeze them shut again.

From a click, Emma sensed the lights had been turned off. She tried again, prying her eyes open.

The room was still lit, with just a single lamp, making it easier to adjust.

"Thanks," she rasped, trying to sit up.

Everyone, with the exception of Taryn and her brother, had creased brows and frowns. Even Axel looked apprehensive.

Blaze gently slid his hands beneath her back and helped lift her to a sitting position. She glanced over her shoulder at him. His lips were a firm line and his eyes looked like dark storm clouds. They always seemed darker when his mood changed.

"Is it gone?" she asked again. She knew it wasn't inside her anymore, but she had seen it outside of her body. Whatever it was, letting it roam around and terrorize humans was far from ideal.

"Yes," Gertie whispered to the silent room.

Emma licked her lips, but it was just sandpaper on her already cracked skin. Blaze rose from the bed she sat on and walked into the adjoined bathroom. Water ran from the faucet and into a glass that he carried back for her.

She took it with a weak smile and downed its contents. He watched her, arms folded over his large chest, muscles tensed.

"I'm not going to attack you again," she said, attempting levity.

"How long?" Blaze demanded, low and rough.

She swallowed the lump that rose in her throat. "How long…?"

"Were you under a Shediem prince's control," Sergei offered gently, but he wouldn't quite meet her gaze.

Emma stared into the empty glass in her hand, for once feeling the freedom to speak about such things. Her eyes burned with tears.

"Since I got back."

Blaze lowered his eyes, shielding his emotions from her.

"I didn't have a choice," Emma said, wishing the tears would dry up, but instead they leaked out. She wiped them away angrily.

"We know you didn't, dear," Gertie replied.

Taryn snorted. "You don't know that for sure. She could be a Shediem sympathizer—"

"I'm not!"

The room fell silent again, but Taryn stared at Emma, her lips still tilted to the side in a smirk. Emma lifted her chin, refusing to let Taryn or anyone else accuse her of willingly betraying the Giborim.

No. She sighed. *I did betray them willingly. I agreed to join them to save my mother.*

"My mother," she said quietly. Another tear burned a trail down her cheek, but this time she made no move to clear it away. Her head lifted and she looked at Sergei. "They're torturing her. She's…She's not…" A sob broke free, and Sergei's face paled. Emma hunched over, head in her hands, and she wept.

Blaze released a long breath as he came to kneel before her. He placed a hand on her knee, but she didn't look up at him.

"I need to know everything, Emma. How much information was betrayed; everything you know."

She nodded, wiping her nose with the back of her hand.

"How did the Shediem get inside the wards?" he asked, and she stopped abruptly, eyes tearing to him in both horror and anger.

"What are you talking about?"

"There have been two Shediem attacks on the compound in the past few days. In one of them, they were cloaked and able to pass through the wards without lowering them."

Emma started. "Oh my god, is Breanna okay? And Isaac?"

Blaze searched her face. "You didn't know anything about them." It wasn't a question.

She shook her head anyway. "Are they okay?"

"They're fine," Blaze assured her, clasping her biceps with his large hands. "Emma, I need to know the truth now. How much information did you give away? Every last bit."

Emma was opening her mouth to answer when shrill, animalistic howls pierced the usually quiet property. No one dared breathe. Expressions ranging from concentration to fear lined each face in the room, and Emma's heart began to pound again. The sounds weren't from a dog or a wolf—they were cries of desperation and bloodlust.

A cacophony of the shrieking howls sounded again, and confirmation registered on nearly everyone's faces.

"Gargoloscks!" Blaze and Axel dove for their swords at once.

Taryn, Sergei, and Gertie all lifted their hands, and colored glows began to illuminate the room.

Footsteps thundered on the other side of the house. Gwyndoline and Constance burst into action but didn't head toward them, going for the front door instead. Gertie's face pinched with concern, glancing toward the open door—she clearly wanted to help them, but more devilish cries drew her attention back. They were much closer. From Emma's estimation, they'd made it through the wards already.

"Ugh, this is exactly what I wanted to be doing tonight," Taryn sneered as she raced out the door and down the hall. Darren followed close behind, but he sent Emma a wink before leaving.

The next round of beastly wails told Emma the creatures had the house surrounded. Her father's words snapped into perfect clarity: he wanted them all dead here and now.

"What do we do? There must be at least fifteen of them," she said, staring at the window across from her. The curtains were drawn, and briefly she wondered exactly what she'd see if she pulled them back.

From what Haddie had told her about Gargoloscks she had no desire to see one, let alone a horde of them snarling for blood.

"Stay here," Blaze shouted to her. "You two try putting up more wards to keep them out of the house," he ordered Gertie and Sergei before following Axel out the door.

The second they were gone, the first crash of shattering glass came from somewhere further in the house. Sergei let loose a string of words that were decidedly Russian.

He moved to the door, palms pulsing and flaring with light, while Gertie did the same to the window.

A rough snarl rumbled on the other side of the window. They all watched with bated breath.

"Get back—" Sergei was cut off with a thunderous crash.

A massive grey creature burst through the window. Glass, jagged and sharp, flew through the air. The beast's maw was wide with black, razor-sharp teeth that flashed in warning. It pounced at the closest person: Gertie.

Emma dove to intercept it, not thinking. The Gargolosck looked to be larger than a wolf, and when she wrapped her arms around its middle, its skin was cold and hard, like stone. She tackled it, both of them hitting the floor with enough force to crack floorboards. Emma's teeth knocked together painfully, but she ignored it.

Any pain from the hard landing was muted by euphoria. The pull of its power feeding Emma was instantaneous. Its raw, carnal hunger for blood and death filled her veins, streaking her vision with red. It was animalistic. Wild. Stiff skin grew brittle and crackled beneath her.

She hissed in anger and jumped to her feet. *More*, her body demanded.

When she stalked for the exit, a man moved to block her way. *Rip his head off*, her blood sang.

"Emma, honey, I know you're in there. Let us deal with these

177

creatures, okay?"

"Move," she snarled.

Fear flashed in his eyes, making her lips curve upward, but still he didn't move.

As if her prey heard her call, Sergei was knocked out of the way when the doorframe shattered. Tiny shards of wood and sheetrock rained on the floor. Two more massive Gargoloscks fought to enter the room before their solid black eyes switched to her, glittering with anticipation.

A tingle of excitement, mixed with glee, raced up her spine. From her, their soulless eyes fell to the man now unconscious on the floor, then to the woman who sent a blast of blinding magic at them. Their skin deflected it, a large, charred spot marring each of their furless bodies. Yet they seemed unaffected.

They each locked onto their selected targets, foamy saliva dripping from their jaws.

Emma jumped to action before they had the chance, lunging with a grace that rivaled Blaze's. She rolled over the top of the first one and landed on her feet between the two beasts.

Touch them. She didn't need the wicked voice to tell her what to do.

Her gut clenched with a hunger that only their power could sate. She jumped, gripping the Gargolosck around the neck, and let her legs kick out in front of her. The momentum swung her up as she tried to straddle its back, but it thrashed.

The flow of energy hit her bloodstream like a shot of adrenaline, and she hissed. She kicked her feet back in the air, still clinging to the beast's neck, but it dropped to the ground and its front legs crunched to dust. Its weight landed atop her, lasting only a moment as she drank the last of it.

The second beast had gone for Gertie, going from the cry she let loose. Emma rolled, sprinting for it.

Sensing her from behind, it turned and swiped its paw that was easily the size of her head at her torso. An audible, sickening crunch sounded.

The air snapped from her lungs, fabric and flesh giving way to its steel-like claws. Pain seared in her ribs as she staggered back a few steps. She wheezed, feeling the heat of her power-laced blood spill down her belly, soaking the tattered scraps of her shirt. Assessing the damage, she cupped the gaping wounds as best she could.

Her breaths came in pants, the effort of drawing in air nearly overwhelming.

The creature circled her with a snort. Was it...smiling? Glancing to her left, she saw Gertie sprawled on the floor, her own pool of crimson staining the carpet. Sergei knelt at her side, his magic working. Emma couldn't worry about them now. The pain already began to ebb, the skin and muscle threading back together. At least one rib was broken but soon it wouldn't be.

Attack! the voice in her mind demanded.

Emma staggered close to the beast, and it moved back, expecting her to fall. Her lips pulled back in a vicious grin. Then she spun, a strange, animalistic sound rumbling from her chest and leaving her mouth before her body pasted itself against the beast's cold, stony back.

The pain had eased enough, her shattered bone fused back together the moment the power hit her veins. The creature's roar vibrated the entire length of Emma's body, drawing a giggle forth from her. Its chest gave way first, bone and sinew turning to ash in her hands. Another giggle. When the rest of its body crumbled the giggles turned to a full belly laughter. It made her recently healed rib ache, but she couldn't stop.

Tears streamed down her face while she languished in the evidence of the Gargolosck's death. Dimly, she registered a male voice, but all she could make sense of was her laughter. The uncontrollable hysteria that poured out of her. She sat up, hugging her knees to her chest and burying her face between her knees as more hot tears tracked down her cheeks.

A hand brushed against her shoulder. She snapped around to face the offending touch, baring her teeth, the laughter dying instantly in her chest.

The haggard and bruised man that stared down at her with wide, violet eyes gave her pause. "Remember who you are, Emma."

"I know who I am!" It was the hungry voice inside her mind that spoke. "I am the bringer of death. Power incarnate!"

Sadness pushed away the purple hue in his irises, leaving a dark blue that was familiar.

Sergei.

Emma blinked.

A boom shook the house, followed by a roar. She turned to the mangled doorway, casting what she hoped was an apologetic look to Sergei before she got to her feet and took off.

Shoes crunching on debris, Emma flew into the hall with jerking limbs just as another beast pounced like a tiger, narrowly missing her. It smashed into the wall, crushing it like a tin can.

The second it was down her eyes flared wide, the ravenous hunger taking her again. Her arms wrapped around its neck and squeezed. And squeezed.

It bucked and thrashed, fighting her wildly while she drank its energy deeply. Warm relief spread through her veins, chasing the cold down.

Down.

Down.

Though she was stronger, it fought hard. It kicked its hind leg out, catching her calf. White-hot pain exploded in her leg. She hissed but didn't let go until it crumpled—nothing more than dust.

Again she felt the shredded skin and material leak her own life-force. It filled her sock then her shoe, and she groaned.

Getting to her feet, she limped deeper into the house. Fire blazed in the kitchen, licking searing-hot tongues through the open door, blackening the ceiling. But it didn't bother her. Fire was hers to command. With a thought, she pushed the flames back, commanding them to hiss out of existence.

Voices shouted to each other; blades shrieked in the air.

She entered the living room area. Magic flew through the air, but it did little more than knock the beasts back a few paces. At least twelve Gargoloscks lunged, snapped, and swiped at the two Giborim and two Spellcasters.

She smiled wide and her blood hummed possessively. "Leave them! It's me you want."

Every head spun in her direction. Twelve sets of bottomless black eyes fixed on Emma. A collection of snorts and sounds that seemed suspiciously like laughs passed from beast to beast. Then they prowled forward.

BLAZE

The Gargoloscks couldn't have seen the power in her eyes. Couldn't have seen the fury and hunger lighting her up like some righteous goddess. If they had, they'd have run. Even Blaze felt his muscles urging him to launch into action. Against her, *his* Emma. The one he vowed to protect.

He imagined the beasts saw a small, fragile girl entirely outnumbered. There was nothing farther from the truth in that moment.

Black smoke trickled into the room behind Emma. Neither Sergei nor Gertie had followed her, and it made his gut twist with worry. He extended his hearing and heard the crackling of flames combined with Sergei's and Gertie's voices—they were safe.

Constance and Gwyndoline stared at Emma from the other side of the room. He didn't need to look at them to know their fear and shock. He'd seen Emma's power in action before—the hunger for more, the way her eyes glowed green, the predatory way she locked in on her prey—and they hadn't.

Axel was still breathing heavily at least twenty feet away from him. The smoke and the brutal effort of attempting to kill the creatures had winded him. Blaze glanced over at him, and his brother gave a sharp nod to let Blaze know he was fine. Finally Gertie and Sergei spilled into the room, stopping abruptly at the scene unfolding. Gertie looked the worst of the two, with blood running from her temple and left thigh.

The Gargoloscks circled Emma. Flames undulated around her hands, licking at her flesh, almost affectionately. They moved in tighter, closing off any gaps between their ranks, intimidating their prey into going down easily.

There were too many—at least ten. She'd be ripped to pieces. He needed to distract them, draw some of them away.

This time when Blaze looked around to his brother and the now-four Spellcasters, they held his gaze. With a jerk of his head toward the beasts, he mouthed the word *distract*. They all nodded in understanding.

Slowly, they stepped toward the Gargoloscks closing in around Emma. If they could make the numbers more manageable for her, she'd be able to kill them all.

And what will she be like when there are no more? He pushed the thought aside. No matter what, he'd be there to help Emma find herself again. They had a war to fight, therefore she needed to be able to overcome a pack of Gargoloscks if she planned to survive.

Flames erupted from the hallway with a whoosh. It was like someone stood on the other side with a blowtorch. Thick, black smoke penetrated the air above them. The house would soon collapse—if they didn't all die of smoke inhalation first.

"Your daddy isn't happy with you, little girl," one of the Gargoloscks jeered.

This made Emma's spine straighten. Blaze, too, froze in place. He'd never heard them speak before. Not that he'd faced Gargoloscks before tonight, but he'd done plenty of research on them to know the softest places that his blades could penetrate.

But more concerning were the words it had spoken. *Daddy.* Who was her father? Blaze's brows dipped. He'd known Emma's father was a Shediem, but only two ranks could engage in proper physical intimacy with women: generals and princes. A man possessed could as well, but as far as he knew, that wouldn't result in a Shediem-blooded child.

Was it Levaroth? Is that why he was obsessed with her?

"How did you do it?" another Gargolosck asked.

Emma didn't respond, though he noticed how her gaze flicked up to meet his for a brief moment. He didn't stop his slow advance, and neither had the others.

"We were told not to kill you. Just hurt you. But your friends have to die."

"You are of no use to our master as you are."

"How sweet your blood will taste. Giborim blood always does. Like honey."

Blaze felt a growl echo in his chest, tearing away the attention of the beast closest to him. He shot forward and brought his sword down into the soft space where its strong jaw and neck met. When he pulled his sword free, the wound hissed, and thick, black, oily blood fell to the floor. The creature groaned in pain when Blaze stabbed through its soulless black eye. The change of its tough hide was instant, turning to solid stone that hit the floor with a *thunk,* then cracked.

Chaos erupted once more.

Flashes of brilliant colors shot toward the beasts. Axel was a blur of singing blades while Blaze moved in a rhythm, slashing at every beast that moved closer to Emma, until he was standing beside her.

She dove at the creature closest, knocked it to the ground, and yanked its heavily muscled front legs at an impossible angle with a crack that turned his stomach. He barely had time to glance at the dried blood staining one of her calves before another beast lunged.

His sword sunk into the thick skin and when he withdrew it, it brought the Gargolosck crashing to the floor at his feet. It shrieked an awful high-pitched noise that made his eardrums ache.

In his periphery he saw the Gargolosck she held claw and buck. Then it went rigid. Blaze spun, carving his sword through another's soft belly as it sprung at him. Claws sliced easily through his forearm. He gritted his teeth, slashing a second blow to its neck. The blade hit rock before cutting through the softer skin, drawing an ear-splitting scream from its unholy maw.

Emma didn't seem to hear it. Or Blaze, when he shouted a warning at her. A Gargolosck prowled toward her back, foamy, crimson saliva coating its teeth. Piles of ash dusted the floor and clung to her clothing. She got to her feet after draining yet another creature, her attention fixed on the floor where its body had been. Blaze yelled her name, and this time she looked up a breath before the creature swiped a giant clawed paw at her head.

A smile that made the hairs on the back of his neck stand on end spread across her face. She rolled just in time, then roundhouse-kicked its face. It staggered just enough for her to shove her fists into its eye sockets. Blaze's stomach clenched violently. Something like a laugh erupted from her throat.

The Spellcasters and Axel had four beasts detained between the five of them. They were using visible glimmering shields to hold them back, though each time a Gargolosck lunged and clawed at it, a bit of its light diminished. They couldn't hold them back for long. The place was filling with too much smoke, making it difficult to see. Difficult to breathe. The heat was draining Blaze of energy, while it only seemed to fuel Emma.

There were four more Gargoloscks that watched her, preparing to pounce. Blaze started forward, spinning both swords around at once. Two of the ugly beasts looked away from Emma. His first sword drove into its neck, then the other followed suit with the second creature. Emma took the distraction as her chance. Her power crackled in the air and his vision blurred. His lungs were tight. He coughed, stumbling forward.

Emma drained the two closest to her in the space of a breath. Her eyes flared bright. Their remains, mixed with blood that could only be hers, coated her forearms. Her eerie green glow highlighted the tumbling, whirling smoke that was choking them all.

The house groaned, before a deafening crash sounded. The top floor collapsed and the ceiling above them rained chunks of sheetrock and dust. Above the roar of the flames that consumed the entire house, surrounding them, beams groaned and cracked.

"We need to leave! This place is going to collapse any second," Blaze called to Emma. Behind him, he bellowed to the others, "Get out, the house is coming down!"

Emma got to her feet, leaving the other two Gargoloscks as heaped piles of ash on the floor, then walked with slow, even strides past him. Her eyes were fixed on the creatures behind the Spellcasters' shields.

"So go." Her voice was soft. Melodic. She walked through the shimmering shield, and it flickered out of existence. All three of the caged beasts leapt for her at once. Her movements were almost too fast for him to track. She dropped into a crouch, the creatures flying above her, and she spun, catching one by its muscular hind leg. She yanked, pulling it bodily to the tiled floor. It went rigid instantly. The next second, it was dust.

Through the thick smoke, three more barreled into the main room, looking every bit the hellish creatures they were. They charged him and he swung his blades with thunderous cracks, but not a single one went down.

It was still five Gargoloscks against one Emma. Everyone else had fled. The roaring flames blocked out the sounds outside, making it impossible to know what they were facing.

Blaze ran to Emma's side and grabbed her arm. Like in the training room, flames erupted on her skin and scorched his hand. He bit back a yelp, morphing it into an angry grunt. His gaze took in the blistered and charred flesh of his hand.

She looked at him, then at his hand, but there was no sign of emotion on her face, her eyes too blinding to read.

"Leave and let me finish this." Her voice seemed to originate from her chest instead of her lips. Something wasn't right.

"Emma, the whole place is burning down. We need to leave. Even you won't survive smoke inhalation."

"I am made of fire. We are one." The melodic quality of her voice was eerie. The beasts snickered.

186

"Dammit, Emma, I'm not going to let you die in here."

"He won't let me die. He'll never let me go."

This time, Blaze heard the slightest quiver of fear.

The walls shook, and he wondered if she had done that, or if the building was even closer to collapsing than he knew.

"Blaze, let's go!" Axel shouted behind him.

As if in answer, a chunk of sheetrock the size of a car crashed to the floor behind the beasts. The structure groaned again—a warning and a promise.

"Emma, please, let's get out of here!" Blaze roared.

She didn't reply. Only watched as the enormous creatures stalked closer, ready to end it before they were crushed in the crumbling building.

"Don't make me watch you leave me again, wondering if you're dead or alive!"

Her head snapped back, and the light left her eyes in a flash. A slow dawning of reality crept over her features. Wordlessly he grabbed her hand and they sprinted for the doors. The Gargolosck charged after them, howling and baying behind them. Overhead, the ceiling rained down while they leapt and dodged the pieces. With only fifteen feet until the exit, they ran as fast as they could, feeling the creatures nipping at their heels.

A snarl exploded far too close to them. Without warning, Emma spun, catching the Gargolosck by surprise. She absorbed the force of its hit, just managing to dodge its snapping maw as they toppled end over end. She kept rolling even as its body sprayed ash through the air.

Her eyes glowed anew. "Go!" she bellowed to Blaze.

The house was crumbling. She'd be crushed.

"Sergei! Gertie, Constance, Gwyn!" Blaze roared before choking, the smoke too thick to breathe.

The Spellcasters were through the door in an instant. Their magic shot around them, keeping the house from crushing them both. Emma stood still, and the last of the Gargolosck pack stumbled. Their energy was a barely visible current that flowed into her. She didn't touch them.

Blaze gaped as the creatures' last snarls faded and their bodies churned through the air, particles of dust and nothing more.

For several moments she stood still.

"Blaze!" someone shouted, but his ears were full of his thundering pulse and the fire consuming the structure. His eyes were burning.

He didn't think, but acted, scooping Emma into his arms before he whipped into a speed he had never moved before. They met the rush of cool night air, bursting over the threshold when the deafening crash of the house succumbing echoed in his ears. Relief jolted through him so completely, his knees buckled on the last step. Emma tumbled out of his arms, both of them landing in mud.

He scrambled over to her as she curled in on herself. Her lips moved, and a single word was uttered over and over.

"More. More. More. More. More."

His blood went cold. "Emma?"

Either she couldn't hear him, or she ignored him. Either way, she muttered the same word on repeat.

He swallowed hard and looked around. Taking in the fresh air, his lungs stung. If he'd been human, he would have been dead several times over.

Sergei lay unconscious on the ground not far away. Axel knelt beside him and Gertie held his head on her lap. Taryn and her brother were streaked with soot and a mix of red and black blood. Gwyn wept softly into her sister's shoulder while Constance watched the fire eat the last of her house.

Farther away, the SUV looked dented and scraped, along with the silver Honda that belonged to either Taryn or Derrik.

"We need to get back to Washington," Blaze said to them. To Constance he said, "I hope your coven will join us."

Constance glared at him with pursed lips, but she gave a single nod of her head.

Emma's muttering began to ease, and at last she opened her

eyes to look at him. From head to toe, her body shook violently. Blaze helped her into a sitting position while scanning her for injuries. His wounds had already healed, and other than the burn in his lungs from the smoke, he was fine.

The night was still warm, though he felt the bite of a chill as his skin adjusted from the blazing heat of the burning house to the air outside. Emma's teeth chattered loudly. He would have guessed shock, but he didn't think she could go into shock like a human could.

"Are you cold?" he asked her.

She shook her head. "Power m-makes m-m-me sh-shiver."

He wrapped his arms around her, crushing her against his chest. Another wave of relief washed over him. They were out. They were safe. Well, no one was safe these days, but they were alive and that was all that mattered.

Nodding at Sergei, he told Axel and Gertie, "Get him in the car."

With one swift movement, Blaze lifted Emma and carried her to the SUV. The door stuck, but after a hard yank, it sprang open with a loud creak. He placed Emma into the front passenger seat and closed the door before she could protest. In the trunk he grabbed one of the emergency blankets he carried and draped it over her while everyone else piled into the two vehicles.

Reluctantly both engines sputtered to life and soon, they were speeding away from the smoldering heap that was Gertie's childhood home. He heard her soft sniffling as he sped as far as he could from the area.

No one spoke a word while he drove to the private airfield. The pilot who had remained on standby was already waiting for them, the aircraft prepped and ready for takeoff.

Constance and Gwyn boarded with the rest of them. She'd already begun to make arrangements for the rest of her coven to follow in the next two days. Sergei had stirred at some point, but looked ready to pass out again at the sight of the humming jet.

Once they were piled inside, they all tended to each other's wounds. Blaze used damp cloths to sponge away the dried blood on Emma's leg and torso. Faint white lines marked her otherwise soft, perfect skin where claws had severed skin and muscle.

His throat thickened as he ran a finger down the worst fading scar. "You're too brave." He said the words so softly he wasn't sure she'd heard him.

She gave a raspy, humorless laugh.

He wanted to press her for some kind of response, but his throat suddenly felt as though it were lodged with gauze.

The plane soared down the runway and lifted into the sky with little preamble; an urgency hung in the air to get them all behind the wards of the compound as soon as possible.

After they rested, there would be answers. He'd have to brief everyone, his uncle included. Emma had the sweaty pallor of an addict coming down from a high. It didn't feel right to grill her for information. Yet.

But one thing was for sure: her father was not just any Shediem. Whoever he was, he had access to the Mark of Fallen Flame and dominion over the beasts of Sheol. Which put everyone at risk.

Especially her.

BLAZE

Through the rest of the flight, he watched Emma the way one would watch the countdown clock on a time bomb, waiting for it to detonate. She slept fitfully and a chorus of snores accompanied the engines rumbling, leaving just him awake. Staring at Emma, wondering if he'd ever be able to puzzle her together in his mind.

He had seen her absorb Shediem power before, and the high it gave her. But back at the house, it was as if she had lost herself entirely to it.

Now that the adrenaline had subsided and the jet's rhythmic vibrations had created a lull, Blaze sighed and dropped his head onto his hands. The heavy sensation of dread filled his chest like cement. His uncle along with every regional and national Giborim leader in the world were counting on Emma to kill the entire Shediem race. It was clear to him now that she wouldn't survive it. She could barely contain the power of a few Gargoloscks. How in the seven hells would she be able to kill the princes or Nakosh?

As if his thoughts had been said aloud, Emma's eyelids fluttered open. She met Blaze's stare head-on. His brows knitted in concern and just when he thought to go to her and wrap her in his arms, she squeezed her eyes shut again. As if his concern was painful to behold.

His shoulders slumped and he turned in his seat to watch the dark side of the morning pass the windows. Emma's breathing grew even again, but Blaze didn't allow himself to doze. He looked a few seats down the aisle to where his brother sat, watching Emma. Blaze wasn't sure when his brother had woken, or if he'd truly fallen asleep to begin with.

Blaze kept his voice quiet when he said, "Why don't you get a few hours of sleep? I'll keep watch."

Axel shook his head. "Can't sleep."

Blaze frowned. "Since when? You've fallen asleep on a rollercoaster before."

Axel huffed a breath. "For the millionth time, I did not fall asleep. And it was a boring rollercoaster anyway."

Blaze chuckled softly. "Sure. The fifty or so screaming people around you said otherwise, but whatever you say, man."

His brother rolled his eyes. They were slightly bloodshot and the dark circles had returned.

Blaze's smile fell. "Are you going to tell me what's going on with you?"

"Nothing."

He held silent for several moments. "Is it the stress of planning the wedding? Because you can postpone it, you know. No one will think ill of—"

"We are *not* postponing my wedding," Axel growled. Then he said, almost too quiet for Blaze to hear, "Emerelda would be pissed."

Blaze didn't say any more, but the tightness in his chest doubled. The secrets held between Emma, his uncle, and now his brother felt like walls built when he wasn't looking. And now he was stuck on the outside trying to decide how to climb them. At this rate, their secrets would all kill him before he had the chance to march into battle.

Axel stared out his window too, his usual jovialness replaced with the blank expression of a robot that was wholly unlike him. The hours passed in more silence that seemed to thicken the closer they got to home.

Once the wheels touched down on Washington soil, the knots loosened slightly. They were on familiar ground, and now they had two Spellcaster covens joining them. Their mission wasn't a total failure.

Their entourage disembarked the plane with groggy yawns and heavy-lidded eyes before piling into the waiting SUVs. Blaze drove one; Constance drove the other, only after shooting Taryn a cutting look that silenced her protests.

They began the journey to the compound. Blaze glanced back only once, noting Emma's pallid skin that had a light sheen to it. But at least she no longer shivered, he reasoned, gripping the wheel tighter. He doubted her appearance was due to being sandwiched between Gertie and Sergei. It was still the aftereffects of her power.

Halfway up the rocky, bumpy slope, Blaze's phone rang. Dread cold and heavy dropped into his gut at the sight of the caller's name.

"Garrett?"

The sounds of steel clanging together mixed with a deep shouting voice filled the speaker. "You better get here quick! I don't know how they got through, but they're everywhere!"

The line went dead before Blaze could respond.

Axel's fists clenched on his thighs. He'd heard too.

Blaze's grip tightened on the steering wheel and he punched the pedal to the floor. The ride up the slope was jarring, but he didn't have time to worry about tossing around the occupants in the back seat.

Another attack on the compound. Blaze swore and slammed his hand on the wheel, making more than one person jump. His blood hummed with anticipation and a slight hint of fear. There were close to fifty Giborim females within the compound, and though they were far from defenseless, they were there for protection. Protection that even he clearly couldn't provide. Not to mention Breanna and Isaac, who were fragile humans.

Dominic will protect them.

"How bad is it?" Gertie asked from the back seat.

Blaze's jaw felt too stiff for words, but he forced them out anyway, not caring that they sounded more like a growl. "They're inside the wards. And it was Garrett, not Silas." Which meant his uncle was either too engaged to call, or dead.

"I don't understand—only I can remove them or break them."

Blaze didn't respond. His eyes flicked up to the rearview mirror, taking in the glow of anticipation in Emma's emerald eyes. He bit back another string of curses. It was too soon for her to fight again, but if he knew anything about addicts, it was that they'd do anything for another high.

Morning had painted the edges of the sky in its usual golden glow. The iron gate came into view, and the carnage that lay within made the blood rush in his ears. Swords sliced and swung through the air; Shediem of assorted ranks met or dodged their blows.

Chaos. It was utter chaos.

The gate swung open with a flick of Gertie's wrists as they approached, and the vehicle had barely come to a stop when Blaze threw his door open and leapt out, breaking into a run.

"Stay in the car!" he shouted.

Protests followed him, but he ran, unsheathing the two daggers strapped at his waist.

Beady eyes swiveled in his direction too late—he ran the blades through the bellies of two Shediem. Their top halves thumped to the ground. The hot spray of black, oily blood coated his face, his arms, his hands. It reeked of decay, but by now he was used to it.

Distantly, he could sense the others joining the fray. He wanted to search for Emma, but he focused on helping sever the twelve scaly heads of the serpentine Nickor wrapped around Jonas McEvoy. He was young, just over from Europe to check on his new, pregnant mate. And this was likely his first encounter with this particularly nasty—and rare—sea creature. Even Blaze

194

didn't know much about them, other than the fact that they could survive on land for days at a time.

Once his blade passed clean through its final neck, the long, dark body loosened its hold on Jonas.

"Thanks," he panted.

"Behind you."

The boy turned, his sword meeting the arm of a djinn. Blaze whirled and three Shax lunged for him in unison. He leapt back, bringing a dagger down into the first vile creature's throat. It gurgled and spit green venom that hit Blaze's left hand. It sizzled against his skin, forcing a low hiss from him. He wiped in vain, watching his flesh bubble and burn away. First came the numbness that made the blade slide from his grip. Then came the fire.

He roared in pain, slashing at one of the other two Shax, but the blade didn't sink deep enough. Blaze fell to his knee, the pain flaring up his wrist and into his forearm.

The two Shax closed in around him, their venom oozing from their wide grins.

"Bye-bye, foolish warrior," one chirped in its singsong voice.

It was making a gurgling sound, collecting mucus to launch at his face, when its head fell to the side. Then the other was split in half, inky fluid spraying around him. Covering him. A glint of metal caught Blaze's blurring vision. The venom reached his shoulder, and his entire arm drooped at his side. Already, the necrosis blackened his fingertips.

The two Shax bodies tumbled to the ground, revealing the violet-eyed Spellcaster, with matching purple hair.

She smirked. "Need help, Warrior?"

Blaze attempted a small laugh, but it sounded more like a wheeze. "Sure."

She knelt beside him, careful not to touch his skin. Her palms hovered just above it, a pale pink light dancing around her fingertips. It swirled and coiled up his arm, draining the fire. His vision blackened but he ground his teeth together, searching for Emma in the throng.

There, in a blur of motion, she spun from Shediem to Shediem, draining them. Their bodies piled to the snowy grass in mounds of grey and black. Flames licked her entire body. She was a vision of power and strength. A nightmare hidden inside a petite body with wide, innocent eyes. Yet he couldn't deny she looked especially beautiful. Hair pulled back by the icy wind, cheeks flushed with excitement, and eyes glowing an emerald green, she looked like she belonged beside the Spellcasters and their magic.

So striking. In a way that a goddess looked when smiting her enemies, he thought.

The venom withdrew from his veins and sinew, leaving a bone-chilling cold.

"There. Do you think you can manage to just take its head off next time, instead of swapping spit with it?"

Blaze narrowed his eyes at the girl, who grinned before jogging back to what remained of the Shediem. Emma picked them off one by one, leaving the remaining Giborim warriors with little to do.

Blaze got to his feet, leaving his venom-coated blade on the ground. It steamed and curled up as though it was little more than aluminum foil.

Many of the Nysroghs edged their way to the wards, clawing and screeching for release. Only ten or so remained, but they couldn't be allowed to go free. Emma stalked toward them, grinning viciously. He could see the power inside her. The enjoyment that was more than the thrill of battle. The same hungry bloodlust he'd seen in her only five hours ago. An addiction that empowered her as long as the high lasted.

She didn't bother with a sword, and he hadn't given her back the dagger he'd commissioned for her. Her hands lifted for the creatures.

A boom sounded, knocking Blaze back. The cold ground forced the air from his lungs on impact. When he lifted his head, not a single Shediem remained—only piles of ashes.

Emma's hands lowered. He couldn't see her face, but he felt the heat pouring from her. The scent of smoke and charred flesh wafted in the wind, assaulting his nostrils. Many of the Giborim who got to their feet stared at the dark angel of death. They covered their mouths and noses to block the smell. Blaze stood once more, caught between equal parts trepidation and awe. Those that surrounded him wore the same mixture in their expressions.

Including his uncle, he noted from a quick scan.

Emma's shoulders heaved with ragged breaths. He walked toward her tentatively. Her powers were numerous, and he felt certain that not even she knew the full extent of them. Moving toward her too quickly might trigger something that was deadly to himself or his people, and he couldn't allow that.

He scanned the faces he passed, searching for his brother's. But Axel was not among them. His heart picked up its pace as he eyed each of the fallen, but still his brother couldn't be seen.

"Axel?" His mouth was dry, and the word barely scraped out.

Taryn met his gaze. "I think I saw him run into the house."

Most likely to check on his soon-to-be bride. Blaze nodded, relief sweeping through him. But the blank, unseeing faces of the dead caused a shiver to run through him. At least twenty of his men, men he had known for decades—if not centuries—were gone. Behind him, the face of the boy Jonas stared up at the dull early morning sky, unblinking.

His throat burned with emotion. To the Giborim now looking around, doing the same, taking stock of those that didn't make it, Blaze said, "Let's get the fallen warriors inside and notify their families. But try to keep them out of sight."

Nods and murmurs of agreement spread through the men and women that began to come together to lift the bodies from the cold, bloodstained ground.

His uncle hurried toward him. "We must investigate this attack. Find out how the Shediem were able to make it inside the wards with them still intact. I think if we—"

"Give me a damn moment, Silas!"

His uncle fell silent, eyes wide, then huffed a breath before spinning on his heel and stalking into the manor.

Blaze exhaled, his breath a curling white wisp in the air. He stepped closer to Emma, noting the way her shoulders had fallen and her arms wrapped around herself. Her sniffles reached him, yanking on his heart and moving his feet faster.

Warmth still radiated from her, but her body began to shiver once again.

"Emma?"

She didn't turn around, only looked beyond, out the open gate. Soft flakes began to fall again—a peaceful white blanket to cover up the slaughter that took place. It seemed wrong. Each frozen tear melted on Emma's feverish skin, and her shivers grew more violent.

"Let's get inside," he said, and brushed his knuckles along her back.

She stilled. Then turned and looked at Blaze, making him suck in a sharp breath. Around her pupils, bloodred stained her irises, the green only visible on the edges.

Her voice cracked as she asked, "What's happening to me?"

Words had escaped him, and he could do nothing but watch in fascination and shock while the red cleared away, leaving her bright green eyes shining with tears.

She bit the inside of her lip, though her jaw still stuttered from the aftereffects of using her powers. "I can feel myself changing."

"I saw it too. With the Gargolosck. It's like you weren't even in your body. You *enjoyed* killing them. Their power, or energy, or whatever it is you take, it was too much for you. You were willing to let the building collapse on you—you didn't care." He gripped her biceps, forcing her to meet his gaze. She winced, but he didn't let go.

"I was trying to save you, to distract them so everyone could get out," she replied. Tears tracked clear paths through the dust and grime coating her cheeks. Bits of snow had begun to stick to her hair and dust her shoulders.

Despite her tears, her words angered him. "It was foolish! If Gertie and Sergei and the others hadn't held up the roof, you'd be dead. Why was it so important to finish them off?" He wanted the truth. The truth of what happened in Sheol, about everything that she had been silent on. He knew now that the mark had forced her silence, but now that she was free of it, he wanted to know. He needed to know.

"I don't know," Emma snapped, huffing a frustrated breath. She pulled back her arms from his grip to swipe her tears away, creating murky streaks. "I don't think straight when I have their power inside me. I'm sorry, okay?"

He softened his gaze. She was right: she wasn't in control. But that frightened him more than the fearless power-hungry person it was turning her into. His fingers ran through his hair, pushing back the too-long strands from his eyes. "What's important is that you come back to me every time."

He sighed. He hoped she always would. But from the way sadness had overtaken her expression again, he wondered if it were possible. If, when this was all said and done, she'd still be the Emma he was falling for.

"Tell me what happened, Em. I want to know everything."

She swallowed hard. Then her gaze met his, and the words that came from her mouth felt distant and disconnected. "Your sister is alive."

It took a second for the words to register. Then his breath evaporated in his lungs. He staggered back a step, eyes wide while his pulse hammered through him. "What did you say?" His voice was so low, he wasn't sure if it had actually crossed his lips. He cleared his throat and tried again. "What did you say?"

Fresh tears fell from her eyes, and she smiled. "Haddie is alive. We became…friends."

"How do you know?" he ground out. His eyes searched her

face for the lie. The trick. Maybe the venom had reached his brain, and this was all a hallucination. Hadessah was dead.

Surely she was dead.

"William," Emma whispered.

He blinked, feeling like his chest was about to explode.

"That's your name, isn't it?"

His knees gave out, landing on freshly fallen snow, but he didn't feel it. His head bowed to the cold earth, pain ramrodding through his chest. It wasn't the physical pain of an injury or an ailment, but one he hadn't felt in decades.

"She's alive?" His accent was thick as he stared at the glittering white ground, his hands fisting the fresh powder. He didn't care that red and black coated the layer beneath.

"Yes," she breathed. Then she knelt before him. Slowly, she lifted her hand, placing it on his cheek. The rough stubble audibly scraped her palm, but she didn't seem to notice. Sliding her hand to his chin, she lifted his face.

Her fragile smile cracked, no doubt at seeing the tears that fell from his eyes. "I'm sorry I couldn't tell you earlier," she said, and a sob broke from her chest.

Blaze's throat bobbed. Then he crushed her to his chest, wrapping her tightly in his arms. She cried against his leather jacket that was caked with dried blood. The dam burst open and together, wrapped around each other in the snow, they wept. His lips were gentle and reverent on hers, on her cheeks, on her closed lids, on her jaw, on her neck. She melted against him and he wished they were somewhere more private. If anyone came out and tried to strip her of her much-needed emotional unloading, he'd threaten them away.

He let her pour out unintelligible words and tried to keep her warm in the wintry downfall.

When at last her shivers were truly from the cold, he swept her into his arms, cradling her before he trudged to the manor. She didn't fight him, only buried her face into the space between his neck and shoulder. Her wild, matted hair still somehow

200

smelled of sugar and cinnamon, making him smile.

He carried her up the stairs and pushed open her door. Laying her gently on the bed, he tugged off her wet shoes and socks. He was undoing the button on her jeans when her eyes flew wide.

"Calm down. You can't go to bed in wet clothes."

"I can undress myself," she said, springing out of the bed.

He rolled his eyes but couldn't help but smile when she snatched up fleece pajama bottoms patterned in little latte cups and a sweater before closing the bathroom door behind her.

He heard the shower turn on, stood, and decided to head to his room to do the same thing.

The hot water stung his left arm, which was still slightly colder than the rest of his body, but at least he wouldn't die from Shax venom.

After emerging from the steam-filled room he crossed to his desk and pulled open the top drawer. The rose-gold hilt glinted in the light pouring from the window above. He ran a finger over the thorny vines that wrapped around the curved grip.

The decision was easy: he'd give it to her. But before he'd even dressed, the sound of Emma's quiet breathing reached his ears—she'd already fallen asleep. He lifted the sheathed dagger out of the drawer and slid it closed, before turning to get dressed.

Entering her room with all the stealth of a thief, he smiled at her sleeping form and crept to her side table, where he laid the dagger. She didn't so much as stir when he walked over to the bed to pull the duvet up to her shoulders. She no longer shivered, her features relaxed with sleep, allowing him to sneak out into the hall.

He needed to find Axel and let him know their sister was still alive.

LEVAROTH

L evaroth roared as the icy dagger pierced his side. His warm blood flowed from the newest wound. Yet he shivered with cold.

He was so cold.

"You helped her, didn't you?" Asmodeus bellowed. The sound bounced off the stone walls, floor, and ceiling, and shook the chamber like booming thunder.

Levaroth's jaw snapped, and he snarled, "I don't know what you're talking about."

His master circled him, still clutching the dark, stained magical blade that glowed and pulsed with blue, icy light. The smile that curved his lips was triumphant and wicked. "Who is Emma Duvall?"

Levaroth groaned inwardly. This was the fifth time the prince had asked. "I told you, I've never heard that name before," he gritted.

The frosty blade trailed his spine while Asmodeus pondered where to drive it in next. "Who is Rowek Zennett?"

Levaroth blinked. A cord of familiarity seemed to press on the walls of his mind, but drifted away as if redirected. "Who?"

The prince smiled with satisfaction before turning to face the wide-eyed Spellcaster. His brother, Tlahaz, stood behind her like some protective guard dog, but there was something in his dark eyes that made Levaroth's gut clench. Both Tlahaz and Prince Asmodeus were in human forms, perhaps so as not to frighten the witch. Levaroth's wings pinned to the wall behind him flexed, trying to draw her attention to them.

To frighten her.

To feed from her fear.

His stomach tightened with hunger. How long had it been since he last fed?

"Good work. Are the memories gone, or can they still be accessed?"

Memories?

"Th-there is a b-block on them," she explained, twisting her hands together, trying to distract herself from her own fear. "Hidden behind a wall, kind of." At the prince's bored look, she stammered, "I-I can access them."

Levaroth wanted to ask what she needed to access. In fact, he couldn't remember who she was or why she was here. *Why am I here?*

"Twist them," his master said, smiling wide and cruel. "I want him so thirsty for her blood that he will stop at nothing to rip her throat out."

The Spellcaster shivered but didn't dare refuse.

"Forgive me for my failings, my prince." Levaroth dipped his head as much as his stiff shoulder would allow. "I do not know why I am here."

Asmodeus's smile widened, his sharp teeth glinting. "Never forget that you are a weapon, Levaroth. And I am the master that wields you."

"Yes," he breathed.

The Spellcaster walked toward him, her head bowed. He could smell her tears, but he couldn't taste her emotions. He strained against his bonds, against the magic that held him.

Taste her.

Feed.

So weak.

Her head lifted, eyes glowing with violet light, then she raised her palms. They too illuminated the blackness.

Pain filled his skull, ripping a scream from his charred throat.

BLAZE

Blaze strode down the wide corridor, grimacing at the trails of mud and wet marking the Victorian-style carpet. His mother would have had a fit if she saw it in such a state, and he made a mental note to have it cleaned as soon as possible.

His uncle rounded the top of the marble staircase, face red and splotched, his eyes full of rage. "Finally! Dare I ask what you've been doing all this time?" Silas didn't wait for his response. "The other elders and I demanded answers from the soldiers on watch here, and one of them led us to a particularly interesting item. He insisted that Axel, *your brother*, had given this to him to place at the back edge of the wards this morning." His uncle's long, gloved fingers dove into his suit pocket and procured a small parcel wrapped in lavender cloth. From its edges, Blaze spied stones and herbs, and the reek of magic assaulted his nostrils.

His brow slammed down as he observed it, but he didn't dare touch it without gloves. "Have you spoken to Gertie about it?"

Silas gave a long-suffering sigh, like Blaze was a small child. "Of course we spoke to the Spellcaster. She claims it wasn't of her making, but she did confirm that it would weaken a portion of her ward enough to allow Shediem through."

Blaze headed for the staircase. "Where are Axel and Gertie? And which soldier did you speak to?"

"All three have been secured. For the safety of everyone in the compound, of course."

Blaze whirled on his uncle, who nearly crashed into him. "They're locked up like criminals?" he growled.

"Until we ascertain what went on here, yes. It is for the best, nephew. Do not think to interfere. I have the backing of all the elders and regional leaders barring one."

"Who?" Blaze's voice was harsh and grating as he took the stairs three at a time, barreling past Emerelda, whose eyes were red and puffy, hiccupping after him. Fresh tears poured down her face. But Blaze didn't stop—he needed to get to his brother.

"Dominic," Silas answered dryly.

Blaze fought a smile. He'd known it was Dominic, but it gave him a bit of amusement to hear his uncle confirm it. His friend always made a show of going against whatever Blaze's uncle demanded. Dominic had helped hunt the Shediem that killed his mother and Haddie. *No, Haddie is alive.*

But what state she was in, he wasn't entirely sure. Emma had said they had become friends, which made him dare to believe she was okay. No doubt she was scarred and a little broken, but she was strong. And once they got her back, he and Axel could help her deal with whatever demons now haunted her.

Axel. He shook his head. His brother wasn't a traitor. He couldn't be. And he had been in New Orleans for the past few days. But he hadn't seen his brother during the fight or after. So where had he gone?

When his ears finally registered that Emerelda had been speaking, he stopped abruptly, just as his uncle said, "Your fiancé is perfectly safe, my dear. You need not worry yourself—we just want to find out what's going on, that's all."

She nodded, then met Blaze's stare, before offering a small smile and curtsy. He ignored her. He couldn't deal with drama right now.

Down the steps he went, behind a false wall in the supply cupboard, down, down, down. The air was significantly colder with a hint of mildew, and the rattle and clinking of chains met Blaze when he descended.

The underground keep was different from the enchanted cells on the grounds where the Shediem were held. This one was meant to be a safe bunker for disasters, or a prison for traitors. Its chains were designed to be able to hold even the strongest Giborim and neutralize Spellcaster magic.

Only a single bulb lit the large, dank space. Three people were bound in separate cells, and every single one looked to Blaze and his uncle when they came into view on the bottom landing.

Gertie sighed with relief, but Blaze only had eyes for his brother. Axel didn't look away, not a trace of guilt on his face. His body trembled like Emma's had after feeding from the Shediem.

At last, Blaze looked at the third person, Oliver Philips. His eyes were glazed over, and a light sheen of sweat covered him, dampening his T-shirt. Blaze stalked toward him slowly, tilting his head to the side. Oliver tracked Blaze's movement, but nothing registered in his face.

"Did you let the Shediem in, Philips?" Blaze asked, coming to a stop a few feet from the bars of Oliver's cell.

"Naw, I didnae," Oliver said in his deep, Scottish brogue. There was little inflection in the words. Almost robotic.

Blaze's patience snapped, and he lunged for the bars with a loud *clang*. "Who gave you the anti-ward charm, Philips?" he demanded with fury.

Oliver didn't so much as flinch. With painful slowness, his head turned, and his eyes landed on Axel, who watched with a scowl.

"Axel gave it to you? Did he say where he got it?"

"Naw, he didnae."

Axel scoffed, but Blaze ignored him. "When did he give it to you?"

"Five days ago. In the mornin'. Just after breakfast."

Gertie made a choked sound that sounded like a sob. Blaze pushed away from the bars and went to stand in front of her, ignoring his brother's sputtering altogether.

"Did you make an anti-ward charm for any reason, Gertie?"

Blaze asked. He didn't allow his voice to be gentle, and it grated on his heart. Especially when she sniffled.

"No! No! No! I'd never do that! I didn't even possess the necessary ingredients!"

Blaze sighed, rubbing the bridge of his nose.

"And how do you know what ingredients it requires?" his uncle snapped.

Gertie narrowed her eyes at Silas. "I know a great many things, and how to remove wards is one of them. It's part of my job description."

"Can you make a list of the necessary ingredients for me, Gertie?" Blaze asked, cutting off his uncle's sharp retort.

She nodded, squeezing her eyes shut.

Blaze moved back to the middle cell, which held his brother. Axel gave him a haughty look, but his eyes burned with anger.

"Did you give Oliver Philips an anti-ward charm, for any reason?"

"Of course not," his brother spat.

Blaze sighed. "Even if it was for another reason, Andrew, I need to know."

His brother started at the use of his real name, but quickly recovered. He leaned forward, as far as the manacles secured above his head would allow. "I. Didn't."

He wanted to believe his brother. And something about Oliver didn't seem quite right.

Blaze looked back to Gertie. "Is there any way Philips is under some kind of spell?" he whispered, even though he knew Oliver could hear him. But Oliver didn't so much as look in their direction.

"I-I don't know," she replied. "I suppose it's possible."

Blaze nodded, then straightened, looking toward his uncle. "Release Gertie. She's coming with us."

"For what?" his uncle asked, incredulous.

"Sound the evacuation alarm. I want everyone out of their rooms and in the courtyard. Don't give them time to grab or hide anything." Blaze ignored his uncle's confused expression, wishing he didn't have to wake Emma too. "I'm going to search the rooms, and Gertie is going to help. We'll see if anyone in this house left behind anything that was used to create the anti-ward charm. I doubt anyone would be that stupid, but it's a starting point."

Axel's eyes widened, though he didn't say anything when Silas unlocked Gertie's cell and let her walk ahead of them both.

With his foot on the bottom stair, Blaze cast a final glance at his brother. "For your sake, I hope you weren't lying."

His brother didn't speak when Blaze ascended the stone stairs, leaving only the echoing sound of his boots scraping on each step and the worry that one of his own may have betrayed them all.

The alarm soon screamed through the upper levels, drawing wide-eyed, fearful faces from the rooms.

"Don't worry, we're safe, just make your way to the foyer please. Leave your belongings." He gave reassuring smiles to those they passed, even though his face felt like a rubber band stretched too thin. When Emma's face appeared in the sea of women and children making their way to the staircase, Blaze intercepted her.

"Hey, are you okay?" she shouted over the siren.

"Yeah, I'll tell you everything in a bit. Just head downstairs."

She nodded, though she looked reluctant to go, and headed downstairs.

"What's going on?" Emerelda asked, throwing herself into Blaze's arms. Her cloying perfume reeked of ginger and something fruity. "Are we under attack again?"

Blaze shook his head. "Go downstairs and stay there. I'll come find you in a bit."

She bit her plump bottom lip that was stained bloodred. "Where's Axel?"

He opened his mouth, then hesitated. "He's looking into something for me."

She nodded, then brushed her hand over his arm before starting down the stairs.

"Head down to the foyer, everyone, don't worry! Please move in an orderly fashion!" Blaze called over the siren and din of worried voices. Over the balcony and down below, he caught sight of Breanna clutching Isaac in her arms and Dominic hovering behind her, looking ready to spring into action. He hadn't had time to catch up with his friend yet, and made a mental note to speak to him about his recollection of events once he and Gertie were done searching the rooms.

When the corridor was cleared of people, they started in the first room, his. Though he knew there wouldn't be anything to find, he wanted to be fair. Gertie swept her palms out. A faint greenish glow emanated from them, but nothing happened. She shook her head.

They went down the line, checking room after room. A few doors were locked, but Gertie made quick work of opening them. After no success, they entered the last room: Axel's.

Gertie repeated the motion, and this time, items shifted. The fine remains of several herbs appeared from under his unkempt bed and zoomed into Gertie's awaiting palm. Blaze's heart stuttered to a stop before shooting into his throat. Then a small fragment of what looked like a peach crystal rose from the pocket of a balled-up pair of trousers shoved in a corner.

"What's that?" he rasped. He was surprised his voice carried at all with how he felt his throat growing tighter and tighter.

She turned to him, eyes brimming with regret and sadness. "The three primary ingredients in an anti-ward charm: ferretanis root, oxetant flower, and a dolokai stone."

They gave off an odor that was both sweet and sour, making Blaze's stomach churn.

"Please tell me there's a perfectly logical explanation for why he had these that don't involve being a traitor." His voice was pleading.

Gertie shook her head. "I'm afraid not. If it had been just oxetant flower, it wouldn't have been suspicious because it's often used as a sleep aid when brewed in tea. But together, I'm afraid they are very clearly for an anti-ward charm."

Blaze swore under his breath, his heartbeat faster. He'd have to tell his uncle. No, tell everyone. That Axel was the reason their loved ones were dead. That his brother was the reason their safety had been compromised.

He didn't want to believe it.

He couldn't.

My brother isn't a traitor.

He isn't.

He'll die! The elders will demand his death.

His breaths came faster and his fists clenched, his vision spotted.

He had just found out their sister was alive, and now, he'd have to fight to hold off his brother's execution.

EMMA

Once Blaze and Gertie reappeared in the foyer to announce that everyone could return to their rooms, Emma tried to catch Blaze's eye. To figure out why she had awoken to a shrill siren, and why his jaw flexed, and why his hands were balled into fists at his sides. Why his eyes were brimming with barely controlled rage, and why he spoke only in a low voice to Gertie, seeming to forget that Emma existed altogether. Whatever this whole thing was about, he was barely holding himself together.

Before everyone had made their way back to their rooms, Blaze had taken off again. She sighed and headed up the staircase, bare feet slapping the cold, marble floor. She was too tired to chase after him. If he didn't want to involve her, then she would wait. It seemed urgent anyway. And from the way her body swayed, she imagined she was close to passing out. She needed the sleep. Having the mark removed and absorbing so much Shediem energy had drained her. *Rest*, she told herself. Then she'd check on him.

Back in her room, she collapsed on the bed, falling into unconsciousness before her head had hit the pillow.

Screams echoed in her head, familiar. A figure huddled in a stone chamber. Hands spotted with purple, green, and yellow splotches gripped her head. Matted hair a dull reddish color jolted Emma with recognition. She tried to scream, but instead, it was the woman's screams that reverberated through the cell.

Her mother's screams.

Incoherent mumbling came from her shaking, rocking form.

"Look at me!" a voice of booming thunder echoed, and her mother shook harder.

Emma knew whom it belonged to, though she couldn't see him. Her mother's head lifted, looking directly at Emma. Or through her. Dried blood caked her temple. Fresh blood oozed from her nostrils. Her lip was split and one of her eyes was swollen shut, black and purple staining the skin around it. Her face, though beaten nearly beyond recognition, held a fiery hatred that seared into Emma's soul.

"That's it. You're going to look at me when I kill you. Your daughter won't be able to save you. I'm going to kill you slowly, and she's going to watch." Her father's voice was close, as if just behind her. She spun, but there was only blackness.

Emma's chest heaved; her lungs wouldn't fill with air. Why couldn't she wake? It was just a nightmare. Just another nightmare.

Her mother looked around, trying to find her. "Emma," she moaned with a pained expression.

Emma screamed for her, to try to get her mother to hear her. "Mom! MOM!"

"Don't bother." Her father chuckled. "You can't see Emma. But she can see you."

"How?" her mother demanded, though her voice was hoarse. Like she had been screaming for days. She glared directly at Emma.

Why couldn't her mother see her? The answer came to her just before her father spoke the words.

"I have her consciousness held within my mind through the remnants of my mark. She is seeing what I see. She won't be able to look away." His cruel, rumbling laugh echoed through the chamber while her mother screamed.

"Wake up, Emma! Don't watch, baby!"

Emma fought to breathe. This wasn't happening. How was this happening? The charred black skin veined with glowing red, like

213

rivers of lava weaving down his arm, and his fingertips were now elongated claws. He was in his true form.

He slashed across Laura's arm, carving deep gashes that gushed with blood. Her mother's scream was deafening. Backed in a corner, she cried words that weren't in English, and Emma wondered from the accented sounds if her mother had slipped into Russian—her native language. It was the first time she'd ever heard her speak it.

Then her mother looked directly at her, though the eyes she looked through did not belong to her. "I love you, Emma," each word a pained gasp.

Emma reached for her. Tried to run to her to staunch the bleeding. To throw her own body over her mother's.

NO! Emma fought against the tether that bound her to her father. Take me, I'll come back, I'll be your slave, she pleaded, hoping her father could hear her.

"You broke your vow," he hissed. "You slaughtered my Gargoloscks. Your use has ended, and now I will kill everyone you love. When no one is left and you are begging for mercy at my feet, I will feed you to my brothers and you will suffer, just like your mother has, for all of your days. Death will be the only thing you think about. It will be all that you crave, but I will not give it to you. You will endure my wrath with every breath. Death will never claim you. I will heap unending agony upon you until you are the cruelest and vilest of beasts. Then you will serve me."

She couldn't speak. She was roaring in his mind, but he shut her out. Still she screamed "I will destroy you!" over and over while she watched, unable to look away from her mother, who resembled a small child mentally removed from the physical suffering. She hoped her mother couldn't feel the pain.

Asmodeus stabbed his massive claws into her mother's thigh, then her abdomen. When Emma lunged for him, he flung her back with a mighty force. She hit the stone wall and collapsed in a heap, silent.

"Would you like to see her, daughter?" her father crooned. "I shall let you."

She awoke thrashing beneath a heavy weight, her throat raw

from screaming.

Air. There was no air.

She was suffocating.

Dying.

"Emma!" Blaze shouted, cutting through her terror.

"Get off!" she screamed.

Blaze lifted himself from her, his gaze intense as she flung herself off the bed and retched the meager contents of her stomach onto the lush carpet.

"Bloody fucking hell, Emma, you wouldn't wake up," he said shakily. He crouched beside her. Gently, he swept back her hair from her face and she heaved again. "It was just a dream," he said more soothingly.

She shook her head, retching once more, so violently her entire body felt like it was being turned inside out. She didn't spare a thought for the carpet. Her mother was dying, if she wasn't already dead. She needed to get to Sheol to save her.

"Levaroth," she croaked.

"What?" Blaze bit out harshly.

"I need to summon Levaroth," she replied, wiping her mouth with the back of her hand. Shooting to her feet, she raced for the door before hitting a solid wall of muscle. She bounced off Blaze's chest with a snarl—a feral sound that should have surprised her—but she didn't care, even at the sight of Blaze's stunned expression. "He's killing my mother for removing the mark. I need to go to Sheol and save her."

"Who is? Levaroth?"

"No, my father!"

Blaze's brows rose. "Who is your father?"

"Asmodeus," Emma said, trying to push past him. This time he let her go, swearing as he followed behind her. She flung the door open and sprinted down the corridor.

"Emma, wait! You can't just go back to Sheol. You won't be able to leave."

"I'm going to kill them all!" she shouted. If Blaze answered, she didn't hear.

The grand double doors burst open before she approached the bottom of the winding stairway, and at least ten guards rushed in, many looking ashen faced. Blaze had her by the bicep and yanked her to a stop. She growled at him, but he ignored her.

"Sir! You have to come, there's a—" The guard she recognized as Gerald fell silent, and a ripple of unease swept through the cluster of men.

Her heart pounded. She ripped herself free of Blaze's grasp and was out the door, running faster than she ever had. The glow of late morning set the sky in gold and red. Her brain refused to process what she was seeing, ignored the deadly cold that gripped and squeezed her lungs, threatening to steal her breath. Her father, the beast he was, stood outside the gate. Red stained the ground around him like a gruesome welcome mat. A handful of guards, ripped into pieces, were strewn all around the prince, who smiled at her.

Vaguely, she registered Blaze tearing after her, shouting at her to stop. She came to a halt just before the closed gate. Her mother's body was limp in her father's arms. Blood soaked the threadbare gown that hung from her starved frame.

Bile rose in Emma's throat. Red tinged the edges of her vision. She loosed a roar that could match any beast's. The cold smile that curved her father's lips grew. His bloodred eyes matched the ground beneath his massive, clawed feet. He looked more dragon than man.

Emma saw the shallow rise and fall of her mother's chest, and faltered.

"I'll come willingly," she said. "You can punish me for all eternity. Put her down. Let her go. Please," she begged. Every inch of her shook with desperation.

"I will have you, daughter. But first, you will watch her die." He shot into the air before Emma could process his movement.

A pair of strong arms locked around Emma's waist, spinning her away.

But still, she saw it happen.

She still saw the steel spikes impale her mother's frail body.

She still heard the squelch of flesh that tore her stomach to shreds.

She heard the sickening crunch of bones splintering.

Her mouth opened on a silent scream. Her chest spasmed as she fought to draw in the breath to let her screams break free.

She fought the grip on her waist. Her nails clawed into the hot, steely arms that caged her. She was frozen.

Broken.

Being torn away from the bloody sight of her mother's body.

Heat roared beneath her skin. The searing hot in her veins was a welcome sensation to the cold that filled her chest where her heart used to be.

The arms that held her back released her. And at last she sucked in a breath.

And screamed.

The sound ripped through the sky. The ground shook. Iron bars bowed outward as Emma sprinted toward the man that murdered her mother.

Her father's eyes widened. Then his voice spoke directly into her mind. *I will see you soon, daughter mine.*

She tried to claw it out of her head. Still she screamed. A cry for blood. For death.

Then she doubled over as fresh agony tore through her body, consuming it. Threatening to split her skin.

When it eased enough, she jumped to her feet. But her father was gone. Still, the cold and crushing weight in her chest increased.

Her gaze cut back to the top of the fence, where her mother hung, cold and still, only fifteen feet from where she stood.

And then the world went black.

Her lids were heavy, her mouth dry. She didn't open her eyes. Images of her mother's body impaled on the steel spikes of the gate flashed. Grief pummeled into her, knocking the air from her lungs. She sobbed softly, turning back into her pillow and begging sleep to claim her again. Her mother was dead. Living was pointless. She had failed. Her father won.

Behind her, a weight sank onto the bed. Blaze's warmth pulled her around to face him. She buried her face in his chest, letting silent tears fall.

"I wish I could take it away," he whispered. "I know you feel like you're drowning now, but you will surface because you must. The fight isn't over." He stroked her hair and soon her sobs subsided. The steady rhythm of his heart lulled her into a dreamless sleep.

The warmth around her shifted, making her conscious of the fact that Blaze was still in her bed, limbs entwined with hers. His lips brushed her forehead.

"You need to get up, my love," he said.

She swallowed hard, then nodded. She would shower, dress, then she would face her new reality. Her mother would be furious to see Emma losing the will to live when the world was on the brink of a supernatural war that she was the key to.

She would bury her mom. Grieving could take place once she made it through what was to come...*if* she made it through what was to come.

Her mother's life had been the cost of freedom. War was declared the second the Mark of Fallen Flame had been removed.

But who had removed it? She hadn't been consciously trying to do so, yet it happened. Somehow.

It surprised Emma that the whole world hadn't been devoured by darkness while she slept as retribution for her betrayal. Perhaps he had yet to make his next move.

She extricated herself from Blaze's embrace, pushing herself up to a sitting position. She glanced at the pity in his pale blue eyes. Another pair of blue eyes filled her mind and she asked, "How is Sergei?"

He swallowed hard before rubbing large circles on her back. "He came out right when"—he sucked in a long, steadying breath—"when it happened. He's in rough shape."

Emma's eyes burned. She'd been so focused on herself that she hadn't paid any mind to those around her. The event itself was burned into her memory. But everything else was hazy, as if it'd happened years ago instead of days.

"I'd like to bury her," she told him, her voice wobbly.

He inclined his head. "Of course."

"But first I'd like a shower." She got to her feet, using what little strength she had to keep her spine straight.

Blaze assessed her. Then he nodded, getting to his feet as well. He strode around the bed, stopping in front of her. The back of his hand brushed against her cheek before he leaned forward and pressed a gentle kiss to her dry and cracked lips.

"I'll have food brought up as well."

Emma didn't bother protesting. She cast him a grateful look before he turned to leave. When the door clicked shut, she undressed and headed for the shower.

A hot shower, in Emma's opinion, could refresh and soothe away deep aches. But that was before she had watched her mother die in the most heinous and gruesome way possible. She was numb to the way the heat pounded into her taut muscles, and she didn't bother lingering.

Back in her room, the spicy, sugary scent of cinnamon wafted toward her. The smell reminded her too much of her mother, of the cinnamon rolls she often surprised Emma with. She staggered into the wall, using it to hold her up while she fought to keep her grip on the tattered remains of her composure.

The tray sitting on her table was piled high with eggs, bacon, toast, and sautéed vegetables. Beside it was a warm, glazed cinnamon roll. Gertie had prepared a small feast for her. Emma stared at the food for a long moment. Blaze still hadn't returned, making it easy to consider tossing the entire tray out her window. Instead, she picked up the mug of coffee—already prepared to her liking—and gulped it down, ignoring its sweet taste and the burn that scraped down her throat. It settled heavily in her stomach, warm and unsatisfying. She grimaced.

Deciding not to risk throwing up again, she turned to change, carefully selecting the ruffled black top her mother had chosen for her first day of senior year. She swallowed back the prick of tears and smoothed her hands over it.

Her movements were slow and sluggish while she finished dressing. She had to force her body to move, each step a challenge when all she wanted to do was collapse to the floor and weep until her heart gave out.

"Enough," she growled to herself. She stomped back to the table and snatched a slice of buttered toast, tearing off a chunk. She chewed the bite that stuck to her dry mouth like glue and nearly gagged before forcing herself to swallow it. Once she'd made herself consume two slices of toast that absorbed the coffee, her stomach felt weighted, but full. It was enough for now.

A knock sounded on her door, and she didn't need to look up to know it was Blaze. He opened the door and walked in. She lifted her gaze to meet his. He stared at her hard, and she desperately tried to take the strength he was offering.

"Are you ready?" he asked her.

She nodded, then started toward him. He held up her winter coat, and she slid her arms in. Placing a hand on the middle of her back, he ushered her out into the corridor.

The manor was unnaturally silent. Christmas decorations were strung from nearly every surface, the colors bright and offensive to her eyes. There were lots of children that lived there, but not a single one ran through the halls, laughing as they normally did. Emma didn't know why the place was so quiet, but she was grateful for it.

At the bottom of the staircase, a large tree stood proud in the corner. It was decorated with handmade ornaments and garlands of popcorn and cranberries.

She stopped, staring at it. Her chest felt hollow. "What day is it?" she whispered.

Blaze was silent for a long moment, staring up at the tree beside her. Grasping her arm, he gave her a light squeeze. "It's Christmas eve."

She nodded. She expected to feel something, but she was emptied of emotion, and she was almost certain she'd never be able to feel again. Tomorrow would be her first Christmas without her mother. The first of as many as Emma would live to see, though she doubted there would be another in her future.

Without another word, they walked out the mansion's doors. The frigid winter air nipped at her nose, stabbing the insides of her lungs. The pain was welcome, because at least she could feel that.

Her heart began to pound at the sight before her.

In the center of the garden's snow-dusted labyrinth, several chairs surrounded a dark wooden casket covered in vibrant flowers that Emma knew were magically grown. She halted, her breath hitching. The casket would contain her mother's remains.

Horrific images filled her mind again. Her mother's limp, bony, bloodied body being run through with spikes. Her form dangling morbidly from the rods. Blood pouring onto the white ground, staining it. Emma couldn't stop her gaze from swiveling to the gate. Somehow the ground glittered white and pure, as if challenging her memory of what had occurred there. Her jaw clenched painfully, her teeth grinding together.

A pair of strong, warm hands cradled her face, gently turning her eyes from the spot, forcing them to Blaze's face.

"Hey," he whispered.

"Where will she be buried?" she asked.

"I thought…since you loved the gardens so much…"

Emma nodded. "Thank you."

Blaze pressed a quick kiss to her forehead. "Come," he said. He led her by the hand to the front row. The temperature instantly warmed, no doubt the work of one of the Spellcasters. They passed faces she knew, and some she didn't. One made Emma trip, and Blaze steadied her. There, sitting in the middle row, was her mother.

"Mom?" she gasped.

Strawberry-blond hair tied up in a perfect knot on top of her head, a slender face, and bright blue eyes that glittered with unshed tears.

Blue eyes. Not green.

It wasn't her mother. *But then who—?*

Blaze hurried her forward, whispering words she didn't quite hear. They took their seats and Emma fought the urge to turn and gawk at the woman sitting behind her.

Every chair was filled, and Emma wondered how many of these people actually knew her mother. Beside her sat Sergei. His eyes were red-rimmed and puffy. He reached for her hand, taking it in his much larger one, and squeezed. Then he rose, shuffling to stand in front of the casket. He wore a clean black suit that looked slightly too big for him. It was creased with wrinkles that she imagined he just hadn't bothered to use his magic to smooth. His tie was yellow, matching the roses that decorated her casket perfectly. Her mother's favorite color.

Suddenly her eyes burned again, and her chest felt tight.

Sergei cleared his throat. "Thank you all for being here," he said, his voice wavering. Then he cleared his throat again.

Emma pressed her eyes shut. Blaze's warm hand clasped hers.

"Some of you knew Laura Duvall; others knew Nadia Ivankov. Whomever you had the pleasure of getting to know, she was a woman loved by all. I knew both," Sergei continued, voice cracking.

A hot tear leaked out and spilled down Emma's cheek, landing in her lap.

"I knew her from a young age...and I loved her more than I loved anyone else on this Earth." Sergei's voice broke into a whisper, and then he paused for several moments.

Emma looked up and met his brilliant blue eyes. They shined with a raw grief that she felt deep in her bones. A grief that made it hard to breathe. Hard to function. But they couldn't afford to fall apart now. Her mother wouldn't want them to. The two people who loved her most in this world had to find a way to carry on. Asmodeus wasn't going to let them grieve. Her mother's death was proof that any fragile peace they had kept was now obliterated.

"She loved me back," Sergei said, his voice stronger. "But her daughter was her entire world. Nadia went to great lengths to protect her, because that's who she was. To be loved by Laura Duvall, or Nadia Ivankov, is to be fiercely protected."

The words tore the air from her lungs and fresh tears streamed down her face.

"And so." Sergei took a deep breath. "Wherever her eternal resting place is, I imagine it filled with all the beauty she gave to this world."

Tiny yellow petals from what Emma guessed were daisies floated down gently around them. Her lips quivered into a small smile. She wasn't sure if Gertie or Sergei was doing it, but the gesture was beautiful. Their warm, enchanted enclosure was scented like a summer breeze. It smelled like her, and Emma couldn't help but breathe it in deeply, letting her tears fall freely as Blaze squeezed her hand.

"Do you want to say anything?" he whispered, his breath tingling her ear. Emma's head snapped to face him.

"Sure," she said, voice strained. She stood and Sergei smiled gently at her. First she walked to the beautiful wooden casket, and placed her hand on the smooth surface. Sergei pressed a soft kiss to her temple before taking his seat.

Emma turned to face everyone, looking at the people seated there. Gertie, Constance, Gwyndoline, Emerelda, and a few other faces softened. Axel wasn't among them, but she didn't linger on that fact. The woman that had startled Emma had her head bowed, and her shoulders shook.

Emma offered those looking back at her as much of a smile as she could muster. "I know many of you didn't get the chance to really know my mom, so I'll tell you a little bit about her. I didn't understand why she seemed so strict most of the time, and I could see she didn't want to always tell me that I couldn't stay the night at a friend's house, or go to a birthday party or a school dance. But now..." She sucked in a deep, steadying breath, pushing back the next surge of threatening tears. "I suppose all moms just want to keep their kids safe, and she was no exception. She had a hard childhood herself, and she made a lot of sacrifices for me." Her eyes found Sergei's. "But I'm so thankful she had someone she could love in a different way. She needed that. And sometimes she would come home with a smile that lasted for days or hum a tune, and I didn't pay much attention to it at the time, but it makes sense now. She did love me, but she loved you too. I wish she had introduced us herself, but I'm glad I got the chance to know you."

She looked back to the small crowd and met the eyes of the woman who once again jarred Emma with her striking likeness to her mother. "My mother was the most beautiful woman. She was my best friend. We would watch movies and eat takeout on the weekends, and she always took me to get coffee or hot chocolate on my first day of school. We drank it by the gallon on other days too, which is probably why I have a caffeine addiction."

Several people chuckled. Emma glanced at Blaze, who stared at her with a mixture of awe and amusement. She swallowed hard before turning to brush the casket. "I'm going to miss you so much, Mom. There's so much I wish I'd said—"

Her voice broke and she swallowed again. She raised her hand to her lips and pressed a kiss to her fingertips that she placed on the cherry wood. A tear slipped out, then another. Her lip trembled. She couldn't control the tsunami of emotion rising within her. The dam was breaking, spilling over, and her frame shook.

"Lunch will be inside. Thank you all for coming," Blaze said gruffly from behind her. Then his arms were around her, catching her just before the wave crashed over her once more.

Her ragged sobs stole through her. The sounds of her anguish were nearly inhuman, but Blaze held her through them. She clung to him, fighting for breath. Her mother was gone.

Forever.

Never again would she see her smiling face or hear her laugh. They'd never again go shopping together or load up on junk food. Her best friend was dead.

"Strong Emma," Blaze whispered, rocking her back and forth. "Brave Emma. Your mother loved you so."

The waves grew smaller, and Emma listened to his reassuring words.

"Go in peace. Your work is done," Blaze said with a strength that shocked her into silence. "By the angel's blood, be lifted to new life. May your wings be restored."

Emma raised her head, her gaze meeting his. "That was beautiful."

"It's our death rite. We send off our fallen soldiers in hopes that they are honored in their afterlife."

Her lips pulled up in an attempted smile. It was sweet of him to speak the sacred words of his people over her mother. She'd truly been a soldier her entire life. Fighting for safety, fighting for the life she wanted for herself and her daughter.

Wiping the drying tears from her face, Emma glanced over to the edge of the empty chairs where the peculiar woman stood. She cried silently into a square of white, embroidered cotton.

"Who is she?" Emma asked.

"Your aunt. I should have warned you first, I'm so sorry. I sent a jet for her while you slept."

A chill unrelated to the cold brushed over her. "My mom's… sister?"

Blaze nodded, still holding her tight. Emma pushed away from his chest then got to her feet, before striding toward the woman.

Her eyes that snapped up to Emma's approach were truly a stunning shade of blue—so different than her mother's seafoam green.

She stopped several feet from the woman, stunned by how similar they looked. There was a difference in height. While her mother was nearly six inches taller than Emma, the woman had only three or four inches on her.

"Hello," the woman whispered in a heavy accent.

"I hear you're my aunt," Emma offered lamely.

She nodded with a small smile. "My name is Natalya." A pale hand extended for Emma to shake.

She looked at it for a moment then threw her arms around Natalya. Her aunt poorly stifled a sob as they hugged. Whatever her mother's reasons for cutting out her sister, Emma didn't care. Natalya was the last remaining family she had.

"I knew you looked familiar," someone said behind her aunt.

They broke apart to face Emerelda, who smiled with satisfaction. "You're Natalya's niece. We're cousins."

Emma glanced at her aunt, who pursed her lips. It was not the expression of friends. "Yes, she is," her aunt said proudly.

Linking her arm with Emma's, Natalya steered her around Emerelda—who looked like she had a great deal more to say— and they headed inside the manor.

Though Emma didn't want to speak with anyone, see their

sympathy, or hear their well-meaning but pointless condolences, she was glad when Breanna ambushed her, barreling into her and wrapping her in a tight hug.

"Emma, I'm so sorry. I heard about your mother," Breanna said in a rush. Emma peered over Breanna's shoulder, wondering where Isaac was. Her question was answered by Dominic standing several feet back, watching Breanna like she might shatter if Emma squeezed too hard, while holding the tiny bundle that was Isaac. It was almost amusing to see such a large, intimidating man so gently cradling the infant.

When Breanna released her, Emma couldn't help but give a knowing smile. Breanna's cheeks were stained red, and Emma gave the girl's hand a reassuring squeeze. She was happy that Breanna had come so far from the terrified, broken girl that had been taken in only a few weeks ago.

Clearly Dominic had a healing effect with his gentle-giant ways.

Emma introduced Breanna to her aunt and in turn, introduced her aunt to the peacefully sleeping babe in Dominic's arms.

For a while, Emma felt the pieces of her heart come together, held in place by the smiles and laughter of the friends she'd made and the woman who reminded her so much of the mother she'd lost. From her laugh to her love for coffee, it was somehow easier to pretend that her mother wasn't really gone. And in a way, it allowed Emma to imagine what her mother would have sounded like with a Russian accent.

Sergei was able to smile too, not a full smile, but one that proved he was trying to be okay. Just like she was.

Before long, exhaustion closed in on her and she said her goodbyes, hugging Natalya once again. Her aunt agreed to stick around instead of flying back to Russia right away, and Emma looked forward to spending time with her.

Blaze swept Emma into his arms and carried her up the stairs. Every step he took felt like a knife digging into the cracks of her heart, prying them open further and further. She felt the weight of her grief settling into her bones yet again and she buried her face into Blaze's warmth. It wasn't her room he entered several minutes later. Too tired to take in the details, she vaguely registered that the bed he placed her in was his. Dark covers were draped over her, and Blaze's warm body settled behind hers.

She rolled to face him, keeping her face pressed into his chest, letting his earthy scent fill her. Softly, she cried the last of her tears.

"I'm so sorry, Emma," Blaze said against her forehead after what felt like an hour of silence.

She didn't reply. She never understood why people apologized when someone died. There were no words to take away the pain of losing someone precious to you, and the words *I'm sorry* seemed to be a grossly inadequate thing to say.

As if he could read her thoughts he said, "I know that does nothing for your pain. I know it won't bring your mum back, but I was in your shoes many years ago. When I say I'm sorry, what I mean is I know what it feels like to be so overwhelmed by grief that you feel unable to breathe. Everything aches and you feel as if you're drowning. When I say I'm sorry, I mean I know that no amount of time will make it better, but I'll do everything in my power to help you get through, until it gets easier. I can kiss you until you forget, or I can listen to stories of her, or you can rage at me and hit me until you're so exhausted you collapse."

Her throat tightened.

"I'm sorry is the shortest way of saying 'Let me do whatever you need. Let me be whatever you need.' You *will* get through this, Emma. Turn your tears to rage and let's stop the monster that took her from you. Help me stop this war before it starts, and end the vile beasts that put you both through hell." His accent was thick, and anger laced his tone.

Emma didn't reply. Instead, she lifted her head and brought her dry lips against his. Her hand brushed the stubble on his jaw, and she kissed him. Softly at first. Then his arms wrapped around her, drawing her tightly to him, their bodies flush, deepening the kiss.

She didn't want to think. Didn't want to feel as she undid the buttons of his shirt before pushing it off his corded biceps. She wanted to lose herself in this. In him. For as long as possible.

Her shaking hands fumbled with the button of his jeans and he stilled.

"Emma," he rasped.

"Please," she whispered against the base of his throat.

He pressed his eyelids shut, taking in a deep breath. The sting of rejection had already begun to set in when his eyes opened again, the grey a rolling storm.

"It won't make you feel better, Emma."

Her eyes narrowed. "You said you'd kiss me until I forgot."

He chuckled. "I think you were intending more than that."

Emma bit her lip, her eyes burning, but there were no more tears to cry. Did she want this? Was she ready for this? She knew the answer almost instantly: she did want it. And she hoped one day it would be him. But masking her grief by throwing herself into a situation that would likely cause her more pain wouldn't help.

So she sat up, looking away, and heaved a sigh.

Blaze sat up beside her, taking her hand in his. "I don't want you to hate me for taking advantage of your grief."

She shook her head, unable to speak. Tears somehow welled in her eyes, yet they didn't fall. They burned, and her head ached. "You're right," she breathed.

He pressed a kiss to her temple. "You deserve the world, Emma. Dates, random flowers, and chocolates. You deserve to be courted. To be made certain of my affection for you. Ideally, I'd ask you to marry me. And only then, when you know without a shadow of a doubt that I would split this world in two just to see you happy, would I show you my love in such a tender way."

Emma's lips parted. Marriage? Had she planned to wait for marriage before having sex? Maybe... Even with her mother's overprotectiveness, an opportunity could have arisen, if she really wanted it. But she hadn't. In the back of her mind, life after leaving her mother's house would allow her to discover whether or not she wanted to wait. Assuming she met the right guy. But now…

With her mother gone and the world in danger of being taken over by the entire Shediem race, things like sex and marriage hadn't registered on her list of priorities.

"I'm not ready to get married," she said. She was barely eighteen, and she had known Blaze for only a few months.

He laughed, a warm, rich sound that made her heart flip over in her chest.

"I wasn't asking you to marry me, Emma. I just wanted you to know, that if we should ever share a bed in that way, it would only be when both of us were ready."

She nodded, staring down at the blanket scrunched up in her fists.

Gathering her in his embrace again, he lay back and she forced herself to relax, trying not to think about how she'd just thrown herself at him.

"Sleep now," he said.

And she did.

Emma awoke to the scent of pine and snow, cocooned in warmth and feeling slightly better than she had the day before. Blaze's fingers lazily played with strands of her hair. His voice was warm and husky with sleep when he said, "Happy Christmas, Emma."

Her throat tightened, choking off any response she might have made.

"Did you sleep okay?"

She forced a single word out. "Yeah." Her vocal cords felt charred and strained, her mouth dry. Clearing her throat, she added, "Did you?"

"Not terrible," he answered.

They remained silent for several moments. Then Emma said, "About last night—"

"Don't trouble yourself. Truly, what you've gone through—what you'll continue to go through—is awful. Losing a parent is tragic, especially when they're so young."

She nodded, looking down at the plain, navy duvet. "I'm still sorry."

He pressed a kiss to the top of her head. "Accepted."

Blaze stilled, and she felt his attention move to the door seconds before a knock sounded. He slid out from under her before grabbing the shirt she had flung to the end of the bed last night, and slipped it back on, covering the golden, chiseled perfection that was his chest. With each button he fastened, Emma had to resist the urge to pout.

Noticing where her attention was, his eyes visibly heated, but he didn't speak.

Gertie entered seconds later, holding a silver platter with an arrangement of foods on it. Her eyes were red-rimmed, a sadness in them that Emma felt in her every molecule.

Gertie didn't smile when she sat the tray on the bed, casting a look of sympathy at her.

"Thank you," Emma said, wishing for another hug, one that would ease the tight knot of pain in her chest.

"Thought you might be hungry."

Blaze nodded. "Thank you."

Gertie returned the nod, then headed for the open door. At the threshold, she paused and turned to meet Emma's gaze. "If you need anything, child, don't hesitate to ask."

Then she departed, closing the door behind her with a soft snick.

Blaze reached over a heaping pile of mini donuts for a sliced

English muffin, before slathering it with butter and jam. Emma stared at the closed door feeling her pain intensify.

He held the muffin out to her. "Eat."

She briefly considered arguing but thought better of it, and accepted with a small smile. All her stomach could manage was a few nibbled bites.

He set the muffin down and wiped his hands on his pristine slacks. "I'll be right back."

Emma sipped her coffee, watching with furrowed brows while he stalked to the set of doors that joined their rooms. He pulled open the unlocked doors, stepped inside, and returned only a moment later carrying her dagger.

She lit up with joy. "You found it!"

He smiled, nodding. "I kept it, waiting for the right moment to give it back. When you returned, I could tell something was off, so I waited…But since it's Christmas day, I figured this was as good a gift as any."

Emma nodded, then frowned. "But I didn't get you anything."

Blaze shook his head. "I don't want anything but you, Emma."

Her heart swelled, causing tears that she quickly blinked away. She took the beautifully crafted blade from his outstretched hand, admiring the tiny roses and thorns carved into the hilt. "Thank you." She was glad he hadn't given it to her while she was under her father's control. The unimaginable pain she might have caused with such a weapon made her stomach turn.

"You're welcome," he answered gruffly before running a hand through his hair. "We can start training with it as soon as you want."

She nodded again, setting the dagger in her lap. "What did Axel say when you told him about your sister?"

Blaze seemed to flinch. "He doesn't know yet."

Emma's jaw dropped at the information. "Why not?" She'd been so consumed with her mother's death, she hadn't noticed or cared that Axel was absent.

"He was caught with items that indicate he is responsible

for weakening the wards and allowing Shediem to attack the compound."

She gasped. "When?"

"Right after we returned. We triggered the alarm so Gertie and I could search the rooms."

She clapped a hand over her mouth. "So where is he now?"

Blaze rolled his neck, no doubt trying to alleviate the tension coiled through his body. "He's in the basement. I was able to suspend his trial for a few days after everything with your mother, but I won't be able to hold it off for much longer."

Her words were hushed when she asked, "What will happen to him if they find him guilty?"

His steely gaze locked onto hers, and she sensed his own inner turmoil as easily as her own.

"If he's found guilty, he'll be put to death."

LEVAROTH

I t had been centuries since Levaroth had been to the king's private estate. Since it was located in the heart of the Pit, few were willing to get close. Even for Shediem—immortal creatures that thrived in chaos—it was too overwhelming. A nightmare especially for those that fed on emotion.

Like a broken bottle of rich perfume, the air was thick with terror. It made his nose wrinkle. From the looks on the princes' faces, they were similarly affected. Beside Asmodeus, at least two dozen children—ranging from eight to preteen—that looked entirely human stood still. Dressed in black robes embroidered with silver and red thread, the small soldiers had vacant eyes.

The Anakeem, a race of hybrids gifted with extraordinary powers. At that thought, something twinged in his mind, sending a jolt of pain through his skull. He rubbed at the spot, and whatever he'd been thinking about floated away.

Prince Amon, who couldn't be bothered to leave his harem back at his mansion, wore a sour expression even while the half-dressed, giggling females stroked his bare chest. His eyes glittered like rubies as he smirked at Levaroth with triumph. As though he knew something Levaroth did not.

More Shediem of lower ranks began to appear, crowding the stone courtyard. The sky was black and starless, the area around them lit only by pits where cobalt-blue flames danced at least five feet high, randomly placed throughout the courtyard. Stone pillars surrounded them, reaching up to the dark abyss. Most of them were crumbling and decrepit. Nothing lasted in the Pit. Nothing grew here. Nothing natural, anyway.

He recalled the vibrant, lush plant life and starry nights on Earth but dismissed them all with a scoff. There was nothing the Earth held that they would not soon possess. Every star and distant planet would exist because the king, Nakosh, desired it.

Sheol had its benefits. Like the fact that it did not have "weather." No freak snowstorms, no hurricanes, no tornadoes. Thus, it was colorless. And rotting. It was where they were meant to rot. Sheol was their eternal punishment, as well as punishment for the wicked.

There was a lake. *The* lake of damnation. Where Nickor and other creatures lived. The same lake that surrounded them on the island the king resided on. It was a murky grey and stagnant. From the pungent scent of decay and blood, Levaroth knew the beasts of the deep had crawled up from their depths to join their gathering.

Their unholy group spoke amongst themselves as if meeting in the center of their world were an everyday occurrence. Asmodeus and Mammon leaned together, discussing something in hushed tones. Levaroth scanned over the basin of crackling flames to his left. When everyone had supernatural hearing, it was imperative you didn't overhear a conversation you weren't supposed to. And they certainly looked as if they did not want to be heard.

A smooth deep brown shoulder moved beside Levaroth, and he turned, noticing the general's rarely used human form. Levaroth blinked.

"Tlahaz."

The man who was not a man dipped his head by way of greeting. A headful of black dreads was tied on the top of his head, spilling down to his ears. *How odd*, Levaroth mused. Tlahaz's faux brown eyes flashed gold, then his already impressive built expanded, ivory spikes protruding from his skin that dulled to a leathery grey.

"Been to Earth then?" Levaroth asked with a smug grin.

Tlahaz grunted.

"Still not much for their languages, I take it."

The general rolled his golden eyes. "They are hairless apes capable of speech." Though something flickered in his gaze that Levaroth couldn't decipher.

"Indeed. But they have their uses." He cast a glance at the near-naked human women pawing at Amon. "And their beauties."

Levaroth felt Tlahaz's body go rigid, noting it with mild curiosity. Perhaps Tlahaz had sampled some of the beauty Earth had to offer. "They will soon be dead or enslaved. Their beauty will matter not."

Levaroth didn't want to point out that the beautiful among them would be the first to suffer, forced to entertain his kind until their feeble hearts gave out. Earth would be a blackened smudge beneath the Shediem princes' thumbs.

But first, he'd kill the Shediem-Slayer.

His vision streaked bloodred and his fists clenched.

When the haze receded, Levaroth saw Tlahaz watching him. There was something *off* about his comrade.

Without another word, Tlahaz turned and melted into the crowd, finding a pillar somewhere in the shadows to hide until his master arrived.

Black mist snaked along the floor, weaving between every creature standing in the dilapidated courtyard. Silence descended upon them. They felt their king draw near. Inky black tendrils slithered and swirled into place on a raised platform, taking the shape of a man. Levaroth knew that even for them, it was safer for him to appear in his human skin. His true form was far too terrible; unleashing it even in his lair would cause catastrophic consequences. There was a reason he was named *World Breaker*.

But his human skin was safe enough to display for them all. He was tall and lean, every bit of him sharp angles, his cruel

236

eyes cutting through the space and demanding submission. In unison, every creature bowed.

A chilling smile tilted the king's lips. "Welcome, my children. My brothers." His eyes sought the five princes, who looked up one by one to acknowledge his attention.

The space was packed with every level of Shediem, the breezeless air stifling with churning violence. After they all rose at the king's command, they waited, enraptured.

"For millennia, our kind have hunted in the shadows, unable to allow our true selves to be seen. To be known. Most of us have remained in Sheol for the majority of our existence, fearing the filthy angel-born brats that hunt us."

Tremors of agreement and grunts of outrage lifted from those surrounding Levaroth. The living shadows that curled around Nakosh almost protectively swirled faster, caressing the king's lithe body in answer.

His voice rang with power. "The time of the Giborim is at an end. We will slaughter their numbers and the kingdom of Sheol will reign on Earth!"

The Shediem cheered so loudly, the ground shook. Every prince raised their fist into the air, the visage of their power glowing and lighting the space. Another surge of bloodlust snaked through Levaroth's veins, and he saw only one face.

One woman.

The Shediem-Slayer.

Kill her.

King Nakosh waited for the crowd to quiet again. His voice took on an eerie, ominous quality as he said, "The one with the blood to unify us all has given the ultimate sacrifice, and that sacrifice will carve out a new rule." His silver eyes pierced the silent crowd, landing on Levaroth. A snarl rumbled in his throat.

Then Nakosh looked out on all his creatures. "Princes, I release you from your chains. It is time to place your kingdoms on Earth."

The roars of excitement and the thrill of bloodshed filled the place. Shediem began to disappear, and when the first prince shed his bond to their world, the ground trembled and bolts of vibrant energy split the sky like fire shooting along a line of gasoline. Levaroth's ears rang. The second prince left, then a third; Sheol mourned its loss with thunderous booms and streaking light.

Asmodeus pulled Levaroth away with him, but before he was lifted from his homeland, he caught sight of the king's dark, liquid silver eyes locked on him.

EMMA

E ach morning when Emma awoke, she and Blaze trained until her limbs shook and her mind became blissfully blank. Though her flames burned beneath her skin when she and the Giborim sparred, she kept them down. He taught her how to hold the knife. How to attack best at close proximity and how to dodge weapons directed at her.

Only Blaze ever called it quits—which Emma at first thought he did to prevent her from pushing herself into unconsciousness. But she realized from his heavy breathing and his skin bright with exertion that he might actually be exhausted too.

After they parted ways to shower, they'd have breakfast in her room, then walk down to their morning meeting. But since her mother's funeral, all was quiet. No abductions, and no more attacks on the compound.

Emma tried to keep the nervousness she felt each and every morning at bay, when there was still no news besides a letter from the cave giants in the south that they would defend against the Shediem. Constance's and Taryn's covens both arrived, preferring to set up camp on opposite sides of the grounds.

With the Shediem's silence, the regional leaders used their meeting time to either argue about when Axel's trial should be held, or grill her for information. She was happy to keep the topic away from Blaze's brother and provide any information that could help them. The constant questioning and reliving the horrors she'd faced grated on her, though. *What does Sheol look like? What do the princes look like in their human forms? What do they look like in their true forms? How do your powers work?*

She detailed her murder of the Prince of Greed, Belphegor, and the eerie shadowy king who looked on in delight. There were certain things she didn't say; for instance, she didn't tell anyone about the crown the king of Sheol left for her. Or the dreams she shared with Levaroth. Though Blaze's hard stare seemed to find each and every piece she kept to herself stamped on her forehead for the way his jaw clenched.

The morning after her mother's funeral, she told them about her father's hybrids. Every face had morphed into one of horror and rage—Blaze's included. While she spoke, his icy blue eyes stayed fixed on her, and every inch of his corded, muscular body tensed.

She didn't, however, share that Haddie was pregnant. After the meeting, when Blaze had thawed from his statue form, he'd grabbed her hand and squeezed it gently. That's when she spoke the words that turned his kind expression to stone again.

His throat had bobbed, then without a word, he'd stalked past her with jerky strides. She didn't see him the rest of the day. Not that she blamed him. The news was horrifying and devastating. It haunted her because she hadn't gotten Haddie out in time. But thinking about the half-Shediem child in her womb only led to thoughts about how it got there. Who put it there…

Such thoughts led to rage that made her skin heat and her veins sear with power. Power that strained for release.

Since that day, Blaze had been quiet. Anger and something darker churned in his stormy eyes. Emma let him be, offering small smiles and gentle touches when she could. When they trained, she allowed him to unleash on her, just as she did on him. Although, to be fair, all she had to do was touch him when her control was frayed and he'd catch fire, so it wasn't quite accurate to say that she unleashed fully.

In her afternoons she checked on Breanna and Isaac. Already

240

she noticed how much Breanna's son was growing. Breanna too had begun to lose the sharpness of her limbs. And Dominic's attentions toward her never wavered. Often, Emma would find her friend in the gardens, she and Isaac bundled up against the harsh winter and Dominic strolling beside her. Though he was intense around her, he never entered her rooms. Emma had to admit she enjoyed seeing the way Breanna's eyes lit up whenever Dominic was near, the shadows of past trauma receding for a while.

Dominic was always quick to part with Breanna when Emma was around, allowing the two of them time to talk. They spent their evenings together, and ate dinner in Breanna's room, watching movies while Breanna taught her how to crochet.

It kept Emma's grief at bay.

At least until the night, when she'd climb the marble staircase and feel the weight begin to settle on her chest yet again.

Her nightmares had resumed with full force: always her father's glowing red eyes and her mother's lifeless broken body speared above her. When Emma inevitably awoke screaming, Blaze would come and wrap her in his arms. But they didn't speak. Neither of them had to— being in each other's company was enough.

That morning, however, it was not a nightmare that drew Emma from her sleep. Her body shook, and a loud rumbling jerked her upright. Darkness still lingered on the other side of her drawn curtains; the clock on her side table read two in the morning.

The bed shook again, and Emma heard the doors vibrating in their frames. The entire mansion swayed, making her dizzy. Screams filled the hall just as Blaze burst through her door, his dark hair mussed with sleep.

"An earthquake?" she asked, throwing off the blanket and getting to her feet.

Blaze didn't answer—he grabbed her arm and sprinted for the door. Emma glanced down at her short sleep shorts and thin tank top and willed them into a sweater and jeans. The material covered her body like a second skin as Blaze rushed with her into the hall. People ran for the front doors, clearly not understanding proper earthquake procedure.

Another violent tremor rocked the house, and the stairs beneath Emma felt like they'd been pulled out from under her.

Screams grew into a crescendo. Bodies tumbled and rolled on the hard, cool marble. Everywhere, people clutched those around them. Blaze's arms wrapped around Emma, crushing her to him. Plaster and dust showered them, the ceiling groaning, threatening to collapse.

"Hold on!" a woman shouted, and Emma distantly recognized it as Taryn.

Bursts of color lit the foyer better than the few sconces on the walls. More joined in, the Spellcasters' magic repairing the damage even while the rumbling grew.

Nausea rolled through Emma, and she gripped a marble column with both hands to steady herself.

A loud crack sounded.

Then the stairs she and Blaze occupied began to move.

A voice shouted, "The staircase is splitting, everyone stay back!"

Emma tried to crane her neck to look, but Blaze's hold was an iron vice. Several people shrieked, and then the trembling stopped.

Between the stone rungs, she tried to spy Breanna and Isaac, but it was no use. Too many people were moving again. *They're okay*, Emma told herself. *Dominic will make sure they're okay.*

"Come on," Blaze demanded, pulling her to her feet. She swayed and stumbled as he helped her down the last few stairs. When she turned her head to look back at the wreckage, her stomach tightened, and her vision swam.

The beautiful, shining marble staircase was torn in half, the giant slabs cracked and caved into the closet beneath it. Emma swallowed down her sick, trying to regain her composure.

Gertie and Sergei brushed past them, glowing palms raised. A moment later she spied Taryn and several other Spellcasters she'd never seen before. They all worked to stitch the staircase back together, but Blaze continued to lead her through the crush of bodies.

In the room where all their meetings were held, he finally released his tight grip. Many of the elders were already waiting there, dressed they had been when the earthquake woke them, their faces stricken.

"Get me eyes on Seattle and contact all of your bases," Blaze growled, storming to the head of the table where a laptop sat. Dominic and several other elders entered the room, shutting the door behind them.

One of the men—Donovan, she recalled—grabbed the computer, and began hammering away at the keys.

Everyone except Emma and Silas took out their phones, typing furiously. Someone dropped their phone with a loud clatter. One of the leaders fell into a nearby chair.

"Holy…" Donovan trailed off. His skin went white, and his hands shook as he turned the screen toward Blaze.

Emma's heart had only begun to return to a semi-normal pace when it kicked back into gear at the way Blaze's eyes went vacant. The hard set of his jaw slackened, his Adam's apple bobbing.

"What is it?" Silas demanded.

Blaze shut his eyes for a moment. Emma didn't move. Didn't breathe, waiting for him to respond.

When his eyes opened again, there was violence in his gaze. He looked around at each of his fellow soldiers. His fellow leaders.

"How many?" Blaze's voice was low.

"All of them," Donovan whispered. His eyes snapped up to Emma. "All five of them."

The room spun, but not from another earthquake.

Blaze gripped the edge of the table so hard his knuckles went white. "This is it, everyone." Then his eyes met Emma's. They shared an intense look, communicating his meaning before the words left his lips. "The princes of Sheol have arrived."

The room went from utter chaos to poring over maps, marking each prince's arrival point, cataloguing the damage across the globe. Blaze had ordered Silas and Dominic to calm everyone down and send them back to sleep. He didn't want anyone knowing just yet.

The earthquake they felt had nearly leveled the mansion… yet the prince that had surfaced was in the middle of Kansas.

"It was likely the combined shock of all five surfacing at once, and of course Seattle is right on a fault line, that's why we felt it so strongly," Donovan told the room when Blaze asked about the state of the rest of the country.

Which meant other states like California were likely completely toppled. Emma tried not to think about the death toll while staring down at the map before her. Red X's marked where the princes surfaced: Europe, South America, China, and Africa. Smaller black X's surrounded each point like swarming insects. Those marked the blackouts—no electricity, no contact.

Black zones. Did anyone within those areas survive?

Around her, the men shouted back and forth, their words far from her ears. Emma watched Blaze pointing at another paper, several men leaning around him, countering his statements loudly.

They were nowhere near having a plan formed.

Emma backed slowly toward the open door, but no one looked up. Even after she was out of the room, her footsteps were light, hurrying through the foyer. The midmorning glow illuminated the large space. She passed Breanna's closed door and faltered for a split second before carrying on. It was best if no one knew what she was about to do, but she loathed not to say goodbye.

Emma marveled at the smooth staircase. How only hours ago it had been split in half, yet now looked as glossy and perfect as it had before the earthquake.

In her room she grabbed her backpack and upturned the contents onto her bed. Racing around, she tossed clothes and some toiletries into the bag. Enough for a week—any more would be too much for her to carry. After strapping her dagger to her waist and putting on her thickest, warmest jacket, she looked around the room, feeling the familiar weight of loneliness settling in her chest.

She swallowed hard then headed for the door. She paused in the doorway, gripping the handle tightly. Her palms heated and she blinked away the moisture that sprung to her eyes. Then she shut the door, striding down the hall.

Emma held her breath until the front door closed, then released it in a torrent. The biting winter wind blasted against her face, and she pulled up her scarf past her nose to shield it. Snow crunched beneath the boots she'd changed her Converse to. Down the stairs she went, over the snow-dusted gravel, past the cluster of tents erected for one of the covens. Their soft chatter along with the crackling of fire helped to muffle Emma's steps all the way to the gate.

She strained to hear any sounds of alarm at her departure, but none came. Not even birds chirped nearby. Only the wind rustling through the labyrinth of rose bushes could be heard once she was far enough. Never before had silence sounded so much like death.

The Giborim guarding the gate still hadn't noticed her. They spoke to each other in hushed tones. She kept out of their periphery, ducking low to the ground and veering far left. When she reached the gate, she laid her hands on the locking mechanisms and closed her eyes, imagining what she wanted.

The bolts disintegrated into sand that poured through her fingers and onto the crisp, snowy grass. The gate gave a subtle groan before swinging in an inch or two. Both guards on the other side fell silent, whirling to see what had caused the gate to move.

Emma yanked the gate open, slipping through when their eyes found her. One began shouting into his headset, but she whirled, spinning a kick that connected with his helmet. The other guard charged at her, a look of hatred stamped across the parts of his face that were visible. She sidestepped then wrapped her arm around his throat, and squeezed. He flailed with the strength of an angry bear, but Emma held firm until his body went limp. She released him gently into the snow and whirled for the other guard, only to spin in a circle. He wasn't there. Boot prints led back to the mansion, making her gut clench.

She'd have even less time to escape Blaze's fury now. The thought made her heart pound before she kicked into a sprint down the slippery, rocky mountainside.

Her only companion was the sound of her footfalls cracking the icy layer coating the ground. Wending her way through the trees, the groan of their weighted limbs chased her. Air whistled above in the treetops. More than once she thought she heard the snap of a twig or an extra set of footfalls over her thumping heart, but she didn't slow. Twice she glanced over her shoulder, but hidden in the forest was nothing but shadows. When they seemed to shift Emma told herself that it could be anything—an animal, or snow falling from a branch.

A chilled burst of air caressed the side of her face and she ground to a halt, digging her heels into the loose rocks. She stumbled forward, sliding over ice. Her hands flew out just in time to catch herself, the bite of cold stinging her palms and soaking into her jeans.

A harsh breath sounded in front of her, and her head snapped up.

Blaze stood in front of her, eyes churning like storm clouds. He had a sword in each hand, their tips mere inches from the ground. His chest rose and fell with heavy breaths that Emma figured had more to do with the palpable anger rolling off him.

"What in the blasted skies did you think you were doing?" His voice was gravelly.

Emma got to her knees, the weight of her backpack pulling her shoulders back. She lifted her chin. "None of you were even remotely close to coming up with a plan. Besides, I'm the only one that can kill them." She brushed the snow from her knees, but it was no use—she was soaked through. She willed a fresh pair of jeans in place of the wet ones, and it warmed her instantly.

Blaze watched, his anger not dissipating in the slightest. He stepped forward, sword brushing a mound of white powder. "You can't just run headfirst into your father's grasp, that's what he wants. As much as it might irritate you"—he took another step forward, quickly eating up the distance between them—"you *need* a plan. Foolish, rash decisions will get you killed." She opened her mouth to argue, but he sheathed his swords without looking. "Would you allow your mother's death to be in vain? Getting yourself killed because you couldn't wait is doing just that."

She bristled. "Don't you dare use my mother's death against me. It's a long way to Kansas; I'd have plenty of time to come up with a plan."

Blaze took the last step between them. His heat and earthy scent washed over her, and she fought against the urge to lean into him. It was soothing in a way that few things were.

Though his voice was hard, making it easier to resist his nearness. "By now, the Shediem will be crawling everywhere, killing and kidnapping anyone they find. Where would you sleep? How would you keep warm? You're not safe on your own."

Emma's shoulders drooped. She hadn't thought about that. "I can't just sit and wait."

Blaze's eyes glinted like metal. "Trust me, I'm anxious to find my sister and see these princes exterminated, but the number one thing I've learned in my century and a half of seeking revenge is that you need to be calculated."

She could see it in his eyes: the pain, the anger. They burned hotter than any flame.

In the distance, the rumbling of a vehicle's engine carried through the trees. Emma glanced in the direction of the sound when it didn't pass, then back at Blaze, whose lips tilted up in half smile. "Since I can't convince you to come back, we'll come with you."

"We?" Emma asked, brows creased.

"Sergei, Gertie, and myself."

She swallowed hard. "I don't want them to get hurt."

Blaze took her hand in his, the heat of it near searing. "They know the risks. This is everyone's fight. We all want the world to be safe from the Shediem."

She let out a long breath, seeing it curl through the frigid air. "Okay. Let's go."

He raised her hand and pressed a gentle kiss to her knuckles before tugging her closer and pressing his lips to hers. He was so warm. His arms around her waist felt safe despite the fact that she was anything but.

EMMA

They raced for the Washington border, Blaze expertly weaving through abandoned cars and wreckage. For the first thirty minutes or so, they all sat in silence, until Sergei cleared his throat.

"So what's the plan?"

"Get as close to the prince as possible and kill him," Emma answered without hesitation.

Gertie spoke next. "And how do you plan on getting close to such a powerful Shediem? There may be tens of thousands of Shediem protecting him."

"We need to get the lay of the land first," Blaze offered, not taking his eyes from the dangerous road ahead.

Sergei leaned forward to squeeze Emma's shoulder, and she gave him a small smile in return. "The route we're taking is going to lead us through Colorado, part of the blackout zone. From there, we'll get a pretty good idea what we're dealing with."

"How long will it take us to drive?" Emma asked, biting into her thumbnail while she stared out at the I-90. It looked like a plague had spread over it, killing all living things.

"With no stops, nineteen hours, but we'll have to find somewhere to get fuel and possibly switch drivers so we can all get enough rest. We could have flown but I think it'll be wise to keep to the ground for now. Assess the damage and see how bad the Shediem infestation is," Blaze answered. "So settle in, everyone—it's going to be a long trip."

They made it to La Grande without incident, stopping only to find an abandoned gas station that Gertie could use her magic on. Then Sergei took the wheel while Emma tried to get some sleep in the back next to Blaze. Their legs bumped together in a soothing rhythm, and the next thing she knew, she was blinking her eyes to adjust to the bright light in front of her. Blaze held a flashlight as he leaned forward, speaking quietly with the others. He pointed at a map held by Gertie, who hummed in disapproval.

"What's wrong? Where are we?" Emma asked.

"Utah," Blaze said distractedly. "There should be another fuel station in Ogden."

"Will we make it that far?" Sergei asked, looking down at the fuel gauge.

Blaze tilted his head side to side in contemplation. "I have an emergency fuel can in the back to get us to Salt Lake City if need be. It's out of our way, but it's guaranteed that there will be petrol there."

Gertie sighed as she folded up the map. "I'll take the next shift as well. I'm well rested."

"I can do it, Gertie, it's not—"

"Hush, young man. No arguments. You barely slept a wink." She glanced back at Emma. "You looked like you had a good rest though. Seven or so hours."

Emma's eyes bugged out of her head. "I slept that long?"

Blaze sent her a wry grin. "It was clearly needed, and not one nightmare."

Gertie's face fell. "You're still having those?"

Even Sergei's eyes lifted to the rearview mirror. Though she could barely make them out in the dim lighting, she could still see the concern that flashed in them.

Emma nodded, not bothering to hide the truth.

"You know, I can make you a sleeping draught," Sergei said. "I made them for your mother. She had nightmares too."

She shook her head, unable to speak against the tightening of her throat. Her mother no longer had nightmares—she didn't have dreams of any kind. They fell into a heavy silence, each of them keeping watch outside the windows.

The vehicle turned down an exit, winding through several abandoned cars. When they approached a small town, only the outlines of buildings could be seen in the dark. Not a single light indicated life within.

Perhaps the Shediem had already gotten to all of them. Emma shivered at the idea.

They slowed in the streets, the tension in the car suffocating. Sergei spotted a gas station on the edge of town and rolled to a stop. For a moment, they didn't move, searching for signs of movement—Shediem or human.

When it seemed like the coast was clear, Sergei unbuckled his seatbelt and opened his door. Blaze followed suit, casting Emma a sidelong glance just before she reached for her door.

"Stay inside the car," Blaze commanded.

"Not gonna happen," she replied before she jumped down, the sound of her shoes slapping the cracked pavement loud in the echoing silence. Gertie was the last to get out, and she sighed her disapproval.

Sergei lifted the pump and inserted the nozzle. Gertie raised her hands and a soft yellow glow danced from her palms to the pump, and at once, fuel audibly flowed into the tank. Emma let out a breath of relief, feeling her shoulder sag slightly.

Less than a second later, a growl rumbled behind her.

Blaze was in motion before she could react, blades drawn, the cold-soldier mask slipping into place. She whirled around, taking in the sight of the Nybbas as it raised its long spindly arms, its dark, soulless eyes locked on her.

The sound of blade severing bone and tendon filled her ears, followed by a shrill screech that no doubt summoned more of its kind. The oily spray of thick, black fluid coated her torso and the side of her face.

Already she felt the stir of her power rising through her—a welcome sensation.

More growls and hisses filled the darkness behind the tall creature. She leapt past it, dodging its amputated limbs to charge the approaching Shediem. It was difficult to make out the ranks of beasts with only the moonlight to show her enemies, but she sensed them. Whether it was a residual effect from the mark or her powers growing stronger, she didn't know, or care. She counted them under her breath.

"Six Nybbases, three Shax, two Drudes, four Nysroghs." The words had barely passed her lips when she ducked, sliding beneath the tangle of limbs that creaked, reaching for her. She ignored the burn of the pavement on the side of her leg, gripping two creatures at once. They hissed, blindly stabbing for her, but she maneuvered her body out of the way just in time.

Their energy was little, but it fuelled her.

The night came into focus.

Her body felt supercharged.

"Move, you useless oafs. I'll finish her."

It was a feminine voice, yet it grated on Emma's eardrums like the high-pitched whine of gears grinding together. She looked up just in time to see the Drude that had spoken raising a long, broad sword.

The final dregs of the Nybbases' powers flowed through Emma and their ashes rained down on her, sticking to her skin and hair. She grinned right before the blade cut through the air, and she rolled back. The clang of metal on road erupted less than a foot from her.

She leapt to her feet, still smiling at the ugly Shediem. The other creature closed in tighter, making it so her back was exposed. From the corner of her eye she saw Blaze carving his way to her.

The Drude swiped the long blade at Emma's chest, and she jerked back just in time to avoid it. Emma sensed the second Drude only a few feet behind her. Two Shax stood to her sides, caging her in.

With a deep breath, Emma drew her Shediem-roasting power into her center. Before Blaze could get too close, she released it.

The small pulse of energy shot out around her, and the strangled screams of each of the Shediem were all that remained—besides the clouds of ash that floated to the ground. It almost seemed too peaceful, too quick a death. She wanted to punish them for taking her mother from her.

Emma breathed in the remnants of their life-force in the air and the heat licked through her.

Blaze watched her carefully less than ten feet away, blade dripping gore. She offered him a small smile to show that she was herself, and he let his blade drop to his side. "We better get moving before more make an appearance."

Emma nodded and wordlessly followed him back toward the vehicle, stepping over the severed limbs and other body parts of more than one Nybbas.

Blaze took over driving through the night. Emma didn't bother sleeping, too pumped with adrenaline to be able to rest. They were quiet. Watchful.

All around, she felt their presence. She felt their numbers in the hundreds. But the Shediem that followed them did not attack. Either they knew it was fruitless, or they had received orders not to. Emma didn't think that was likely considering she'd betrayed her father. He undoubtedly wanted her dead.

So why weren't they attacking?

Once they crossed the border into Kansas, the road was blown away, the terrain too rough to carry on by vehicle. They pulled over and Gertie spelled the vehicle so no one could try to scavenge it for parts. When they disembarked the SUV, Emma felt at least a hundred sets of eyes on them, causing her to shiver.

The sky had gone from a subtle glow to looking as though it burned red and orange—like flames.

Still, the air was brisk. Not as cold as winter in Kansas should have been. An effect from the princes rising or something else?

Slowly, the morning sun lit the scorched earth. The closer they trekked into areas where civilization had once been, the more Emma felt her heart twist. There was barely anything left as proof. A blackened pair of children's shoes, small hunks of splintered wood…

There were a few people sorting through the wreckage. All of them were dirty and wore blank expressions. They hardly looked at Emma and the crew when they passed.

With each step they took, every mound of churned soil they climbed, the sense of dread grew inside her. Her shivers from the cold subsided after an hour of walking on foot and soon her body began to ache. Sergei and Gertie seemed to be in far worse condition, occasionally using their magic to heal blisters on their feet or push a cloud of warmth to stem their trembling.

"Save your magic," Blaze barked after the third time, making all three of them jump. "You don't know when you'll need it."

"Better to use a little magic than freeze to death," Sergei argued. "Not everyone here has the supernatural ability to survive the cold for so long."

Blaze didn't respond nor say anything at all for many hours, even when they stopped to consult their only map.

By the time the sun was at its peak in the sky, Emma barely felt the cold. Even the two Spellcasters seemed to have thawed slightly.

The Shediem that stalked them kept their distance, though they didn't hide. Their creepy eyes watched them.

Watched her.

By nightfall, the chill had returned and not even her heavy jacket could keep the cold away. They still had another half day of walking before they reached the prince's camp. It felt like a lifetime away.

"Let's stop here for the night," Blaze said, his tone more pliant than it had been earlier, though the tight set of his jaw was still apparent.

"Oh, thank goodness!" With a gust of breath Gertie sat heavily onto a large mound of earth. Sergei followed suit, wiping the sweat from his forehead.

The two of them set to work on conjuring a fire and logs out of thin air while Blaze started to unpack the two tents they'd carried. Fighting the sense of longing she felt when flames began to crackle nearby, Emma forced herself toward him and began setting up the second tent.

"You okay?" she asked Blaze in a low tone, trying to avoid drawing their companions' attention. The two of them hadn't had a proper conversation since she tried to disappear on her own.

He grunted noncommittally and Emma pursed her lips, watching him jam the poles right through the fabric then toss the mess to the ground. She crossed over to where he crouched and took the material from his hands before he could dislodge the pole. Finally his eyes met hers, and she felt her heart crack at the fear she saw in them.

"I can't lose you too," he said thickly.

She swallowed hard, feeling tears prick her eyes. "You aren't going to lose me."

He scoffed and shook his head. "You don't bloody know that, Emma. Dammit, why are you always so quick to rush into danger? Do you not have any self-preservation instincts?"

Emma couldn't stop the laugh that burst out of her, but she quickly squashed any further laughter when his steely eyes darkened. "Of course I do. You just don't trust that I can take care of myself." She kept her tone level. It wasn't an insult, it was simply a fact.

He shook his head, then checked the impaled tent lying on the uneven ground. With a deep breath he met her gaze again. "I do think you can take care of yourself, but the fate of the entire world rests on your shoulders. It makes me feel helpless. I want to shoulder as much of the burden as I can. It's not much, but I'll take whatever you give me."

She smiled before reaching up and cupping his scruffy cheek. "I can't do this without you." A knot formed in her throat as soon as she spoke the words. Even with his help—with everyone's help—it wouldn't be enough. She might not survive this war, but she couldn't bring herself to admit that out loud. Especially to Blaze, who looked like he could hear her thoughts. His cool grey eyes seemed filled with all the anguish Emma felt.

She cleared her throat then looked at the tent before helping him set it up. After retrieving her sewing kit, she sewed the hole closed. One of the two Spellcasters could make it waterproof.

They ate their meager rations, Sergei entertaining them by singing a classic Russian lullaby. It brought a smile to Emma's face, listening to the tune her mother had hummed to her throughout her childhood. She hadn't heard the words before now.

For a moment, she felt her mother's arms wrapped around her. An unexplainable sense of comfort blanketed her, warming her better than the fire.

She took the second watch so the others could get some rest. Only Sergei's snores and the Shediem that circled their camp kept her company, until an hour or so into her watch, when Blaze emerged from the tent.

"What are you doing?" she asked, brows raised in surprise.

"Can't sleep," was his only response before he sat beside her and stared into the dwindling flames.

"You should really try; we all need to be rested for tomorrow."

Blaze glanced sidelong at her. "If any of us needs to be a hundred percent, it's you."

She shrugged. "I'm not tired. I feel like I've been doing nothing but sleeping."

A rare smile curved his lips and it felt like warm sunshine—the sight was infectious. All too soon it faded, and with it, the warmth. "I'll take over your watch. Go get some more sleep."

Emma sighed. "I'd rather stay out here with you."

He nudged her shoulder. "Go on, I'll be here when you wake."

She wanted to argue. What better excuse would they get to have a moment alone? But as soon as she glanced toward the tent where Gertie slept soundly, she felt another wave of exhaustion wash over her. After pressing a soft kiss to Blaze's cheek, she rose and walked to the tent, turning to smile at him before disappearing inside.

His answering smile was forced, but she understood why.

Tomorrow she'd enter the lion's den.

EMMA

The four of them peered down the ridge where their encampment was to see a massive, crater-like hole punched in the earth where a city had once been, though there was no evidence of it any longer.

Shediem crawled all over the place. Hunting, no doubt. Humans dressed in the same pitiful rags she'd once worn trudged here and there, carrying anything from baskets of food to linens. Where they'd gone to get such things, Emma didn't know.

She stared down into the valley, trying to make out any familiar faces. Her chest felt like an icy hand had punched straight through it, and she sensed which prince was below before he stepped into view. He looked every bit the handsome, well-dressed prince, almost human in appearance except for his bloodred eyes.

On her left, she heard Gertie suck in a sharp breath, and on her right, Blaze's body went rigid.

"Asmodeus," she whispered. Her father.

From the distance of several football fields, his eyes met hers, and a slow smile spread across his sadistic face. For several beats no one breathed. Then with a simple hand gesture, every Shediem faced them too, eyes glowing and fangs bared.

Then they launched into movement, sprinting straight for them.

Sergei let loose a string of angry-sounding Russian. Then Blaze got hold of her arm and was dragging her back so fast, her feet scrambled beneath her.

"Stop!" she screamed.

Blaze didn't listen. The unholy snarls and taunts rising from the valley made her insides churn. At least a thousand Shediem were moments away from cresting the hill.

"Gertie, Sergei, a wall!" Blaze demanded.

The two Spellcasters spun, lifting their hands, and colored light streamed from their palms, creating a barrier around them.

Emma finally managed to get her legs righted, and jerked out of Blaze's grasp. "We can't outrun them, we have to fight," she said, bracing herself. The familiar tingling mixed with heat in her veins spread through her body, warming her.

Blaze pulled his sword from over his shoulder, watching the ridge with equal parts determination and hunger. There was no denying he craved the battle as much as she did. "Then we'll fight." To Sergei and Gertie he said, "When they get close enough, break the wall. We're going to be overwhelmed by the numbers so keep the majority away as long as possible."

"Got it," Gertie said.

"Will do," Sergei answered.

A sea of monstrous creatures flooded the horizon. Their cries of bloodlust were deafening. Emma smiled—giddiness at feeding on so much power made her want to lunge toward the beasts. But she remained rooted. She had to hold her position. Follow the plan.

The first wave hit the barrier and was thrown back with pained yelps, knocking down the second row too. While they got to their feet—some with long arms swaying and others brandishing weapons of their own—a steady sound of marching made all four of them turn.

Crash.

Crash.

Crash.

A wall of red enclosed the clearing from behind, trapping them. Emma's smile vanished. These were not Shediem. Even with their hoods pulled low over their faces, she knew they were Spellcasters.

"What in the—" Those were the only words from Sergei before a bright light shot at them.

With a boom that knocked the four of them to the ground, their protective barrier disintegrated. Then chaos was unleashed.

Emma's ears rang as she leapt to her feet. Sergei and Gertie stepped toward the line of Spellcasters while Emma and Blaze advanced on the Shediem.

They were outnumbered, she knew that. Exchanging a final glance with Blaze, they launched into the fold.

Emma sent a jet of power around her, which burned through the Shediem closest to her. Their energy filled her. She moved on, latching onto two dazed Shax and sucking them dry before they could blink.

She turned, finding an axe above her head preparing to come down, a grinning Drude holding the particularly brutal weapon. Emma jumped back just as the zing of the blade missed her chest. She launched her foot into the Shediem's face. Spinning again, she caught a Nybbas by its gangly arm and absorbed its power into herself. She used her new special abilities for herself, blinding those around her—forcing illusions into their minds. A sword swiped for her abdomen and she easily leapt out of the way, bringing her elbow down on the blade. Her foot met the meaty hand that held it and its owner shrieked when its fist, along with the sword, landed on the ground.

Her power grew with each Shediem she drained; so too did the wicked voice in her head, demanding more. She became faster, whirling and striking like a supernatural tornado. After a while, she forgot what her purpose was beyond the call for more power. *More. More. More.* Shediem crowded around her, falling almost as fast as they crowded in.

When she spun for her next prey she missed the glint of

metal coming her way, and it sliced into her side. With a gasp she clutched the wound. Blood hot and thick poured from it, but she didn't care.

Her eyes locked onto the creature responsible and she lunged with an inhuman snarl. Baring her teeth, she wrapped her fingers around the Drude's bony wrists, and realization dawned on its face a moment too late.

She pulled, tearing its arms from its body. They smacked into two feathered creatures that leapt for her before Emma grabbed the Drude's face. It fell to its knees, catlike eyes wide while power filled her. She laughed coldly, the wound on her side already knitted shut. The Shediem's ashes burst as another Drude stormed forward to take its place.

She barely had time to react, rolling to the side before the sword swung down. It was immediately clear this Drude was older, more experienced, from the frighteningly fast way it moved. Emma had the dagger at her hip, but she wanted to feel the Drude die in her hands.

Each time she dodged or tried to get close to the Shediem it seemed to anticipate her moves, landing an especially hard blow to her temple with its bony elbow. She went down hard, breaths coming in short bursts.

How long had they been fighting? It felt like hours and her strength was waning. The power she'd absorbed burned through her much quicker than it usually did. The throng of grey and bluish skin seemed endless. She cast out her power, a smaller radius than before, but it was enough.

Their power wasn't as strong as it would be directly from the source—a sip when she needed the full glass.

Through a gap, Emma caught a glimpse of Blaze fighting twenty yards away.

She was forcing herself back to her feet when a scream rang over the rocky clearing. A scream that sounded familiar.

Gertie.

Several shouts went out and then Blaze roared, "Gertie!"

Emma fought harder then, managing to land a blow on a Shax's chest that made it stumble. With a sweeping kick she sent it to the ground and pounced. The Shediem let out a gurgling laugh just before she siphoned the last of its power. What was so funny about dying, she wondered?

The heady rush was everywhere, and suddenly she tore through the masses, leaving a coating of ash in her wake. When at last she emerged, Blaze's blood-splattered face was filled with fury as he fought toward the monster standing serenely on top of a boulder.

What was he doing? He couldn't fight a prince!

Sergei sent blast after blast of magic at the wall of remaining Spellcasters. Briefly, Emma wondered if Adrianna was somewhere in the line of red cloaks.

She took off at a run for her father, leaping over the carnage Blaze's fury had wrought. "Asmodeus!" she screamed, never breaking stride.

The eerie man's face split with a smile. "Hello, daughter. How I've missed you."

In a blink he vanished from the boulder. She faltered, only for her father to appear directly in front of her, now donning metal armor that looked like scales. The tip of a massive sword pressed into her neck.

"Kneel, or I'll massacre your friends with nothing but a swipe of my hand."

Emma's chest rose and fell while she considered her options. Behind her, the Shediem closed in again. A shout came from behind her, causing her to look over her shoulder. The blade dug painfully into her skin, and she saw a blinding white light cocooning both Blaze and Sergei, lifting them into the air for Emma to see.

She swallowed hard. Where was Gertie?

Her gaze returned to the Shediem prince, rage spiking through her, blurring her vision. Slowly, she lowered herself to her knees while glaring up at the monster that was her father.

"I've been expecting you," the cruel prince crooned. His eyes flashed with hunger. Bloodlust.

He was going to kill her.

She didn't flinch when the blade withdrew from her throat, a trickle of blood—hot against her cool skin—soaking into her already torn sweater.

He raised the weapon high, preparing her for her execution. "It's a pity you didn't desire to serve me willingly."

With a swoosh, the sword cut through the air. She lifted her hands and sent another blast from her body. It tossed him back with a shout.

Her temples throbbed. Leaping to her feet, Emma whirled, preparing to kill her way through a horde of Shediem only for another blast of light to send them flying. She couldn't see where it'd come from.

Shouts rang out as a final burst of light sent the cloaked soldiers flying too. Blaze and Sergei fell to the snow, Blaze landing a little more gracefully than the Spellcaster did.

They rushed toward her, but Emma frantically searched for whoever had helped her. The answer came when the only standing cloaked person pushed back their hood—black, not red.

Adrianna's curly dark mane bounced free, and her friend's dark eyes landed on her. She inclined her head in a nod, but Emma was too stunned to move.

"Emma, we've got to go," Blaze shouted, though it sounded distant. He pulled her by the arm, leading her away.

She remained transfixed, both girls staring at the other. Emma couldn't believe it. Her friend had magic. She was here.

But why?

It was only a matter of seconds before other sounds trickled back in: shouts, the snarls and snaps of Shediem, her father's roaring commands.

"Come with us!" Emma called. But her friend just shook her head.

Emma's heart cracked when she was pulled away. They

sprinted away as fast as they could. Blaze had let go of her to take the limp form Sergei had been carrying, and Emma's heart froze.

Gertie, grey and lifeless, hung in his arms. He cradled her to his chest while they ran, the Shediem in desperate pursuit. Emma glanced over her shoulder, spying the prince stalking after them. A charred black hole in the center of his chest smoked. Her stomach churned at the realization that she could see *through* his body.

"There's nowhere you can run, Shediem-Slayer!" he bellowed, stumbling to his knees. The ground shook from the strength of his voice. "Your death is coming!"

They didn't stop, but the sounds of their pursuers eventually did. She couldn't believe they'd managed to escape. Her power hadn't killed him, but it had at least wounded him enough to let them get away.

Even after their surroundings fell silent, they didn't stop jogging their way back to the vehicle until it looked like Sergei would pass out. Their break was short-lived, and Sergei panted and wheezed beside them. But he didn't complain.

Blaze strained to continue carrying Gertie at their hurried pace, but from the hard determination in his expression, Emma didn't try to stop him.

When they made it back to their vehicle, they stood in silence, staring at the SUV. It felt harsh to flop Gertie's body down in the back seat, but what choice did they have? Blaze set her in the seat as gently as he could.

Emma reached for him, hoping to offer him comfort, but he jerked away from her touch before stalking a little ways from the vehicle. She watched him fall to his knees before he screamed a deafening, horrid sound that made Emma's gut clench.

Another body.

Another person she cared for, dead.

She shook her head, unable to stop her angry tears.

"I'll get him, Gertie. I'll kill him for you," she promised the lifeless woman through the window.

Emma dragged herself to her room, sore and mentally strained. She felt as if the threads of her being were still unraveling and only a few strands remained. Her eyes burned, already puffy from shedding so many tears on the trip back.

Gertie.

She was not only a powerful and gifted Spellcaster; she was also an immensely kind woman. She had children. Grandchildren. A family. And now she wouldn't be there to help protect them from what was coming.

The destruction wrought on the world thus far was proof enough that too many would die for this war. For a war that wasn't even theirs to fight.

Hot tears spilled over Emma's cheeks, burning the cool skin. It was a familiar sensation these days.

Pushing open her bedroom door, she froze.

The air inside was icy. Her breath plumed in front of her and her skin pebbled. Wrapping her arms around herself, she stepped inside and shut the door.

There on her bed, like a dark beacon, was the source of the cold. She walked closer, slowly. Hesitantly. Her breath came in ragged puffs.

Its power pulsed as she drew near. The glittering onyx stones crudely carved into the spires that made up the crown winked at her in the dim light. Black shadows rose from the crown and into the air above it. They swirled and melded into letters that became words.

The tears on Emma's face froze and her breath hitched.

The message from the King of Death stilled in the air for her to read:

For you, my queen. I'll see you soon.

Another crown. Another message. It wasn't just King

Nakosh's insistence that made her lunge for the black crown, but the rage that shot through her. Gertie was dead. Her mother was dead. How many more people that she cared about would die too in the sick game the Shediem kept playing with her?

The moment her fingers brushed the carved stones, ice shot up the crown, blanketing the black onyx in crystalized blue. It rushed up her hands and arms, but her flames leapt to her skin in defense, melting the ice with a long hiss.

Then she heard his voice in her mind, as clear as if he stood behind her. *Just to give you a little taste of what to expect. You may wield flames now, but when you take your place in Sheol, only ice and cold will be your constant companions.*

Emma whirled around, making sure the king of Sheol wasn't truly standing in her bedroom, but she was alone. With a stunning black crown that matched the gaping darkness in her chest where her heart had once been.

BLAZE

They held a small funeral for Gertie. He was so damned sick of funerals already—it seemed nearly everyone was grieving someone these days. Her sisters' grief suffocated the place. Gertie had left information on how to contact her children for such events, but that was before the Earth had become home to the five princes of Sheol.

Now, the best he could do was send two of his guys to track down at least one of them, to let them know their mother had died. Not many had known Gertie as well or as long as he and Axel had, but she was the kind of woman that everyone adored. If for no other reasons than her decadent cooking and compassionate heart.

His throat was thick and he swallowed hard, coming back to his surroundings when his uncle called for a vote on Axel's trial.

"All those in favor for getting this done with today?"

His uncle and nearly every other leader raised their hands.

Blaze's fists clenched under the table. "I buried the woman that was like a second mother to my brother and me only yesterday. Can I not get a goddamned minute to come up for air?" Axel had been allowed to attend the funeral—in shackles no less—but at least he'd had his brother with him.

Silas shook his head, adamantly. "This needs to be done with, boy, and you know it! My goddaughter is heartbroken over her broken engagement *yet again*."

Blaze's answering laugh was harsh and bitter. "I stopped being a boy the moment my mother died. And any tears Emerelda sheds is for the loss of the extravagant party she won't get to throw, not because she loved my brother."

Silas went from red to purple in a click, seeming to swell with indignation. But slowly, he let out his anger in a huffed breath. "Regardless, the motion passes. Axel's fate will be decided this afternoon."

Even though Blaze wanted to lash out in retribution for Silas's betrayal, he couldn't afford to lose focus right now. He had a matter of hours to prove his brother's innocence. It wouldn't be much time, but he just needed to keep his brother alive until he could sort the mess out.

Vaguely he heard his uncle speaking again, but Blaze tuned him out. He needed to get to the cells and talk to his brother. Gertie would have slapped him silly if she could see how distracted he was now. The thought almost made him smile.

"I think Beleez is a safe bet," Emma agreed, her voice harder than he had ever heard it.

His gaze snapped to her, attention back in the room.

"If I can dangle myself in his direction just enough, maybe he'd offer an invitation to his territory. I can pretend to want to get in contact with my father again or something."

Blaze made a choked noise in the back of his throat. "Are you insane?" he snapped. She met his stare, eyes burning with green light. "Did you learn nothing from yesterday? Your father wants you dead!" He softened his tone when she no longer seemed to be looking at him, but through him. "I know you're in pain, Emma, you've lost your mum and now Gertie is gone. But throwing yourself to the wolves is only going to ensure I have to grieve *your* death too." His voice broke, Adam's apple bobbing.

She blinked, seeming to return to herself. "Do me a favor, Blaze," she whispered. "Don't cry for me when I'm gone. It's a waste of time." Then she met everyone else's gazes before turning and striding from the room.

His blood pounded in his ears, and he shook his head. But he couldn't chase after her now and tell her just how foolish she was to think he wouldn't shed a tear for her. And that she would die. He wouldn't allow it. He had to stay and make sure Silas didn't try to pull any other wild ideas from his top hat.

"Personally, I think that's a great idea," Silas drawled. "Much better than the last attack."

Blaze's fists clenched so hard his knuckles cracked.

"We cannot offer up our greatest weapon as a sacrifice, with no backup," Dominic said from further down the table. His friend held Blaze's gaze for several moments—a promise to him as well as a warning to the rest of the room.

No one objected, though Silas was opening his mouth to do so until Dominic folded his arms over his bulky chest and leveled a challenging glare in his direction.

"Fine." His uncle rolled his eyes. "Five men. Don't forget that we need all the help here we can get."

"Ten," Blaze countered. "And I'll need Taryn and Derrik." Silas sputtered until Blaze abruptly cut him off. "Volunteers to accompany us on our mission to South America?"

Dominic's hand rose first, followed by two others.

Blaze nodded. "I'll ask the others. Dom, can you get the plane prepped? We leave tonight."

That gave him just enough time to try to stop his brother's execution and convince Emma not to so flippantly offer up her life to every powerful Shediem they crossed.

For some reason, he had the feeling the former would be easier.

Blaze halted outside his brother's cell, arms folded across his chest. Axel lay on the hard, stone floor with one arm thrown over his eyes. Blaze wasn't fooled into believing his brother was asleep, however. His chest was still, holding his breath.

Unwilling to break the silence, Axel finally turned his head, his arm falling onto his abdomen instead.

"Evening," he drawled. The gaunt, sunken look of his face had only worsened since yesterday, which Blaze was sure could be, in part, attributed to Gertie's loss. The frailty of his brother's usually strong form still made his gut twist.

Something was not right.

Possession?

Magic of some kind?

He planned to find out.

"Good to see you're still in such good spirits, considering your execution is meant to be decided in two hours."

His pale blue eyes widened imperceptibly. "Well…good. Has Emerelda asked about me?"

Blaze cocked his head in silent contemplation. "When did she last visit you?"

Axel scrubbed a hand down his face, the coarse hair on his chin sounding like velcro. "I saw her at Gertie's…" He swallowed hard. "I saw her yesterday, but we didn't talk."

Blaze nodded. He hadn't let his brother out of his sight for even a moment yesterday. "And before then?"

"Uhh," Axel mused aloud. "I guess the day after I was thrown in here."

"What did she say to you?"

His brother's features darkened. "Why is that any of your business?"

Anger rose inside him so quickly, he couldn't control it. Blaze shot forward, banging his palms against the bars, sending a bellow through the chamber. The prisoner next to them, Oliver Phillips, groaned before sitting up. "I'm trying to save your life, you idiot!" Blaze snarled, making his brother flinch.

Odd. He's never flinched away from me before.

"I don't see how that's relevant," Axel said calmly. Then he sighed. "She said to be strong and that she loved me." He winced, holding a hand to the front of his head. "This damn headache won't go away."

Blaze exhaled his frustration. "I'll get you some aspirin later. Now think: did anyone give you *anything* the day before or the morning we left for New Orleans? Run through everything you remember."

Axel hissed, gripping his head with both hands. "I already told Silas everything. It was all normal. I had breakfast with Emmy, I went to training, but then I felt sick so I took a nap. After dinner, we went over wedding preparations and then I went to bed. That morning, I packed, had breakfast, kissed Emmy, and then we left. That's it."

Blaze chewed on his cheek for a moment, thinking. "Who did you train with?"

Axel's jaw visibly tightened. "A bunch of the guys."

"Was he there?" Blaze gestured to the cell next to him. Oliver swayed, looking in worse shape than Axel did before he curled up in a ball again, facing them.

Axel paused before grinding out the word "Yes."

Blaze kicked the bars of Oliver's cell, forcing him to sit up again.

He moaned a pained sound. "What?"

"Walk me through everything that happened before and after you went to the training room."

"I don't remember," he sobbed.

"Bollocks! I think you're hiding something, Phillips. What is it?"

"Nothing!" the man wailed.

Blaze grimaced. He was definitely hiding something. That, or he was spelled to forget. Without a second glance he tore up the stairs, sprinting for Sergei's quarters. He banged on the door unceremoniously, only ceasing when it was pulled open, out of his reach.

Sergei looked alarmed, his blond hair rumpled and the lines

on his face indicating he'd been sleeping.

"I need you to come with me," Blaze said.

To his credit, Sergei didn't argue. He simply nodded and shut the door behind him. His clothing was wrinkled, the sleeves rolled up to his elbows and his bottom partially untucked. But Blaze didn't say anything as he led the way back into the basement.

Sergei faltered on the landing, looking apprehensively at the cells. "There's magic down here."

Blaze nodded. "I know. What I don't know is are both of them spelled, or just one?"

With a sharp exhalation through the nose, he walked closer, stopping in front of his brother's cell.

"Brought in backup, did you?" Axel asked mockingly before returning his gaze to the ceiling.

"Why didn't you send for Taryn or even Constance? As coven leaders, they're far stronger in their magic than I am," Sergei said softly before moving to stand in front of Oliver's cell.

"Because Taryn is kind of a loose cannon and Constance just lost her sister. I didn't want to ask any more of her right now."

Without looking at Blaze, Sergei nodded his understanding. "What's his name?"

"Oliver Phillips," Blaze supplied.

"Oliver," Sergei called to the now-sleeping prisoner. When he didn't stir, Blaze stepped closer.

"He started coughing right after you left," Axel said. "Choking on his spit or something. Hasn't said anything since."

Blaze's heart whipped into a frenzy as he fumbled for the correct key, then slid it into the lock. He pulled the door open, ignoring the echoing creak as he shuffled inside. The man's frame was still.

Blaze touched his shoulder, attempting to turn him.

His skin was like ice.

Flopping him onto his back, Blaze knew before he saw the ring of blue and purple staining the skin around Oliver's lips that he was dead.

Frozen in place, he stared down at the man who'd been alive only ten minutes ago. Possibly even less.

Sergei entered the cell cautiously to glance at the dead man. When Blaze glanced at him, he nodded, confirming what Blaze suspected: the magic that had been used so Oliver didn't share any useful information had "disposed" of the threat. Now there was a corpse who'd supposedly died of asphyxiation.

Axel now stood with his face between the bars, observing the dead man too.

"Why didn't you call out for help?" Blaze asked.

He scoffed. "Who would have heard me? That guy cried for help every night, all night long. He kept begging to be freed, saying he'd been promised that."

Blaze pondered that. It made sense with how out of his mind Oliver had been that he'd want to be released from the cells, but who had promised him that he would be freed? Did he mean when Silas had said that if he provided useful information he'd be released, or something else entirely?

His gaze fell back to the lifeless man who likely hadn't done anything wrong besides be in the wrong place at the wrong time. Now, whatever information he'd held onto was lost.

Blaze shook his head. The evidence that Axel was innocent was compelling enough for him, but would it be for the council of leaders?

Turning to Sergei, he asked, "What do you think?"

The Spellcaster crouched, careful not to touch the man while taking in every detail. "He was spelled. I can smell it on him, but it's faint. There was likely a word or a phrase that had been triggered to kill him when spoken. Something that was indicting to whomever placed the spell."

Blaze shook his head. "The only Spellcaster here at the time was Gertie."

"Is it possible he left the grounds at some point?"

"It's possible," he confirmed, nodding. "But highly unlikely."

"That's enough for reasonable doubt." Sergei stood. After a moment, he fixed his attention on Axel, who looked on with mild interest. "There's something deeper in you. Not demonic...I can't put my finger on it, but it's like..."

"Like what?" Blaze prompted, feeling his agitation grow. What little he had to combat the charges against his brother might be enough to prevent an immediate execution, but he likely wouldn't be leaving this cell.

Sergei turned to him instead. "Like a poison."

Blaze paced in the conference room like a caged tiger, prowling back and forth, likely wearing a groove into the carpet. No doubt Gertie would tell him off later—

He stopped abruptly, the cold punch of grief hitting him square in the chest.

Gertie wouldn't tell him off ever again. Or fret over his hair or bake him cookies with the first snowfall of the season. He'd never again make her laugh or be a part of her life, because she was dead.

While he struggled to draw in a full breath, several leaders stalked into the room and took their place around the table.

Emma strode in with Sergei and just her presence was like a balm on a wound. Blaze offered her as much of a smile as he could manage, though he was sure it appeared to be more of a grimace. Either way, she returned the gesture before taking a seat two chairs down from his with Sergei between them.

Silas filed in with the rest of the council next, looking irritated. "What is it, nephew? The trial is meant to start in an hour."

Dominic led a cuffed and chained Axel to the front of the room, stopping against the wall behind Blaze.

"I have evidence that suggests my brother has been framed for a crime he did not commit."

When everyone was seated, including his bull-headed uncle, they all waited for him to continue—though Silas's face slowly turned a nice beetroot color.

"Without my primary Spellcaster, I asked the help of Sergei to confirm the use of magic."

Protests rose, but Blaze silenced them all with a hand.

"Oliver Phillips, who had claimed my brother gave him a charm to weaken the wards, was very much alive and out of his mind when I visited the cells only an hour ago. His behavior indicated a level of interference with his choice of words, so I sought out the help of Sergei to see if he could break the enchantment. However, when the two of us arrived at his cell not even ten minutes later, Oliver was dead. Cause of death would appear to be asphyxiation, but Axel claims that Oliver regularly called out to be freed, saying that he had been promised his freedom. By whom, you ask? My guess is whoever spelled him to begin with."

Silas stood, smirking. "That's all just hearsay. There's no proof."

"I smelled the magic on him," Sergei interjected, rising to his feet as well. Emma smiled up at him with pride. "It was old, but my guess is that the spell included a self-destruct, meant to silence the victim should any line of questioning get around the enchantment. A fail-safe, so to speak."

"Gertie was the only Spellcaster here at the time, and Axel didn't leave the compound without me at any point in the past few weeks. It's next to impossible that he could have been spelled without my knowing. Oliver Phillips, however, was reported leaving the grounds nearly a dozen times in the past week, and he was always alone," Blaze finished.

Murmurs spread around the table, growing in volume until Silas scoffed, loudly. "Still, this proves nothing. Axel must have been involved in some way, or else why would the ingredients for the charm have been found in his room?"

"They could have been planted there. Besides, the ingredients themselves won't automatically weaken the wards—they have to be bound by a Spellcaster, causing the ingredients to work together to become the charm used to create holes within protections. And again, Gertie had no involvement with that."

"That we know of," Silas spat, and Blaze was around the table before he knew what he was doing.

He gripped his uncle by the lapels, forcing their faces only inches apart. "You will not speak ill of the only woman that has cared for me and my brother these past decades. Just because she was a Spellcaster does not mean she was not loyal. You cannot blame everyone else for your inability to gain anyone's loyalty or affections."

His uncle, for once, was speechless.

Emma's sweet scent reached Blaze a moment before her dainty hand rested on his back. Centering him. Comforting him.

He released his uncle, turning to address the room. "I call to a vote the action decided upon for Andrew Thomas—"

Emerelda burst into the room right at that moment, causing all heads to swivel in her direction.

"Wait! I was told the trial was in an hour. No one told me it had been moved up." Tears streamed down her face, and her bright blue eyes locked with Axel's.

"This is a private council meeting," Blaze said. "You may wait outside the room."

She sniffled. "I want to be here for him…in case…in case…" She sobbed into her hands, still standing in the doorway.

Emma's body was tense at his side, but he didn't spare her a glance.

When Emerelda glanced up, her eyes and Axel's connected.

Then Blaze heard his brother's snarl.

Whirling around, he saw his brother's face screwed up in animalistic fury as he lunged for Emma. Axel's hands went around her throat and they both fell to the ground. Blaze's utter stunned confusion evaporated a second later, and he and Dominic moved at the same time. His friend pulled at Axel's degenerating body while Blaze fought to keep Emma away, but his brother's grip was unnaturally strong—even for him.

Her eyes were wide and she gaped in shock, her face red.

Dominic grabbed a chair and sent it crashing against Axel's skull. He went limp, slumping to the floor beside Emma.

She gasped, desperately trying to draw in air. Blaze pulled her up, crushing her to him in a strong hug, and she immediately pushed against him.

Realizing she had just been choked and likely didn't want to feel any sort of restriction of her person, he released her. "Are you all right?" he asked.

She nodded but didn't speak. Discoloration already bloomed on the slim column of her neck, and a hot searing anger burned in his veins. Why had Axel attacked her unprovoked? And why did he wait? If he'd been desperate to kill her, why not attack her the moment he walked through the door?

Nothing made sense.

Blaze looked to Dominic, before shifting his attention to the doorway. Emerelda, hands clasped over her mouth, stood with wide, tear-filled eyes. "Is he okay?" She hiccupped a sob. "Oh they'll surely kill him now! My Andrew! My love!" She spun on her heel and ran from the room, her wailing echoing through the house.

Blaze might have won everyone over and helped free his brother until this happened. Now, it was almost guaranteed that Axel would be put to death. Not for attacking Emma, but for seeming unhinged. As his uncle often said, "Any chink in one's armor is a weakness you cannot afford."

His brother was a weakness.

But Blaze didn't care. "Take him back to his cell and make sure he's secured," he instructed Dominic, who nodded before hefting his brother up.

Getting to his feet, Blaze scanned the faces shaken with

shock and fear. "What you just witnessed is evidence of Spellcaster magic at play. I beg you to allow me time to prove his innocence before you cast judgment. Allow me to find whoever is responsible so that we might bring them to justice instead."

"You cannot be ser—" Silas began, but Blaze shot him a look that had the words dying on his tongue.

"All in favor of granting me a two-week reprieve to find the person responsible for this mess? If by the end of those two weeks, the culprit is not found…" He heaved a steadying breath, then forced the rest of the words out. "I will submit to whatever form of justice you decide upon."

Emma's hand rose, though he could sense her reluctance. Sergei's followed, and one by one half a dozen hands went up. Majority ruled.

Hope flared in his chest, and he released a sigh of relief. "Thank you." Those were the only words he spoke before grabbing Emma's hand and leading her out of the room and up to hers.

When the door was shut and it was just the two of them, he brought his lips down on hers as gently as he could. When he pulled away, he bent at the knees, lowering himself to examine the bruises forming on her neck. They were black and purple, stirring a sickness in his gut that churned with anger.

If his brother wasn't under some kind of spell or influence, he'd march down into the basement and break Axel's nose a second time.

"I'm okay," she rasped.

He frowned. "You don't sound okay."

With a shrug, she said, "He's not himself."

Blaze swallowed hard. "I know." He ran a hand through his hair, tugging at the knotted strands hard. The bite of pain helped clear his mind. "We will go to Brazil, attempt your plan, and then be back here searching for clues as to who messed with my brother."

She shook her head, a sad smile curving her lips. "You should stay here and look for leads. I'll be okay without you."

"I won't even consider letting you face a prince without me," he retorted. If she lost herself to the high that the power gave her, she might become a danger to his people. With him there, he could reach her. He would always try. The growing connection they had—his increasing affection for the girl—made it impossible to allow her to face Beleez on her own. "I know it's really bad timing, but there's a war approaching. The Shediem cannot be allowed to terrorize the Earth. As much as I love my brother, my very existence demands that I protect the Earth first. He would want that too."

She reached up, cupping his cheek with her soft, warm palm. "We'll do it all together." Standing up on her tiptoes, she let her lips brush against his, sparking an intoxicating sensation that made him crave more. But he forced himself to pull away.

"Pack lightly. We will leave as soon as possible."

She waited for his knock on her door twenty minutes later. After the bruising on her neck faded to a putrid yellow-and-green combo, he felt the weight of guilt lift slightly. He should have been faster. He should have pulled her back and kept her safe. She bore the marks of his failure, and they faded all too quickly. It felt like an excuse to dismiss the attack. Once the bruises faded completely, there would no longer be physical evidence of his shortcomings. But he would not soon forget.

"Stop looking at me like that. I'm fine, really. Strangely enough, I've grown accustomed to people trying to kill me."

Her comment was meant for levity, but it served only to darken his mood further. With a sigh, she steered him out the door, and they made their way down to the foyer.

The human, Breanna, held her squirming infant while speaking softly with Dominic.

When Emma caught sight of her, she ran down the remaining steps toward her friend, heedless of the conversation she had been having with Dominic.

His friend reluctantly bowed to both girls and stepped away, intercepting him on the final step. "Plane is fueled and ready."

Blaze nodded. "We'll have to bring as much food as we can from the kitchens, given our numbers. Gertie usually did that…" His words dissolved on his tongue.

Emma turned, no doubt hearing him even from twenty feet away. "Breanna and I will go scrounge up supplies," she suggested.

The human nodded, glancing again at Dominic, her cheeks flushing pink. Blaze fought a smile when his friend's gaze followed her until well after both women had disappeared from view.

"It's interesting how fate decides to make fools of us all, eh?" Blaze said.

His friend was silent for several moments. "A man struck with Cupid's arrow will go into war fighting to protect his loved ones, but also with the hope of something to return to. If anything, I consider myself lucky."

Love. That was quite the declaration. It'd only been a few weeks since Breanna was given a new life at his manor. Already his friend was in love. It seemed there was a lot of that going around lately.

He thought of the strong, powerful girl with wild auburn curls and depthless emerald eyes who had captured his attention from the moment he'd laid eyes on her. And how her bravery and sometimes stubborn will had endeared her to him.

Did he love her?

His heart didn't take long to answer that question. He did love her.

Her compassion, her tenacity. Even the darkest parts of her, he still found that he couldn't help but love her more for them.

Blaze clapped Dominic on the shoulder. "Yes indeed. We are the luckiest of men."

The roar of the engine dulled the moment the door was shut.

Blaze was the pilot this time, not trusting anyone else to navigate the harsh winter conditions.

Emma sat in the seat beside him, awed, as they flew over snow-covered mountains and into the clouds.

"How long is the flight?" she asked once they reached cruising altitude.

"Twelve hours. We'll be landing about a day's hike from the blackout area."

Her eyes were wide. "Will we have enough fuel for that?"

He nodded. "Without any extenuating circumstances, we'll be fine."

She worried her bottom lip. "Are you going to fly the whole time?"

"I'll switch with Dominic for the last half. We'll all need to get some rest for what's to come."

She nodded, turning in her seat to glance back at everyone else, who were no doubt settling in for a nap.

"Try to get some sleep. I'll wake you before we land."

"I'll stay up with you. I'm not tired."

Blaze didn't argue, and after an hour of nothing more than idle chatting, she'd finally fallen asleep.

When Dominic came to relieve him six hours in, Blaze took out a flannel blanket from an overhead compartment and covered Emma before taking his place in one of the chairs further back.

Whether it was from the grief weighing heavily on him or just the fact that he hadn't slept well in days, sleep claimed him almost instantly.

The touch that woke him was feminine. His eyes were sore when they opened, revealing Emma leaning over him. She smiled slightly—a nervous smile. Her hand cupped his face and before she could react, he pulled her onto his lap. His lips claimed hers in a hard, urgent kiss. She responded in kind, threading her fingers through his hair and pulling him closer still.

The plane jostled them, but their desperate embrace was unaffected by the movement. When at last he broke the kiss, her lips were red and swollen, but pulled into a wide smile that made her eyes sparkle.

"I should wake you up like that more often," she said breathlessly.

He couldn't help but laugh, only for the gravity of what was to come to hit him full force and knock away any traces of levity.

A glance outside along with the adjusting pressure in his ears told him they'd just broken through the thick grey clouds. They'd be landing soon.

"You should buckle up." He unlatched his seatbelt and stood in one swift move before scooping her up and depositing her in his empty seat.

"Still warm," she commented with a laugh.

He didn't smile; instead he pressed another kiss to her forehead. "We're nearly there." To the rest of the rousing soldiers and Spellcasters he said, "Get ready." Then he strode for the cockpit.

"Need me to put her on the ground?" he asked Dominic, who gripped the controls hard enough for his knuckles to turn white.

"I've got it." His friend flexed his fingers, loosening his hold before rolling his shoulders back.

"Rough night?" he asked.

"The bloody sky is filled with Veemuris."

Blaze's brows rose. The large, bat-like creatures were rarely seen. Though there had been recorded instances during old wars where the sky filled with them, only for them to rain down on soldiers and tear them apart, leaving fields littered with nothing but bones. It was among the myths of his kind that only the king of Sheol himself could release them.

Perhaps he had.

"I don't see any now," Blaze said, his gaze scouring the black sky. Their lights were bright, but still it was difficult to make out any shapes around them.

"Hopefully they're far behind us. I'd hate to face the damned creatures the second we land."

"They didn't damage anything, did they?" He sat forward, trying to glimpse the dashboard.

"No. We got lucky, I think."

Blaze sat back and fastened his seatbelt. "We'll see as soon as we land if luck is really on our side."

The ground came into view. The same sort of destruction as they had seen in Kansas lay beneath them, with the ground rolling in an outward pattern, like a massive fist had struck the earth. Towns and cities were demolished with little to nothing left to show for their existence.

The lower they got to the ground, the more Blaze began to wonder how they'd ever land.

"Looks like this is going to be a bit bumpy," Dominic said dryly, maneuvering toward the only space that was relatively flat. It certainly wasn't a runway, but it was all they had.

"Just don't break my damned plane," Blaze grumbled, bracing himself when the landing gear lowered.

The second the wheels hit rocky, bumpy earth, the plane groaned and rattled, shaking them up like a soda can while the engine roared its reverse thrust. Gritting his teeth, Blaze dug his fingers into the armrests while several people in the back shouted. The plane bounced high before crashing back down. The aircraft eventually slowed, and rolled over the uneven terrain with greater ease.

Dominic flashed him a smile. "Great landing, eh?"

Blaze released his breath and ran a hand through his hair, smoothing it back from his face before unlatching his seatbelt and heading for Emma. Her eyes were wide, the grip on her own seat bloodless.

Blaze tucked back her curls and pressed a kiss to her lips.

"It's over. We're safe."

She nodded wordlessly.

A feminine snort drew his eyes farther, to Taryn, who unbuckled herself and stood. "As if I'd ever let myself die in a plane crash."

He shook his head and looked back to Emma, noticing her face was even paler than it had been several seconds ago.

"Suit up, soldier," he said, forcing a smile. "We're going demon hunting."

EMMA

B y the time they disembarked from the plane, strapped with weapons and each hauling a backpack, Emma felt nothing but relief that they'd made it to Brazil in one piece.

Blaze didn't waste any time in reiterating the plan. "Keep together for this part and stay vigilant."

They took off at a light jog with only a single lantern to help guide their feet. Emma found herself tripping over the craggy, broken earth on more than one occasion, but each time she vaulted forward, Blaze caught her by the bicep and righted her.

She quickly became thankful for her supernatural stamina, especially when the Spellcasters' breathing grew louder. Sergei kept pace with them well enough, though she could tell after two hours that he was flagging.

Blaze called for a quick break to allow everyone to catch their breath and drink some water from their limited supply.

"We need to keep going," he said after only ten minutes of rest, and they were back to traversing the hellish landscape. But the sky began to fill with an early morning glow. It wasn't long before the sun peered over the horizon as though it were a perfectly ordinary day.

Even with the earth under attack—with millions of people dead—the sun rose, painting the sky in rich, luscious colors.

How did the universe stand to create beauty in the midst of terror?

But perhaps that's why, Emma mused. *Finding beauty and peace offers hope to those that feel unable to go on.*

They slowed to a stop hours later, and even Blaze's breathing was labored. She let herself drop to the ground, leaning on her hands as she fought to catch her breath.

Others buckled too, the sound of their exhaustion mixing with the rushing of blood in her ears.

"Ugh, are we there yet?" Taryn complained from several feet away.

Someone gave a harsh bark of laughter, but no one said any more for several minutes. Emma wrestled a protein bar from her pack, unwrapped it, and stared at it, wondering if it was even worth it since she'd probably throw it up anyway.

Slowly, she managed a few bites, then a few more. By the time Blaze got to his feet, she'd swallowed the last bite. She desperately wanted to chug more water, but she needed to save as much as possible.

He looked to her, holding her gaze. His eyes held all the strength and reassurance she needed. "Are you ready?"

Emma took a deep breath and got to her feet. She nodded, before swallowing hard and glancing over her shoulder at Sergei walking toward her.

He pulled her into a tight hug, and she felt her resolve grow. "Go give them hell, girl," he whispered.

Emma's lips lifted in the faintest of smiles before she turned back to Blaze. He held her face in his hands gently, searching. To spot the fear she had stuffed down deep? She hoped he couldn't see it. Finally, he kissed her, and she fought the urge to deepen it in front of so many people.

With a nod, she stepped back, and Blaze gave the order. Ten Giborim fanned out behind her, Blaze and the Spellcasters somewhere behind her as she began to jog again. She hoped the protein bar wouldn't find its way back up.

Emma didn't bother to look behind her to see if anyone was there, because before long, it was only the sound of her footsteps and her breathing with her. The sun had warmed the early afternoon, and combined with her exertion, sent sweat trickling down her forehead, burning her eyes.

A high-pitched wail caused her to stumble to a stop. She looked skyward, trying to locate the source of the noise, but couldn't spot anything. There was only the pale blue sky and the odd, lazy-drifting cloud.

Her brows furrowed but she shuffled forward again, wondering if dehydration had already set in, causing delusions.

Another sharp cry pierced the near silence. Then another.

Emma looked up again, this time to see a black cloud move in front of the sun. The screeches grew louder, and she realized it wasn't a cloud. They were birds of some kind.

The creatures barreled right for her, their long wingspans kicking Emma's heart into high gear. She took off at a sprint, glancing behind when their screams grew deafening.

There were at least twenty huge bats with visible fangs and clawed feet. What the hell were they? She'd never seen bats that big before.

When the first one collided with her back, it sent her sprawling to the ground, mouth full of dirt. It grabbed her hair, whether with its feet or its fangs she wasn't eager to find out.

Emma rolled to her back hard, trying to knock the creature loose. It wailed directly in her ear and she winced, but it scrambled back from her, disorientated. The winged animal had solid black eyes to match its black leathery skin.

The others dove for her face and she batted them away. A trickle of Shediem energy lit up her veins and her eyes widened—they were from Sheol.

Knowing how to kill the nasty beasts, Emma grabbed for them when the next wave of assault came, though their sharp fangs bit into her flesh. She cried out as they surrounded her, tearing through clothing and ripping her skin.

With bloodied fists, she knocked each of them off her, only to grip them and suck their feeble energy away. They died still shrieking, though her ears were ringing so loud she could barely register their sounds. With an explosion of dust, their bodies were no more.

The last two she gripped at the same time, their teeth still buried in her bicep and calf.

"Take me to your master!" she demanded. When nothing happened, she ripped them from her flesh with a wince. "Take me to Prince Beleez."

Still they didn't react, their jaws snapping and their claws scratching, trying to make purchase. Emma gritted her teeth and sucked away their energy in an instant, letting the ash fall on her.

A man appeared draped in a silver brocade robe, standing several yards away. His jaw was sharp, his eyes red. Straight golden hair fell past his shoulders.

"Emma," he purred, lips curved into a sensual smile. "Daughter of the Prince of Wrath. Shediem-Slayer."

"That would be me," she answered.

He looked around. "There was no need to kill my Veemuris. Although, unfortunately for you, they're spawned from ashes."

Emma glanced down right as her hands began to itch. The blackened ashes smeared on her skin began to move. Horror struck her and she wiped at the soot, trying to scrub it off her faster.

It fell to the ground like grains of sand, rolling and sliding over the broken earth to form small piles. One by one they rose in the air, taking shape. Black eyes blinked into existence, all of them looking from her to the prince and back.

Beleez stepped toward her, forcing her to focus on him instead of the prehistoric-looking bats. She saw the caution in the tense set of his shoulders. "What brings you to my kingdom?" he asked.

She kept her stance attack-ready, watching the prince and the Veemuris with caution. "I-I need to speak with my father."

The prince raised a pale, slender brow.

Licking her lips to wet them, she didn't have to pretend to be nervous. When the prince stopped just beyond her reach, she saw that his eyes were not wholly red. A thin black slit ran through the center, giving him an even more wild and animalistic quality. Her heart raced and her palms were damp. She rubbed them on her jeans, still feeling the itch as though something moved beneath her skin. "The Giborim want me dead the second they've used my powers against you all."

The Veemuris surrounding the prince stirred. A few emitted shrill screeches, but he held up a hand to silence them. His smile grew. "You've seen the error of your ways, have you?"

She couldn't decide if his tone was genuine since he tended to sound mocking in everything he said.

"More like, I've accepted what my role in all of this is to be. If the Shediem are to rule over the humans then I will scorch the betraying, backstabbing angel-spawns. Every single one." She lowered herself to one knee, feeling like she'd choke on her next words as flashes of her kneeling before her father filled her mind. Her shoulder gave a phantom twinge in remembrance of the mark he'd forced on her. "I will serve my father and the king as they see fit." Her eyes never lowered, never left his. She wouldn't give him or his minions the opportunity to strike without her knowing.

Beleez cocked his head to the side, studying her. "Asmodeus has ordered you to be executed instantly."

Emma swallowed hard, fingers tingling with power that swirled inside her like a hungry beast. She kept it leashed, containing her own personal demon—a demon of death. Only it wasn't as the Mark of Fallen Flame had been, like a separate entity inside her. This was just the darkest parts of herself charging to the surface at even the faintest hint of blood.

"However," he said, stilling her heart, "should you swear loyalty to *me*, I will let you live. My brothers will not touch you if you are mine."

She blinked up at him, blood rushing in her ears so loud she was certain the prince could hear it too. "As your soldier?"

His grin turned wicked and he took another step toward her. "As my bride."

The air left her in a rush, her mouth agape.

Perhaps her shock had made him bolder, or the fact that she hadn't refused him immediately made him comfortable with being reckless. Whatever the case, he offered a hand to her.

Foolish, she thought, letting her lips split and bare her teeth in a vicious smile. Then she lunged.

His eyes widened, grin vanishing, and realization hit him a fraction of a second before her skin met his.

A brush—just a simple brush with her skin and he disappeared, yet his power snapped her control. The beast inside her was awakened and ravenous. She spun with a snarl, searching for the prince.

His power came first. Heady, washing over her like a gentle wave—Beleez.

She turned, finding him behind her, too far to touch.

His smile returned. Kind. Loving.

She wanted to run to him. To love him. Serve him.

"My prince," she whispered, dropping in one swift movement to press her forehead to the rocky earth.

Long, slender fingers slipped through her hair, his touch a soothing balm to the way her heart pounded. Distantly she felt the desire to wrap her hands around his throat and drain him of every ounce of his energy—

No, why would I do that? I love Beleez. His face was sculpted by dark angels. Everything about him is beautiful.

His soft laugh rumbled through her like silk caressing her insides.

"I don't see why Wrath had such a hard time taming the mighty Shediem-Slayer. Look how she bows before me." Eerie laughter filled the thick air. "Not even she can resist my power of obsession."

Emma's head snapped up, the haze clearing for a moment of clarity. Why was she kneeling? What was happening?

Then the fog coated her mind again, and she sighed contentedly while her prince stroked her head.

"Rise, my little rebellion."

She obeyed, glancing over his shoulder to see a dark blur zip into view and then out again. Several Veemuris rumbled their discontent and snapped their wings, clearly sensing a shift in the air as well. Emma strained her eyes to see what it was, and she felt the warmth and intensity of Beleez's power trickle away yet again.

"Don't look away from me, my love."

Emma forced herself not to gag. Before he could overwhelm her again with his obsession, she cast him a demure smile, hoping her expression seemed like the stricken devotee he assumed her to be.

Blaze sped a distance away yet again, and Emma leapt for the prince. She secured her hands around his slender neck, sending his power rushing through her. Every cell felt supercharged, her body light.

Beleez clawed at her arms, trying desperately to dislodge her grip, but she squeezed harder. His red eyes bulged, the slit pupils widening.

She sucked in his life energy, feeling his skin grow brittle. Her vision shifted, granting her view of a farther distance.

He let out a croaking sound, then his skin turned grey. Her gums ached; her canines lengthened. She pulled her lips back, baring them to her dying prey.

His feeble body collapsed.

Emma took a ragged breath. She was powerful.

So powerful.

The newest ability added to her arsenal, obsession.

More, her hunger cried.

More.

More.

More!

The Veemuris around her were stunned in place. As soon as a streak of black hair and dark clothing flashed in her periphery, she sprang into action once more. Her dagger was tucked into the sheath at her back. She drew it at the same time a sword cut through the air with a melodic sound.

Then came the squelch and snap of severed skin and bone. Chaos ensued.

Emma sliced and stabbed the large creatures that flapped in the air, dive-bombing her head and her arms. Her body was fluid, the power zinging through her like crackling bolts of lightning. She craved their pitiful scraps of power and tasted it in the air, inhaling deeply. They dropped from the sky, crashing to the ground in explosions of ash. A man's steel-blue gaze caught hers, and he froze.

More Shediem appeared, spurring the Giborim into movement. Her power roared inside her and her enhanced vision zeroed in on each of her prey. Their bodies crumbled one after the other until none was left. Spinning in a circle, she let out a battle cry.

The handsome, familiar face of the Giborim entered her line of vision, and she snarled. *How dare he steal my prey! They were mine!*

Tentatively he lifted his hands to cup her face. His skin was hot.

"It's over, Emma: you did it. Beleez is dead." His accent was thick, his voice like warm honey.

The prince's power caressed her mind and she gripped it tightly, giving it a tug in her mind.

The nonhuman's eyes became glassy, unfocused. He dropped to his knees, arms out in front of him as he kissed the dirt.

A triumphant smile curled her lips. *Yes, bow, creature.*

"Emma, fight it," the angel-spawn gritted out.

Emma?

"I am the Shediem-Slayer." Her voice sounded strange to her ears.

The man bowing at her feet lifted his head, expression filled with adoration—except for his eyes. They were hard.

He was fighting her power.

Anger snapped through her, and she pushed more of it into him.

His breath hitched, tears streaming down his sharp cheekbones. "Emma," he rasped.

A chill raced up her spine at his tone. It knocked something loose in her mind. His utterance of her name was both a plea and a prayer, and it reached something inside her. She withdrew her power, pulling it back into herself.

"Blaze," she whispered. A shiver wracked her body, jerking her muscles painfully.

He leapt to his feet and gripped her face, crushing his lips to hers.

A sob escaped her. "I can't do this. It's too much."

"No," he murmured against her lips. "I'm here. You did so well. You did it all on your own."

She shook her head, pulling back. "What if I'd forced you to run yourself through with your sword?"

His lips twitched. "I wouldn't have. I could sense your power. It feels different."

She lifted a brow quizzically. "What does?"

"I'm already yours, heart and soul," he said with a slow smile. "Your power is a forced emotion. It feels wrong."

Emma's heart swelled and she thought it might burst. She jumped into his arms as they came around her. He held her tight while she shook, her teeth chattering. After his confession, she felt like she should issue one of her own.

That's when she felt another prince's energy a moment before she heard the feminine whimper.

They broke apart, whipping around, and Emma's stomach plummeted.

Amon, Prince of Lust—looking every inch the regal, sexual immortal he was—held a golden-haired woman against his chest, a gloved hand over her mouth. Tears coursed down her cheeks.

"Haddie!" Blaze charged toward the prince, swords drawn.

The prince and the woman both vanished, then appeared behind him. "Leash the Giborim or I'll snap her neck," the dark, sensual prince growled.

Blaze stopped abruptly, glancing from Emma to his sister. His gaze lowered to her full, rounded belly and Emma felt the heat of his rage rolling off his rigid body.

She kept herself ready for an attack, though an anxious dread unfurled inside her. Could she handle another prince's power so soon? She'd have to try. "What do you want?"

"And why do you have my sister?" Blaze ground out, swords clenched in each hand.

Amon's glittering ruby-red eyes appraised Emma with blatant hunger. "I felt my brother's demise. Congratulations are in order, I think, flower."

She scoffed. "Why would you congratulate me for murdering Beleez?"

His smile was a cruel slash of white on his hauntingly beautiful face. "I can feel your power. It's dark. Heady. Its siren song calls to me." He licked his lips, and Emma felt herself cringe.

Haddie sobbed harder in his hold. Emma took an involuntary step forward, stopping when Amon hissed.

"Don't move, Shediem-Slayer."

She lifted her hands in placating gesture. "Why are you here?"

The prince seemed to regain some composure, and straightened. "I want to make a trade."

"Great, how about you piss off back to Sheol where you belong, and I won't remove your head from your body?" Blaze snarled.

Amon smirked. "What would you give to have your sister back, Giborim?" Emma could have sworn she heard Blaze's teeth grinding together. "As much as I've enjoyed her company, it's the Shediem-Slayer I want."

Blaze opened his mouth to respond, but Emma held up a

hand. "Me for Haddie?" She stared at the prince that made her skin crawl. She didn't want to be anywhere near him, but for Haddie, she'd do whatever he wanted.

Despite the rest of their companions having drawn in behind them at some point, no one moved.

Amon's eyes sparkled with wicked delight. "Will you come quietly, flower?"

Blaze began to speak but Emma raised her voice, drowning him out. "Yes."

Murmurs passed through the people at her back, but Sergei's and Blaze's voices rose above them, their protests lost to her ears. All she saw was the fear and desperation in Haddie's eyes while she frantically shook her head.

Emma stepped forward. "Release Haddie. Let her walk to her brother and I'll come to you willingly."

Amon hesitated for a moment, assessing every possible outcome.

Blaze turned, and gripped her forearm tightly. "Emma, don't. We'll fight."

"She's pregnant, Blaze," Emma said sadly. "You could harm her or the baby."

"That's not a baby, it's a demon," he spat.

Emma recoiled, forcing herself from his grasp, and immediately his eyes filled with regret.

"You're different. You're special."

She shook her head. "Even with all of us, we won't win like we did with Beleez. We had the element of surprise then, and your sister wasn't a hostage. I have to do this."

With a nod to Haddie, she brought her gaze to the prince once again. "Release her."

"Drop the knife," he demanded. "And step away from them first."

Emma narrowed her eyes. She'd forgotten about the dagger in her hand. Reluctantly, she released it, letting it fall to the dirt with a soft *thunk*. When she saw him nod his approval, she took a single step forward, watching Amon carefully. "Now let her go. I'm coming to you of my own free will."

When he didn't react, she tried again, taking another step closer. "Let her go."

She stopped just out of the prince's reach. In a blink Amon pushed Haddie away, sending her shrieking as she scrambled forward. Emma didn't have time to catch her—Amon's arms were already around her.

Then Blaze and the group were gone.

BLAZE

A long growl tore from his throat as he clutched the frail, pregnant girl to his chest, still staring at the spot where Emma had disappeared from. It took a moment for him to reign in his fury. His entire body pulsed with rage and his vision edged with red.

Damn her and her heroic antics.

Damn her for not thinking anything through.

She was with Amon, the Prince of Lust.

And they still didn't know which point was Amon's new lair.

His teeth ground together, a new wave of anger crashing into him.

Looking down at the girl that resembled his mother in almost every way, he felt his breath catch. She'd been a captive to the Prince of Lust. Her big, rounded belly was proof enough of that.

She stared back at him, blue eyes swimming with tears.

"Are you hurt?" Blaze managed to ask.

Haddie shook her head slowly. She lifted a trembling hand and brought it to his cheek. A tear spilled over, tracking through the dirt on her gaunt face. He closed his eyes as emotion pummeled him all at once like a raging hurricane.

"William," she whispered.

Forcing himself to swallow the lump that was lodged in his throat, he opened his eyes again.

"Hadessah."

With a laugh that sounded more like a sob, she wrapped her arms around his neck. He held her, feeling her small frame shake while she cried silently. His grip increased more and more as reality set in.

She's alive.

His little sister was alive. She was here, in his arms.

At last his sister pulled back. "Where's Andrew? What name does he use now?"

Blaze offered a tight smile. "Axel. He's back at the compound in Seattle."

"Seattle? I have missed a lot, haven't I?" She searched his gaze for whatever had flashed in it, but he schooled his features. He'd tell her eventually, but not yet.

"I'll fill you in on it all in due time," he assured her.

She nodded. "We have to go after Emma. Amon is obsessed with her. She was all he'd talk about; sometimes he'd just mutter her name over and over. He's deranged."

A sick sense of dread bloomed in his gut. "Do you know where he is?"

She bit her lip, considering. "I don't know where exactly but—"

Dominic spoke up then. "We have maps of each prince's location. Do you think you'd be able to help us identify which continent at least?"

"Asia," she said in a rush. "They're in Asia. The humans were primarily Asian. That's all I know."

Blaze exchanged a look with Dominic. Then he nodded. "All right, everyone, let's get back to the aircraft. We'll have to steal some fuel from an abandoned airport. Taryn," he barked.

The Spellcaster looked at him with a lazy grin. "Yes, warrior?"

"Stay with my sister. Heal any injuries she has. You'll have to protect her when we land."

She made a noncommittal sound of acknowledgement before spinning on her heel and stalking away. Blaze led Hadessah and the rest of their group back, and though he desperately wanted to pick her up and carry her over the rough terrain, she insisted on walking.

Stubborn, just like she'd been as a child.

He still couldn't believe that she was here—that she was alive. He'd always suspected. Hoped. Andrew—Axel—would be shocked.

As soon as they were back on the aircraft, they were up in the air. With an insane amount of luck, they were able to find an abandoned airfield not too far away where they refilled the plane, before making it back to Seattle in record time.

When he stormed into the compound, his uncle met him in the foyer, pug-like face red and lips pursed. Blaze tightened his arm around Haddie's thin waist protectively.

"Well?" Silas demanded. "Did the girl manage to take out the prince?"

"Yes."

Silas's eyes flicked back and forth between Blaze and Haddie several times before lingering on her, a hint of suspicion in them. "Who is this, pray tell?"

Blaze sucked in a slow, calming breath. "I'll tell you later. For now, we need to move. I need to debrief the council while we refuel and plan for our next journey." He started to maneuver around his uncle, only for Silas to step into his path, blocking him.

"What is going on, nephew?"

"Gather everyone and I'll tell you." Blaze's voice was harder than he'd intended, but every second that Emma remained in Amon's clutches was another moment she was likely suffering untold abuse.

As if his uncle sensed the urgency in the way his body tensed defensively or from the bark of his tone, Silas thankfully stepped away with a small bow. With a final backward glance at Hadessah, he stalked up the staircase.

"Is that…Uncle Silas?"

Blaze nodded stiffly and gently guided her up the marble staircase toward Emma's room. At the door he said, "Go ahead and shower or nap or whatever. I'll have some food sent up. Emma has some clothing that might fit you in her wardrobe. Just make yourself comfortable." He pressed a kiss to her forehead. "I'm so glad you're safe." The words were barely a hoarse whisper, each one filled with emotion that he thought might choke him.

"Me too," Haddie said softly.

When Blaze pulled away to look at her, her sapphire blue eyes were already brighter than they'd been when he'd first seen her. Unable to help himself, he lowered his gaze to her swollen belly. A lash of disgust and despair whipped through him, turning his lips upside down.

Her swallow was audible. "I'm okay, big brother." She rubbed the large bump affectionately. "We're both okay."

He couldn't speak, for fear that something hateful would escape, so he simply nodded. Then he spun on his heel and hurried back down to the main level.

After instructing the girls working in the kitchen to take up some sandwiches to Haddie, he headed for the meeting room, where everyone waited. Their hushed voices fell silent when he entered.

"Ah," Silas said, clearing his throat. "Finally. What's this about, nephew?"

Blaze rolled his shoulders and strode for the head of the table—his usual spot since his father abdicated his seat with the council. "Our mission was successful in part." His eyes roved over each member at the table. Dominic gave him a reassuring nod, and he continued. "Emma was able to destroy Beleez, Prince of Gluttony."

Murmurs ran through those gathered but Blaze spoke over them: Emma needed him, so he didn't have time to waste. "However, Amon, the Prince of Lust, appeared not even a minute later"—he inhaled deeply—"with my sister, Hadessah, as his captive."

A cacophony of shouts and questions assaulted his ears. Even saying the words out loud made his gut clench. For almost two hundred years she'd suffered at the hands of the Shediem. Her womb was filled with a demonic child that he was certain had not been willingly put there.

Finally Dominic barked out, "Hush! Let him speak!"

Blaze gave his friend a grateful nod. "The prince insisted upon a trade, and once again our Shediem-Slayer sacrificed herself. She is now his captive. My sister rests upstairs." He didn't wait for anyone to speak before rolling on. "We believe Emma is being kept in China and we need to infiltrate the camp to rescue her—"

A harsh laugh from his left cut him off. Silas sneered. "We will not waste our men for her. Let the Shediem kill her and be rid of the threat she poses to us all. She's far too powerful, that one."

Blaze's fists clenched on the tabletop. "Not another word, Uncle."

Silas went quiet, but his smug expression remained.

"Emma is one of us, and we wouldn't leave one of our own to be tortured by their kind. She is invaluable to our cause. Only she can kill a prince. We need her." Blaze swallowed thickly, meeting his uncle's gaze. "I need her. She will be my mate when all of this is done."

Another chorus of murmurs spread around the table, skipping a smiling Dominic. "I will be honored to join this mission, *rodnoy bret.*"

A tense silence followed before four more men volunteered. Blaze felt his uncle's glare on the side of his face like a laser, but didn't acknowledge him.

"We'll round up the men and get a few more on board. Rodriguez, can you call ahead to the Orlando compound? We'll need to top up on fuel there."

The man addressed nodded, already pulling out his satellite device.

"The rest of you get packed as quickly as you can. We leave in thirty minutes."

Blaze turned to go, but his uncle gripped his arm tightly. Silas hissed, "You know that girl cannot survive the power of all the princes and Nakosh. You'll lose her. Best be thinking about how you'll put her down when the time comes."

Blaze jerked his arm free and strode away without a backward glance, though his every muscle was coiled tight.

Because a small part of him, no matter how hard he tried to hide it, knew his uncle might be right.

EMMA

They materialized inside a thick, canvas tent. It was almost amusing that the spoiled princes of hell, who'd toppled cities and destroyed the height of modern civilization, who were accustomed to castles and grand furnishings, were reduced to tents and the findings of their human slaves. Emma cast her gaze at the thick, soft rug she stood on. It was like stepping back in time. Though looking around at the large, elegant four-poster bed and chaise lounge chairs—all of which were occupied by what appeared to be drugged, nude humans— she was certain the slaves would be living in less-than-ideal conditions.

"All of you, out!" Amon barked, still holding Emma tight. She noted that his arms, even his hands, were covered so that her skin wouldn't touch his. Clever.

Lazily the lust-high humans with far too much skin on display ambled out of his tent, some eyeing her and giggling. Others stayed silent, like thoughtless zombies. Emma hated Amon for enslaving them and taking away their free will. For treating them as little more than puppets forced to dance until their bodies broke.

When the tent flap fluttered closed, an invisible hand of dread wrapped around her throat and squeezed.

He pushed her toward the bed. "You've been naughty, little flower. Killing my brother."

Emma caught herself just in time from bashing her head against the wooden post. She whirled around to face her captor. "But oh, how strong you must be now." His eyes flared bright with excitement and he licked his full, sensual lips. "That young, slight body containing the power of two of my brothers. What can you do, little flower?" His lips curved in a wicked smile. "Show me."

She tried Beleez's power first, sending a tidal wave toward the prince. His body stiffened and he swallowed thickly.

But instead of throwing himself at her feet in worship, he only grinned wider. "My, my, little flower," he purred. "That's something indeed."

He blinked away the remnants of obsession she'd flung at him. With a long, graceful stride, he closed the distance between them. In a blur of motion, he had her chin firmly in his gloved hand, holding her still so she couldn't force skin-to-skin contact while he leaned in close. His lips hovered just beside her ear when he whispered, "I'll let you in on a little secret, though. I'm already enamored with you." His other hand brushed up the side of her arm, causing her to shiver, and he smiled knowingly. With the gentle stroke of a lover, the backs of his gloved fingers caressed her cheek. "You can't force obsession that's already there."

Emma tried to jerk her head away, but his fingers dug in tighter. She bit back a cry of pain.

He inhaled her scent, no doubt tasting the tang of her fear. "I have big plans for you, little flower," he rasped. "I'm going to feed you my blood until you're intoxicated with my lust. You'll be begging me to have my way with you."

A snarl-like sound tore from her throat as she fought against his hold. "It's pathetic that you have to force people to want you, don't you think?" She knew it was foolish to goad him, but the words poured from her mouth without thought. "No one ever willingly gets on their back for you. What's worse is the minute you've finished with them, they're already seeking pleasure somewhere else. You're not memorable or desirable.

You're nothing."

Her words hit her mark, his grin vanishing, replaced with fire in his red eyes while his body began to tremble with rage. His hold on her jaw flexed, and he pulled her forward then slammed her head against the post.

Dots spotted her vision, but she brought her knee up, connecting solidly with his crotch. His sharp intake of breath was her only reward before he backhanded her. She fell sideways, looking for something to use as a weapon. She missed her dagger. A twig no thicker than her thumb sat an inch or so from her hand, and she grasped it just before Amon clutched her by her jacket and hauled her to her feet.

"Just for that, I'll let my men have their turn with you too," he snarled.

Emma barely heard the words, focusing all of her concentration on her other ability, keeping her hand hidden behind her back. Her heart jackhammered in her chest and she hoped he couldn't hear it. The twig grew, filling her hand with cool metal, and lengthened. When she knew it was done, she thrust the curved dagger toward his chest, the glint of steel just a flash before she buried it in the prince's chest.

It was a distraction and nothing more; she knew a blade wouldn't kill a prince. No sooner had she shoved it to the hilt through his sternum did she release it and run. He was too fast, too strong for her to touch his face. She'd remain his prisoner forever with that tactic.

Her best chance was to try to escape.

His gurgling laugh made the hairs on her arms stand on end. Her heart pounded harder, her steps seeming impossibly slow even with her superhuman speed.

She'd made it within reach of the slit in the tent when arms of steel banded around her waist and tossed her. Landing hard on her back, the wind forced from her lungs, she blinked up at the peak of the tent. Amon's face came into view above her.

A stream of red stained the shirt beneath his princely coat.

Her dagger was clutched in his hand, an exact replica of the one Blaze had given her. Blood dripped from its tip and onto her neck, her face. She squeezed her lips shut, remembering his promise, but his smile was filled with all the sick, twisted glee of a hunter whose prey was caught in a trap.

No! she screamed internally. Her limbs flailed until the prince straddled her waist, pinning her arms painfully beneath his knees.

He bent over her with the dagger still dripping blood onto her lips. "I love how you fight me, flower, but our game is at an end...for now."

His fist was a blur before pain erupted in her temple and the world went black.

When Emma came to, her body was hot. Parts of her ached in ways that made her pant with desire.

"Amon," she gasped.

A dark chuckle sounded behind her, chafing against her heavy, needy breasts and sending tingles between her thighs.

"Amon," she said again on a moan. Why was she so warm?

"Yes, flower?"

Her mouth was dry, a sweetness on her tongue that she craved more of. Every cell in her body was alight with pleasure. She strained against her bonds, loving the delicious rub of leather against her skin. Looking down, she noted that she wore only her underwear. Still, it felt like far too much fabric.

"Take these off," she begged. "Where are you? Let me see you."

She wanted her prince. Wanted to feel his touch. Wanted him to soothe away the unbearable aches.

His laugh came again, raising goose bumps along her arms and legs.

Finally her shirtless god came into view. Her mouth watered

at the sight of his golden skin. She wanted to lick every inch. His head cocked to the side, taking her in from head to toe with his eyes that sparkled like beautiful rubies.

Smiling, he stopped in front of her. His bare thumb rubbed over her bottom lip, and she stifled a groan of pleasure.

He licked his own lips hungrily, sending a thrill through her body. "I admit I love it when you're all teeth and claws. A rare, poisonous flower planted in the garden, its illusion of innocence set to draw me in. Then once you get close, it's almost too late to avoid the strike. Your thorns are your best attribute, flower. But under the right circumstances you bloom into something even more beautiful. Your center is filled with the sweetest nectar, and I must confess I am dying for a taste."

His last words were a breath against her lips, and Emma struggled to get closer. To press her body against his.

"Touch me," she begged.

He chuckled. "Will you hurt me if I do, flower?"

She frowned in confusion, even as a niggling sensation began in the back of her mind—a warning of some sort that she couldn't reach.

She didn't want to.

"Why would I hurt you?" She looked around as though there were others that might hurt her prince. Her god. She'd kill them before they could even try.

"That's right," he said, tentatively stroking her arm.

Why was she bound?

Danger. Kill him.

She shook her head to clear the unwanted voice. *No, I need him. He's mine.*

His caress continued to her chest, running over the swell of her breast.

Fire licked through her: hatred. The flames slid through her veins like a serpent. Her memories flicked back into place all at once and the prince halted, his hand cupping her.

He'd fed her his blood after knocking her out.

He'd stripped her.

A slow smile curved her lips as their eyes met. "You're going to die."

The low, lethal quality of her voice was foreign to her own ears, but immediately she felt the flood of Amon's powers rush through her.

In the past his sexual energy had been too much for her to take. But now with the powers of two other princes occupying her body, she drank it down greedily, eager for his death.

He stumbled back, face contorting into anger. Behind him on a desk lay the dagger she'd stabbed him with. The blade was clean now. He grabbed it and rushed to her while she fought against her bonds.

The leather groaned, the stitches snapping one by one. She was almost free. Her ankles were bound still, but she just needed her hands. The prince had enough skin on display that she'd be able to easily find some part of him to feed from.

More, her beast chanted.

The blade swiped for her throat. Her chest. She squeezed herself back as far as her restraints would allow. The bedframe creaked, and the wood protested her strength, especially with the Prince of Lust coursing through her veins.

Wildly the prince swung the dagger. When he aimed for her face, she turned her head to avoid losing an eye. Sharp bursts of pain bloomed on her arm, her cheek, her stomach. Emma gritted her teeth and at last yanked her hands free, the leather snapping audibly.

A screech filled the tent, and other Shediem filed in. Her ankles were still bound but she sank down, ignoring the hot crimson from her wounds smearing her thighs.

The first one that dared get close was a bulbous-headed Shax. Her hands wrapped around its thick neck and she forced it to the floor. Hovering over it, she drew the energy from its body so fast it became dust in her hands in a blink.

Yes, the beast inside her crooned. *More. Kill. You are the goddess of Death.*

Emma let loose a war cry, swinging her arms for each Shediem that got close. From behind the throng of soldiers, Amon watched her with fire in his eerie eyes.

"Fight me yourself, you coward," she bellowed, draining his minions left and right. Occasionally their blades cut flesh but with their energy filling her, her wounds knitted back together just as quickly.

Her ankles sprung free and she willed the leather to become sand instead. She sprinted, sucking away the life-force of each demonic creature that got within her range.

Until she lunged for the prince.

He vanished, and her head hit the tent wall, snapping the fabric taut. The impact jostled her.

A sharp pain lanced down her back, wrenching a scream from her. She'd felt this pain before and she knew it well; the crack that followed confirmed that the prince had a whip.

Something guttural rumbled in her throat before she spun toward him.

"I'm afraid I'm not as easy to defeat as my brothers, little flower." His tone was colder than usual, all light of excitement extinguished. "Shall I tell you how I forced my seed inside that filthy Giborim's womb?"

Emma froze, lips curled back, exposing her teeth.

"Do you want to hear how she cried silently, not uttering a sound when I raped her over and over for weeks while you played the hero with her brother?"

Her scream of fury came from somewhere so deep in her soul that she thought she felt the ground quake. Lunging for him again, she dodged the whip that sliced through the air. It caught her hip and tore her flesh but she didn't pause. Didn't stop. With a thought she changed her undergarments, letting the dark, thick material wrap over her entire body. She didn't have to look down to know she was now wearing a wicked-looking jumpsuit.

Again and again Amon cracked the whip, though her new

attire protected her from the worst of it. She'd tear him apart over and over until she was sated. Until she'd gotten justice for every woman he'd ever hurt.

The monster would burn in the wrath of her vengeance.

She knocked him back and jumped on top of him, pinning him the same way he'd done to her while she drove her fists into his face, ignoring the crunch of bones and spurts of blood. His screams were drowned out by her own anguished cries.

Her fists turned to claws and she tore at his skin, determined to pull him apart.

Distantly, she knew this was madness. That she was as much a monster as he, but she couldn't bring herself to care. She'd be the avenging angel, even if her wings were blacker than her soul.

The tent burst open and at least a dozen Spellcasters rushed in. Their magic threw her backward, her spine cracking when it hit something hard. Air wouldn't come to her lungs and she gasped like a fish out of water.

The blinding light wrapped around her, its icy touch at war with her fire. She was held immovable. Utterly still, with air still evading her.

Blackness edged her vision, and she knew she'd die.

She could barely make out the prince getting to his feet. His body was battered, offering a tiny spark of satisfaction before the darkness swallowed her whole.

BLAZE

Every hour that passed was like a knife carving another slice into his heart. When they entered Chinese airspace, they had to provide security clearances, because at least part of China was somehow still operational.

It wasted time, circling above while their fuel dwindled and the right people verified the codes that gave them clearance everywhere in the world.

When at last the crackly voice had granted them access, Blaze flew the plane harder than was probably good for its engine, but desperation clawed through him. His uncle's words had haunted him for the entire journey.

What would he find when they got to Emma? Would she be able to kill Amon without losing herself?

How much more could she take?

It went against his protective nature to ask her to save them all. To ask her to risk herself for them. But the fate of humankind was on the line. A supernatural war would begin at any moment. And when it did, every single Shediem in existence would gun for her.

They didn't have to worry about where the soldiers needed to be. It was clear that the war would come to them, wherever Emma was. She was the ultimate threat.

The only problem was she was becoming an increasing threat to Giborim and humans too. With each prince she absorbed, the more she became like them…

He shook his head, forcing away any further thought on the subject before he began the descent.

When they landed, Blaze barked out his commands and they disembarked the aircraft with their weapons and supply packs.

It was just as cold as it had been back in Seattle, with a wicked wind whipping across the abandoned airfield. Unlike in Kansas and Brazil, cities loomed in the distance in every direction, the skyscrapers reaching for the grey sky like iron fingers.

Wordlessly they set out. The distance they'd need to cross was far greater than in the other two locations because the damaged zone was so much smaller—meaning they'd had to land farther to avoid still-standing cities. Yet the closer they got to the nearest city, the more the silence around them became deafening.

He could sense the humans, though they hid from view. Some—most likely the homeless—congregated around metal barrels where fire crackled, offering a sliver of warmth against the harsh cold.

Blaze ignored them and the gazes that followed as they passed. A few faces peered through foggy windows, but no one interfered. For that he was grateful. He couldn't do anything for them right now. Until he rescued Emma, she was his only priority, selfish as it was.

Something mixed with the light shuffle of their footsteps. Gently, a song reached his ears at the edge of the city. Its melodic sound carried on in the wind, as though Mother Nature herself sang to the people. He knew immediately what it was.

"Shax ahead," he whispered to his companions. A few murmured their confirmation.

From the buildings, a steady stream of enthralled humans filed out, marching toward the source of the sound.

Blaze heaved a sigh. This, he couldn't let go. Stopping along a sleek brick building that might have been a coffee shop at one time, he pressed his back against it.

Slowly, he peered around the side, and spotted the Shax

whose wide, ugly mouth opened to spill the crescendo of his woeful tune. Drudes, djinn, and a Zemnion stood watch, roughly keeping the mindless humans in line while they marched out of the city in rows of three.

Blaze cursed under his breath. There were at least two dozen Shediem they'd have to slay. But with ten Giborim and three Spellcasters, it would be a piece of cake. The thing that bothered him was the humans' proximity.

They'd get hurt. Many would die.

But weighing the risks, he knew it'd be worth it. They didn't have a choice. Tens of thousands of humans were being led to their deaths and they didn't even know it.

There'd likely be more Shax every mile or so to keep the humans under their spell.

He whispered his plan to the rest, and a round of nods passed through them.

"Ready?" he asked. Not waiting for their response, he lunged around the corner and sprinted headlong toward the creatures. The weight of his blades was familiar. They cut through the air in their own sweet melody before severing flesh and bone.

The Shax was first down. His sword met the heavy clang of another blade, this one from a Drude. A leathery smile twisted the vile creature's lips as they traded blows in a rapid flurry. Their predictive nature made it hard to best them in combat, but Blaze had an ace up his sleeve. Clearing his mind the way his father taught him, he let his body move fluidly, the ancient swords moving him of their own accord.

The Drude's eyes widened before its own head was lobbed from its body, rolling into the panicked crowd of humans backing away. The pavement was wet with both red and black blood, proving his theory correct: humans had died.

His eye caught on movement and he spied the Zemnion—a creature that looked like a rhino and a lion had a baby, though it ran on its thick, furry back legs, thin tail slashing back and forth, projecting its fear. It sprinted away from them, pushing the much smaller humans out of its way in its race to warn the Shediem ahead.

Blaze shot after it, his speed far surpassing the large, thundering creature's. Leaping into the air, he came down on top of it, his blades glancing off its stony skin.

They both tumbled to the ground, and its feline eyes snapped to him before it hissed. A large ivory horn adorned its snout. Blaze didn't move when it barreled toward him, the horn poised to impale him through the chest.

Once the creature was close enough, he jerked a blade through the softer part of its bottom jaw. The sword pierced its skull, erupting with a crack on the other side.

The scent of rot filled his nostrils, and black, oily blood sprayed his face and chest. He kept his mouth clamped shut to avoid ingesting it, and withdrew the blade from the now-dead Shediem with a noise of disgust.

Others jogged over to him, offering to help him to his feet. In the distance, he saw Dominic and Taryn calming the humans and instructing them inside their houses or as far from the city as possible.

Ignoring the proffered hands, Blaze climbed to his feet and accepted a cloth from Zachary to wipe the Shediem gore from his face. "We can't spend too much time here. We're losing the light already."

The sky was darkening. Emma had been on her own for far too long.

To a group of shaking, huddled humans he said in Mandarin, "Take care of your fellow man. Protect each other and stay away from here as far as possible."

They nodded and wisely got to their feet, then ran back toward the city.

When Dominic and Taryn caught up with the group, they carried on. But they didn't encounter any more Shediem, leading Blaze to believe the Shediem knew they were coming.

The sun had begun its descent on the horizon when they

reached the outskirts of Amon's camp. Soon they'd be thrown into darkness, and though Blaze and his fellow Giborim could see just fine in the dark, the Spellcasters could not. And, as much as he wanted to charge in like a bull in a china shop, he forced himself to wait. To watch.

The patrols were random—a smart move on their part. And Amon's hiding place was likely at the center, away from direct view, which would make locating it that much more difficult.

"On the next rotation we'll strike. Stealth is key." Blaze's eyes flicked to Sergei, Taryn, and her brother. "I need you to make us all look like Shediem. Physical changes and not just illusions, because we'll all have to go in at different locations."

Taryn made a choked noise and Sergei's eyes grew wide.

"Sergei, I know you helped doctor Emma's mother for close to two decades. I'm sure this will be easy for you."

His shoulders slumped. "I used potions to do most of it. And I don't have any with me. Besides, changing red hair to blond isn't the same as changing a humanoid to a Shediem."

"You still know how to alter one's appearance. Whatever you can do will help."

Taryn looked like she might protest, but clamped her mouth shut instead. *Smart girl.*

"You better not make me a Shax," Dominic muttered, stepping forward to volunteer first.

Taryn's lips split in a sly grin. "Oh come on, Russian brute, you'd look great as a Shax."

It was eerie how quickly and accurately the Spellcaster altered his friend, shrinking him from six foot one to three feet tall. It took everything in Blaze not to laugh while Dominic gave a gruff sigh of resignation.

"Don't speak or make any sounds. Your voice will be a dead giveaway," Taryn added.

"Not to mention the Shediem can sense our presence," Dominic retorted.

"I've done my best to mute everyone's energy," Taryn said in a tone that might have seemed soft on the surface, but a cord of steel ran through it. The Giborim met her gaze, and they held each other in a stare-off that radiated tension.

Blaze cleared his throat, trying to diffuse the situation. "That's great, Taryn, thanks. Derrick, Sergei, get started."

Sergei stepped in front of him, his palms glowing with buttery yellow light. "This might burn a little," he said before a thousand pinpricks touched Blaze's skin. It was both itchy and uncomfortable, but he fought the urge to scratch while his bones rearranged. His skin pulled tighter, his muscles burning.

When Sergei stepped back to observe his work, Blaze glanced at the squat, scowling Shax nearby. "How do I look?" he asked.

Someone sniggered, snapping his attention to the creepy, leggy Nybbas on his left. "You make an almost attractive female."

Glaring at Sergei, who fought a smile, Blaze huffed, examining the rest of their company. The Spellcasters were working on each other, and soon they, too, were identical to the vile creatures he sought to slice to pieces.

The sky had morphed from an orange-red glow to dark blue hues, and finally to inky black that blotted out their light.

They had to move now.

"Spread out. Head for the biggest tent—that's where Amon will be. We'll meet back here when we're done."

Their backpacks and weapons were piled behind a lonely bush where they'd hopefully go unnoticed.

His comrades fanned out, staying low through the boulders and rubble until they were out of sight.

Blaze, crouching behind a split boulder, waited for two guards to pass in opposite directions. In his normal form his bulk wouldn't have been concealed, but as a Drude, it worked perfectly. Once both guards were far enough, he rose from his hiding spot, twin swords in hand, and crept toward the light of the campsite.

It was the size of a small city, lanterns, torches, and fires illuminating as far as the eye could see. The raucous laughter and jeering reached his ears long before the first tent came into view. Unlike Asmodeus's camp, which sat in a valley, Amon's sat atop a hill. Though he was certain the hill had not been there before the prince's emergence, which destroyed most of Wuhan.

Cresting the hill at last, Blaze lowered himself, watching groups of Shediem and humans writhe and pulse as one. It was not unheard of—humans fraternizing with monsters—but he couldn't fathom how they lusted for creatures so far from the human form. His sharpened teeth ground together audibly. The pull inside him to slaughter was almost irresistible, but he forced himself up. He needed to blend in.

Adopting the swagger of a high-level Drude, he sheathed his blades and stalked into the hornet's nest. He looked like one of them, but that was as far as the façade went. If any of them questioned him, his cover would be blown.

Thanks to the drinks and drugs being passed around, very few eyes turned his way, making it easier than it should have been to slink around tents and wander deeper. After what felt like an hour, the familiar flutter of heat and comfort dropped into his chest.

Emma was near.

His speed increased, and a faint, familiar grunt of pain reached his ears. The sound of a whip cutting through the air then slicing through flesh shredded the calm he'd forced in place. Emma's muffled cry called to him, carrying his steps faster. Everything was a blur until he burst into the massive canvas tent that he knew held her. The scene before him had him halting, the breath leaving his lungs in a sharp exhalation.

Tied on a wooden cross with her arms wide was Emma. Her mouth was taped, and blood trickled from her split eyebrow, pooling in her eye that had swollen shut. In a black jumpsuit torn and hanging in tatters, it gave him full view of her massacred flesh.

Arms, legs, stomach…all of her, bloodied.

The prince panted, gripping a whip and grinning like an idiot when he spun to face Blaze. "About time you arrived." His creepy red eyes sparkled like the psychopath he was.

Before Blaze could move, he heard the muttered command, then bright light flashed and ice gripped him with jagged claws. He fought against the Spellcasters' hold but his body didn't move an inch.

"I've captured all your little friends as well. I plan to simply kill them, but you..." The prince moved with fluid grace and stopped in front of Blaze, flashing his teeth in an expression between disgust and a feral show of dominance that made Blaze want to laugh.

Yet nothing about the situation was funny. They were caught with no form of backup on the way. His friends and fellow soldiers would die for his mistake.

The prince continued. "You get to watch me break your precious Shediem-Slayer." He turned to Emma, still clutching the bloodied whip, but with a gentler, almost tender smile. It was a stark contrast to his violent words. "I'll snap every bit of defiance in her pretty little face until she's mine. If that pathetic dog Levaroth can stay her wrath enough to touch her, then I will be able to as well." He chuckled. "With a little persuasion."

Emma struggled against her bonds, muffled sounds of anger coming from behind the duct tape.

"Shhh, little flower," the prince crooned. His hand lifted for her cheek and the moment his skin met hers, he hissed. When he jerked his hand away, her eyes flared with emerald light.

Blaze would have smiled at the fire lingering in her gaze if the magic encasing him would allow him any movement. Even while being tortured she was still a viper. It gave him hope that she wouldn't break, no matter what Amon did to her. His eyes met hers and he hoped they conveyed what he was thinking.

To fight.

To never give up.

As confirmation, she gave a slight nod that warmed his chest.

Amon tsked at their silent exchange, and without warning

raised the whip and snapped it across her abdomen. A small cry escaped her lips. Her eyes shone with tears that she quickly blinked away.

The sound seemed to excite the prince because he groaned, low and throaty, making Blaze want to burst from the magic holding him and snap the prince's neck.

"The pain will stop when you are ready to behave. Are you ready to behave, flower?"

Her muffled curse was clear enough for both of them to make out and the prince sighed, feigning weariness. However, the creep's eyes glittered, proving he enjoyed her fight. Sick bastard.

"Master?" a raspy voice called from the entrance of the tent.

"What is it?" Amon barked.

"News, my lord."

A growl echoed in the prince's throat before he stalked past Blaze and through the opening of the tent.

Blaze's eyes returned to Emma. He wished he could speak, to reassure her. Of what, he didn't know. He just wanted to comfort her.

Faintly he heard, "—all of them except the witch. The brother surrendered without a fight though—"

Amon cut the Shediem off. "Execute them all. And if the Spellcaster comes back, kill her too."

Apparently he wasn't even trying to hide that Taryn had slipped through the cracks. And if Blaze knew anything about the young Spellcaster, it was that she would try to save her brother. Which meant they could still be rescued.

Emma's eyes narrowed, and he was certain she'd heard him too. A sigh left her, and she hung her head. In relief or exhaustion, he wasn't sure.

"I'll see you soon, flower," Amon called to her, though she simply lifted her head to glare at him.

The prince's chuckle and barked orders to have Blaze bound too were the last things he heard before unconsciousness swept, unexpected and strong, forcing him into the darkness.

ADRIANNA

A slow jazz tune emanated from outside her room. The twins argued in the room next to hers and she sat up with a slow smile. Warm, golden summer sunshine streamed through her window. Outside, someone mowed their lawn.

Everything was perfect. Peaceful.

The smell of bacon and maple syrup wafted into her room before her mother peered inside with a smile. "Morning, doll face! Breakfast is ready."

"Be right there," she murmured through a yawn.

Getting to her feet, Adrianna saw a girl appear and lean against the wall opposite her. Her hair was short, and a wild shade of teal green. With her sharp chin and high cheekbones, she resembled what Adrianna assumed could only be a fairy.

"Who are you?" she asked.

"Taryn," the girl answered casually, looking for all the world as though it wasn't strange she'd just appeared in Adrianna's bedroom.

"How did you get in here?" she asked bitingly.

"Magic, obviously." Taryn pushed off from the wall and sighed. "While I hate to interrupt such a happy dream, I don't really have a choice. Emma is in trouble: you need to rescue her."

Adrianna blinked, feeling the earlier joy beginning to trickle away. Sadness crept in in its place. This wasn't real. Her mother was dead, her family far away.

The room's brightness dulled, the colors fading to grey.

"How do you know Emma?" she asked, her nose wrinkling. "How do you know me? I've never seen you before."

Taryn shrugged. "You're a pretty hot topic amongst the Spellcasters: the most powerful Spellcaster to ever live was abducted by the General Tlahaz and forced to serve King Nakosh. How is the king, by the way? Be sure to give him my utter hatred." She smiled sardonically. "We were supposed to be busting your girl Emma out of Amon's little slice of Earth, but everyone was caught. Except me, of course."

Adrianna stared at the strange fairy-like girl. Slight in build, but tall. And the closer she got, the more Adrianna could feel her power.

Her brows raised. "Emma is with Amon?"

Taryn nodded. "I gotta save my brother before he's executed, and I don't have time to spring Emma too. I need you to do it."

Adrianna scoffed. "I've already intervened once; now I'm on lockdown. How the hell am I supposed to save her?"

Taryn rolled her eyes. "I've heard the rumors of Tlahaz's obsession with you. Having a general wrapped around your finger has its uses, am I right?" She gestured outside the bedroom door, to Adrianna's family.

Her eyes narrowed at the girl. "You seem to know an awful lot."

"I run my own coven, so yeah, I'm in the loop you could say. Anyway, they're in China. Wuhan. Go save them." Taryn paused. "And how *is* Levaroth? Say hi for me." Her grin turned wicked.

Then she was gone.

Adrianna jolted, her dream vanishing, and the heavy arm that held her against the warm, solid body at her back tightened reflexively. Pushing off Tlahaz's arm, she sat up. With a groan, he followed suit.

His lips pressed to her exposed shoulder. "What is it?" His voice was rough with sleep.

She fought back a shiver before tossing her blanket and getting to her feet. "Go back to sleep."

Tlahaz's golden eyes darkened. "I know that tone. What are you up to, Witch?"

Adrianna huffed as she threw on what clothing she could find discarded on the floor. "I can either force you to go back to sleep, or you can do it of your own free will."

He chuckled. "I could force you to tell me what's wrong, or you could do it of your own free will."

Her ire sparked. "When have you ever given me free will?"

His expression hardened but he didn't respond.

"Exactly."

In an instant, the shirtless, chiseled perfection that was Tlahaz stood before her, cupping her face gently. His eyes darted between hers. "What is it?"

She swallowed hard. "I can't tell you."

He growled. "Why?"

In a whisper she said, "Because you'll try to stop me."

"You aren't leaving, Adrianna."

Licking her lips, she stepped back, trying to breathe in something other than his tantalizing scent. "I'll be back. I swear."

With a rough sigh, he said, "Let me come with you."

She shook her head, "I can't."

"You can't fix Levaroth. It's too late for that."

She rolled her eyes and crossed her arms over her chest. "I know that."

He ground his teeth audibly, and she cringed. "What if I swore not to intervene as long as it didn't directly violate an order from my king?"

Her eyes narrowed while she considered. Freeing Emma wasn't a violation of any orders the king had given either of them. If she had to guess, she'd imagine Nakosh had no idea that Emma was Amon's captive.

She took a deep breath. "Fine."

His grin was bright, making her stupid heart flutter, which she of course ignored.

Holding out her hand, she sighed. "Let's go."

EMMA

Sleep was almost impossible in her position. Everything hurt, and her healing was slowed by the magic that kept her bonds in place. They weakened her. But eventually exhaustion won out after several hours of watching an unconscious Blaze bound on a cross that was bigger than hers, his feet suspended off the ground.

Amon had taken his harem outside, thankfully, though the moans and grunts were loud enough to make her teeth grind. But it gave her the chance to work the fabric stuffed into her mouth. She shoved the dampened scrap against the tape covering her mouth over and over, hoping to create enough of a gap so she could speak to Blaze when he woke.

Her eyelids had begun to droop but after what felt like a few minutes, they snapped open when the prince threw open the tent flaps and stepped in. His chest glistened with sweat and his eyes shone from the high of sexual energy he'd fed on.

The light around the tent told her the sun had risen at some point.

"Good morning, flower." The prince eyed her hungrily. "I must say, I love to see you bound and at my mercy. Are you ready to behave today?"

"Never," she spat behind the tape, though it was still muffled.

Amon chuckled lightly. Servants came in with a large metal tub that they set in front of her. They poured in steaming buckets of water. For a bath, she realized with confusion. Then her stomach clenched. Amon wouldn't try to bathe her, would he?

Her answer came when he picked up a sponge left on his table, dipped it into the slowly filling tub, and stepped toward her. She thrashed against the rope holding her, not caring that it cut into her wrists, making them bleed. Her entire body was crusted with dried blood and she itched fiercely, but she preferred that to the prince touching her in any way.

He shot her a warning look before he lightly dabbed at her left arm. The warm sponge burned her torn, aching flesh. She bit back the whimper that tried to escape, clamping her jaw tightly shut.

Amon's eyes flicked up to her face and pinned her gaze beneath his lethal stare. His tongue darted out to wet his lips while he continued his gentle washing of her body, turning away from her only to rinse the sponge and start again. Each time forcing her to stare into his eerie eyes.

"We can make a deal, flower," he said in a voice like velvet. "Would you like that?"

She tried to shake her head, to snarl, but her body was too tired.

He smiled. "I will spare your friends if you give yourself to me." His free hand lifted, fingertips hovering over her cheek for a moment until she felt the light touch of his skin.

Her power didn't shoot to the surface like it normally did—it didn't surprise her since she was completely worn out. The magic was draining her, and she currently healed at the same rate a human did.

Amon smiled triumphantly, and a choked noise came from her throat when he leaned in, pressing his lips to her cheek. A jolt of anger shot through her, but her power was vacant.

"One by one I'm plucking your petals, little flower," he whispered, his breath hot on her cheek. "You're mine."

A cough sounded beside them, jerking her attention to Blaze lifting his head. Amon's lips brushed against her neck and a chill ran up her spine.

"Ah, you're awake. Good."

"Are you okay, Emma?" Blaze asked, his voice hoarse and scratchy.

She nodded as best she could.

"I was just washing the Shediem-Slayer." Amon's grin turned wicked. "You're welcome to watch. But first"—he turned back to Emma—"let's get these clothes off."

"Don't you dare!" Blaze snarled.

The prince laughed heartily. "While you were napping, my little flower and I made a deal. I will spare the lives of your comrades and in exchange, Emma will remain here with me, forever."

Emma wanted to shake her head, to communicate with Blaze that she'd never surrender to the prince, but she couldn't sentence the others to death for her sake. When her eyes met his, she tried to inject the words she'd been too afraid to say out loud.

I love you.

Blaze's eyes softened. "I love you, Emma. Don't ever stop fighting."

Her heart swelled in her chest at the words he spoke.

He loved her.

She loved him.

Amon rolled his eyes with a drawn-out groan. "Give me a break—Giborim don't fall in love. They stake their claim and impregnate the woman gullible enough to bed them."

"Don't you ever claim to know my kind, Demon!" Blaze seethed.

Emma's breath caught. The pure rage burning in Blaze's steely blue gaze was remarkable.

Fixing his sensual gaze on her, Amon brushed her bare collarbone. "Let's get you clean, flower."

With a snap of his fingers a small woman with glazed eyes breezed inside the tent.

"Yes, Master?" she asked, her voice scratchy, either from

disuse or because she was under his spell and hadn't had a drink in far too long. Her plain white dress was formfitting but stained and beginning to fray.

"Fetch a Spellcaster to gag this one," he gestured to Blaze, and she bowed before disappearing through the slit.

"You can silence me all you want, Shediem—just know your death is inevitable," Blaze said, resting his head against the wood. His eyes closed, for which Emma was grateful because Amon went back to sponging her off.

A few minutes later a Spellcaster entered and cast a spell that wrapped a thick band of light around Blaze's head, covering his mouth. He didn't fight it, but his glare was as sharp as any blade.

Despair began to trickle in when Amon pushed away the torn scrap of material that covered her more sensitive areas to clean her. She closed her eyes, unable to see if Blaze watched. Trapped in the darkness of her mind, she fought to dredge up her power, but it remained silent.

"Broken so soon, flower?" Amon whispered just above her lips, and her eyes jerked open. His smile spread slowly across his face. "There she is. Would you like me to unbind you?"

Hope sparked. If she pretended to be beaten and he let his guard down, she could try to kill him, assuming her power came back the moment the magic was lifted.

Emma nodded.

He took his time uncoiling the ropes. When the first slid away like a python unwrapping her from its deadly hold, she flexed her wrist, the telltale tingling of power skating beneath her skin. Amon worked on the other, and Emma cast a glance at Blaze.

His dark, wavy hair hung like a curtain, hiding his eyes from her, but she felt his gaze regardless.

She gave him a small smile, her split lip stinging in the process.

The coarse rope fibers scratched her raw skin when the last enchanted binding coiled to the floor, and Emma was on Amon in an instant. They tumbled back, the prince's head slamming into the edge of the steel tub before crashing to the floor. She straddled him, his eyes wide and for once, fearful. Her hands wrapped around his throat, a feral snarl tearing from somewhere deep and dark inside her.

Heavy, sensual, lustful power burst through her veins, filling her.

"You can kill me, flower, but I'll never be gone. I'll be inside you, haunting you," Amon choked. "I'll make sure you're every bit the wicked demon you hate so much."

Fire raged inside her; she was sure he could see it in her eyes when she pulled a hand back. With a crack, her fist came down on his face. Then another.

Cool black liquid splashed her face.

The prince's face crunched, his power so drained his skin was papery and sallow. Yet Emma's fist raised to deliver another punishing blow.

Finish it, the monster inside her hissed.

She grabbed the sides of his face, fingers buried in his pale, blood-slicked hair. Her nails dug in, deeper. Deeper. Drawing blood.

A laugh bubbled up from her lips, shaking her frame.

"That's it, Prince. Give in and die."

Though his face was too distorted to be sure, she thought he smiled.

With a dry crackling noise, she fell through his chest, every inch of him crumpling to ash on the shaggy rug. Amon's energy pumped through her thick and slow. She gritted her teeth, forcing herself to bear it.

Everything was warm, her clothing too tight. Too restrictive. Emma didn't move, letting his power settle inside her.

"It's mine now," she told the clumps of ash with a satisfied smile.

So powerful.

Inhaling deeply, she felt like a goddess. Three princes' energies flowed through her. It was intoxicating. The world would bow at her feet with just a crook of her finger.

Three more, the voice in her mind cooed. *Then the king. After that, they'll all worship you.*

She stared at her hands, examining the black that coated them. Her heart beat hard but steady. Calm.

You were made for this. Your touch is lethal. Death is your blade. The voice spoke truth in her mind, and she let its words sink in.

I was made for this.

She smiled at the blood on her hands. It looked good. Looked right.

"Emma?" a familiar female voice spoke from the tent opening.

"Get out," she said quietly.

"Emma, come on, we've got to get you out of here."

She turned to see a wild, dark beauty with violet eyes. Behind her stood a tall, sexy man with a head full of dreads that hung past his shoulders. His chest was bare though blades were strapped on his back, daggers and throwing knives holstered in perfect view.

A warrior.

Emma licked her lips and stood.

The familiar girl watched her with hesitation before glancing sidelong at the man still hanging from a cross.

He was familiar too, especially when she met his piercing grey eyes. A band of light wrapped around his mouth, making him unable to speak.

Cocking her head to the side, she stepped toward the intruders. "Who are you, warrior?" she asked the muscular ebony-skinned man.

He grunted a sound that might have been a laugh. "General Tlahaz, Shediem-Slayer. Listen to the witch: we need to get out of here, now." With a disdainful look at the man on the cross he added, "I suppose you'll want to take the Giborim with you. Levaroth spoke of the filthy angel-blooded soldier that had managed to steal your affection away from him."

Levaroth. The name made her stagger back a step as though

she'd been punched in the chest. Her vision swam briefly, and she shook her head, trying to clear it.

"Emma, please, what's going on? This isn't like you."

Ringing in her ears made her grind her teeth. *Don't let go. Drain the Shediem. Feed.*

"It's the princes' power," Tlahaz answered. "She's part Shediem, so the more she feeds on them, the more she becomes full Shediem. And if I'm reading her energy right, she has at least three princes' powers rioting inside her."

She snarled at the voices breaking through her bloodlust.

"What do I do?"

It was that voice. Her friend's voice, filled with despair, that burned away the last of the haze.

Emma's head shot up. "Adrianna!"

Her friend let out a choked sound of relief and she rushed to Emma, throwing arms around her neck. Emma returned the embrace, squeezing hard enough to hear a squeak of pain. She eased her grasp but didn't let go.

Tears formed in her eyes. "You're here." A sob broke from her chest, and Adrianna's own frame shook while they both cried.

"Witch, we need to hurry."

Emma whipped up her head, shooting a menacing glare at the general. "Move, A. I'll kill him."

Tlahaz barked a laugh at the same time her best friend shouted, "No!"

Emma blinked in shock, meeting her friend's gaze. Her irises were no longer purple. Sensing Emma's surprise, Adrianna turned sheepish.

"Are you...?"

Adrianna looked over her shoulder, then shrugged. "We kind of have an alliance."

The warrior stepped up behind her, gripping her shoulder possessively. "The witch is mine." He paused as Emma quirked a brow. "Did I say that right?"

Adrianna giggled. "Sure, Demon."

Rustling sounded next to Emma, and she snapped her gaze from the confusing—and somewhat concerning—scenario in front of her to Blaze struggling against the ropes binding him.

"Crap, sorry. Uh…" She reached up, attempting to pry the knotted rope untied.

"Here, let me," Adrianna said, bumping her hip against Emma's.

Her brows furrowed but she stepped to the side, giving her friend some space. At Adrianna's back, Tlahaz stood, arms folded over his chest, somehow managing to not tear his arms to shreds on the weapons strapped there.

Dark violet light drew Emma's attention. The ropes that tied Blaze to the cross vanished, as did the magical gag.

He dropped to his feet gracefully, eyes fixed on the general with murderous rage.

Emma threw herself in front of Blaze, hugging around his middle. "Are you okay?"

After a few tense seconds, he hugged her back. "I'm fine. Are you all right? That looked rough."

Emma shrugged, not wanting to discuss it yet.

"We really need to be going. Everyone in sworn service to Amon now knows he's gone and will be thirsting for your blood," Tlahaz said in his deep, gravelly voice. Adrianna nodded her agreement.

Slowly the muffled sounds of chaos outside reached Emma's ears.

Before she could ask, Adrianna said, "I cast a protection spell over the tent to keep everyone else out."

"Right, yeah. Makes sense." In truth, she still couldn't wrap her mind around the fact that her best friend was a Spellcaster.

The general led the way out and Adrianna followed. Emma grabbed Blaze's hand, pulling him along, hoping she'd be able to stop him from killing the Shediem if need be.

She didn't particularly like the fact that her best friend was in some sort of relationship with a general. Distantly she recalled her unconventional relationship with Levaroth. It wasn't even a friendship; it was complicated. She wondered where he was, but a pang in her chest had her pushing all thoughts of him away. She didn't miss Levaroth, but the last she'd heard from him was when he'd told her Adrianna was attempting to tamper with his memories. Then his mark had disappeared.

Hundreds of Shediem rushed around, angrily and desperately trying to penetrate the invisible barrier that enclosed the tent.

"Now what?" Blaze asked with a huff.

Tlahaz flashed him a grin. "Surely you know this part, Angel-blood. We fight."

As one, they surged into the throng. The sticky feel of magic coated Emma's skin in one moment, and the next, it was gone.

Then Shediem were everywhere. Snarls, blades, teeth all around her.

Emma took a deep breath and dove into action. Between the four of them, they easily carved a path through the Shediem, and when they were through Adrianna sent a blast over her shoulder, erecting an invisible wall that Shediem and humans alike collided with.

Emma's stomach turned. "Wait, the humans. We need to rescue them."

Tlahaz shook his head. "Sorry, Shediem-Slayer. None of those humans look like they want to be free."

Though their contorted faces seemed to confirm his words, Emma snapped, "They're enthralled, they don't know any better."

Digging her heels in, she came to a halt, then spun and sprinted back to the line of clawing, thrashing monsters. With a deep breath she lifted her arms and sent a blast of her power out, never slowing.

A rumble shook the hilltop, and hundreds of ugly creatures turned to ash in an instant. Feeling for the newest power in her arsenal, she tugged on it, hoping she could reverse the lust-driven power Amon had enslaved the humans with.

She kept running, even when they went still, blinking

dazedly. Weaving in and out, she repeated the steps over and over, combing through the unending camp. She took what little power was offered to her through their instant annihilation, but it wasn't enough to sustain her.

Blaze and Adrianna shouted after her, but she didn't stop.

Her temples throbbed and her knees locked before she tumbled to the icy ground with a cry.

Around her, everything went quiet.

Her breathing was shaky. Her vision blurred. She'd expended too much power, she needed to feed again.

Or sleep.

Rolling onto her back, she groaned.

"Emma!" Adrianna skidded to a stop beside her, panting. "What's wrong? What happened?"

"Tired," she murmured.

"You're drained, aren't you?" Blaze asked with an admonishing tone.

Emma nodded, blinking up to find Tlahaz standing just out of reach.

"Don't even think about it, Shediem-Slayer."

"So hungry," she grumbled.

"We'll get you back on the plane and you can rest. But you need to get up," Blaze said above her.

Adrianna brushed a lock of hair away from her face. "Can you sit up?"

With her friend's help, Emma pushed forward to a sitting position, though she swayed.

Voices sounded behind them, but before she could utter a word, Blaze spun. "Taryn? Over here!"

A group of Giborim soldiers as well as Sergei and two other Spellcasters came into view. She didn't notice it right away, but behind them, they dragged a large blue-and-yellow Shediem. A thick tail swung wildly beneath it. It thrashed its legs trying to get to its feet, which were tied, and Emma almost felt sorry for the beast.

The voice in her mind spoke through her lips, startling everyone around her. "Bring the prisoner to me. I need to feed."

Taryn scoffed. "Looks like you've got a nice snack right there."

It was then the Giborim soldiers recognized Tlahaz for what he was: a Shediem general.

The tension was palpable. Tlahaz bared his teeth and hissed, but Adrianna moved in front of him, attempting to block his body with her much smaller frame. It was almost laughable, except for the look of possessiveness in her eyes that glowed with violet light.

"You should go," Blaze said in an eerily quiet voice.

Adrianna bent down to whisper to Emma, "Levaroth sacrificed his memories of you to break your father's mark. He has been warped to want to kill you, but there's a fail-safe. Only you can trigger it." She stood before Emma could ask what the trigger was, an apology on her face. "I'll see you soon, Em."

Then they were gone.

"What the hell was that about?" Dominic asked.

"I'll explain later," Blaze said quietly.

Emma got to her feet slowly, everyone's gaze on her, and a ripple of unease surrounded her. Ignoring them, she walked around to where the prisoner stilled. It looked like a cross between an alligator and a bull, with thick, muscled limbs, a yellow, hairy snout, and black, emotionless eyes. Yet blue alligator skin covered its bottom half. Definitely one of the ugliest Shediem she'd ever encountered.

It grunted when she drew close.

Before it could react, she dove on top of it, letting its dark power fill her. It was over all too soon, its body vanishing in a puff of ash that the breeze broke apart.

The throbbing in her head had ceased, and she straightened. She felt better already. Still tired, but she'd make the trek back to the plane without passing out.

"What the crap! We were going to question that," Taryn shrieked.

More, the voice in her mind demanded.

Later, she found herself answering.

Whatever monster had developed inside her, it huffed its disappointment.

Was she going crazy? Was it a lingering effect of the mark her father had given her?

The scariest possibility—one she couldn't entertain—was that it was really just her.

The hunger.

The bloodlust.

It was all her.

Her gaze lowered to her hands, still stained with black, and the pride that rippled through her made her spine jerk. She followed Blaze and the group, not letting them see the truth written on her face.

That deep down, the monster was her.

EMMA

They were on the plane—each of them exhausted and most of them wounded—when the bone-deep cold seeped in. Wrapped in a thick, coarse, woolen blanket, Emma shivered uncontrollably. The high that the Shediem blood had given her was more powerful with three princes' energies flowing through her veins, yet it seemed like her body was normalizing faster, though the effects were still harsh.

Like all addicts, she required more to sustain her craving.

Emma tried not to think about how she'd be affected when she consumed the last three princes' powers.

With her teeth chattering loudly over the roar of the engine, eyes watched her wearily. Sergei was among them, his brows drawn in concern. She ignored them all, attempting to force her jaw shut.

After an hour—when the shivers had mostly subsided—she shuffled toward the cockpit, where Blaze piloted the aircraft. She took the seat beside him, and they stared ahead wordlessly. His hand brushed her exposed fingers where she still clutched the blanket closed over her shoulders.

Emma looked at him, studying the rough, dark stubble of his beautiful face.

I love you, Emma.

Her mouth was opening to say the words she'd been unable to vocalize earlier when Blaze spoke. "How are you feeling?"

She gave a humorless laugh, her eyes casting down to her lap. How did she feel? Besides stiff and sore from the violent shaking she'd endured for the past hour, and the aching in her chest from seeing her best friend with Tlahaz, what was left? Her lips parted, letting the words spill out without any fear of judgment. "I'm tired. My mom is dead, Gertie is dead, my best friend is dating a Shediem general or something. I'm becoming more and more like the monsters I kill. I crave their death. So many people have gotten hurt, Haddie included"—Blaze's jaw flexed, and his eyes darkened— "and I don't really know how to feel. Maybe when this is all over, I'll be able to figure it out."

She sagged back in the chair, feeling like a physical weight had been lifted, making her boneless.

Blaze was silent for several moments, staring above the clouds. "One day at a time. You did well with Amon. I mean, you broke through the haze, or whatever you called it."

Emma bit her lower lip and shook her head. "It wasn't easy. If Adrianna hadn't been there, I don't think I would have."

"I know you would have."

His firm tone, mixed with the raw emotion in his gaze, made her heart constrict. "Maybe."

"What did Adrianna say to you before she vanished?"

Emma swallowed hard before meeting his gaze. "That Levaroth sacrificed his memories in order to free me from my father's mark." She couldn't bring herself to repeat the other part—how only she could trigger his memories to return.

Blaze looked away, jaw flexing. "How very noble of him."

She sighed. "I guess." After several moments of awkward silence, she asked, "What's the plan now?"

"Regroup at the compound. I need to check on Haddie and find some lead to help my brother. Then in a few days we'll head to the next base. We'll keep picking off the princes one by one and hope the king doesn't make an appearance any time soon."

She nodded, though deep down she knew that wasn't going to happen. Nakosh knew she was killing princes. Sooner or later, he'd stop her and then there would be a war.

"Get some sleep. It's a long flight."

She didn't need to be told twice—exhaustion was settling in again. Snuggling into the chair, she let her eyelids droop.

Emma came down the stairs, the scent of sausage gravy and buttery biscuits permeating the house with its heavenly aroma. She smiled when she entered the kitchen, her mother's shiny curtain of strawberry-blond hair shimmering in the morning sun that poured in through the open window.

The scents of warmth and summer drifted in, mixing with the aroma of her mother's superior cooking, and her heart expanded in her chest. Humming to the beat of an old eighties rock song, Laura Duvall plated a fresh tray of steaming biscuits.

"Morning," Emma greeted, pecking a kiss to her mother's cheek. She snagged a mug from the cabinet and proceeded to fill it with the half-empty pot of coffee—still hot, which meant her mother had already had several cups.

She smiled warmly at Emma, not a trace of worry or fear lining her young and beautiful face. "Morning, sweets! Load up your plate and I'll get you some gravy."

Emma was grabbing the first hot biscuit when she felt the punch of ice to her chest, signaling a Shediem. But not just any Shediem. His ancient, dark, and fearsome power radiated through the house, and she turned slowly.

Curling wisps of inky black shadowed the king of Sheol. His silver eyes were a stark contrast to the darkness shrouding him.

As the living shadows danced across his face, she caught sight of the faintest trace of a smile. It didn't appear to be cruel or malicious. If anything, she thought it looked...remorseful.

"I am truly sorry to interrupt what I'm sure is the best dream you've conjured for yourself in many weeks. However, I've come to tell you that your little game of eliminating my brothers has come to an end."

Emma glanced over her shoulder toward her mother. But she was no longer there.

The pain of recalling that her mother was dead hit her anew. The dreamscape darkened, her subconscious receding. But the King of Damnation held her firm, determined to deliver his message.

She swallowed hard, feeling the floor tremble. Her lips felt glued shut when she tried to speak, so instead she glared at the demon that broke her one moment of happiness—even if it was just an illusion.

"Time is up, little Shediem-Slayer." His hands were in his pockets, and from the small flashes she saw of his lean, muscular body—or rather, the form he chose to don—he almost looked like a normal man. Long, black hair, sharp jaw, and haunted eyes. He was handsome yet ethereal.

Terrifying.

The house shook, the dream fracturing.

"We'll continue this little chat face to face, shall we?"

With a smirk, he vanished, and Emma jerked awake.

Snapping up in her seat, she saw they were in one of the black SUVs. It rocked and bounced along the snowy, mountainous terrain. The vehicle drove through a carved-out path in the thick blanket of white that reached the side windows.

Outside it was grey, so Emma had no concept of what time it was. But if she had to guess, she'd say she'd been unconscious for at least twelve hours.

Beside her, Sergei's head rested against the seat, his eyes closed, and face more lined than she'd seen it in the short time she'd known him. His rigid posture along with the creases between his brows made her suspect he wasn't actually asleep.

Next to him was Derrik, who did appear to be asleep, if the violent swaying of his body with each bump they hit was any indication. In the front, silent and exhausted, were Blaze and Taryn. The Spellcaster stared out the side window, her body tense.

Sensing that Emma was now awake, Blaze gazed at the rearview mirror, inspecting her. She smiled slightly, letting him know she was okay. Though she desperately wanted to tell him what had just happened, she knew it needed to wait until they were alone.

When their vehicle crested the mountain, the ground leveling out before the compound gates, Emma felt a flicker of warmth spread through her chest. They were home.

Several Giborim dressed in their usual black fatigues and armed to the teeth approached their vehicles, and after a brief exchange, the gates swung open.

The push and pull of the wards made her skin feel tight, but once they were through, a gasp escaped her.

All through the grounds, tall tents were erected. Hundreds of people milled around. Some were obviously soldiers; others were shooting jets of light at each other, forcing their opponent to sharply throw a shield up or counter with their own blast of magic.

Spellcasters. Lots of them.

"What is this?" she asked, eyes wide.

Taryn smirked at Emma over her shoulder. "A few of my sister covens."

"And all the compounds on the West Coast have been moved up here," Blaze added.

"That's incredible," she breathed. "But why?"

"The war will come to you when it starts. You're the number one target. We need to be ready when it happens."

Ice dropped into her gut at his words. Nakosh had warned her that he was coming, and soon. She half expected him to burst out of the ground any second.

She had fully understood what was coming, but seeing those people gathered, preparing, made her pulse spike. Was she prepared for this? Were any of them truly ready to face the reality that they could die soon?

Yet their faces looked light—if perhaps determined. Especially the Giborim. Many cleaned and sharpened weapons.

When they stepped out, Emma felt the warm air wrap around her like a blanket. *Magic*, she thought with a pang of sadness. Gertie had been the one to enchant the compound's grounds to keep the rose bushes and garden crops at the back of the property in season. Now, the heat inside their protected space rivaled a Californian summer.

As they wound through the tents on the outskirts of the compound, sounds fell to a hush, and all eyes were on them.

On her.

She couldn't decipher many of their expressions, but she offered them what she hoped was a grateful smile as she passed.

Blaze wound his fingers through hers, and his show of affection bolstered her courage. Taryn and Derrik broke off before the doors to speak with a group of Spellcasters that rallied toward them.

The rest of them filed into the compound, weariness clear in their slumped shoulders. Dominic, however, clapped Blaze on the shoulder and sent Emma a warm smile. "Glad you are safe, *draga*. Now this one will not act like a snarling animal." He smirked at Blaze, who scoffed, and Dominic headed for the first door just out of the foyer.

Breanna's room.

Emma couldn't help the smile that curved her lips.

Blaze glanced down at her, and his own smile spread over his face. "Disaster usually creates the most daring of love stories."

She nodded, then sobered, looking at the others who set off to their separate chambers.

Leading Blaze up the wide marble staircase, she said, "I need to tell you something."

Without preamble Emma closed the door to her room, shut them both inside, and launched into her visit from Nakosh.

Blaze's gaze hardened, his jaw ticking when she finished. "There's no time to waste"—he started past her—"if the king of Sheol has made it clear he's ready to make his appearance. We need to be prepared."

Emma grabbed his arm, pulling him to a stop. "You and everyone that came on the rescue mission are exhausted. Take a few hours to get some sleep before you go charging in without even knowing when or where it's going to take place."

Blaze shook his head. "We felt the tremors of all the princes surfacing and it nearly destroyed the compound. Imagine how much stronger the shock will be when the king of Sheol surfaces. Everyone needs to be on guard and alert." He ran a hand through his dirty hair and grimaced. "Besides, I need to check on Haddie and Axel."

Emma sighed. "I appreciate that. But without rest you won't be at a hundred percent."

Blaze gave a low chuckle before pressing a kiss to her temple. "I've fought in more wars than is good for a man. I know what true exhaustion feels like, and this is nowhere near it."

"What do you need help with?" she asked. "I'll help any way I can so you can get cleaned up and sleep. I've just slept half a day, so I'm more than ready to go."

The amusement in his eyes dimmed. "Are you truly okay? I've never seen…" He cleared his throat. "You've never needed to feed off a Shediem's energy like that before. It was like you needed it to function."

She swallowed hard and nodded. "I'm okay. It was just from having so much and then expending it all so quickly."

Which is exactly what will happen on the battlefield. The thought remained unspoken, but she saw it reflected in his eyes.

She reached out, squeezing his hand lightly. "It's going to be okay. Now go see your sister."

He kissed her again, this time lingering for a moment, then breezed out of the room.

342

LEVAROTH

*I*n darkness the king was made. So shall I serve the darkness
and my king.

The girl's face flashed in his mind for the millionth time
as the sharp slice of pain shot through his brain.

Find her.

*In darkness the king was made. So shall I serve the darkness
and my king.*

Kill her.

*In darkness the king was made. So shall I serve the darkness
and my king.*

Drain her.

*In darkness the king was made. So shall I serve the darkness
and my king.*

"Who is your target?" his prince's voice boomed over the
chanting in his mind.

*In darkness the king was made. So shall I serve the darkness
and my king.*

"Emma Duvall," Levaroth gritted out.

This time the pain was an icy blow to his side, and he roared.

In darkness the king was made. So shall I serve—

"Who is your target?" Asmodeus repeated.

—the darkness and my king.

"Emma Duvall!" His mouth foamed with the taste of his
own blood.

"What will you do when you find her?"

The beast he'd kept chained deep inside snapped free.

"Kill. Her."

The prince smiled, satisfied. "You're ready."

Levaroth rattled his chains.

In darkness the king was made. So shall I serve the darkness and my king.

Find Emma.

Kill Emma.

Tear her apart.

Find Emma.

Kill Emma.

Drink her blood.

The madness gripped him, and the beast reveled in it.

He'd find Emma Duvall and kill her for making him suffer.

EMMA

T hough night fell on the compound, everyone inside its grounds was bustling. Preparing. Emma had showered off the horror of the past few days, before heading downstairs to see Breanna and Isaac.

She knocked on her friend's door softly, so as not to wake the baby if he was asleep. Breanna cracked it open, observing her with red-rimmed eyes.

Emma's brows slammed together. "What's wrong?"

The door opened further. Breanna sighed, then stepped out of the way and gestured inside.

When the door shut behind them, Emma spun to face her. "What happened?"

The girl swallowed hard. "Dominic told me what you are. What they all are." She gestured with her chin toward the entrance of the house, where hundreds of Giborim soldiers and Spellcasters mingled. "He told me where you guys have really been going and what's happening."

Emma bit her lip. They'd all been careful around her, but since the covens arrived, Emma guessed it hadn't been long before she'd seen them using magic. "I'm sorry we couldn't tell you."

Breanna nodded, hugging her arms around herself. "But it means that Dominic will go on living for hundreds of years after both me and my son are gone. There is no future for us. Not anymore." Her lip trembled, and Emma rushed to hug her.

"Look, right now"—Emma swallowed hard—"things are uncertain enough. Don't dwell on the reasons you can't let your heart feel love. Dominic cares about you and Isaac. I don't know Dominic very well, but everyone can see that you've made him smitten."

Breanna made a sound somewhere between a sob and a laugh.

"Do you care for him too?"

Breanna nodded. "More than I ever thought I could."

Emma smiled to herself. "For now, let that be enough."

A knock sounded at the door, making them release each other. Emma went to answer it, finding Blaze on the other side.

"Meeting in five minutes," he said.

"Okay." She closed the door and turned back to Breanna, who sat on the edge of her bed, staring at her son with a pained expression. "I have to go."

They embraced once more before Emma turned to leave. "Stay here and stay safe."

Breanna nodded, swiping away a single tear that rolled down her porcelain cheek.

Emma entered the conference room, which was already packed with Giborim and Spellcasters, including Taryn, her brother, and Sergei. When Emma came to a stop beside him he draped an arm over her shoulders, squeezing her to his side for a moment before letting go.

Blaze met her gaze with a nod before all chatter died down and he began.

"As you can see, our mission in Asia was a success. Emma eliminated the prince Amon. As of now, only Mammon, Levian, and Asmodeus remain."

A dagger of rage sliced her heart at the mention of her father. Eyes cut nervous and excited glances in her direction.

"On our journey back to the compound, the king of Sheol made contact." The room nearly burst with gasps and murmurs, but Blaze pressed on, raising his hands to calm the group. "He has made it abundantly clear that he intends to make an appearance soon. Any minute, really." The collective held their breaths. "We need a strategy. Emma will need to focus on the princes and Nakosh. The rest of you should be able to hold your own against the Shediem ranks."

Taryn stepped forward, placed her hands on the table, and looked around. "Without their beloved king, slaying them should trap them in Sheol. It's my belief they are able to return to Earth only when Nakosh is there to keep the door open, so to speak." Murmurs of ascent went around. "I think it's safe to say none of you should have a problem holding your own; just remember to avoid their venom."

Out of the corner of her eye, Emma saw Emerelda—who had stood in the back, by the door—slip out.

Blaze watched her go before looking around the room. A solemn air wrapped around them all. "No matter what happens, it has been a pleasure to serve and protect with you."

Dominic beat his fist to his chest at the opposite end of the table, drawing Emma's attention to him. "By angels' blood we were made!" His accent was thick, his voice booming. The other Giborim followed suit, their fists slamming against their chests.

"To serve and protect as it was decreed!" The answering shouts resembled a thunderclap.

Only the Spellcasters remained silent.

When Blaze spoke again, his eyes were filled with storm clouds. "May the angels protect us." His voice was low, with an edge of violence that Emma knew all too well. The Giborim were warriors—meant for war and bloodshed.

Her heart thundered.

Without another word, Blaze hurried from the room. Emma made to follow, but Silas stepped in front of her, a smug smile curving his thin lips.

"So, I've been dying to ask: what does it feel like to defeat three impossibly powerful Shediem princes? It's truly a miracle what you're able to do considering the angels themselves created us to keep the filthy creatures in check."

Emma would have laughed at the man's backhanded insults, but instead she smiled sweetly. "I guess they just needed something more powerful to get the job done."

Lip curled, he was raising a hand to strike when Sergei gripped his arm from behind and twisted it sharply. A crack sounded and Silas screamed.

The room fell silent. Suddenly Taryn and Derrik stood to Emma's left behind Sergei, hands raised, and the Giborim stood to her right.

In a low, growly voice, Sergei said, "If you try to strike her again, I'll chop off your head, you self-righteous prick."

Silas's red face purpled, his mouth gaping as Dominic gripped his shoulder. "Whatever your judgments are, Silas, let them go. The girl is the key to surviving this war and you know it."

With a sneer, Silas jerked from Dominic's grasp before spinning on his heel. The other Giborim parted to let him pass. He threw the double doors open with a bang and stalked out.

The others followed suit, except for Sergei and Emma.

When the last person was gone, he looked her over. "You okay?"

She nodded with a sigh. "I get why he hates me. I hate myself sometimes."

Sergei's thick dark brows furrowed. "Why do you hate yourself, *draga?*"

Emma's fists unclenched. "I'm the daughter of a Shediem prince. I don't just kill the Shediem, I absorb their power. And I love it. When I'm feeding on their energy, I crave it, and..." Her voice cracked. With a deep, shuddering breath, she tried again. "I feel like a monster too."

Sergei smiled, a gentle, understanding smile. "I see your mother's goodness in you, Emma. No matter what, I'll never believe you're a monster. You couldn't be." He rubbed her biceps, warming the goose bumps that erupted over her skin. "Where does your power to kill Shediem come from?"

Her brow furrowed. "What?"

"Where does it come from?"

Emma thought for a moment. "Uhh…"

"It's angelic, Emma. You have both light and dark power in you, as we all do." A ball of pale blue light filled his palm, and he held it out for her to see. "Spellcasters are said to be a balance. A perfect neutral, born of the elements to keep both light and dark in check. Why would there need to be a balance, do you think? Why not just wipe out all the darkness?"

Confused by where he was going with this, she answered, "I'm not sure."

"Humans are not wholly good nor bad, correct?"

Emma nodded slowly.

"The secret is, we all have a bit of both in us. There is no way to erase the darkness completely. If the Giborim were to wipe out all of humanity and the Shediem so only they remained, there would still be darkness. Though they serve a noble cause, not even the Giborim are entirely righteous."

The blue light turned to a glowing white sphere. She watched as inky black crept in, winding snakelike fingers through the ball of light, trying to smother it. But the light grew brighter, beating back the darkness until the sphere was coated equally with shadow and light.

Emma couldn't help but smile sadly. She'd seen the hatred and prejudice of the Giborim. And in tiny sparks, she'd seen goodness in one Shediem in particular.

Levaroth.

As Rowek he'd been kind, sweet, and loving, though as Levaroth his need to protect her was suffocating.

It was true that they were all capable of both light and darkness. She just hoped the darkness wouldn't consume her.

The words spilled out before she could stop them. "I just hope whatever light is inside me isn't blotted out by the darkness. The more Shediem power I take, the more I feel like there's only darkness inside me."

The sphere vanished when Sergei closed his fist, and his hand came to rest on her shoulder. "So long as you fight to remain who you truly are, you'll never be evil. Keep your mother in your heart. And if it gets to be too much, those of us that love you will fight to bring you back to the light," he said.

Her eyes burned with tears. She nodded, and Sergei pulled her into a tight hug.

"Never forget, dear Emma, who you truly are."

She clutched to that hope. The hope that she'd survive this and remain who she was.

No matter how small the fragment might be.

BLAZE

As soon as the meeting was over, Blaze hastened to follow Emerelda. It was a whim, he knew. A suspicion that he couldn't shake. But if he was going to save his brother, he'd follow every lead until his deadline was up.

The air was warm and inviting—so different from the true temperature outside the wards—when he slipped into the night. Slinking through the shadows, he rounded the side of the house, detecting the low voices. Through the maze of rose bushes and neatly trimmed hedges, Blaze crept low enough to not be seen to the fence line. The temperature dropped further with each step.

"No one has a single clue about you or how you've been breaking into the compound." Emerelda's whisper made his body tense just before she came into view. Wrapped in her thick fur, breath curling in visible puffs in the moonlight, she leaned against the tall, lean frame of a stranger.

A dark, velvety voice floated through the night. "Pinning any suspicion on your fake fiancée was a smart move, I'm impressed."

What little warmth Blaze's body managed to hold onto vanished when the faint illumination reflected in the Shediem's dark red eyes.

A prince. Inside the wards.

"I fed him your blood like you instructed, painting him as the madman." She laughed. "Soon we can be together, Mammon.

I'll be your queen and we'll rule over these simple creatures."
Emerelda leaned forward, stretching up to press a kiss to his
lips, but he drew away.

"And what of the Shediem-Slayer? She needs to die. Tonight."

It was pure reflex that had Blaze gripping the blade at his
hip. Every part of him raged to leap out and slaughter both the
traitor and the prince she was consorting with.

"I've been working on it. Axel tried like I *persuaded* him to
do, but that girl is almost impossible to get close to. Everyone
is constantly fawning over her. And she only just got back from
China." The venom in her voice rose with her volume.

"Get it done, Emerelda, and then we'll be together. It's how
it has to be."

She sighed like a petulant child but said, "It will be done."

"Good girl," Mammon praised. "Now go before you're
discovered. The wards will detect me soon."

His mouth lowered to hers, kissing her lazily. Tamely.

Bile burned the back of Blaze's throat. She'd framed Axel and
he'd fallen for it. All the interest Emerelda had taken in Emma
made so much more sense.

Emma. He needed to protect her.

And he needed to get to his brother. Emerelda's confession
was proof of his innocence. The reason he'd been looking like
he was poisoned was because he was—with a prince's blood.

Blaze turned, preparing to sprint back, when a sharp pain
erupted in his temple.

"Well this is an interesting turn of events," Emerelda crooned
before his body slid sideways and everything went black.

EMMA

E mma lay in bed, staring at the ceiling. Sleep wouldn't come so she waited for Blaze to return to his room, but so far, at just after midnight, he hadn't. After a few more minutes, she decided to use the excuse of going to the kitchen to get some tea to help her sleep and hoped she'd run into Blaze on the way.

With a sigh, she rolled to the edge of the bed and climbed to her feet. She'd just reached for her favorite thigh-length cardigan when the first boom sounded.

Distant shouts followed, and she froze.

Another boom. Then another.

In an instant, Emma raced out of her room and down the hall. People began to poke their heads out of their doors, awakened by the commotion.

Down the glossy marble staircase, another crash came from outside the manor. The ground shook. Gritting her teeth, Emma knew what she'd find before she reached the giant mahogany door.

Other Giborim raced after her, armed and ready to face the threat outside their borders.

She leapt over the stairs, skidding to a stop in the gravel.

The covens of Spellcasters were spread out along the edge of the fence line, pushing their colorful magic into the wards.

On the other side, flaming boulders assaulted the barrier of magic.

"It's starting!" a Giborim yelled next to her before taking off running toward the border.

"Where's Blaze?" someone else shouted.

Her heart sank. Where was he? There was no way he didn't know what was happening right now...

Unless something had happened to him.

Soldiers flooded from the manor, rushing past her with blades drawn. Using what little light was available from the campfires and blasts of magic, she tried to scan for Blaze, but there were too many people.

She spun on her heel and returned inside, stopping at Breanna's room. Her door was ajar. Emma didn't pause before pushing her way in.

Breanna clutched a whimpering Isaac to her chest while Dominic hugged them both. They looked up at the sight of Emma and she cleared her throat, suddenly guilty she'd intruded on a tender moment.

"What is it, Emma?" Dominic asked before Breanna could.

"Have you seen Blaze?"

His brows drew together. "Not since the meeting. I assumed he was with you."

Emma's chest tightened. "That was the last time I saw him too." Her voice wavered.

Shock registered in the Russian's cold eyes. He pressed a kiss to Breanna's loose waves, then released her. "Stay safe, *regina mea*."

Breanna offered him a small smile before turning to Emma. "You be safe too."

She nodded stiffly. "I'll try."

Dominic nudged her out of the room and shut the door gently behind them. "Quick, this way."

He led Emma to the back of the manor, through a small door she'd thought opened to a supply closet. Instead, a set of wooden stairs led down into pitch blackness.

Dominic took the lead yet again, reaching above to tug on a chain she hadn't noticed. A light clicked on, casting a faint glow over the stairs before he began descending them.

"Where does this go?" she asked.

"Prison cells," was his only response.

Her eyes widened in surprise when they reached the bottom, finding a long row of cells stretching into a narrow hall.

They passed the first two cells and came to a stop in front of the third.

Emma gasped, spying Axel. His wrists were chained above his head, which hung limp against a pale bicep.

"Has your brother come to visit you recently?" Dominic asked.

Axel snorted before slowly lifting his head. His cheeks were gaunt, his eyes so pale they were almost white. "Haven't seen him in…well, I haven't really been able to keep track of time in here."

Dominic gusted a breath before cursing low. "Your brother is missing."

Emma snapped her gaze to the Russian, swallowing hard. She hadn't wanted to accept that fact, but now it stared her in the face.

Axel's expression turned grim. "Well I didn't kidnap him. I've been a little tied up." His tone was humorless, but he still smirked as though there was anything that could possibly be amusing at a time like this.

"We didn't check with Haddie," Emma whispered. "Maybe he went to see if she was safe."

Dominic shook his head. "She was in the kitchen helping with dishes." Then he cocked his head. "Although it's possible Blaze didn't know that."

"Haddie?" Axel croaked. His face filled with disbelief, then with raw anguish.

"You didn't know," she whispered. It wasn't a question; his expression told her as much. "Blaze didn't tell you."

"After dropping off Haddie here, we left straight away to rescue you," Dominic explained.

Something like a sob escaped Axel. "Oh god, she's alive?"

Emma nodded, her eyes pricking with tears.

His chest heaved with a rattling breath. "I want to see her."

Dominic rested a hand on the cell bars. "The compound is under attack. Nakosh and the remaining princes, along with their armies, are going to be marching up to our borders any second. There's no time now, but I promise she's safe."

Axel didn't appear to be listening. A wail tore from him, desolate and broken. It broke Emma's heart.

"Did you help the Shediem attack the compound? Did you let them inside?" she asked in a cold, hard voice.

"No," he sobbed. "No, no, no. I'd never betray my kind."

Emma looked to Dominic. "He's telling the truth. Maybe he can help us." Axel didn't seem like he'd be able to fight, but perhaps he was capable of helping in some other way. He had trained alongside Blaze; if anything, he'd know how his brother fought.

Dominic looked at her wearily. "He could be lying. I think it's best he stay here until we find Blaze. Besides, he *did* attack you."

"I'll be fine. Axel knows his brother better than anyone else. He can help with strategies. Help rally the Giborim—"

"The Giborim voted for his imprisonment. They believe he is a traitor. Letting him out will only incite infighting. We can't afford that right now."

Emma huffed in frustration. "Fine. I'll find Blaze, then I'll be back to get you out, Axel." He deserved to see his sister. "I need to find Haddie to see if she's seen Blaze." She ran for the stairs again.

At first, Dominic didn't follow, but after a few seconds, she heard his footsteps on the wooden stairs behind her. They ran through the manor, which was now mostly empty.

A cry of pain jerked her to a stop. "Oh god, no, please! Not now!"

Haddie.

Emma took off, faster than before, skidding to a stop in the kitchen where Haddie crouched on the floor, clutching her belly. One woman was pressing a damp cloth to her forehead; another rubbed her back. They murmured words of encouragement.

"What's wrong?" Emma asked.

Haddie's eyes lifted to hers. "The baby is coming."

Emma could have laughed at the absurdity of it all. Instead she knelt in front of her friend. "Have you seen Blaze?"

"No," Haddie panted, her face relaxing slightly.

Emma dropped her head. Her anxiety ratcheted up further. Something was definitely wrong.

"I'm going to check outside, see if anyone has seen him," Dominic offered, looking uncomfortable.

She nodded to him. Then to Haddie she said, "We need to get you upstairs to a bed."

Despite Hadessah's protests, the group of women hefted her to her feet and started for the stairs.

Another echoing boom shook the walls.

Emma grimaced. "I have to see if they need me outside, but I'll come check on you in a little bit, okay?" she said behind her friend.

One of the women assisting Haddie turned to her. She was older than Emma had seen most Giborim look, possibly late thirties, which Emma was sure meant several hundred years old at least.

"Don't worry, dear, I've delivered many babes in my life. Go." She smiled kindly, and Emma nodded before heading for the door again.

Outside, Giborim fought hordes of Shediem beyond the protection of the wards. They continued to be bombarded with hit after hit.

The closer she got to the edge, the more she heard the Spellcasters bracing for each blast. They looked strained, as though they were physically blocking the objects being flung at the barrier.

When a particularly large flaming object in various shades of purple came sailing into the wall, hitting with a thunderous crash, several Spellcasters were knocked backward.

The gap allowed Emma to spy the line of cloaked magic-wielders leading the charge. Together they formed the glowing, burning spheres that were hurled at the wards.

It was magic.

Emma bit down on her lip so hard she nearly drew blood.

"Hold strong, this is a big one!" Taryn shouted from twenty feet down the line. Her palms glowed bright before she injected a vibrant green streak of magic into the sky.

"Taryn, have you seen Blaze?" she asked.

One Spellcaster screamed and crumpled to the ground while many others were flung back when the next wave of magic hit. Taryn whipped around to look at a young girl, who didn't appear to be moving.

When others crowded around her, Taryn reluctantly turned to Emma, her palms lifted to keep her magic flowing. "No, I haven't seen him. Haven't seen my brother in a while either." Worry creased her face.

"Maybe they went together to do something," Emma suggested, the words to soothe herself as much as the Spellcaster. But Taryn didn't look convinced.

"I'm sure they'll turn up. For now, we follow the plan he outlined. You're not to interact until one of the princes shows up. Stay behind us, just in case the wards fail."

Emma's heart hammered painfully. "It can't fail. There are kids and unarmed women inside."

Taryn winced as yet another blazing ball of magic hit. "We're not going to let anyone past us. Just stay back until it's time."

Emma nodded, turning on her heel to rush back into the house. She climbed the stairs and knocked on the door where Haddie's grunts and moans emanated from.

"Enter," the same Giborim woman from earlier spoke.

Emma strode inside, finding Haddie kneeling waist-deep in an inflated kiddie pool. Her beautiful face screwed up in pain, but only the slightest cry escaped. Emma wanted to rush to the girl and help in any way she could. But it was birth. There was nothing to be done for her.

"How far along is she?" Emma asked softly.

"Eight centimeters," a younger girl answered. She held Haddie's hand, helping her through the contraction. "Not too much longer. She's progressing really quickly."

Emma nodded. "Can I get you anything?" she asked Haddie, who sagged when the wave of pain receded.

She shook her head. "I can do this."

A smile pulled at Emma's lips. "Of course you can."

The boom that shook the manor had everyone stiffening, and Haddie cried out suddenly.

"I have to go help, but I'll be back soon."

"Emma," Hadessah gasped.

She turned.

"That bastard Amon is dead, right?"

She nodded slowly.

"Did he suffer?"

Emma's smile spread. "Yes."

Haddie smiled then too. "Good."

If there had been any question as to who the father was, the answer was clear now. Emma wished she could resurrect the prince and kill him again for her friend. For the suffering he inflicted on her.

"Go kick some Shediem ass," Haddie snarled, then her face scrunched in pain while she rocked back and forth, breathing it through.

"I will," Emma vowed.

She stopped by her room to grab her dagger then holstered it to her thigh. Back on the grounds, she found Taryn.

The Spellcaster's arms shook and her breathing was shallow. "Change of plans. We need to trust that the wards are going to hold, and go on the offensive."

Emma nodded. "I'll help."

The Spellcaster cast her a disapproving look, but didn't argue.

"Coven of Skyes and Coven of Marauders!" Her voice boomed with magic to reach throughout the grounds.

The Spellcasters turned their attention to her, awaiting instruction.

"Attack!"

With a collective roar to the dark, starless sky, they charged. Emma sprinted through them, hoping to go unnoticed by the opposing Spellcasters. An icy blast of winter air hit her the second she stepped over the barrier.

A wall of red-cloaked figures blocked her path less than ten feet from the wards, but she didn't stop. Emma knocked through them as hard as she could, sending at least two sprawling.

Once she was through the first line of defense, she saw the Giborim hacking at Shediem. There were hardly any left, but Emma charged for the first one she saw. Her hands gripped rubbery grey flesh, and a surge of angry energy flowed through her.

The familiar hunger awakened with the first spark.

Power roared through her veins, making her vision sharper. Her hearing clearer.

Emma zipped to the next, sucking out the creature's energy so fast its body turned to a brittle black husk that she drove her fist through.

The ashes shattered, coating her.

She reveled in the feel of their death on her skin.

I am power.

I am death.

Everything around her melted into a cacophony of colors and muffled sounds. Only the hunt remained.

Kill.

Drain them.

Just as she absorbed the last bit of power in the vicinity, the ground shook.

Boom.

Boom.

Boom.

Emma shuffled through the snow, peering into the darkness.

360

A wall of dark figures marched up the mountain, their steps thundering.

Wild excitement danced through her, and she smiled. Leading the charge, in a chariot pulled by massive bony creatures that resembled horses with skeletal wings tucked into their sides, was the sleek, leather-clad Prince Levian. The beasts bared their pointed teeth and snarled. Their empty eyes, as white as the snow, were locked on her. Beneath their hooves, tongues of flame sizzled in the snow, licking up their black legs. They trotted on, unaffected.

Thousands of Shediem stormed behind the prince and his dramatic war chariot. His dark, slicked-back hair and sneer were illuminated by the fire dancing in front of him.

"BY THE ANGELS' BLOOD WE WERE MADE," a booming voice echoed over the beating of marching footfalls.

"TO SERVE AND PROTECT AS IT WAS DECREED!"

The Giborim's war cry made the hairs on the back of her neck stand on end.

Utter chaos ensued, but Emma's thirst for Shediem power had her charging forward as well, her eyes fixed on the prince.

The winged beasts pulling the chariot kicked up into a canter, huffing and snarling. Steam curled around their bodies from the live flames. But Emma was a creature of fire too.

Slightly changing direction, she ran parallel to the prince. Once she spotted her opening, she took it, lunging through the air.

Hands reached for the anticipated surge of power that didn't come.

She hit an invisible barrier with a crash that sent her shooting backward. Her body barked in pain when she landed on her back in the snow, staring up at the dark night.

It took several moments before she could draw in breath again. But when she did, Emma's gaze zeroed in on the dark, cloaked figure that marched behind the chariot.

A Spellcaster.

Leaping to her feet, she took off at a run. Not toward the prince whose back was turned, his sword slicing through the arm of a Giborim who misjudged their own swing, but toward the Spellcaster who conjured a shield around Levian.

Emma pulled out the dagger from her thigh holster automatically. It wasn't until she drove the blade into the Spellcaster's chest and their hood fell back—revealing a slender, feminine face with dark eyes—that Emma registered what she'd just done.

She'd murdered a human.

Not a monster. Not a demon. A person.

Her face contorted with agony. Warm liquid pooled around the dagger's hilt, coating her hand. It bubbled up between the girl's thin, parted lips.

"I'm sorry," Emma gasped. "I'm so sorry."

The Spellcaster fell back, and Emma caught her before she hit the snow. The girl appeared to be around her age, and from the way confusion marred the girl's brow, Emma didn't think she spoke English.

"I'm sorry, I'm sorry." Her words poured out on repeat. With a sickening crack and gurgle, Emma wrenched the blade from the Spellcaster's sternum. Then her hands went to the wound, trying to staunch the blood flow. But there was too much.

The girl's face took on a greyish hue even in the small amount of light. Then her eyes flicked to the sky, where they stayed.

Unseeing.

A sob bubbled up Emma's throat.

Arms hauled her to her feet. "Leave her," Taryn hissed. "There's nothing you can do now."

She pushed Emma away and she stumbled, the chaos of the fight coming back to full volume.

The prince circled around, grinning at Emma's tear-streaked face.

This was *his* fault.

All of the Shediem race's fault.

She'd killed because she'd seen no other option.

The blood on her hands was more than just the Spellcaster lying dead in the snow. It was the hybrid children she'd burned. It was every Giborim that died or would die because of this war. She wiped her sticky hands on her jeans, thankful for the black material. After cleansing the dagger in the snow, she straightened, eyes narrowing.

Emma let out a snarl and took off at a run, dodging weapons and Shediem alike. Animals fought too—familiars, she thought. Some flew in the air; others crashed into each other in the snow, clawing and biting.

It was a brutal bloodbath.

Levian's grin faltered. His hands lifted at his sides, palms raised, but nothing happened.

The prince's realization struck only moments before she leapt up, barreling into his carriage.

She knocked into him with the force of a raging bull, her hands tearing at his face and neck, drawing blood.

His power soared through her. A scream of retribution scorched her throat.

Haunting and heady, his dark energy was a tornado. It tore apart her insides and forged them anew.

She was remade in the darkness.

Yes, more, her inner beast demanded.

The prince's body crumbled, his blood still wet on her fingers as his ashes scattered.

Behind her eyes, it felt like thousands of needles pricked and stabbed. She winced at the pain, covering her eyes while they fought to adjust.

The new addition to her power begged to be used. And as the chariot rocked over mounds of packed snow—or perhaps bodies, she wasn't interested in finding out which—she focused on the massive, bulky beasts still pulling the chariot around the battlefield.

Sleep, she willed.

Their hoofbeats slowed, their muscular bodies seeming lethargic. They stopped, and at once, lay down.

Emma jumped out of the carriage and moved to stand in front of them. Without another thought, she laid a hand on their foreheads one by one.

Their deaths were quick, and their energy fueled her.

Looking around at the feast of Shediem, she smiled.

By the time I'm done, my power will never again fade. I am a goddess of darkness and death, reaping the wicked as I see fit.

No one will stand in my way.

ADRIANNA

T he Shediem outside the tent chanted, calling for death. Adrianna burrowed deeper into the thin blankets, trying desperately to get warm. Athena curled up against her stomach, the size of a medium-sized dog. Her small spikes poked Adrianna in the belly, but she didn't mind. Her familiar was warm and comforting.

Sensing Adrianna's unrest, Athena lifted her beautiful violet head. The creature's magnificent eyes searched hers before she nuzzled Adrianna's cheek.

"People are going to die, Athena," she said sadly. "Innocent people. The people we should be fighting with, not against."

Tlahaz chose that exact moment to tear into the tent, his body armor glinting. "Still abed, Witch?"

Adrianna ignored him, pulling up the cover over her and Athena completely. The wyvern huffed a puff of smoke in indignation. "If he can't see us, maybe he'll go away," she told her familiar.

"Not going to happen, Witch. Get up." To punctuate his words, he ripped the blanket off, and she squealed.

Athena whipped her head around and blew a gust of hot steam in his direction. Tlahaz waved it away, his lip curling.

"What have I told you about feeding the beast fish? Its breath reeks for weeks after."

Adrianna stuck her tongue out. "You told me I'm not allowed to feed her any of the Shediem out there"—she pointed outside the tent—"so I gave her what we had."

Tlahaz's golden eyes swirled with a hint of amusement. "I also said to keep the creature off the bed. It tears the sheets." He turned, heading for the armor hanging in the corner. The attire *she* was meant to wear.

Adrianna snorted as she sat upright. "You tear the sheets more than she does."

He flashed her a rare grin over his shoulder before laying the armor at the foot of the bed. "Get dressed," he instructed.

She folded her arms across her chest, feeling particularly unruly. "I don't want to wear that."

He leaned onto the bed, resting his weight on his fists. "If you don't put it on yourself, I will do it for you. Would you like that, Witch?"

She sniffed. "I don't see why I have to wear *that* in particular. I'm a Spellcaster; can't I just use my magic to protect myself? I'll be in the air anyway."

"Other familiars will be in the air, as will the Veemuris."

"But they won't attack me," she pointed out. Her gaze fell to the sheets that she twisted in her fingers.

Silence remained like a heavy cloak over them.

Then Tlahaz spoke. "What is it, Adrianna?"

She still didn't look at him when she whispered, "I can't do this." She didn't have to elaborate.

Tlahaz stood to his full height and inspected her. He didn't make threats or belittle her. Instead, he walked around to the side of the bed and sat down beside her.

Taking her hand in his, he brought it to his cheek and kept it there, drawing her gaze up to meet his. "Your spirit is kind and good, Adrianna. I'm not commanding you to kill unless it's truly necessary. But you know what the prophecy states. It knew which side of the battle you'd stand on. Your job is to stay alive and to fulfill the prophecy."

"Doesn't it bother you?" she asked. "That I'll bind your king back in Sheol for all eternity?"

He didn't answer for several moments. "My duty is to my king," he said softly, "but it is also to you. For whatever twisted reason, fate has created a bond between us that is unbreakable. I live to help you fulfill your destiny."

His lips kissed the faint silvery mark on the column of her throat where he had taken her blood. Where he'd seen the future. Their future.

She blushed.

"Don't kill anyone," she begged, and he let her hand slip from his face.

This time he looked down. "I cannot make any promises. It's war. People will die. There is nothing you or I can do to change that."

Adrianna stroked Athena's back when she started to edge onto Adrianna's lap. To comfort her.

Tlahaz reached over and stroked the spot between the familiar's eyes that made her go boneless. Every time she did it, it made Adrianna laugh. "Traitor," she admonished her wyvern playfully.

"Come, Beauty. We need to get you ready before the troops head out."

She wrinkled her nose at the raucous jeers and laughter ensuing right outside her tent, but she got to her feet, determined to see this through.

When she was fully dressed—her hair pulled back in a braid—she observed herself in the mirror, looking every bit the warrior princess she always aspired to be.

Horns sounded all through the camp, freezing her blood.

Tlahaz took her hand in his and pressed a kiss to the back of it, before heading out to join the hellish soldiers.

BLAZE

A sharp slap hit his cheek. "Wake up, sleepyhead. I have something fun planned."

Emerelda's cheery voice brought back the scene he'd spied of her kissing a prince of Sheol, and his blood returned to a boil.

They'd mentioned killing the Shediem-Slayer.

Emma. Blaze's eyelids—heavy and dry like coarse sandpaper on his eyes—flitted open at that thought.

Emerelda came into focus. But beside her, with his arms folded over his chest, eyes bloodshot and a cruel smirk twisting his full lips, was Derrik. Blaze sat in a chair, tied with thick rope around his chest, ankles, and wrists—no doubt enchanted rope to keep him from busting through the fibers.

Blaze shook his head, stopping abruptly when nausea crashed into him like a tidal wave. "Derrik," he sighed. "You too?"

The Spellcaster sneered. "Oh don't be so surprised. There are far more Shediem sympathizers than you realize."

His attention returned to Emerelda. "What did Mammon promise you? Riches? Power?"

She scoffed.

"You have to know he'll kill you the second you're of no use to him."

She flipped her golden hair over her shoulder in that vain, flippant manner of hers. "This is not a new alliance, *William.*"

She spat his name, glaring down at him. "Mammon and I met by accident in Tahiti some thirty years ago. I could have killed him, but I didn't. He didn't try to kill me either. We were cautious of each other, but the attraction was instant and so intense, we couldn't deny it." Emerelda sighed dreamily, and Blaze's stomach turned. "It was the best night of my life. After that, we kept in contact, mostly through his messengers. But I visited him in Sheol after getting wind of the Shediem-Slayer. I planned to kill her, but you kept her under such a close watch that I couldn't get close without alerting you." She barked a laugh.

"And anyway, Jake might have succeeded if you hadn't intervened. Then there was your brother." Still smirking, she added, "I didn't have to kill her myself; I just had to ensure that everyone hated her. Your uncle especially. It didn't take much to convince him that she's too dangerous. Too volatile. Don't be surprised if the Giborim tear her apart for me. Especially once they see her kill another prince.

"Levian is here now. He's useless, really. No love lost there. But with his power added to her arsenal, our people will see her for what she is. A monster."

That meant Emma was still alive. He couldn't hold back the surge of relief he felt.

It must have shown on his face because Derrik slapped him hard enough to taste blood. Blaze didn't make a sound.

"What's your part in this, Derrik?"

The Spellcaster's chest puffed with pride. "I worked the magic needed to get through the wards and helped pin everything on your brother."

Blaze's jaw clenched. "What's in it for you? Surely you're not Mammon's lover too?"

Derrik hit him again, this time with his fist. The punch connected with his nose, and a slight crunching sound made Blaze's teeth grind together.

"What's in it for me is a world free from judgment and condemnation. You Giborim sit on your pedestals thinking it's your job to police every little thing we do." Derrik bent close, his rancid breath making Blaze gag. "News flash: you're nothing."

When Derrik straightened, Blaze wheezed for fresh air. There was something very wrong with the Spellcaster. It wasn't a lack of personal hygiene that made him smell so foul. No, there was something else at play. Something demonic. Possession maybe? Though he couldn't sense anything beyond the fact that the tunnel they were situated in was filled with Shediem in cells.

"Giborim don't police Spellcasters," Blaze said at last, cocking his head to the side to look at the two.

The faint illumination from the sconces on the walls flickered. Derrik glared, the wrath of the Spellcaster filling the chamber with the scent of magic and fury. "Taryn and I have different dads, but we share the same mother. My sister's two years older than me and pretty much raised me while our mother worked constantly, trying to provide for us. Our coven didn't like our mom much because she was willing to take whatever jobs came her way. Many of them were from Shediem. One day when she was working a potion for one of her clients, the Giborim burst into our house. They killed her because of who her client was."

Derrik's body visibly shook, his words growing louder and louder, echoing in the tunnel. "They said that she was trash because she deemed to work for the Shediem, and when they were done beating her until she didn't even look like my mom, they threw her in a dumpster. If they knew she had kids, they didn't care. They didn't look for us. Taryn had hidden in a closet with me. The bastards destroyed our home and set it on fire with us still in it."

He lifted his T-shirt, revealing thick, gnarled scars on his left side. Turning, he showed that the scars waved over his back. *Burns.* Blaze tasted bile.

"Taryn got burned too. Worse than this. But she healed her scars. She tried to heal mine, but I wouldn't let her." He dropped his shirt, turning to face Blaze again. "I wanted a reminder of who the real enemy is. You." He punctuated the last word with a hard jab to Blaze's chest.

"Look, I am so sorry that happened. I would never order something like that to be done. If we ever got word that a Spellcaster was working a particularly nasty spell for a Shediem, we'd seize it, but we never killed anyone."

"LIAR!"

The sound reverberated through the narrow hall, and the beasts slumbering in their cells began to screech and wail at the sound.

"There were four men that beat my mother to death. You sent one of them. Jakob Bernal was *your* man. Under *your* command."

Ice sluiced through every inch of Blaze's body.

It couldn't be true. He kept a close eye on his men, and though Jake was a hothead, he wasn't a murderer. Was he?

They were friends, but there had been several occasions where Blaze had wondered just how many secrets his comrade carried.

"I'm sorry," he said. "I had no idea that happened. That's despicable. Unforgiveable. He and anyone else involved will be tried for their crimes, you have my word."

"Don't worry," Derrik snarled. "I already exacted their justice."

Flames leapt to the torches lining the walls, lighting the deeper parts of the tunnel.

Four figures hung from ropes tied to the ceiling, their bodies limp.

Horror shot through Blaze. Thanks to his angelic eyesight, he could make out every broken bone. Every bruise and cut.

Jake's body was the closest, his skin dull and grey.

Dead. His friend was dead.

The other three weren't facing him, so he couldn't make out who they were.

Blaze shook his head, trying to quell the urge to roar in anger.

"Well, it's been a blast, Blaze. Now for the fun part." Emerelda nodded to Derrik, who lifted his hands toward the corridor. The groaning protest of metal locks breaking and cell doors swinging open filled Blaze's ears, along with the furious beating of his heart.

More than a dozen Shediem of all shapes and sizes barreled into the tunnel. Some leapt for the swaying bodies overhead until Emerelda clucked her tongue.

"Leave those. We've got a live one for you. Perhaps you'll recognize him as your jailor."

They turned in unison. Snarls and growls rumbled the concrete floor beneath Blaze's shoes. Emerelda and Derrik headed for the stairs while every beast clawed their way toward him.

Tied and defenseless, he was unable to protect his brother or Emma. He was of no use to anyone now.

The first Shax opened its wide jaws, venom dripping dangerously close to his feet. It sank its knifelike teeth into his thigh, and he clamped his jaw shut to keep his scream locked inside.

He heard Emerelda titter up the stairs.

Another Shediem's claws flashed in the flickering light just as the door at the top of the stairs burst open with a boom.

"What the—" came Axel's voice.

"Grab them!" Dominic demanded.

A scuffle ensued as Blaze fought away from the jaws of the creatures attacking him. Pain seared through his leg. Already the venom penetrated his veins, making the room hazy.

A blast of green light sent the Shediem attacking him shooting back. Sergei rounded Blaze's chair, and when his eyes fell on Blaze's leg he immediately placed a hand just above the wound to draw the venom out.

A body thumped to Blaze's side—Derrik. Bound and gagged, squirming. His curses were muffled.

A second thump, and Emerelda landed on the other side in the same position.

Axel ran past, flashing a grin over his shoulder at Blaze. "Got yourself in quite the pickle, I see."

"Just a bit," Blaze grumbled.

Dominic appeared in front of him, and both he and Sergei undid Blaze's bonds.

Once the coils of rope slid free, he turned to his friend. "Weapon?"

Dominic smiled, handing him one of his swords, which must have been discarded somewhere in the chamber.

He leapt into action beside his brother, cutting through the Shediem like the team they were.

"You okay?" Blaze asked him.

Axel nodded. "A little weak, but I'll recover. Dominic figured out something was amiss when Emerelda and Derrik were both missing, as well as you. Never thought my ex would be a Shediem sympathizer though." He grunted, then drove his sword through the neck of a Drude.

Blaze hacked at the many spidery arms of a Nybbas, and he lobbed its head from its body. "It's worse than that—I'll fill you in on everything once we're done here."

"Including Hadessah, right?" Axel's tone was grim, and Blaze nearly lost his footing, dodging a swipe from a snarling Drude.

They shared a look, then Blaze nodded.

When the final spray of black blood coated the wall, Axel lowered his sword, breathing heavily. After weeks of being locked up, he was no doubt exhausted.

It was Dominic that spoke first. "Who in the bloody name of—is that Connor? And Malachi?"

Axel turned, staring down into the tunnel. He took a step forward as if to rush to their friend. "Jake?"

Sergei frowned. "What happened here?"

There was no mistaking the muffled laughter coming from Derrik bundled on the floor. Axel spun and launched his foot into the Spellcaster's gut.

Blaze grabbed his brother and pulled him back. "Stop! He'll face tribunal."

"Jake is dead," Axel snarled.

Blaze nodded, still holding his brother steady while Dominic waited for him to say more. "He killed them out of revenge." Pushing his brother toward the stairs, he said, "I'll explain on the way out. We have to get moving."

The four of them hastened from the underground prison, gulping down fresh air before sprinting toward the manor, following the sounds of war and death.

EMMA

Her eyes burned.

Her throat felt thick with cement.

Ashes blackened her hands until she no longer recognized them. Were her nails longer?

She raced to her next opponent, though their scent was different. With a hiss, she lunged.

"Emma, what the hell!" the female's voice grated like marbles in a blender, and Emma gritted her teeth. Faintly, she registered the pixie-like Spellcaster.

Not Shediem.

"Hmph," she huffed before turning to find more prey.

Just as she did, a solid wall of red, black, and gold marched up the hill. One prince glided on a platform raised in the air above the Shediem's heads as though riding a magic carpet, only he was sitting regally on a throne. His face was snakelike and pointed, and his skin was made up of gold and black scales.

Her gaze lowered to the prince with molten, lavalike skin leading the formation: her father. He looked in his element here. The beast of war, charging into battle with the newest wave of Shediem.

In one massive fist he clutched a chain, and a winged beast walked beside him.

It was his golden eyes she noticed first, and her breath

caught. Recognition fired in his eyes, but only rabid hatred was reflected back at her. His tattooed skin was marred with gashes and bruises. Foam flew from his mouth when he bared his teeth and snarled loud enough for Emma to hear, even with the fifty yards between them.

Levaroth did not look like himself. He resembled a dog starved and beaten, then set loose in a pen with a weaker dog to bloody before killing.

Though she was no longer weaker than the general. Of that she was certain. But could she kill him? She should, she knew that, but she'd shared so much with Levaroth. And though his tactics of protection were extreme, there was no denying he'd once cared for her. He'd traded his memories for her.

But now, it was clear his sacrifice had backfired. Adrianna had warned her what he'd be like. He'd warned her himself too.

Now, the proof was before her.

Her father's beastly face split with a triumphant grin. When his troops halted with thirty yards spanning the gap, Asmodeus's booming, commanding voice rumbled into the sky that glowed with the first rays of morning sun.

"Shediem-Slayer! Murderer of your people!" Silence rang in his pause. Even Levaroth held still, his glare still trained on her. "This dawn I bring you your one ally among us." He lifted the chain that led to the steel collar around Levaroth's neck.

Jeers and murderous shouts rose from the Shediem, followed by howls from none other than the grey, stony beasts that padded closer—Gargoloscks. A row of at least fifty children stood behind them, their eyes void of emotion.

"Let's see if you can tame my monster this time!" Asmodeus tugged the chain and it vanished, along with the collar.

Levaroth sprang into action, sprinting toward Emma like a blur of lightning. At the same time, both sides charged at each other.

"Emma!" a voice rang out behind her.

She whirled, spying him rushing to her. "Blaze."

Relief coated her voice, but she didn't have time to react—Levaroth knocked into her, toppling them both to the icy, blood-soaked ground.

He snapped his teeth at her neck. She pushed him back, fingers digging into the hot skin of his torso. Before Levaroth could lunge for her again, Blaze's solid body connected with his, sending him flying into the snow. The Shediem growled low and animalistic.

If there was any hope that the man she'd come to know remained somewhere inside, it vanished at the crazed look in his eyes. For the first time ever, she truly feared him.

Blaze raised his sword, poised to strike, and Emma screamed at the same time Levaroth burst into motion. She felt his iron-tight grip on her arm, ripping her away from the center of the battlefield. Her feet swung wildly, trying desperately to gain a foothold, but rocks and ice continued to move beneath her.

"Leva—" She screamed when her back hit jagged, cutting rock. Her lungs struggled to draw in a breath.

He was still ethereally beautiful, even in his madness. His windswept blond hair covered one golden eye, but she felt the full weight of his hatred.

"Ready to die, traitor?" he growled.

Emma sucked in the frigid morning air before answering. "There was a time you threatened a man for calling me that."

His eyes narrowed. "Don't speak, Witch, you'll only fill my head with lies."

Emma cocked her head to the side, sadness trickling in besides her fear. "What did they do to you?" She reached for him.

Levaroth jumped forward, hands on either side of her head, caging her. "They fixed what you did to me!" His bellowed words had her recoiling into the sharp rock that bit into her back. Before she could say anymore, he gripped her throat and squeezed.

Though fear rioted through her, she didn't immediately try to steal his power; she fought against the voice in her head that screamed at her to kill him.

Her eyes burned with shame before she unleashed her hold on her power, letting Levaroth's dark, intoxicating energy fill her. It eased the exploding pain from his hands pressing in on her throat.

With a harsh grunt he released her, staring at her in shock. As if remembering something.

Blessed oxygen entered her lungs again. "I'm sorry," she said on a gasp that turned into a cough.

"You really are the villain, aren't you? I'm so stupid for not seeing it before."

Her voice was rough. "I don't know. But you thought of yourself as the villain once, and then proved to me that you aren't."

His brows furrowed. For a moment he didn't respond. He shook his head, clearing it of whatever memory had surfaced.

When his eyes met hers again, they burned hot.

He's gone. I can't reach him. Emma heaved a breath, preparing to spring into action at the same time he did.

They collided, clawing, snarling. Pain ruptured in her arm, and a warmth soaked the sleeve of her shirt. Emma gasped, trying to get a grip on him. But he was too fast, batting her away without allowing their skin to touch.

She looked to his lips in a burst of clarity. It might be the only way.

But before she had the chance, her body was snatched forward by the collar of her jacket. He slammed her back against the rock, the jutting edges cutting into her, and her head hit with a solid thunk. Stars dotted her vision. A sound somewhere between a cry and a groan escaped her lips.

Levaroth slammed her against the rock a second time and her limbs turned to jelly. Everything blurred.

When she crashed into the rock a third time, blackness consumed her.

LEVAROTH

Kill her.
    Drain her blood.
    In darkness the king was made. So shall I serve the darkness and my king.

The traitor went limp, falling to the snow. Behind her, the rock was painted with her blood, and he breathed in the scent deep. It smelled like his—dark and powerful, but tinged with something lighter.

Sunshine.

He spit at her prone, unmoving form. She was unconscious, and he so hated killing when he didn't get to watch the life leave their eyes, but he'd have to make do. His orders were to kill her as fast as possible. Already she healed much faster than she should. Soon she'd wake and be at full strength again if he didn't hurry.

Kill her.

Spill her traitor blood.

He cupped her face, palms brushing against her cool cheeks, preparing to snap her delicate neck. "Such a pity," he whispered to the unconscious girl, "I fell in love with you, only for you to be my downfall. And now I'll be yours."

There was a time when he believed he'd have done everything over the same way just to meet her. To feel her presence, her warmth. To smell the sunshine in her blood.

But now he'd kill the pitiful creature that caused him so much pain.

He smiled at the thrill of her approaching death.

"Levaroth!"

The voice that echoed on the mountaintop behind him was familiar but difficult to place. When he stood and spun, he spied the Giborim filth that had no doubt secured the Shediem-Slayer for his mate.

He hissed. "Stay back, filth!"

The Giborim halted, his eyes first fixing on the streaked blood coating the rock, then down to the heap that was the girl. When he lifted his gaze back to Levaroth, the coldness in his grey eyes turned into a tumultuous storm, raging and unpredictable.

Her sweet blood froze in the winter air, her wounds already sealed.

He was running out of time. Unsheathing his only blade, he raised it above his prey.

And brought it down.

A roar rumbled over the mountain before the Giborim's body crashed into his, knocking the knife from his hands less than an inch above the traitor's chest.

He tumbled back, the two of them landing blows, dodging others. Blood and spittle went flying. He hoped his blood infected the Giborim's wounds.

Let him suffer a million agonies while dying a slow death. *Pathetic self-righteous creature.*

Another crack to his cheek sounded, but he didn't feel the pain. He wasn't capable of feeling pain anymore.

They rolled again and he was pressed into the cold, wet snow, the Giborim's face screwed up as the rage took over.

"You're no different than me," Levaroth spat just before a punch landed to his throat and he wheezed.

"I am nothing like you!" the Giborim roared, his fists pummeling Levaroth's flesh. Cracking his bones.

"Blaze, stop," a small, weak voice rasped.

The Giborim didn't even pause.

"Blaze, stop! You're killing him!"

He couldn't die, she needn't have worried. He'd never die. Forever he'd be trapped in his infernal existence.

In darkness the king was made. So shall I serve the darkness and my king.

The Giborim brute did pause then, just realizing the Shediem-Slayer was conscious, though she swayed where she sat.

That, or his own vision swayed. He couldn't tell the difference anymore.

"He deserves to die!" the Giborim choked out. "He nearly killed you."

The girl crawled on her hands and knees toward them—likely too weak to walk. Laying a hand on her mate's shoulder, she said, "His mind is all messed up. It's not his fault."

"Should've killed you while you were lying there all helpless," he said, blood gurgling in his mouth and running down his throat. He wasn't sure where the blood was coming from. His healing was slower than usual. He hadn't fed in weeks.

So weak.

The traitor had the gall to look at him pityingly. She touched his face and he flinched away, certain she would finish the job.

But no pain came.

His energy wasn't being siphoned from his skin. She tried again, stroking his cheek, and felt instead a prickling of heat.

"What are you doing?" the Giborim asked accusatorily, his brows crashing together.

Her skin visibly paled, the pink disappearing from her cheeks while he felt his healing increasing in speed. His wounds knitted closed, the bones fusing back together.

She was giving him her power. But why?

Her shoulders slumped and her hand fell away, her breaths coming in labored pants.

"Why would you do that?" the Giborim shouted. "Now he has the strength to try to kill you again!"

She shook her head slowly. "He won't."

He barked a laugh. He wouldn't just try; he'd succeed.

"I need you to come back to me," she whispered, bending over him. Her lips were so close, and her scent muddied his senses. "Adrianna told me you made a deal for me. You sacrificed yourself to help me. You used to love me, I think. Or care about me, anyway."

Her words were absurd. He never loved her. They'd always been enemies. Yet something flickered to life in his mind: a flash of the ebony-skinned Spellcaster and his bargain. To break her father's mark in exchange for his memories of her.

He didn't know what she was doing until her cool lips pressed to his.

More memories flooded his mind, rolling in wave after wave. He sucked in a sharp breath. The wall that held it all back crumbled, and soon his arms wrapped around Emma, pulling her to him, deepening the kiss.

She opened for him, tasting him as he tasted her. Her sweetness, her beauty.

She saved him.

Her feelings for him were in every dip of her tongue, in the sheer riot of emotions he tasted rolling off her—relief, bliss, trust.

Love.

Emma Duvall loved him.

She broke the kiss first, her breathing heavy for a different reason. A sound of disgust came from behind her. She turned to look at the Giborim and Levaroth followed suit, catching sight of the hurt and anger written on his face. He stood a ways away now, no doubt spiraling at what he'd just witnessed.

Smug satisfaction that Levaroth didn't try to quash lit his chest.

"Blaze, I had to. Adrianna hinted that only I could break the spell. It was just a guess, but—"

"I get it," Blaze said, voice icy like the wind. "We need to go. The others will need us."

"I can help you get to Asmodeus. I'll have to pretend I'm still a mindless killing machine, but I can get you close enough to kill him."

Emma nodded, guilt plainly written on her face. His chest ached. It wasn't just the kiss that was causing the guilt. He'd felt her emotions, tasted them on the air.

She loved him and she was conflicted because he was sure she loved the Giborim too.

But they'd have to deal with that mess later. They had a war to end.

"Come on." Levaroth helped her to her feet. "Let's get this over with."

EMMA

H er heart felt fractured. She'd meant to break the spell only, and if she'd told Blaze what she planned to do, he'd have tried to stop her. But once it'd started, she couldn't stop.

Everything had vanished, and it was just the two of them: a flicker of warmth in the biting cold. In his arms she'd been assaulted with the truth of her feelings for the demon.

He was stubborn and possessive and had caused her all sorts of grief, but he'd also sacrificed himself for her. He'd protected her. Cared for her.

She hadn't been brave enough to acknowledge it before, but now it was undeniable. And Blaze had seen everything she'd felt, she had no doubt. She didn't want to hurt him; if there had been any way to shield him from the kiss, she would have. Now she was plagued with shame. And what would happen now? They had discussed a future together when all of this was over. Would he still want a future with her after what she'd done?

The battle-strewn chaos came into view, and Emma was forced to push away her lingering thoughts.

"Okay, I've got to rough you up a little, but I promise to kiss it better," Levaroth whispered, flashing her a wink. "You better go help your friends, Muscles, or I'll have to put you down for real because I'm not kissing *you* all better."

Blaze leveled him with a murderous glare, ignoring her completely before slipping into the clashes of metal on metal and the screams of the dying. Emma's heart sunk further in her chest, feeling the space between them morphing into a gaping chasm.

Levaroth's face transformed without warning, and he knocked her into the snow. Her arm whacked into a cold, lifeless body and she whimpered.

"Let's put on a show for them, eh, sunshine?"

His nickname warmed her marginally, and she nodded subtly before leaping to her feet, snarling like a caged animal.

The children of destruction let their powers loose, dropping people to the ground without touching them, making their eyes bleed. Emma sent out a wave of power, coaxing them to lie down and sleep. She tried to keep her focus on Levaroth and the children, but her distraction sent her flying backward when she didn't block his kick.

He hissed through his teeth, face flashing with an apology before he stalked toward her. She got to her feet, checking to make sure the children had all fallen asleep. The crowd of confused expressions told her they had.

She and Levaroth performed their dance, sometimes drawing blood while they battled toward where the massive glowing beast that was her father fought. His massive blade cut through two or three people in one swipe, and the spray of hot blood made her gag.

Levaroth's hands wrapped around her neck, but he didn't squeeze like before. Then he shoved her back, and she whirled.

Her father's bloodred eyes met hers, and she smiled. She grabbed him, throwing her entire weight onto his exposed skin. It was hot, burning her skin. She smelled it in the air but she held fast.

And all at once her father's roar filled the sky while his powerful, putrid energy sliced into her. Like the lethal creature that he was, it tore through her, and she sucked out every last bit of his nightmarish essence—an ocean of blood that he had poured out. It was eviler than a million deaths in his name.

"This is for my mom," she spat.

"You damned bitch!" His voice was hoarse, his eyes bulging. Rivulets of red blood trickled from the corners of his eyes.

Emma felt the shift in her body: nails elongating, turning into claws that matched her father's. She smiled down at them. They were black, like the ashes of the Prince of Wrath that fell to the snow, inconsequential. Nothing.

Yes, the voice within her purred. *More.*

Slowly, other sounds began to filter back in, and she heard her name being called.

She turned to face Levaroth. The concern she saw there turned to disbelief before he swiped away all emotion.

"Did you know what I'd become?" she asked without a hint of anger. This was right. Now she looked like the monster that was caged inside her.

After a moment's hesitation, he answered. "No."

With a slow smile, she turned, then stalked through the throng, eyes locked on the final prince. The second-to-last piece of her.

She'd be whole soon.

Complete.

Mammon used the Shediem and Spellcasters to do the killing for him. His chiseled jaw was splashed with blood and gore, his regal brocade jacket coated in death, flapping in the wind.

Sensing her, he turned. His eyes met hers before sliding to Levaroth, behind her. "So the faithful dog is back with its rightful master, I see," the prince sneered in his chilling voice.

"He's not my dog, Mammon," Emma replied sweetly. "He's my angel of death."

With a snarl, Levaroth lunged for the prince. Mammon dodged away, but not quickly enough. For all his effort, he struggled valiantly, but Levaroth held the prince firm.

Emma clapped her palms to his cheeks hard enough to sting,

and giggled at the sound. His energy flowed into her, filling her already heated blood to the point of boiling. It burned, scorching a path through her. Emma didn't stop.

Hungrily, greedily, she drank it all, and his snakelike skin grew taut before hardening and disintegrating in her hands.

She breathed in deeply. Her skin was tight. There was so much Shediem power flowing within her, it made her head spin. But it was oh, so delicious.

Licking her lips like she'd just consumed the most delicious meal, she straightened.

Buzzing began in her veins, causing her to wince. It grew like thousands of bees stinging inside her. She doubled over, clutching her abdomen.

Levaroth knelt in front of her, trying to get her to meet his eyes. "Emma, push it into me, push it into me."

No, he just wants it for himself, an angry voice snarled.

"It's mine!" she shouted. Still, the buzzing worsened, making her veins feel as though they'd explode.

She flung her head back, arms out. And screamed to the sky.

A burst of energy surged from her body, creating a powerful wind that lifted her several feet from the ground. When she looked down, a cold sweep of terror carried away the last of the uncomfortable heat.

Levaroth, blood-streaked hair blown away from his eyes, stared up at her in wonder.

"You're okay," she whispered.

He nodded, getting to his feet.

All around them, the fighting had stopped. There wasn't a Shediem in sight. Either she'd killed them all, or whatever ones had survived had retreated.

He brushed the back of his fingers against her cheek, his touch like ice to her fevered skin. "Your eyes…"

She frowned. "They're red, I know."

"No." The corners of his lips twitched, the amusement faded. "They…changed."

"How?" she asked.

"Emma!" Blaze hurried to her, stopping just out of arm's reach. The fear in his gaze turned to ice in an instant.

Distantly she felt a tug of emotion, though she couldn't place it.

"I felt the blast..." He stared at her eyes, then his attention snagged on her hands. More specifically on the claws still protruding from her fingers, which twitched under his scrutiny.

"I'm fine."

"So is he, I see," Blaze added with no shortage of disdain.

"She had the opportunity to kill me and she kissed me instead," Levaroth said with a growing smirk. "Let's face it, I'm just that irresistible."

Before Blaze could snipe a reply, Emma barked, "Enough."

Just then, the ground began to shake violently. She grabbed both men to steady herself. Shouts and cries rose all around them, and people tumbled to the ground.

Emma's chest tightened. She knew what was coming.

She could feel him.

"Finally," she breathed.

The ground split with a thunderous crack that echoed all around. A wide pillar of light less than a mile away shot into the sky.

Everything stilled. Emma straightened, releasing both guys that were still gripping her.

The pillar was not light.

It was fire.

BLAZE

H e knew it was coming. He'd been anticipating it. They all had.

Yet the all-consuming horror and rage still battled inside him at the sight of the king of Sheol coming to Earth.

Emma would fight him next. Already, she was different. Colder. More brusque. Not to mention the demon claws and her eyes. They'd changed to a golden green, her pupils now vertical slits.

She looked like a human-beast hybrid. Terrifying, yet—damn him for thinking so—beautiful.

He still couldn't fathom that she'd willingly kissed the Shediem general, but perhaps she was changing inside just as much as she was on the outside. And where would that leave him? Them?

He had just blinked away his morose thoughts when Emma took off at a sprint for the funnel of flames rising like a beacon.

"Emma, wait, dammit!" Blaze called after her, taking off too.

Levaroth followed after her, but he didn't call for her to stop. His expression was set, hard.

The general knew what she had to do. Blaze did too, but he wasn't ready to say goodbye. He wasn't ready to lose her.

The three of them raced toward the king—toward certain doom—while cheers rose from the Shediem, praising their king.

Challenging the mighty Shediem-Slayer to try to defeat him.

"Emma!"

She stopped abruptly, hardly giving Blaze time to dig his heels in and come to a stop. Throwing her arms around his neck, she whispered, "I have to do this. Only I can. So don't follow. Go live a good life, William. I'll miss you."

She pressed a kiss to his cheek, then nodded to Levaroth, who pulled Blaze's arms behind his back and held him in place. Then she took off again, running away.

Away from him. Away from his screams of protest.

She'd said goodbye.

She knew she wasn't coming back.

When she disappeared from sight, lost in the mess of people and beasts, he felt his fractured heart shatter once again, and with her the pieces he needed to put it back together.

ADRIANNA

A drianna's heart pounded at the sight of the massive swirling pillar of flames. Her grip on her sword went slack, sweat trickling down her forehead, burning her eyes while she watched a lone figure running in a blur of motion toward the fire that kissed the heavens.

When Nakosh had surfaced, most of the ground had fractured and cracked. Bodies fell into the crevices.

She and Athena had mostly kept to the sky, where she'd battled in favor of the Spellcasters. Tlahaz would have shot her down himself if he'd seen her fighting for the Giborim, whom she had no true loyalty to. But she'd chosen to fight for her own race.

She'd protected her people and other familiars to the point of exhaustion, but until the king had surfaced, she'd forgotten the true reason she was there.

When the blurred figure slowed, approaching the column with more caution, Adrianna spurred Athena on with a gentle kick to her sides.

They flew closer. Adrianna's breath hitched.

Emma—her best friend—marched fearlessly forward, stopping just outside the roaring tower of fire.

And she, Adrianna, was to bind the ultimate darkness.

Isabella's light, airy voice filled her mind, her words drowning out every other sound: *And when the earth is split by dark and light, there is one—the most powerful magic-wielder, who flies through the air on immortal wings. For if she can bind the ultimate darkness, then the world will not die. But if she cannot condemn the ruler of death, then darkness will swallow the world forever.*

She just had to bind Nakosh before he killed Emma. However she did that...

"Faster, Athena!" Adrianna shouted, and her faithful, colorful familiar obliged. Her wings pumped harder, carrying them faster.

"Emma, don't!"

Emma whipped her head around, searching for the reason behind Adrianna's warning.

Something hit Athena with a sickening *thwack* that crunched when it hit bone. Athena shrieked a horrid sound that made Adrianna's heart stop. Looking to her side, she saw a massive javelin-like weapon careening up to meet her familiar.

Adrianna screamed as Athena fell sideways, but she held tight, funneling her magic into the wyvern to heal the wounds as best she could.

Her familiar gave another gurgling cry before curling her wings in, sending them spinning.

Down.

Down.

Down.

Adrianna lost her grip, screaming. Her heart tore in half for her familiar, mixing with the terror of the ground racing up to meet her.

The bond between her and Athena snapped, and Adrianna felt like every rib in her chest had shattered.

She couldn't breathe.

She let herself fall, letting grief crush her as surely as the ground soon would. Her body impacted with another, sending them both to the ground. Her arm hit hardest, the bones snapping in two, and she gasped from the pain.

Too much pain.

Tlahaz's familiar golden eyes stared down at her, his hands

roving over her, searching for injury.

Tears spilled out of her, soaking her cheeks. "Athena." The word was choked. Hoarse.

Too much pain.

His ruggedly handsome face reflected the pain she felt.

No words were needed. She felt his answer without needing to ask: Athena was dead.

A fresh wave of tears fell, accompanied with a small sob that she swallowed down.

Emma. She needed to save Emma.

Looking over Tlahaz's shoulder at his black feathered wings, she whispered, "Need to get over there…Emma…"

With her eyes she pleaded to Tlahaz's true face. He was not human, but still she cared for him. Had fallen in love with him, no matter how wrong it was. What she was asking was for him to defy his king, but he'd already vowed to help her when the time came.

Tlahaz nodded, his expression set with determination. He cradled her to his warm chest, letting his wings expand before shooting up into the sky, and carried her to where Emma had disappeared inside the wall of fire.

EMMA

E mma followed the smooth, velvety voice beckoning her inside. She wielded fire herself; she wasn't afraid of it as she stepped into the licking, crackling heat.

Inside the cyclone of spinning flames, Nakosh stood.

Looking at the king of Sheol without his cloak of shadows—perhaps they feared the fire—made her brows crease. He looked like a man. An achingly beautiful man with long, straight black hair, cutting silver eyes, angular jaw, and full lips that smiled at her. He had a lean, muscular frame clothed in a simple black suit. Leave it to the King of Hell to show up to a war in a suit with not a single weapon in sight.

Though he was dangerous, and she'd do well to remember that.

The only difference from how she'd seen him in the past were the charred skeletal wings protruding from his shoulder blades. They looked like they'd been burned off.

"Welcome, darling Emma," Nakosh purred. "My, my, you're really coming into your own, aren't you?"

She ignored his comment in favor of finishing what she started. Not to mention that his power was all around her, driving her hunger to the point that her hands began to tremble. "You know how this ends, don't you?"

His smile held a thousand secrets. "Oh dearest," he sighed.

"I know it in far greater clarity than you do." He put his hands in his pockets, looking perfectly at ease. Stalking toward her he said, "I see all. The future." He cocked his head to the side and looked her up and down, his gaze lingering on her eyes. "You will too." Those words were soft, more for himself than for her.

The dip between her brows deepened. "What do you mean?"

"Once you kill me, you'll take my place as ruler of Sheol. All Shediem will be in your command. You'll have more power than your tiny body can contain, and you'll be able to see the future." Her thoughts kicked into a million different directions, but he continued. "It'll take you a few millennia to get used to the power, I reckon, but you'll adjust."

Emma's lips parted, but no words came out. Was he seriously giving up? He wasn't going to fight her?

"What if I don't want to rule Sheol? I've instructed my friends to kill me once I've killed you."

His laugh was shrill. Unhinged.

She took an uneasy step back.

His smile didn't fade, but his laughter did. "If I could die, I'd have done it long ago."

Emma's breath caught in her throat. She'd be immortal?

He stopped in front of her. "I've been waiting for you for so long." Finally the smile turned to something like contentment. "I'm ready, Shediem-Slayer. Free me at last."

Emma's heart hammered in her ears. With uncertainty, she lifted her hands to either side of his face, hovering over his skin.

Touch him.

Touch him!

TOUCH HIM!

KILL HIM!

TAKE HIS POWER!

With that, her skin fluttered against his and a scream tore from her throat.

LEVAROTH

Her scream cleaved through his chest, through the mountain, and into the sky. He and the Giborim were running before either of them could think. In the air, he spied Tlahaz's dark wings, and his panic ratcheted up. He caught a glimpse of the Spellcaster in his arms and heard her calling Emma's name.

He knew of the prophecy. Were they too late? He couldn't sense Emma like he could before, but still he didn't think she was dead.

The ground shook and heaved open further. One jagged gap began to crumble, and he leapt over it, feeling the soil under his boots falling away just before he scrambled to his feet. He kept running. The blasted Giborim was at his side, both of them drawn toward the girl inside the cyclone of flames. It swirled faster and faster, the wind being sucked in to feed the flames.

It was becoming unstable. The ground, too, seemed to be heaving like a living thing. Fire spread in vicious streaks, consuming everyone and everything in its path. If things didn't calm, the whole mountain would crumble and cause innumerable deaths.

He and the Giborim dodged the fingers of destruction that stretched for them. At last they approached as close as they could to the storm of fire and wind. Above, the Spellcaster Adrianna began to work, trying to contain the chaos.

A single dark, lean figure stood in the eye of the fire. It glided closer, but he still couldn't make it out.

The dark outline of wings at their back made his knees go weak.

She's dead.

Nakosh killed her.

Emma is dead.

His breaths came faster, turning to pants until he couldn't breathe at all.

"No," Blaze whispered. "No, no, no, no." His voice cracked, and he backed away.

The elements stilled, the fire freezing when the figure emerged, and the last of Levaroth's composure dissolved.

Emma's new eyes—brighter, animalistic—were rolling back in her head. She stumbled forward. Her lips moved, but no sound escaped.

Behind her, new wings shimmered, starting bloodred at the top of her wing bones and fading to a black—like ink spreading up her new appendages. At the very bottom of the tips, gold feathers reflected the crackling orange flames.

"Emma?"

It was Blaze that spoke. He was too transfixed, too unsure of what to do or say.

She didn't answer. But with every step she took, black shadows leapt from the ground, clinging to her slender legs, wrapping around her body, swallowing her from his sight.

Blaze rushed forward. "Emma, come back to me, you can do it. Fight this."

With a scream, she threw her palms out to his chest. It was her new power that sent him shooting back.

Tlahaz landed solidly to his right, and the Spellcaster scrambled out of his arms.

"Emma, oh god, Emma, let me help you," Adrianna choked out.

Emma fell to her knees, covering her ears, and another scream rocked the ground. The fire extinguished, yet the ground quaked threateningly.

"NOW!" Tlahaz bellowed. "Bind her now!"

"Stop!" Levaroth shouted. "I will take her to Sheol, where she can get used to her new powers. She'll be safe there."

"She's not going with you!" Blaze snarled in his face.

"Do you want her to kill you and all of your annoying little race? Because that's what's going to happen if she loses control!"

"We'll both go, and I'll make sure she stays in Sheol until she's ready." Adrianna's words were directed to no one in particular but she raised her palms, looking to Tlahaz. "Catch me when I fall."

Levaroth lunged for Emma, tugging one of her hands from her head, and wound his fingers through hers. Whether she knew it was him or not, he wanted her to feel someone near when she got to Sheol.

Blaze was starting forward to protest when Adrianna's hands glowed with blinding light. Her body tilted sideways, and Tlahaz caught her before the snowy, brutalized mountain vanished.

When Levaroth opened his eyes, he was in Nakosh's castle. The shadows that slinked over Emma's pale skin wound their way over her head until they formed a jagged, haunting crown.

Her head lifted, eyes glowing with green light.

Levaroth bowed as the Queen of Sheol rose to her feet in front of her throne.

Acknowledgements

Wow! I have so many people to thank, I could literally fill a book. So I'll try to keep it brief. Thank you to my husband, Matthew for cheering me on, supporting me, brainstorming with me, and for letting me ramble all hours of the night about Emma and the crew. Thank you to my Noah, I know you're far to young to understand this, but I appreciate you so much for being patient with me and for learning to occupy yourself most days. I will totally pay for your college, kid.

To my betas, I love you, I love you, I love you! To my critique partner, Kayla, you're the freaking bomb girl, I adore you. Mariz, from the bottom of my heart, thank you for your incredible work on all of my books, you're a Rockstar! To Dean, I hope you read this and know that I am truly thankful for your grace and compassion. You're an immensely talented human and this series would be nothing without you.

Dear readers, you are everything. Your kind messages and support for these books has been overwhelming, I cannot possibly thank you enough. It makes my heart fill to bursting each and every time you sit down to read the words that I put down.

Thank you, a million times and then a million more.
You're all incredible.
Much love,
Brittany

About the Author

Brittany is an American by birth but a Kiwi at heart, living in the wondrous New Zealand with her husband and their son. Writing has been a passion since she was very young. In middle school, she had articles published in the local newspaper, and the school paper in high school. She attended the Institute of Children's Literature with the hope of one day creating stories for the world.